Outstanding Critical Acclaim for Elizabeth Hand

"ACCOMPLISHED!"

—William Gibson

"RARE!"

—Samuel R. Delany

"Ms. Hand is a SUPERIOR STYLIST."

—*New York Times Book Review*

"You want to give her a standing ovation."

—James Morrow

"DYNAMITE."

—*Des Moines Register*

By Elizabeth Hand

Waking the Moon

Glimmering

Winterlong

Published by HarperPrism

LAST SUMMER
AT MARS HILL

ELIZABETH HAND

HarperPrism

A Division of HarperCollins*Publishers*

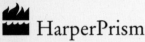

HarperPrism

A Division of HarperCollins*Publishers*
10 East 53rd Street, New York, NY 10022-5299

Individual story copyrights appear on page 325.

Copyright © 1998 by Elizabeth Hand

Cover photographs © by Graphistock & Superstock
Photo composit by Carl Galian

First printing: September 1998

Printed in the United States of America

Library of Congress Cataloging-in-Publication Data

Hand, Elizabeth.
    Last summer at Mars Hill / Elizabeth Hand.
       p. cm.
    ISBN 0-06-105348-1
    I. Title.
  PS3558.A4619L38   1998
  813' .54—dc21   98-6734

Visit HarperPrism on the World Wide Web at http://www.harperprism.com

98 99 00 01 02 ❖ 10 9 8 7 6 5 4 3 2 1

For Stephen P. Brown,
who long ago helped me to find stories in the City of Trees
With love and thanks

CONTENTS

CONTENTS

And do not rely on the fact that in your life, circumscribed, regulated, and prosaic, there are no such spectacular and terrifying things.

—C. P. Cavafy, "Theodotus"

Last Summer at
Mars Hill

Even before they left home, Moony knew her mother wouldn't return from Mars Hill that year. Jason had called her from his father's house in San Francisco—

"I had a dream about you last night," he'd said, his voice cracking the way it did when he was excited. "We were at Mars Hill, and my father was there, and my mother, too—I knew it was a dream, like can you imagine my *mother* at Mars Hill?—and you had on this sort of long black dress and you were sitting alone by the pier. And you said, 'This is it, Jason. We'll never see this again.' I felt like crying, I tried to hug you but my father pulled me back. And then I woke up."

She didn't say anything. Finally Jason prodded her. "Weird, huh, Moony? I mean, don't you think it's weird?"

She shrugged and rolled her eyes, then sighed loudly so that he'd be able to tell she was upset. "Thanks, Jason. Like that's supposed to cheer me up?"

A long silence, then Jason's breathless voice again. "Shit, Moony, I'm sorry. I didn't—"

She laughed, a little nervously, and said, "Forget it. So when you flying out to Maine?"

Nobody but Jason called her Moony, not at home at least, not in Kamensic Village. There she was Maggie Rheining, which was the name that appeared under her junior picture in the high school yearbook.

But the name that had been neatly typed on the birth certificate in San Francisco sixteen years ago, the name Jason and everyone at Mars Hill knew her by, was Shadowmoon Starlight Rising. Maggie would have shaved her head before she'd admit her real name to anyone at school. At Mars Hill it wasn't so weird: there was Adele Grose, known professionally as Madame Olaf; Shasta Daisy O'Hare and Rvis Capricorn; Martin Dionysos, who was Jason's father; and Ariel Rising, née Amanda Mae Rheining, who was Moony's mother. For most of the year Moony and Ariel lived in Kamensic Village, the affluent New York exurb where her mother ran Earthly Delights Catering and Moony attended high school, and everything was pretty much normal. It was only in June that they headed north to Maine, to the tiny spiritualist community where they had summered for as long as Moony could remember. And even though she could have stayed in Kamensic with Ariel's friends the Loomises, at the last minute (and due in large part to Jason's urging, and threats if she abandoned him there) she decided to go with her mother to Mars Hill. Later, whenever she thought how close she'd come to not going, it made her feel sick: as though she'd missed a flight and later found out the plane had crashed.

Because much as she loved it, Moony had always been a little ashamed of Mars Hill. It was such a dinky place, plopped in the middle of nowhere on the rocky Maine coast—tiny shingle-style Carpenter Gothic cottages, all tumbled into disrepair, their elaborate trim rotting and strung with spiderwebs; poppies and lupines and tiger lilies sprawling bravely atop clumps of chickweed and dandelions of truly monstrous size; even the sign by the pier so faded you almost couldn't read the earnest lettering:

MARS HILL

SPIRITUALIST COMMUNITY

FOUNDED 1883

"Why doesn't your father take somebody's violet aura and repaint the damn sign with it?" she'd exploded once to Jason.

Jason looked surprised. "I kind of like it like that," he said, shaking the hair from his face and tossing a sea urchin at the silvered board. "It looks like it was put up by our Founding Mothers." But for years Moony almost couldn't stand to even look at the sign, it embarrassed her so much.

It was Jason who helped her get over that. They'd met when they were both twelve. It was the summer that Ariel started the workshop in Creative Psychokinesis, the first summer that Jason and his father had stayed at Mars Hill.

"Hey," Jason had said, too loudly, when they found themselves left alone while the adults swapped wine coolers and introductions at the summer's first barbecue. They were the only kids in sight. There were no other families and few conventionally married couples at Mars Hill. The community had been the cause of more than one custody battle that had ended with wistful children sent to spend the summer with a more respectable parent in Boston or Manhattan or Bar Harbor. "That lady there with my father—"

He stuck his thumb out to indicate Ariel, her long black hair frizzed and bound with leather thongs, an old multicolored skirt flapping around her legs. She was talking to a slender man with close-cropped blond hair and goatee, wearing a sky-blue caftan and shabby Birkenstock sandals. "That your mom?"

"Yeah." Moony shrugged and glanced at the man in the caftan. He and Ariel both turned to look at their children. The man grinned and raised his wine glass. Ariel did a little pirouette and blew a kiss at Moony.

"Looks like she did too much of the brown acid at Woodstock," Jason announced, and flopped onto the grass. Moony glared down at him.

"She wasn't *at* Woodstock, asshole," she said, and had started to walk away when the boy called after her.

"Hey—it's a joke! My name's Jason—" He pointed at the man with Ariel. "That's my father. Martin Dionysos. But like that's not his real name, okay? His real name is Schuster but he changed it, but *I'm* Jason Schuster. He's a painter. We don't know anyone here. I mean, does it ever get above forty degrees?"

He scrambled to his feet and looked at her beseechingly. Smaller even than Moony herself, so slender he should have looked younger than her, except that his sharp face beneath floppy white-blond hair was always twisted into some ironic pronouncement, his blue eyes always flickering somewhere between derision and pleading.

"No," Moony said slowly. The part about Jason not changing his name got to her. She stared pointedly at his thin arms prickled with gooseflesh, the fashionable surfer-logo T-shirt that hung nearly to his knees. "You're gonna freeze your skinny ass off here in Maine, Jason Schuster." And she grinned.

He was from San Francisco. His father was a well-known artist and a member of the Raging Faery Queens, a gay pagan group that lived in the Bay Area and staged elaborately beautiful solstice gatherings and AIDS benefits. At Mars Hill, Martin Dionysos gave workshops on strengthening your aura and on clear nights led the community's men in chanting at the moon as it rose above Penobscot Bay. Jason was so diffident about his father and his father's work that Moony was surprised, the single time she visited him on the West Coast, to find her friend's room plastered with flyers advertising Faery gatherings and newspaper photos of Martin and Jason at various ACT-UP events. In the fall Jason would be staying in Maine, while she returned to high school. Ultimately it was the thought that she might not see him again that made Moony decide to spend this last summer at Mars Hill.

"That's what you're wearing to First Night?"

Moony started at her mother's voice, turned to see Ariel in the middle of the summer cottage's tiny living room. Wine rocked back and forth in her mother's glass, gold shot with tiny sunbursts from the crystals hung from every window. "What about your new dress?"

Moony shrugged. She couldn't tell her mother about Jason's dream, about the black dress he'd seen her wearing. Ariel set great store by dreams, especially these last few months. What she'd make of one in which Moony appeared in a black dress and Ariel didn't appear at all, Moony didn't want to know.

"Too hot," Moony said. She paused in front of the window and adjusted one of three silver crosses dangling from her right ear. "Plus I don't want to upstage you."

Ariel smiled. "Smart kid," she said, and took another sip of her wine.

Ariel wore what she wore to every First Night: an ankle-length patchwork skirt so worn and frayed it could only be taken out once a year, on this ceremonial occasion. Squares of velvet and threadbare satin were emblazoned with suns and moons and astrological symbols, each one with a date neatly embroidered in crimson thread.

Sedona, Aug 15 1972. Mystery Hill, NH, 5/80. The Winter Garden 1969. Jajouka, Tangiers, Marrakech 1968.

Along the bottom, where many of the original squares had disintegrated into fine webs of denim and chambray, she had begun piecing a new section: squares that each held a pair of dates, a name, an embroidered flower. These were for friends who had died. Some of them were people lost two decades earlier, to the War, or drugs or misadventure; names that Moony knew only from stories told year after year at Mars Hill or in the kitchen at home.

But most of the names were those of people Moony herself had known. Friends of Ariel's who had gathered during the divorce, and again, later, when Moony's father died, and during the myriad affairs and breakups that followed. Men and women who had started out as Ariel's customers and ended as family. Uncle Bob and Uncle Raymond and Uncle Nigel. Laurie Salas. Tommy McElroy and Sean Jacobson. Chas Bowen and Martina Glass. And, on the very bottom edge of the skirt, a square still peacock-bright with its blood-colored rose, crimson letters spelling out John's name and a date the previous spring.

As a child Moony had loved that skirt. She loved to watch her mother sashay into the tiny gazebo at Mars Hill on First Night and see all the others laugh and run to her, their fingers plucking at the patchwork folds as though to read something there, tomorrow's weather perhaps, or the names of suitors yet unmet.

But now Moony hated the skirt. It was morbid, even Jason agreed with that.

"They've already got a fucking quilt," he said, bitterly. "We don't need your mom wearing a goddamn *skirt*."

Moony nodded, miserable, and tried not to think of what they were most afraid of: Martin's name there beside John's, and a little rosebud done in flower-knots. Martin's name, or Ariel's.

There was a key to the skirt, Moony thought as she watched her mother sip her wine; a way to decode all the arcane symbols Ariel had stitched there over the last few months. It lay in a heavy manila envelope somewhere in Ariel's room, an envelope that Ariel had started carrying with her in February, and which grew heavier and heavier as the weeks passed. Moony knew there was something horrible in that envelope, something to do with the countless appointments Ariel had had since February, with the whispered phone calls and macrobiotic diets and the resurgence of her mother's belief in *devas* and earth spirits and plain old-fashioned ghosts.

But Moony said nothing of this, only smiled and fidgeted with her earrings. "Go ahead," she told Ariel, who had settled at the edge of a wicker hassock and peered up at her daughter through her wineglass. "I just got to get some stuff."

Ariel waited in silence, then drained her glass and set it on the floor. "Okay. Jason and Martin are here. I saw them on the hill—"

"Yeah. I know, I talked to them, they went to Camden for lunch, they can't wait to see you." Moony paced to the door to her room, trying not to look impatient. Already her heart was pounding.

"Okay," Ariel said again. She sounded breathless and a little drunk. She had ringed her aquamarine eyes with kohl, to hide how tired she was. Over the last few months she'd grown so thin that her cheekbones had emerged again, after years of hiding in her round peasant's face. Her voice was hoarse as she asked, "So you'll be there soon?"

Moony nodded. She curled a long tendril of hair, dark as her mother's but finer, and brushed her cheek with it. "I'm just gonna pull my hair back. Jason'll give me shit if I don't."

Ariel laughed. Jason thought that they were all a bunch of hippies. "Okay." She crossed the room unsteadily, touching the backs of chairs, a windowsill, the edge of a buoy hanging from the wall. When the screen door banged shut behind her Moony sighed with relief.

For a few minutes she waited, to make sure her mother hadn't forgotten something, like maybe a joint or another glass of wine. She could see out the window to where people were starting downhill toward the gazebo. If you didn't look too closely, they might have been any group of summer people gathering for a party in the long northern afternoon.

But after a minute or two their oddities started to show. You saw them for what they really were: men and women just getting used to a peculiar middle age. They all had hair a little too long or too short, a little too gray or garishly colored. The women, like Ariel, wrapped in clothes like banners from a triumphant campaign now forgotten. Velvet tunics threaded with silver, miniskirts crossing pale bare blue-veined thighs, Pucci blouses back in vogue again. The men more subdued, in chinos some of them, or old jeans that were a little too bright and neatly pressed. She could see Martin beneath the lilacs by the gazebo, in baggy psychedelic shorts and T-shirt, his gray-blond hair longer than it had been and pulled back into a wispy ponytail. Beside him Jason leaned against a tree, self-consciously casual, smoking a cigarette as he watched the First Night promenade. At sight of Ariel he raised one hand in a lazy wave.

And now the last two stragglers reached the bottom of the hill. Mrs. Grose carrying her familiar, an arthritic wheezing pug named Milton: Ancient Mrs. Grose, who smelled of Sen-sen and whiskey, and prided herself on being one of the spiritualists exposed as a fraud by Houdini. And Gary Bonetti, who (the story went) five years ago had seen a vision of his own death in the City, a knife wielded by a crack-crazed kid in Washington Heights. Since then, he had stayed on at Mars Hill with Mrs. Grose, the community's only other year-round resident.

Moony ducked back from the window as her mother turned to stare up at the cottage. She waited until Ariel looked away again, as Martin and Jason beckoned her toward the gazebo.

"Okay," Moony whispered. She took a step across the room and stopped. An overwhelming smell of cigarette smoke suddenly filled the air, though there was no smoke to be seen. She coughed, waving her hand in front of her face.

"Damn it, Jason," she hissed beneath her breath. The smell was gone as abruptly as it had appeared. "I'll be *right there*—"

She slipped through the narrow hallway with its old silver-touched mirrors and faded Maxfield Parrish prints, and went into Ariel's room. It still had its beginning-of-summer smell, mothballs and the salt sweetness of rugosa roses blooming at the beach's edge. The old chenille bedspread was rumpled where Ariel had lain upon it, exhausted by the flight from LaGuardia to Boston, from Boston via puddlejumper to the tiny airport at Green Turtle Reach. Moony pressed her hand upon the spread and closed her eyes. She tried to focus as Jason had taught her, tried to dredge up the image of her mother stretched upon the bed. And suddenly there it was, a faint sharp stab of pain in her left breast, like a stitch in her side from running. She opened her eyes quickly, fighting the dizziness and panicky feeling. Then she went to the bureau.

At home she had never been able to find the envelope. It was always hidden away, just as the mail was always carefully sorted, the messages on the answering machine erased before she could get to them. But now it was as if Ariel had finally given up on hiding. The envelope was in the middle drawer, a worn cotton camisole draped halfheartedly across it. Moony took it carefully from the drawer and went to the bed, sat and slowly fanned the papers out.

They were hospital bills. Hospital bills and Blue Cross forms, cash register receipts for vitamins from the Waverly Drugstore with Ariel's crabbed script across the top. The bills were for tests only, tests and consultations. Nothing for treatments; no receipts for medication other than vitamins. At the bottom of the envelope, rolled into a blue cylinder and tightened with a rubber band, she found the test results. Stray words floated in the air in front of her as Moony drew in a long shuddering breath.

Mammography results. Sectional biopsy. Fourth stage malignancy. Metastasized.

Cancer. Her mother had breast cancer.

"Shit," she, said. Her hands after she replaced the papers were shaking. From outside echoed summer music, and she could hear voices—her mother's, Diana's, Gary Bonetti's deep bass—shouting above the tinny sound of a cassette player—

"Wouldn't it be nice if we could wake up
In the kind of world where we belong?"

"You bitch," Moony whispered. She stood at the front window and stared down the hill at the gazebo, her hands clamped beneath her armpits to keep them still. Her face was streaked with tears. "When were you going to *tell* me, when were you going to fucking *tell* me?"

At the foot of Mars Hill, alone by a patch of daylilies stood Jason, staring back up at the cottage. A cigarette burned between his fingers, its scent miraculously filling the little room. Even from here Moony could tell that somehow and of course, he already knew.

Everyone had a hangover the next morning, not excluding Moony and Jason. In spite of that the two met in the community chapel. Jason brought a thermos of coffee, bright red and yellow dinosaurs stenciled on its sides, and blew ashes from the bench so she could sit down.

"You shouldn't smoke in here." Moony coughed and slumped beside him. Jason shrugged and stubbed out his cigarette, fished in his pocket and held out his open palm.

"Here. Ibuprofen and valerian capsules. And there's bourbon in the coffee."

Moony snorted but took the pills, shooting back a mouthful of tepid coffee and grimacing.

"Hair of the iguana," Jason said. "So really, Moony, you didn't know?"

"How the hell would I know?" Moony said wearily. "I mean, I knew it was *something*—"

She glanced sideways at her friend. His slender legs were crossed at the ankles and he was barefoot. Already dozens of mosquito bites pied his arms and legs. He was staring at the little altar in the center of the room. He looked paler than usual, more tired, but that was probably just the hangover.

From outside, the chapel looked like all the other buildings at Mars Hill, faded gray shingles and white trim. Inside there was one large open room, with benches arranged in a circle around the walls, facing in to the plain altar. The altar was heaped with wilting day lilies and lilacs, an empty bottle of chardonnay and a crumpled pack of Kents—Jason's brand—and a black velvet hair ribbon that Moony recognized as her mother's. Beneath the ribbon was an old snapshot, curled at the edges. Moony knew the pose from years back. It showed her and Jason and Ariel and Martin, standing at the edge of the pier with their faces raised skyward, smiling and waving at Diana behind her camera. Moony made a face when she saw it and took another swallow of coffee.

"I thought maybe she had AIDS," Moony said at last. "I knew

she went to the Walker Clinic once, I heard her on the phone to Diana about it."

Jason nodded, his mouth set in a tight smile. "So you should be happy she doesn't. Hip hip hooray." Two years before Jason's father had tested HIV-positive. Martin's lover, John, had died that spring.

Moony turned so that he couldn't see her face. "She has breast cancer. It's metastasized. She won't see a doctor. This morning she let me feel it . . ."

Like a gnarled tree branch shoved beneath her mother's flesh, huge and hard and lumpy. Ariel thought she'd cry or faint or something but all Moony could do was wonder how she had never felt it before. Had she never noticed, or had it just been that long since she'd hugged her mother?

She started crying, and Jason drew closer to her.

"Hey," he whispered, his thin arm edging around her shoulders. "It's okay, Moony, don't cry, it's all right—"

How can you say that? she felt like screaming, sobs constricting her throat so she couldn't speak. When she did talk the words came out in anguished grunts.

"They're dying—how can they—*Jason*—"

"Shh—" he murmured. "Don't cry, Moony, don't cry . . ."

Beside her, Jason sighed and fought the urge for another cigarette. He wished he'd thought about this earlier, come up with something to say that would make Moony feel better. Something like, *Hey! Get used to it! Everybody dies!* He tried to smile, but he felt only sorrow and a headache prodding at the corners of his eyes. Moony's head felt heavy on his shoulder. He shifted on the bench, stroking her hair and whispering until she grew quiet. Then they sat in silence.

He stared across the room, to the altar and the wall beyond, where a stained glass window would have been in another kind of chapel. Here, a single great picture window looked out onto the bay. In the distance he could see the Starry Islands glittering in the sunlight, and beyond them the emerald bulk of Blue Hill and Cadillac Mountain rising above the indigo water.

And, if he squinted, he could see Them. The Others, like tears or blots of light floating across his retina. The Golden Ones. The Greeters.

The Light Children.

"Hey!" he whispered. Moony sniffed and burrowed closer into his shoulder, but he wasn't talking to her. He was welcoming Them.

They were the real reason people had settled here, over a century ago. They were the reason Jason and Moony and their parents and all the others came here now; although not everyone could see Them. Moony never had, nor Ariel's friend Diana; although Diana believed in Them, and Moony did not. You never spoke of Them, and if you did, it was always parenthetically and with a capital T— "Rvis and I were looking at the moon last night (They were there) and we thought we saw a whale." Or, "Martin came over at midnight (he saw Them on the way) and we played Scrabble . . ."

A few years earlier a movement was afoot, to change the way of referring to Them. In a single slender volume that was a history of the Mars Hill spiritualist community, They were referred to as the Light Children, but no one ever really called Them that. Everyone just called them Them. It seemed the most polite thing to do, really, since no one knew what They called Themselves.

"And we'd hate to offend Them," as Ariel said.

That was always a fear at Mars Hill. That, despite the gentle nature of the community's adherents, They inadvertently would be offended one day (a too-noisy volleyball game on the rocky beach; a beer-fueled Solstice celebration irrupting into the dawn), and leave.

But They never did. Year after year the Light Children remained. They were a magical commonplace, like the loons that nested on a nearby pond and made the night an offertory with their cries, or the rainbows that inexplicably appeared over the Bay almost daily, even when there was no rain in sight. It was the same with Them. Jason would be walking down to call his father in from sailing, or knocking at Moony's window to awaken her for a three A.M. stroll, and suddenly there They'd be. A trick of the light, like a sundog or the aurora borealis: golden patches swimming through the cool air. They appeared as suddenly as a cormorant's head slicing up through the water, lingering sometimes for ten minutes or so. Then They would be gone.

Jason saw Them a lot. The chapel was one of the places They seemed to like, and so he hung out there whenever he could. Sometimes he could sense Them moments before They appeared. A shivering in the air would make the tips of his fingers go numb, and once there had been a wonderful smell, like warm buttered bread. But usually there was no warning. If he closed his eyes while look-ing at Them, Their image still appeared on the cloudy scrim of his inner eye, like gilded tears. But that was all. No voices, no scent of rose petals, no rapping at the door. You felt better after seeing Them, the way you felt better after seeing a rainbow or an eagle above the Bay. But there was nothing really magical about Them, except the fact that They existed at all. They never spoke, or did anything special, at least nothing you could sense. They were just *there;* but Their presence meant everything at Mars Hill.

They were there now: flickering above the altar, sending blots of gold dancing across the limp flowers and faded photograph. He wanted to point Them out to Moony, but he'd tried before and she'd gotten mad at him.

"You think I'm some kind of idiot like my mother?" she'd stormed, sweeping that day's offering of irises from the altar onto the floor. "Give me a break, Jason!"

Okay, I gave you a break, he thought now. *Now I'll give you another.*

Look, Moony, there They are! he thought, then said, "Moony. Look—"

He pointed, shrugging his shoulder so she'd have to move. But already They were gone.

"What?" Moony murmured. He shook his head, sighing.

"That picture," he said, and fumbled at his pocket for his ciga-rettes. "That stupid old picture that Diana took. Can you believe it's still here?"

Moony lifted her head and rubbed her eyes, red and swollen. "Oh, I can believe anything," she said bitterly, and filled her mug with more coffee.

In Martin Dionysos's kitchen, Ariel drank a cup of nettle tea and watched avidly as her friend ate a bowl of mung bean sprouts and nutritional yeast. *Just like in* Annie Hall, she thought. *Amazing.*

"So now she knows and you're surprised she's pissed at you." Martin raised another forkful of sprouts to his mouth, angling deli-cately to keep any from falling to the floor. He raised one blond eyebrow as he chewed, looking like some hardscrabble New Englander's idea of Satan, California surfer boy gone to seed. Long gray-blond hair that was thinner than it had been a year ago, skin that wasn't so much tanned as an even pale bronze, with that little goatee and those piercing blue eyes, the same color as the Bay stretching outside the window behind him. Oh, yes: and a gold hoop earring and a heart tattoo that enclosed the name *JOHN* and a T-shirt with the pink triangle and SILENCE=DEATH printed in stern block letters. Satan on vacation.

"I'm not *surprised*," Ariel said, a little crossly. "I'm just, mmm, disappointed. That she got so upset."

Martin's other eyebrow arched. "*Disappointed?* As in, 'Moony, darling, I have breast cancer (which I have kept a secret from you for seven months) and I am very *disappointed* that you are not self-actualized enough to deal with this without falling to pieces'?"

"She didn't fall to pieces." Ariel's crossness went over the line into full-blown annoyance. She frowned and jabbed a spoon into her tea. "I *wish* she'd fall to pieces, she's always so—" She waved the hand holding the spoon, sending green droplets raining onto Martin's knee. "—so *something*."

"Self-assured?"

"I guess. Self-assured and smug, you know? Why is it teenagers are always so fucking smug?"

"Because they share a great secret," Martin said mildly, and took another bite of sprouts.

"Oh, yeah? What's that?"

"Their parents are all assholes."

Ariel snorted with laughter, leaned forward to get her teacup out of the danger zone and onto the table. "Oh, Martin," she said. Suddenly her eyes were filled with tears. "Damn it all to *hell* . . ."

Martin put his bowl on the table and stepped over to take her in his arms. He didn't say anything, and for a moment Ariel flashed back to the previous spring, the same tableau only in reverse, with her holding Martin while he sobbed uncontrollably in the kitchen of his San Francisco townhouse. It was two days after John's funeral, and she was on her way to the airport. She knew then about the breast cancer but she hadn't told Martin yet; didn't want to dim any of the dark luster of his grief.

Now it was her grief, but in a strange way she knew it was his, too. There was this awful thing that they held in common, a great unbroken chain of grief that wound from one coast to the other. She hadn't wanted to share it with Moony, hadn't wanted her to feel its weight and breadth. But it was too late, now. Moony knew and besides, what did it matter? She was dying, Martin was dying and there wasn't a fucking thing anyone could do about it.

"Hey," he said at last. His hand stroked her mass of dark hair, got itself tangled near her shoulder, snagging one of the long silver-and-quartz-crystal earrings she had put on that morning, for luck. "Ouch."

Ariel snorted again, laughing in spite of, or maybe because of, it all. Martin extricated his hand, held up two fingers with a long curling strand of hair caught between them: a question mark, a wise serpent waiting to strike. She had seen him after the cremation take the lock of John's hair that he had saved and hold it so, until suddenly it burst into flames, and then watched as the fizz of ash flared out in a dark penumbra around Martin's fingers. No such thing happened now, no Faery Pagan pyrotechnics. She wasn't dead yet, there was no sharp cold wind of grief to fan Martin's peculiar gift. He let the twirl of hair fall away and looked at her and said, "You know, I talked to Adele."

Adele was Mrs. Grose, she of the pug dog and suspiciously advanced years. Ariel retrieved her cup and her equanimity, sipping at the nettle tea as Martin went on, "She said she thought we had a good chance. You especially. She said for you it might happen. They might come." He finished and leaned back in his chair, spearing the last forkful of sprouts.

Ariel said, "Oh, yes?" Hardly daring to think of it; no don't think of it at all.

Martin shrugged, twisted to look over his shoulder at the endless sweep of Penobscot Bay. His eyes were bright, so bright she wondered if he were fighting tears or perhaps something else, something only Martin would allow himself to feel here and now. Joy, perhaps. Hope.

"Maybe," he said. At his words her heart beat a little faster in her breast, buried beneath the mass that was doing its best to crowd it out. "That's all. Maybe. It might. Happen."

And his hand snaked across the table to hers and held it, clutched it like it was a link in that chain that ran between them, until her fingers went cold and numb.

On Wednesday evenings the people at Mars Hill gave readings for the public. Tarot, palms, auras, dreams—five dollars a pop, nothing guaranteed. The chapel was cleaned, the altar swept of offerings and covered with a frayed red and-white checked table cloth from Diana's kitchen and a few candles in empty Chianti bottles.

"It's not very atmospheric," Gary Bonetti said, as someone always did. Mrs. Grose nodded from her bench and fiddled with her rosary beads.

"Au contraire," protested Martin. "It's *very* atmospheric, if you're in the mood for spaghetti carbonara at Luigi's."

"May I recommend the primavera?" said Jason. In honor of the occasion he had put on white duck pants and white shirt and red bow tie. He waved at Moony, who stood at the door taking five dollar bills from nervous, giggly tourists and the more solemn-faced locals, who made this pilgrimage every summer. Some regulars came week after week, year after year. Sad Brenda, hoping for the Tarot card that would bring news from her drowned child. Mr. Spruce, a ruddy-faced lobsterman who always tipped Mrs. Grose ten dollars. The Hamptonites Jason had dubbed Mr. and Mrs. Pissant, who were anxious about their auras. Tonight the lobsterman was there, with an ancient woman who could only be his mother, and the Pissants, and two teenage couples, long blonde hair and sunburned, reeking of marijuana and summer money.

The teenagers went to Martin, lured perhaps by his tie-dyed caftan, neatly pressed and swirling down to his Birkenstock-clad feet.

"Boat trash," hissed Jason, arching a nearly invisible white-blond eyebrow as they passed. "I saw them in Camden, getting off a yacht the size of the fire station. God, they make me sick."

Moony tightened her smile. Catch *her* admitting to envy of people like that. She swiveled on her chair, looking outside to see if there were any newcomers making their way to the chapel through the cool summer night. "I think this is gonna be it," she said. She glanced wistfully at the few crumpled bills nesting in an old oatmeal tin. "Maybe we should, like, advertise or something. It's been so slow this summer."

Jason only grunted, adjusting his bow tie and glaring at the rich kids, now deep in conference with his father. The Pissants had fallen to Diana, who with her chignon of blonde hair and gold-buttoned little black dress could have been one of their neighbors. That left the lobsterman and his aged mother.

They stood in the middle of the big room, looking not exactly uneasy or lost, but as though they were waiting for someone to usher them to their proper seats. And as though she read their minds (but wasn't that her job?), Mrs. Grose swept up suddenly from her corner of the chapel, a warm South Wind composed of yards of very old rayon fabric, Jean Naté After-Bath, and arms large and round and powdered as wheaten loaves.

"Mr. *Spruce*," she cried, extravagantly trilling her *rrr*'s and opening those arms like a stage gypsy. "You have come—"

"Why, yes," the lobsterman answered, embarrassed but also grateful. "I, uh—I brought my mother, Mrs. Grose. She says she remembers you."

"I do," said Mrs. Spruce. Moony twisted to watch, curious. She had always wondered about Mrs. Grose. She claimed to be a true clairvoyant. She *had* predicted things—nothing very useful, though. What the weather would be like the weekend of Moony's Junior Prom (rainy), but not whether she would be asked to go, or by whom. The day Jason would receive a letter from Harvard (Tuesday, the fifth of April), but not whether he'd be accepted there (he was not). It aggravated Moony, like so much at Mars Hill. What was the use of being a psychic if you could never come up with anything really useful?

But then there was the story about Harry Houdini. Mrs. Grose loved to tell it, how when she was still living in Chicago this short guy came one day and she gave him a message from his mother and he tried to make her out to be a fraud. It was a stupid story, except for one thing. If it really had happened, it would make Mrs. Grose about ninety or a hundred years old. And she didn't look a day over sixty.

Now Mrs. Grose was cooing over a woman who really *did* look to be about ninety. Mrs. Spruce peered up at her through rheumy eyes, shaking her head and saying in a whispery voice, "I can't believe it's you. I was just a girl, but you don't look any different at all . . ."

"Oh, flattery, flattery!" Mrs. Grose laughed and rubbed her nose with a Kleenex. "What can we tell you tonight, Mrs. Spruce?"

Moony turned away. It was too weird. She watched Martin entertaining the four golden children, then felt Jason coming up behind her: the way some people claim they can tell a cat is in the room, by some subtle disturbance of air and dust. A cat is there. Jason is there.

"They're *all* going to Harvard. I can't *believe* it," he said, mere disgust curdled into utter loathing. "And that one, the blond on the end—"

"They're all blond, Jason," said Moony. "*You're* blond."

"I am an *albino,*" Jason said with dignity. "Check him out, the Nazi Youth with the Pearl Jam T-shirt. He's a legacy, absolutely. SAT scores of 1060, tops. I *know.*" He closed his eyes and wiggled his fingers and made a *whoo-whoo* noise, beckoning spirits to come closer. Moony laughed and covered her mouth. From where he sat Martin raised an eyebrow, requesting silence. Moony and Jason turned and walked outside.

"How old do you think she is?" Moony asked, after they had gone a safe distance from the chapel.

"Who?"

"Mrs. Grose."

"Adele?" Jason frowned into the twilit distance, thinking of the murky shores and shoals of old age. "Jeez, I dunno. Sixty? Fifty?"

Moony shook her head. "She's got to be older than that. I mean, that story about Houdini, you know?"

"Huh! Houdini. The closest she ever got to Houdini is seeing some Siegfried and Roy show out in Las Vegas."

"I don't think she's ever left here. At least not since I can remember."

Jason nodded absently, then squatted in the untidy drive, squinting as he stared out into the darkness occluding the Bay. Fireflies formed mobile constellations within the birch trees. As a kid he had always loved fireflies, until he had seen Them. Now he

thought of the Light Children as a sort of evolutionary step, somewhere between lightning bugs and angels.

Though you hardly ever see Them at night, he thought. *Now why is
that?* He rocked back on his heels, looking like some slender pale
gargoyle toppled from a modernist cathedral, the cuffs of his white
oxford-cloth shirt rolled up to show large bony wrists and surprisingly strong square hands, his bow tie unraveled and hanging rakishly around his neck. Of a sudden he recalled being in this same
spot two years ago, grinding out a cigarette as Martin and John
approached. The smoke bothered John, sent him into paroxysms of
coughing so prolonged and intense that more than once they had
set Jason's heart pounding, certain that This Was It, John was going
to die right here, right now, and it would be all Jason's fault for
smoking. Only of course it didn't happen that way.

"The longest death since Little Nell's," John used to say, laughing
hoarsely. That was when he could still laugh, still talk. At the end it
had been others softly talking, Martin and Jason and their friends
gathered around John's bed at home, taking turns, spelling each
other. After a while Jason couldn't stand to be with them. It was too
much like John was already dead. The body in the bed so wasted,
bones cleaving to skin so thin and mottled it was like damp
newsprint.

By the end, Jason refused to accompany Martin to the therapist
they were supposed to see. He refused to go with him to the meetings where men and women talked about dying, about watching
loved ones go so horribly slowly. Jason just couldn't take it. Grief he
had always thought of as an emotion, a mood, something that pos-
sessed you but that you eventually escaped. Now he knew it was
different. Grief was a country, a place you entered hesitantly, or
were thrown into without warning. But once you were there,
amidst the roiling formless blackness and stench of despair, you
could not leave. Even if you wanted to: you could only walk and
walk and walk, traveling on through the black reaches with the
sound of screaming in your ears, and hope that someday you might
glimpse far off another country, another place where you might
someday rest.

Jason had followed John a long ways into that black land. And
now his own father would be going there. Maybe not for good, not

yet, but Jason knew. An HIV-positive diagnosis might mean that Death was a long ways off; but Jason knew his father had already started walking.

". . . you think they don't leave?"

Jason started. "Huh?" He looked up into Moony's wide gray eyes. "I'm sorry, what?"

"Why do you think they don't leave? Mrs. Grose and Gary. You know, the ones who stay here all year." Moony's voice was exasperated. He wondered how many times she'd asked him the same thing.

"I dunno. I mean, they *have* to leave sometimes. How do they get groceries and stuff?" He sighed and scrambled to his feet. "There's only two of them, maybe they pay someone to bring stuff in. I know Gary goes to the Beach Store sometimes. It's not like they're under house arrest. Why?"

Moony shrugged. In the twilight she looked spooky, more like a witch than her mother or Diana or any of those other wannabes. Long dark hair and those enormous pale gray eyes, face like the face of the cat who'd been turned into a woman in a fairy tale his father had read him once. Jason grinned, thinking of Moony jumping on a mouse. No way. But hey, even if she did, it would take more than *that* to turn him off.

"You thinking of staying here?" he asked slyly. He slipped an arm around her shoulders. "'Cause, like, I could keep you company or something. I hear Maine gets cold in the winter."

"No." Moony shrugged off his arm and started walking toward the water: no longer exasperated, more like she was distracted. "My mother is."

"Your *mother?*"

He followed her until she stopped at the edge of a gravel beach. The evening sky was clear. On the opposite shore, a few lights glimmered in Dark Harbor, reflections of the first stars overhead. From somewhere up along the coast, Bayside or Nagaseek or one of the other summer colonies, the sounds of laughter and skirling music echoed very faintly over the water, like a song heard on some distant station very late at night. But it wasn't late, not yet even nine o'clock. In summers past, that had been early for Moony and Jason, who would often stay up with the adults talking and poring over cards and runes until the night grew cold and spent.

But tonight for some reason the night already felt old. Jason shivered and kicked at the pebbly beach. The last pale light of sunset cast an antique glow upon stones and touched the edge of the water with gold. As he watched, the light withdrew, a gauzy veil drawn back teasingly until the shore shimmered with afterglow, like blue glass.

"I heard her talking with Diana," Moony said. Her voice was unsettlingly loud and clear in the still air. "She was saying she might stay on, after I go off to school. I mean, she was talking like she wasn't going back at all, I mean not back to Kamensic. Like she might just stay here and never leave again." Her voice cracked on the words *never leave again* and she shuddered, hugging herself.

"Hey," said Jason. He walked over and put his arms around her, her dark hair a perfumed net that drew him in until he felt dizzy and had to draw back, gasping a little, the smell of her nearly overwhelming that of rugosa roses and the sea. "Hey, it's okay, Moony, really it's okay."

Moony's voice sounded explosive, as though she had been holding her breath. "I just can't believe she's giving *up* like this. I mean, no doctors, nothing. She's just going to stay here and die."

"She might not die," said Jason, his own voice a little desperate. "I mean, look at Adele. A century and counting. The best is yet to come."

Moony laughed brokenly. She leaned forward so that her hair once again spilled over him, her wet cheek resting on his shoulder. "Oh, Jason. If it weren't for you I'd go crazy, you know that? I'd just go fucking nuts."

Nuts, thought Jason. His arms tightened around her, the cool air and faraway music nearly drowning him as he stroked her head and breathed her in. *Crazy, oh, yes.* And they stood there until the moon showed over Dark Harbor, and all that far-off music turned to silvery light above the Bay.

Two days later Ariel and Moony went to see the doctor in Bangor. Moony drove, an hour's trip inland, up along the old road that ran beside the Penobscot River, through failed stonebound farms and past trailer encampments like sad rusted toys, until finally they reached the sprawl around the city, the kingdom of car lots and franchises and shopping plazas.

The hospital was an old brick building with a shiny new white wing grafted on. Ariel and Moony walked through a gleaming steel-and-glass door set in the expanse of glittering concrete. But they ended up in a tired office on the far end of the old wing, where the squeak of rubber wheels on worn linoleum played counterpoint to a loudly echoing, ominous *drip-drip* that never ceased the whole time they were there.

"Ms. Rising. Please, come in."

Ariel squeezed her daughter's hand, then followed the doctor into her office. It was a small bright room, a hearty wreath of living ivy trained around its single grimy window in defiance of the lack of sunlight and, perhaps, the black weight of despair that Ariel felt everywhere, chairs, desk, floor, walls.

"I received your records from New York," the doctor said. She was a slight fine-boned young woman with sleek straight hair and a silk dress more expensive than what you usually saw in Maine. The little metal name-tag on her breast might have been an odd bit of heirloom jewelry. "You realize that even as of three weeks ago, the cancer had spread to the point where our treatment options are now quite limited."

Ariel nodded, her arms crossed protectively across her chest. She felt strange, light-headed. She hadn't been able to eat much the last day or two, that morning had swallowed a mouthful of coffee and a stale muffin to satisfy Moony but that was all. "I know," she said heavily. "I don't know why I'm here."

"Frankly, I don't know either," the doctor replied. "If you had optioned for some kind of intervention oh, even two months ago; but now . . ."

Ariel tilted her head, surprised at how sharp the other woman's tone was. The doctor went on, "It's a great burden to put on your daughter—" She looked in the direction of the office door, then glanced down at the charts in her hand. "Other children?"

Ariel shook her head. "No."

The doctor paused, gently slapping the sheaf of charts and records against her open palm. Finally she said, "Well. Let's examine you, then."

An hour later Ariel slipped back into the waiting room. Moony looked up from a magazine. Her gray eyes were bleary and her tired expression hastily congealed into the mask of affronted resentment with which she faced Ariel these days.

"So?" she asked as they retraced their steps back through cinder-block corridors to the hospital exit. "What'd she say?"

Ariel stared straight ahead, through the glass doors to where the summer afternoon waited to pounce on them. Exhaustion had seeped into her like heat; like the drugs the doctor had offered and Ariel had refused, the contents of crystal vials that could buy a few more weeks, maybe even months if she was lucky, enough time to make a graceful farewell to the world. But Ariel didn't want weeks or months, and she sure as hell didn't want graceful goodbyes. She wanted years, decades. A cantankerous or dreamy old age, aggravating the shit out of her grandchildren with her talk about her own sunflower youth. Failing that, she wanted screaming and gnashing of teeth, her friends tearing their hair out over her death, and Moony . . .

And Moony. Ariel stopped in front of a window, one hand out to press against the smooth cool glass. Grief and horror hit her like a stone, struck her between the eyes so that she gasped and drew her hands to her face.

"Mom!" Moony cried, shocked. "Mom, what *is* it, are you all right?—"

Ariel nodded, tears burning down her cheeks. "I'm fine," she said, and gave a twisted smile. "Really, I'm—"

"What did she *say?*" demanded Moony. "The doctor, what did she tell you, *what is it?*"

Ariel wiped her eyes, a black line of mascara smeared across her finger. "Nothing. Really, Moony, nothing's changed. It's just—it's just hard. Being this sick. It's hard, that's all."

She could see in her daughter's face confusion, despair, but also relief. Ariel hadn't said *death,* she hadn't said *dying,* she hadn't since that first day said *cancer.* She'd left those words with the doctor, along with the scrips for morphine and Fiorinal, all that could be offered to her now. "Come on," she said, and walked through the sliding doors. "I'm supposed to have lunch with Mrs. Grose and Diana, and it's already late."

Moony stared at her in disbelief: was her mother being stoic or just crazy? But Ariel didn't say anything else, and after a moment her daughter followed her to the car.

In Mars Hill's little chapel Jason sat and smoked. On the altar in front of him were several weeks' accumulated offerings from the denizens of Mars Hill. An old-fashioned envelope with a glassine window, through which he could glimpse the face of a twenty-dollar bill—that was from Mrs. Grose, who always gave the money she'd earned from readings (and then retrieved it at the end of the summer). A small square of brilliantly woven cloth from Diana, whose looms punctuated the soft morning with their steady racketing. A set of blueprints from Rvis Capricorn. Shasta Daisy's battered *Ephemera.* The copy of Paul Bowles' autobiography that Jason's father had been reading on the flight out from the West Coast. In other words, the usual flotsam of love and whimsy that washed up here every summer. From where Jason sat, he could see his own benefaction, a heap of small white roses, already limp but still giving out their heady sweet scent, and a handful of blackberries he'd picked from the thicket down by the pier. Not much of an offering, but you never knew.

From beneath his roses peeked the single gift that puzzled him, a lacy silk camisole patterned with pale pink-and-yellow blossoms. An odd choice of offering, Jason thought. Because for all the unattached adults sipping chardonnay and Bellinis of a summer evening, the atmosphere at Mars Hill was more like that of summer camp. A chaste sort of giddiness ruled here, compounded of equal parts of joy and longing, that always made Jason think of the garlanded jackass and wistful fairies in *A Midsummer Night's Dream.* His father and Ariel and all the rest stumbling around in the dark, hoping for a glimpse of Them, and settling for fireflies and the lights from Dark Harbor. Mars Hill held surprisingly little in the way of unapologetic lust—except for himself and Moony, of course. And Jason knew that camisole didn't belong to Moony.

At the thought of Moony he sighed and tapped his ashes onto the dusty floor. It was a beautiful morning, gin-clear and with a stiff warm breeze from the west. Perfect sailing weather. He should be out with his father on the *Wendameen*. Instead he'd stayed behind, to write and think. Earlier he'd tried to get through to Moony somewhere in Bangor, but Jason couldn't send his thoughts any farther than from one end of Mars Hill to the other. For some reason, smoking cigarettes seemed to help. He had killed half a pack already this morning, but gotten nothing more than a headache and a raw throat. Now he had given up. It never seemed to work with anyone except Moony, anyhow, and then only if she was nearby.

He had wanted to give her some comfort. He wanted her to know how much he loved her, how she meant more to him than anyone or anything in the world, except perhaps his father. Was it allowed, to feel this much for a person when your father was HIV-positive? Jason frowned and stubbed out his cigarette in a lobster-shaped ashtray, already overflowing with the morning's telepathic aids. He picked up his notebook and Rapidograph pen and, still frowning, stared at the letter he'd begun last night.

Dearest Moony,

(he crossed out est, it sounded too fussy)

I just want you to know that I understand how you feel.
When John died it was the most horrible thing in the
world, even worse than the divorce because I was just a kid
then. I just want you to know how much I love you, you
mean more than anyone or anything in the world, and

And what? Did he really know how she felt? His mother wasn't dying, his mother was in the Napa Valley running her vineyard, and while it was true enough that John's death had been the most horrible thing he'd ever lived through, could that be the same as having your mother die? He thought maybe it could. And then of course there was the whole thing with his father. Was that worse? His father wasn't sick, of course, at least he didn't have any symptoms yet; but was it worse for someone you loved to have the AIDS virus, to watch and wait for months or years, rather than have it happen quickly like with Ariel? Last night he'd sat in the living room while his father and Gary Bonetti were on the porch talking about her.

"I give her only a couple of weeks," Martin had said, with that dry strained calm voice he'd developed over the last few years of watching his friends die. "The thing is, if she'd gone for treatment right away she could be fine now. She could be *fine*." The last word came out in an uncharacteristic burst of vehemence, and Jason grew cold to hear it. Because of course even with treatment his father probably wouldn't be all right, not now, not ever. He'd never be fine again. Ariel had thrown all that away.

"She should talk to Adele," Gary said softly. Jason heard the clink of ice as he poured himself another daiquiri. "When I had those visions five years ago, that's when I saw Adele. You should, too, Martin. You really should."

"I don't know as Adele can help me," Martin said, somewhat coolly. "She's just a guest here, like you or any of the rest of us. And *you* know that you can't make Them . . ."

His voice trailed off. Jason sat bolt upright on the sofa, suddenly feeling his father there, like a cold finger stabbing at his brain.

"Jason?" Martin called, his voice tinged with annoyance. "If you want to listen, come in *here,* please."

Jason had sworn under his breath and stormed out through the back door. It was impossible, sometimes, living with his father. Better to have a psychic wannabe like Ariel for a parent, and not have to worry about being spied on all the time.

Now, from outside the chapel came frenzied barking. Jason started, his thoughts broken. He glanced through the open door to see Gary and his black labrador retriever heading down to the water. Gary was grinning, arms raised as he waved at someone out of sight. And suddenly Jason had an image of his father in the *Wendameen,* the fast little sloop skirting the shore as Martin stood at the mast waving back, his long hair tangled by the wind. The vision left Jason nearly breathless. He laughed, shaking his head, and at once decided to follow Gary to the landing and meet his father there. He picked up his pen and notebook and turned to go. Then stopped, his neck prickling. Very slowly he turned, until he stood facing the altar once more.

They were there. A shimmering haze above the fading roses, like Zeus's golden rain falling upon imprisoned Danaë. Jason's breath caught in his throat as he watched Them—They were so beautiful, so *strange*. Flickering in the chapel's dusty air, like so many scintillant coins. He could sense rather than hear a faint chiming as They darted quick as hummingbirds from his roses to Mrs. Grose's envelope, alighting for a moment upon Diana's weaving and Rvis's prize tomatoes before settling upon two things: his father's book and the unknown camisole.

And then with a sharp chill Jason knew whose it was. Ariel's, of course—who else would own something so unabashedly romantic but also slightly tacky? Maybe it was meant to be a bad joke, or perhaps it was a real offering, heartfelt, heartbreaking. He stared at Them, a glittering carpet tossed over those two pathetic objects, and had to shield his eyes with his hand. It was too bright, They seemed to be growing more and more brilliant as he watched. Like a swarm of butterflies he had once seen, mourning cloaks resting in a snow-covered field one warm March afternoon, their wings slowly fanning the air as though They had been stunned by the thought of spring. But what could ever surprise *Them,* the Light Children, the summer's secret?

Then as he watched They began to fade. The glowing golden edge of the swarm grew dim and disappeared. One by one all the other gilded coins blinked into nothing, until the altar stood as it had minutes before, a dusty collection of things, odd and somewhat ridiculous. Jason's head pounded and he felt faint; then realized he'd been holding his breath. He let it out, shuddering, put his pen and notebook on the floor and walked to the altar.

Everything was as it had been, roses, cloth, paper, tomatoes; excepting only his father's offering, and Ariel's. Hesitantly he reached to touch the book Martin had left, then recoiled.

The cover of the book had been damaged. When he leaned over to stare at it more closely, he saw that myriad tiny holes had been burned in the paper, in what at first seemed to be a random pattern. But when he picked it up—gingerly, as though it might yet release an electrical jolt or some other hidden energy—he saw that the tiny perforations formed an image, blurred but unmistakable. The shadow of a hand, four fingers splayed across the cover as though gripping it.

Jason went cold. He couldn't have explained how, but he knew that it was a likeness of his father's hand that he saw there, eerie and chilling as those monstrous shadows left by victims of the bombings at Hiroshima and Nagasaki. With a frightened gasp he tossed the book back onto the altar. For a moment he stood beside the wooden table, half-poised to flee; but finally reached over and tentatively pushed aside his roses to fully reveal the camisole.

It was just like the book. Thousands of tiny burn-holes made a ruined lace of the pastel silk, most of them clustered around one side of the bodice. He picked it up, catching a faint fragrance, lavender and marijuana, and held it out by its pink satin straps. He raised it, turning toward the light streaming through the chapel's picture window, and saw that the pinholes formed a pattern, elegant as the tracery of veins and capillaries on a leaf. A shadowy bull's-eye—breast, aureole, nipple drawn on the silken cloth.

With a small cry Jason dropped the camisole. Without looking back he ran from the chapel. Such was his hurry that he forgot his pen and notebook and the half-written letter to Moony, piled carefully on the dusty floor. And so he did not see the shining constellation that momentarily appeared above the pages, a curious cloud that hovered there like a child's dream of weather before flowering into a golden rain.

Moony sat hunched on the front stoop, waiting for her mother to leave. Ariel had been in her room for almost half an hour, her luncheon date with Diana and Mrs. Grose notwithstanding. When finally she emerged, Moony could hear the soft uneven tread of her flip-flops, padding from bedroom to bedroom to kitchen. There was the sigh of the refrigerator opening and closing, the muted pop of a cork being pulled from a bottle, the long grateful gurgle of wine being poured into a glass. Then Ariel herself in the doorway behind her. Without looking Moony could tell that she'd put on The Skirt. She could smell it, the musty scents of patchouli and cannabis resin and the honeysuckle smell of the expensive detergent Ariel used to wash it by hand, as though it were some precious winding sheet.

"I'm going to Adele's for lunch."

Moony nodded silently.

"I'll be back in a few hours."

More silence.

"You know where to find me if anyone comes by." Ariel nudged her daughter gently with her toe. "Okay?"

Moony sighed. "Yeah, okay."

She watched her mother walk out the door, sun bouncing off her hair in glossy waves. When Ariel was out of sight she hurried down the hall.

In her mother's room, piles of clothes and papers covered the worn Double Wedding Ring quilt, as though tossed helter-skelter from her bureau.

"Jeez, what a mess," said Moony. She slowly crossed to the bed. It was covered with scarves and tangled skeins of pantyhose; drifts of old catering receipts, bills, canceled checks. A few paperbacks with yellowed pages that had been summer reading in years past. A back issue of *Gourmet* magazine and the *Maine Progressive*. A Broadway ticket stub from *Prelude to a Kiss*. Grimacing, Moony prodded the edge of last year's calendar from the Beach Store & Pizza to Go.

What had her mother been looking for?

Then, as if by magic, Moony saw it. Its marbled cover suddenly glimpsed beneath a dusty strata of tarot cards and Advil coupons, like some rare bit of fossil, lemur vertebrae or primate jaw hidden within papery shale. She drew it out carefully, tilting it so the light slid across the title.

MARS HILL: ITS HISTORY AND LORE
BY
ABIGAIL MERITHEW COX
A LOVER OF ITS MYSTERIES

With careful fingers Moony rifled the pages. Dried rose petals fell out, releasing the sad smell of summers past, and then a longer plume of liatris dropped to the floor, fresh enough to have left a faint purplish stain upon the page. Moony drew the book up curiously, marking the page where the liatris had fallen, and read,

Perhaps strangest of all the Mysteries of our Colony at Mars Hill is the presence of those Enchanted Visitors who make their appearance now and then, to the eternal Delight of those of us fortunate enough to receive the benison of their

presence. I say Delight, though many of us who have con-
jured with them say that the Experience resembles Rapture
more than mere Delight, and even that Surpassing Ecstasy
of which the Ancients wrote and which is at the heart of all
our Mysteries; though we are not alone in enjoying the favor
of our Visitors. It is said by my Aunt, Sister Rosemary
Merithew, that the Pasamaquoddie Indians who lived here
long before the civilizing influence of the White Man, also
entertained these Ethereal Creatures, which are in appearance like to those fairy lights called Foxfire or Will O'The
Wisp, and which may indeed be the inspiration for such
spectral rumors. The Pasamaquoddie named them Akiniki,
which in their language means The Greeters; and this I
think is a most appropriate title for our Joyous Guests, who
bring only Good News from the Other Side, and who feast
upon our mortality as a man sups upon rare meats . . .

Moony stared at the page in horror and disgust. *Feasting* upon
mortality? She recalled her mother and Jason talking about the
things they called the Light Children, Jason's disappointment that
They had never appeared to Moony. As though there was something
wrong with her, as though she wasn't worthy of seeing Them. But
she had never felt that way. She had always suspected that Jason
and her mother and the rest were mistaken about the Light
Children. When she was younger, she had even accused her mother
of lying about seeing Them. But the other people at Mars Hill spoke
of Them, and Jason, at least, would never lie to Moony. So she had
decided there must be something slightly delusional about the
whole thing. Like a mass hypnosis, or maybe some kind of mass
drug flashback, which seemed more likely considering the histories
of some of her mother's friends.
    Still, that left Mrs. Grose, who never even took an aspirin.
Who, as far as Moony knew, had never been sick in her life, and
who certainly seemed immune to most of the commonplace ail-
ments of what must be, despite appearances, an advanced age.
Mrs. Grose claimed to speak with the Light Children, to have a sort
of understanding of Them that Ariel and the others lacked. And
Moony had always held Mrs. Grose in awe. Maybe because her

own grandparents were all dead, maybe just because of that story about Houdini—it was too fucking weird, no one could have made it up.

And so maybe no one had made up the Light Children, either. Moony tapped the book's cover, frowning. Why couldn't she see Them? Was it because she didn't believe? The thought annoyed her. As though she were a kid who'd found out about Santa Claus, and was being punished for learning the truth. She stared at the book's cover, the gold lettering flecked with dust, the peppering of black and green where salt air and mildew had eaten away at the cloth. The edge of one page crumbled as she opened it once more.

> Many of my brothers and sisters can attest to the virtues of Our Visitors, particularly Their care for the dying and afflicted . . .

"Fucking *bullshit*," yelled Moony. She threw the book across the room, hard, so that it slammed into the wall beside her mother's bureau. With a soft crack the spine broke. She watched stonily as yellow pages and dried blossoms fluttered from between the split covers, a soft explosion of antique dreams. She left the room without picking up the mess, the door slamming shut behind her.

"I was consumptive," Mrs. Grose was saying, nodding as she looked in turn from Ariel to Diana to the pug sprawled panting on the worn chintz sofa beside them. "Tuberculosis, you know. Coming here saved me."

"You mean like, taking the waters?" asked Ariel. She shook back her hair and took another sip of her gin-and-tonic. "Like they used to do at Saratoga Springs and places like that?"

"Not like that *at all*," replied Mrs. Grose firmly. She raised one white eyebrow and frowned. "I mean, Mars Hill saved me."

Saved you for what? thought Ariel, choking back another mouthful of gin. She shuddered. She knew she shouldn't drink, these days she could feel it seeping into her, like that horrible barium they injected into you to do tests. But she couldn't stop. And what was the point, anyway?

"But you think it might help her, if she stayed here?" Diana broke in, oblivious of Mrs. Grose's imperious gaze. "And Martin, do you think it could help him, too?"

"*I* don't think *anything*," said Mrs. Grose, and she reached over to envelope the wheezing pug with one large fat white hand. "It is absolutely not up to me at all. I am simply *telling* you the *facts*."

"Of course," Ariel said, but she could tell from Diana's expression that her words had come out slurred. "Of *course*," she repeated with dignity, sitting up and smoothing the folds of her patchwork skirt.

"As long as you understand," Mrs. Grose said in a gentler tone. "We are guests here, and guests do not ask favors of their hosts."

The other two women nodded. Ariel carefully put her glass on the coffee table and stood, wiping her sweating hands on her skirt. "I better go now," she said. Her head pounded and she felt nauseated, for all that she'd barely nibbled at the ham sandwiches and macaroni salad Mrs. Grose had set out for lunch. "Home. I think I'd better go home."

"I'll go with you," said Diana. She stood and cast a quick look at their hostess. "I wanted to borrow that book . . ."

Mrs. Grose saw them to the door, holding open the screen and swatting threateningly at mosquitoes as they walked outside. "Remember what I told you," she called as they started down the narrow road, Diana with one arm around Ariel's shoulder. "Meditation and nettle tea. And patience."

"Patience," Ariel murmured; but nobody heard.

The weeks passed. The weather was unusually clear and warm, Mars Hill bereft of the cloak of mist and fog that usually covered it in August. Martin Dionysos took the *Wendameen* out nearly every afternoon, savoring the time alone, the hours spent fighting wind and waves—antagonists he felt he could win against.

"It's the most perfect summer we've ever had," Gary Bonetti said often to his friend. *Too* often, Martin thought bitterly. Recently, Martin was having what Jason called Millennial Thoughts, seeing ominous portents in everything from the tarot cards he dealt out to stricken tourists on Wednesday nights to the pattern of kelp and maidenhair left on the gravel beach after one of the summer's few storms. He had taken to avoiding Ariel, a move that filled him with self-loathing, for all that he told himself that he still needed time to grieve for John before giving himself over to another death. But it wasn't that, of course. Or at least it wasn't *only* that. It was fear, *The Fear*. It was listening to his own heart pounding as he lay alone in bed at night, counting the beats, wondering at what point it all began to break down, at what point It would come to take him.

So he kept to himself. He begged off going on the colony's weekly outing to the little Mexican restaurant up the road. He even stopped attending the weekly readings in the chapel. Instead, he spent his evenings alone, writing to friends back in the Bay Area. After drinking coffee with Jason every morning he'd turn away.

"I'm going to work now," he'd announce, and Jason would nod and leave to find Moony, grateful, his father thought, for the opportunity to escape.

Millennial Thoughts.

Martin Dionysos had given over a corner of his cottage's living room to a studio. There was a tiny drafting table, his portable computer, an easel, stacks of books; the week's forwarded offerings of *Out!* and *The Advocate* and *Q* and *The Bay Weekly,* and, heaped on an ancient stained Windsor chair, the usual pungent mess of oils and herbal decoctions that he used in his work. Golden morning light streamed through the wide mullioned windows, smelling of salt and the diesel fumes from Diana's ancient Volvo. On the easel a large unprimed canvas rested, somewhat unevenly due to the cant of a floor slanted enough that you could drop a marble in the kitchen and watch it roll slowly but inexorably to settle in the left-hand corner of the living room. Gary Bonetti claimed that it wasn't that all of the cottages on Mars Hill were built by incompetent architects. It was the magnetic pull of the ocean just meters away; it was the imperious reins of the East, of the Moon, of the magic charters of the Otherworld, that made it impossible to find any two corners that were plumb. Martin and the others laughed at Gary's pronouncement, but John had believed it.

John. Martin sighed, stirred desultorily at a coffee can filled with linseed oil and turpentine, then rested the can on the windowsill. For a long time he had been so caught up with the sad and harrowing and noble and disgusting details of John's dying that he had been able to forestall thinking about his own diagnosis. He had been grateful, in an awful way, that there had been something so horrible, so unavoidably and demandingly *real,* to keep him from succumbing to his own despair.

But all that was gone now. John was gone. Before John's death, Martin had always had a sort of unspoken, formless belief in an afterlife. The long shadow cast by a 1950s Catholic boyhood, he guessed. But when John died, that small hidden solace had died, too. There was nothing there. No vision of a beloved waiting for him on the other side. Not even a body moldering within a polished mahogany casket. Only ashes, ashes; and his own death waiting like a small patient vicious animal in the shadows.

"Shit," he said. He gritted his teeth. This was how it happened to Ariel. She gave in to despair, or dreams, or maybe she just pretended it would go away. She'd be lucky now to last out the summer. At the thought a new wave of grief washed over him, and he groaned.

"Oh, shit, shit, shit," he whispered. With watering eyes he reached for the can full of primer on the sill. As he did so, he felt a faint prickling go through his fingers, a sensation of warmth that was almost painful. He swore under his breath and frowned. A tiny stab of fear lanced through him. Inexplicable and sudden pain, wasn't that the first sign of some sort of degeneration? As his fingers tightened around the coffee can, he looked up. The breath froze in his throat and he cried aloud, snatching his hand back as though he'd been stung.

They were there. Dozens of Them, a horde of flickering golden spots so dense They obliterated the wall behind Them. Martin had seen Them before, but never so close, never so many. He gasped and staggered back, until he struck the edge of the easel and sent the canvas clattering to the floor. They took no notice, instead followed him like a swarm of silent hornets. And as though They were hornets, Martin shouted and turned to run.

Only he could not. He was blinded, his face seared by a terrible heat. They were everywhere, enveloping him in a shimmering cocoon of light and warmth, Their fierce radiance burning his flesh, his eyes, his throat, as though he breathed in liquid flame. He shrieked, batting at the air, and then babbling fell back against the wall. As They swarmed over him he felt Them, not as you feel the sun but as you feel a drug or love or anguish, filling him until he moaned and sank to the floor. He could feel his skin burning and erupting, his bones turning to ash inside him. His insides knotted, cramping until he thought he would faint. He doubled over, retching, but only a thin stream of spittle ran down his chin. An explosive burst of pain raced through him. He opened his mouth to scream, the sound so thin it might have been an insect whining. Then there was nothing but light, nothing but flame; and Martin's body unmoving on the floor.

Moony waited until late afternoon, but Jason never came. Hours earlier, Moony had glanced out the window of her cottage and seen Gary Bonetti running up the hill to Martin's house, followed minutes later by the panting figure of Mrs. Grose. Jason she didn't see at all. He must have never left his cottage that morning, or else left and returned by the back door.

Something had happened to Martin. She knew that as soon as she saw Gary's stricken face. Moony thought of calling Jason, but did not. She did nothing, only paced and stared out the window at Jason's house, hoping vainly to see someone else enter or leave. No one did.

Ariel had been sleeping all day. Moony avoided even walking past her mother's bedroom, lest her own terror wake her. She was afraid to leave the cottage, afraid to find out the truth. Cold dread stalked her all afternoon as she waited for something—an ambulance, a phone call, *anything*—but nothing happened. Nobody called, nobody came. Although once, her nostrils filled with the acrid smell of cigarette smoke, and she felt Jason there. Not Jason himself, but an overwhelming sense of terror that she knew came from him, a fear so intense that she drew her breath in sharply, her hand shooting out to steady herself against the door. Then the smell of smoke was gone.

"Jason?" she whispered, but she knew he was no longer thinking of her. She stood with her hand pressed against the worn silvery frame of the screen door. She kept expecting Jason to appear, to explain things. But there was nothing. For the first time all summer, Jason seemed to have forgotten her. Everyone seemed to have forgotten her.

That had been hours ago. Now it was nearly sunset. Moony lay on her towel on the gravel beach, swiping at a mosquito and staring up at the cloudless sky, blue skimmed to silver as the sun melted away behind Mars Hill. What a crazy place this was. Someone gets sick, and instead of dialing 911 you send for an obese old fortuneteller. The thought made her stomach churn; because of course that's what her mother had done. Put her faith in fairydust and crystals instead of physicians and chemo. Abruptly Moony sat up, hugging her knees.

"Damn," she said miserably

She'd put off going home, half-hoping, half-dreading that someone would find her and tell her what the hell was going on. Now it was obvious that she'd have to find out for herself. She threw her towel into her bag, tugged on a hooded pullover and began to trudge back up the hill.

On the porches of the other cottages she could see people stirring. Whatever had happened, obviously none of *them* had heard yet. The new lesbian couple from Burlington sat facing each other in matching wicker armchairs, eyes closed and hands extended. A few houses on, Shasta Daisy sat on the stoop of her tiny Queen Anne Victorian, sipping a wine cooler, curled sheets of graph paper littering the table in front of her.

"Where's your mom?" Shasta called.

Moony shrugged and wiped a line of sweat from her cheek. "Resting, I guess."

"Come have a drink." Shasta raised her bottle. "I'll do your chart."

Moony shook her head. "Later. I got to get dinner."

"Don't forget there's a moon circle tonight," said Shasta. "Nine thirty at the gazebo."

"Right." Moony nodded, smiling glumly as she passed. What a bunch of kooks. At least her mother would be sleeping and not wasting her time conjuring up someone's aura between wine coolers.

But when she got home, no one was there. She called her mother's name as the screen door banged shut behind her, waited for a reply but there was none. For an instant a terrifying surge raced through her: something else had happened, her mother lay dead in the bedroom . . .

But the bedroom was empty, as were the living room and bath-room and anyplace else where Ariel might have chosen to die. The heady scent of basil filled the cottage, with a fainter hint of mari-juana. When Moony finally went into the kitchen, she found the sink full of sand and half-rinsed basil leaves. Propped up on the drainboard was a damp piece of paper towel with a message spelled out in runny magic marker.

Moony: Went to Chapel
Moon circle at 9:30
Love love love Mom

"Right," Moony said, disgusted. She crumpled the note and threw it on the floor. "Way to go, Mom."

Marijuana, moon circle, astrological charts. Fucking *idiots*. Of a sudden she was filled with rage, at her mother and Jason and Martin and all the rest. Why weren't there any *doctors* here? Or lawyers, or secretaries, or anyone with half a brain, enough at least to take some responsibility for the fact that there were sick people here, people who were *dying* for Christ's sake and what was anyone doing about it? What was *she* doing about it?

"I've had it," she said aloud. "I have *had* it." She spun around and headed for the front door, her long hair an angry black blur around her grim face. "Amanda Rheining, you are going to the hos-pital. *Now.*"

She strode down the hill, ignoring Shasta's questioning cries. The gravel bit into her bare feet as she rounded the turn leading to the chapel. From here she could glimpse the back door of Jason and Martin's cottage. As Moony hurried past a stand of birches, she glimpsed Diana standing by the door, one hand resting on its crooked wooden frame. She was gazing out at the Bay with a rapt expression that might have been joy or exhausted grief, her hair gilded with the dying light.

For a moment Moony stopped, biting her lip. Diana at least might understand. She could ask Diana to come and help her force

Ariel to go to the hospital. It would be like the intervention they'd done with Diana's ex-husband. But that would mean going to Martin's cottage, and confronting whatever it was that waited inside. Besides, Moony knew that no one at Mars Hill would ever force Ariel to do something she didn't want to do; even live. No. It was up to her to save her mother: herself, Maggie Rheining. Abruptly she turned away.

Westering light fell through the leaves of the ancient oak that shadowed the weathered gray chapel. The lupines and tiger lilies had faded with the dying summer. Now violet plumes of liatris sprang up around the chapel door beside unruly masses of sweet-smelling phlox and glowing clouds of asters. Of course no one ever weeded or thinned out the garden. The flowers choked the path leading to the door, so that Moony had to beat away a net of bees and lacewings and pale pink moths like rose petals, all of them rising from the riot of blossoms and then falling in a softly moving skein about the girl's shoulders as she walked. Moony cursed and slashed at the air, heedless of a luna moth's drunken somersault above her head, the glimmering wave of fireflies that followed her through the twilight.

At the chapel doorway Moony stopped. Her heart was beating hard, and she spat and brushed a liatris frond from her mouth. From inside she could hear a low voice; her mother's voice. She was reciting the verse that, over the years, had become a sort of blessing for her, a little mantra she chanted and whispered summer after summer, always in hopes of summoning Them—

> "With this field-dew consecrate
> Every fairy take his gait
> And each several chamber bless,
> through this palace, with sweet peace;
> Ever shall in safety rest,
> and the owner of it blest."

At the sound, Moony felt her heart clench inside her. She moved until her face pressed against the ancient gray screen sagging within its doorframe. The screen smelled heavily of dust; she pinched her nose to keep from sneezing. She gazed through the fine moth-pocked web as though through a silken scrim or the Bay's accustomed fog.

Her mother was inside. She stood before the wooden altar, pathetic with its faded burden of wilting flowers and empty bottles and Jason's cigarette butts scattered across the floor. From the window facing the Bay, lilac-colored light flowed into the room, mingling with the shafts of dusty gold falling from the casements set high within the opposing wall. Where the light struck the floor a small bright pool had formed. Ariel was dancing slowly in and out of this, her thin arms raised, the long heavy sweep of her patchwork skirt sliding back and forth to reveal her slender legs and bare feet, shod with a velvety coat of dust. Moony could hear her reciting, Shakespeare's fairies' song again, and a line from Julian of Norwich that Diana had taught her:

All will be well, and all will be well, and all manner of things will be well.

And suddenly the useless purity of Ariel's belief overwhelmed Moony. A stoned forty-three-year-old woman with breast cancer and a few weeks left to live, dancing inside a ruined chapel and singing to herself. Tears filled Moony's eyes, fell and left a dirty streak against the screen. She drew a deep breath, fighting the wave of grief and despair, and pushed against the screen to enter. When she raised her head again, Ariel had stopped.

At first Moony thought her mother had seen her. But no. Ariel was staring straight ahead at the altar, her head cocked to one side as though listening. So intent was she that Moony stiffened as well, inexplicably frightened. She glanced over her shoulder, but of course there was no one there. But it was too late to keep her heart from pounding. She closed her eyes, took a deep breath and turned, stepping over the sill toward Ariel.

"Mom," Moony called softly. "Mom, I'm—"

Moony froze. In the center of the chapel her mother stood, arms writhing as she held them above her head, long hair whipping across her face. She was on fire. Flickers of gold and crimson ran along her arms and chest, lapped at her throat and face and set runnels of light flaming across her clothes. Moony could hear her shrieking, could see her tearing at her breast as she tried to rip away the burning fabric. With a howl Moony stumbled across the room—not thinking, hardly even seeing her as she lunged to grab Ariel and pull her down.

"*Mom!*"

But before she could reach Ariel she tripped, smashed onto the uneven floor. Groaning she rolled over and tried to get back up. An arm's-length away, her mother flailed, her voice given over now to a high shrill keening, her flapping arms still raised above her head. And for the first time Moony realized that there was no real heat, no flames. No smoke filled the little room. The light that streamed through the picture window was clear and bright as dawn.

Her mother was not on fire. She was with Them.

They were everywhere, like bees swarming across a bank of flowers. Radiant beads of gold and argent covered Ariel until Moony no longer saw her mother, but only the blazing silhouette of a woman, a numinous figure that sent a prismatic aurora rippling across the ceiling. Moony fell back, horrified, awe-struck. The figure continued its bizarre dance, hands lifting and falling as though reaching for something that was being pulled just out of reach. She could hear her mother's voice, muted now to a soft repetitive cry—*uh, uh!*—and a very faint clear tone, like the sustained note of a glass harmonica.

"Jesus," Moony whispered, then yelled, "*Jesus!* Stop it, *stop*—"

But They didn't stop; only moved faster and faster across Ariel's body until her mother was nothing but a blur, a chrysalis encased in glittering pollen, a burning ghost. Moony's breath scraped against her throat. Her hands clawed at her knees, the floor, her own breasts, as her mother kept on with that soft moaning and the sound of the Light Children filled the chapel the way wine fills a glass.

And then gradually it all began to subside. Gradually the glowing sheath fell from her mother, not fading so much as *thinning,* the way Moony had once read the entrance to a woman's womb will thin as its burden wakes to be born. The chiming noise died away. There was only a faint high echo in Moony's ears. Violet light spilled from the high windows, a darker if weaker wine. Ariel sprawled on the dusty floor, her arms curled up against her chest like the dried hollow limbs of an insect, scarab or patient mantis. Her mouth was slack, and the folds of tired skin around her eyes. She looked inut-

terably exhausted, but also somehow at peace. With a cold stab like
a spike driven into her breast, Moony knew that this was how Ariel
would look in death; knew that this was how she looked, now;
knew that she was dead.

But she wasn't. As Moony watched, her mother's mouth
twitched. Then Ariel sneezed, squeezing her eyes tightly. Finally she
opened them to gaze at the ceiling. Moony stared at her, uncomprehending. She began to cry, sobbing so loudly that she didn't hear
what her mother was saying, didn't hear Ariel's hoarse voice whispering the same words over and over and over again—

"Thank you, thank you, thank you!—"

But Moony wasn't listening. And only in her mother's own mind
did Ariel herself ever again hear Their voices. Like an unending
stream of golden coins being poured into a well, the eternal and
incomprehensible echo of Their reply—

"You are Welcome."

There must have been a lot of noise. Because before Moony could
pull herself together and go to her mother, Diana was there, her face
white but her eyes set and in control, as though she were an ambulance driver inured to all kinds of terrible things. She took Ariel in
her arms and got her to her feet. Ariel's head flopped to one side,
and for a moment Moony thought she'd slide to the floor again. But
then she seemed to rally. She blinked, smiled fuzzily at her daughter and Diana. After a few minutes, she let Diana walk her to the
door. She shook her head gently but persistently when her daughter
tried to help.

"You can follow us, darling," Diana called back apologetically as
they headed down the path to Martin's cottage. But Moony made no
move to follow. She only watched in disbelief—*I can follow you? Of
course I can, asshole!*—and then relief, as the two women lurched
safely through the house's crooked door.

Let someone *else* take care of her for a while, Moony thought
bitterly. She shoved her hands into her pockets. Her terror had
turned to anger. Now, perversely, she needed to yell at someone.
She thought briefly of following her mother; then of finding Jason.
But really, she knew all along where she had to go.

*   *   *

Mrs. Grose seemed surprised to see her (*Ha!* thought Moony triumphantly; what kind of psychic would be *surprised?*). But maybe there was something about her after all. Because she had just made a big pot of chamomile tea, heavily spiked with brandy, and set out a large white plate patterned with alarmingly lifelike butterflies and bees, the insects seeming to hover intently beside several slabs of cinnamon-fragrant zucchini bread.

"They just keep *mul*tiplying." Mrs. Grose sighed so dramatically that Moony thought she must be referring to the bees, and peered at them again to make sure they weren't real. "Patricia—you know, that nice lady with the lady friend?—she says, *pick* the flowers, so I pick them but I still have too many squashes. Remind me to give you some for your mother."

At mention of her mother, Moony's anger melted away. She started to cry again.

"My darling, what is it?" cried Mrs. Grose. She moved so quickly to embrace Moony that a soft-smelling pinkish cloud of face powder wafted from her cheeks onto the girl's. "Tell us darling, tell us—"

Moony sobbed luxuriously for several minutes, letting Mrs. Grose stroke her hair and feed her healthy sips of tepid brandy-laced tea. Mrs. Grose's pug wheezed anxiously at his mistress's feet and struggled to climb into Moony's lap. Eventually he succeeded. By then, Moony had calmed down enough to tell the aged woman what had happened, her rambling narrative punctuated by hiccuping sobs and small gasps of laughter when the dog lapped excitedly at her teacup.

"Ah *so,*" said Mrs. Grose, when she first understood that Moony was talking about the Light Children. She pressed her plump hands together and raised her tortoiseshell eyes to the ceiling. "They are having a busy day."

Moony frowned, wiping her cheeks. As though They were like the people who collected the trash or turned the water supply off at the end of the summer. But then Moony went on talking, her voice growing less tremulous as the brandy kicked in. When she finished, she sat in somewhat abashed silence and stared at the teacup she held in her damp hand. Its border of roses and cabbage butterflies took on a flushed glow from Mrs. Grose's paisley-draped Tiffany lamps. Moony looked uneasily at the door. Having confessed her story, she suddenly wanted to flee, to check on her mother; to forget the whole thing. But she couldn't just take off. She cleared her throat, and the pug growled sympathetically.

"*Well,*" Mrs. Grose said at last. "I see I will be having lots of company this winter."

Moony stared at her uncomprehending. "I mean, your mother and Martin will be staying on," Mrs. Grose explained, and sipped her tea. Her cheeks like the patterned porcelain had a febrile glow, and her eyes were so bright that Moony wondered if she was very drunk. "So at last! there will be enough of us here to really talk about it, to *learn*—"

"Learn what?" demanded Moony. Confusion and brandy made her peevish. She put her cup down and gently shoved the pug from her lap. "I mean, what happened? *What is going on?*"

"Why, it's Them, of course," Mrs. Grose said grandly, then ducked her head, as though afraid she might be overheard and deemed insolent. "We are so *fortunate*—you are so fortunate, my dear, and your darling mother! And Martin, of course—this is a wonderful time for us, a blessed, blessed time!" At Moony's glare of disbelief she went on, "You understand, my darling—They have come, They have *greeted* your mother and Martin, it is a very exciting thing, very rare—only a very few of us—"

Mrs. Grose preened a little before going on, "—and it is always so wonderful, so miraculous, when another joins us—and now suddenly we have *two!*"

Moony stared at her, her hands opening and closing in her lap. "But what *happened?*" she cried desperately. "What *are* They?"

Mrs. Grose shrugged and coughed delicately. "What are They," she repeated. "Well, Moony, that is a very good question." She heaved back onto the couch and sighed. "What are They? I do not know."

At Moony's rebellious glare she added hastily, "Well, many things, of course, we have thought They were many things, and They might be any of these or all of them or—well, none, I suppose. Fairies, or little angels of Jesus, or tree spirits—that is what a dear friend of mine believed. And some sailors thought They were will-o-the-wisps, and let's see, Miriam Hopewell, whom you don't remember but was *another* very dear friend of mine, God rest her soul, Miriam thought They came from flying saucers."

At this Moony's belligerence crumpled into defeat. She recalled the things she had seen on her mother—*devouring* her it seemed, setting her aflame—and gave a small involuntary gasp.

"But why?" she wailed. "I mean, *why?* Why should They care? What can They possibly get from us?"

Mrs. Grose enfolded Moony's hand in hers. She ran her fingers along Moony's palm as though preparing for a reading, and said, "Maybe They get something They don't have. Maybe we *give* Them something."

"But what?" Moony's voice rose, almost a shriek. *"What?"*

"Something They don't have," Mrs. Grose repeated softly. "Something everybody else has, but They don't—

"Our deaths."

Moony yanked her hand away. "Our *deaths?* My mother like, sold her *soul,* to—to—"

"You don't understand, darling." Mrs. Grose looked at her with mild, whiskey-colored eyes. "They don't want us to *die.* They want our *deaths.* That's why we're still at Mars Hill, me and Gary and your mother and Martin. As long as we stay here, They will keep them for us—our sicknesses, our destinies. It's something They don't have." Mrs. Grose sighed, shaking her head. "I guess They just get lonely, or bored of being immortal. Or whatever it is They are."

That's right? Moony wanted to scream. *What the hell are They?* But she only said, "So as long as you stay here you don't die? But that doesn't make any sense—I mean, John died, *he* was here—"

Mrs. Grose shrugged. "He left. And They didn't come to him, They never greeted him . . .

"Maybe he didn't know—or maybe he didn't want to stay. Maybe he didn't want to live. Not everybody does, you know. *I* don't want to live forever—" She sighed melodramatically, her bosom heaving. "But I just can't seem to tear myself away."

She leaned over to hug Moony. "But don't worry now, darling. Your mother is going to be *okay.* And so is Martin. And so are you, and all of us. We're safe—"

Moony shuddered. "But I can't stay here! I have to go back to school, I have a life—"

"Of course you do, darling! We all do! *Your* life is out there—" Mrs. Grose gestured out the window, wiggling her fingers toward where the cold blue waters of the Bay lapped at the gravel. "And ours is *here*." She smiled, bent her head to kiss Moony so that the girl caught a heavy breath of chamomile and brandy. "Now you better go, before your mother starts to worry."

Like I was a goddamn kid, Moony thought, but she felt too exhausted to argue. She stood, bumping against the pug. It gave a muffled bark, then looked up at her and drooled apologetically. Moony leaned down to pat it and took a step toward the door. Abruptly she turned back.

"Okay," she said. "Okay. Like, I'm going. I understand, you don't know about these—about all this—I mean I know you've told me everything you can. But I just want to ask you one thing—"

Mrs. Grose placed her teacup on the edge of the coffee table and waved her fingers, smiling absently. "Of course, of course, darling. Ask away."

"How old are you?"

Mrs. Grose's penciled eyebrows lifted above mild surprised eyes. "How old am I? One doesn't *ask* a lady such things, darling. But—"

She smiled slyly, leaning back and folding her hands upon her soft bulging stomach. "If I'd been a man and had the vote, it would have gone to Mr. Lincoln."

Moony nodded, just once, her breath stuck in her throat. Then she fled the cottage.

In Bangor, the doctor confirmed that the cancer was in remission.

"It's incredible." She shook her head, staring at Ariel's test results before tossing them ceremonially into a wastebasket. "I would say the phrase 'A living miracle' is not inappropriate here. Or voodoo, or whatever it is you do there at Mars Hill."

She waved dismissively at the open window, then bent to retrieve the tests. "You're welcome to get another opinion. I would advise it, as a matter of fact."

"Of course," Ariel said. But of course she wouldn't, then or ever. She already knew what the doctors would tell her.

There was some more paperwork, a few awkward efforts by the doctor to get Ariel to confess to some secret healing cure, some herbal remedy or therapy practiced by the kooks at the spiritualist community. But finally they were done. There was nothing left to discuss, and only a Blue Cross number to be given to the reception- ist. When the doctor stood to walk with Ariel to the door, her eyes were too bright, her voice earnest and a little shaky as she said, "And look: whatever you were doing, Ms. Rising—howling at the moon, whatever—you just keep on doing it. Okay?"

"Okay." Ariel smiled, and left.

"You really can't leave, now," Mrs. Grose told Martin and Ariel that night. They were all sitting around a bonfire on the rocky beach, Diana and Gary singing "Sloop John B" in off-key harmony, Rvis and Shasta Daisy and the others disemboweling leftover lobster bodies with the remorseless patience of raccoons. Mrs. Grose spread out the fingers of her right hand and twisted a heavy fili- greed ring on her pinkie, her lips pursed as she regarded Ariel. "*You shouldn't have gone to Bangor, that was very foolish,*" she said, frowning. "In a few months, maybe you can go with Gary to the Beach Store. *Maybe.* But no further than that."

Moony looked sideways at her mother, but Ariel only shook her head. Her eyes were luminous, the same color as the evening sky above the Bay.

"Who would want to leave?" Ariel said softly. Her hand crept across the pebbles to touch Martin's. As Moony watched them she felt again that sharp pain in her heart, like a needle jabbing her. She would never know exactly what had happened to her mother, or to Martin. Jason would tell her nothing. Nor would Ariel or anyone else. But there they were, Ariel and Martin sitting cross-legged on the gravel strand, while all around them the others ate and drank and sang as though nothing had happened at all; or as though whatever *had* occurred had been decided on long ago. Without looking at each other Martin and her mother smiled, Martin some- what wryly Mrs. Grose nodded.

"That's right," the old woman said. When she tossed a stone into the bonfire an eddy of sparks flared up. Moony jumped, startled, and looked up into the sky. For an instant she held her breath, thinking, *At last!*—it was Them and all would be explained. The Fairy King would offer his benediction to the united and loving couples; the dour Puritan would be avenged, the Fool would sing his sad sweet song and everyone would wipe away happy tears.

But no. The sparks blew off into ashes, filling the air with a faint smell of incense. When she turned back to the bonfire, Jason was holding out a flaming marshmallow on a stick, laughing, and the others had segued into a drunken rendition of "Leaving on a Jet Plane."

"Take it, Moony," he urged her, the charred mess slipping from the stick. "Eat it quick, for luck."

She leaned over until it slid onto her tongue, a glowing coal of sweetness and earth and fire; and ate it quick, for luck.

Long after midnight they returned to their separate bungalows. Jason lingered with Moony by the dying bonfire, stroking her hair and staring at the lights of Dark Harbor. There was the crunch of gravel behind them. He turned to see his father, standing silhouetted in the soft glow of the embers.

"Jason," he called softly. "Would you mind coming back with me? I—there's something we need to talk about."

Jason gazed down at Moony. Her eyes were heavy with sleep, and he lowered his head to kiss her, her mouth still redolent of burnt sugar. "Yeah, okay," he said, and stood. "You be okay, Moony?"

Moony nodded, yawning. "Sure." As he walked away, Jason looked back and saw her stretched out upon the gravel beach, arms outspread as she stared up at the three-quarter moon riding close to the edge of Mars Hill.

"So what's going on?" he asked his father when they reached the cottage. Martin stood at the dining room table, his back to Jason. He picked up a small stack of envelopes and tapped them against the table, then turned to his son.

"I'm going back," he said. "Home. I got a letter from Brandon today,"—Brandon was his agent—"there's going to be a show at the Frick Gallery, and a symposium. They want me to speak."

Jason stared at him, uncomprehending. His long pale hair fell into his face, and he pushed it impatiently from his eyes. "But—you can't," he said at last. "You'll die. You can't leave here. That's what Adele said. You'll *die*."

Martin remained silent, before replacing the envelopes and shaking his head. "We don't know that. Even before, we—I—didn't know that. Nobody knows that, ever."

Jason stared at him in disbelief. His face grew flushed as he said, "But you can't! You're sick—shit, Dad, look at John, you can't just—"

His father pursed his lips, tugged at his ponytail. "No, Jason, I *can*." Suddenly he looked surprised, a little sheepish even, and said more softly. "I mean, I *will*. There's too much for me to give up, Jason. Maybe it sounds stupid, but I think it's important that I go back. Not right away. I think I'll stay on for a few weeks, maybe until the end of October. You know, see autumn in New England and all. But after that—well, there's work for me to do at home, and—"

Jason's voice cracked as he shook his head furiously. "Dad. No. You'll—you'll die."

Martin shrugged. "I might. I mean, I guess I will, sometime. But—well, everybody dies." His mouth twisted into a smile as he stared at the floor. "Except Mrs. Grose."

Jason continued to shake his head. "But—you *saw* Them—They came, They must've done *something*—"

Martin looked up, his eyes feverishly bright. "They did. That's why I'm leaving. Look, Jason, I can't explain, all right? But what if you had to stay here, instead of going on to Bowdoin? What if Moony left, and everyone else—would you stay at Mars Hill? *Forever?*"

Jason was silent. Finally, "I think you should stay," he said, a little desperately. "Otherwise whatever They did was wasted."

Martin shook his head. His hand closed around a tube of viridian on the table and he raised it, held it in front of him like a weapon. His eyes glittered as he said, "Oh, no, Jason. Not wasted. Nothing is wasted, not ever." And tilting his head he smiled, held out his arm until his son came to him and Martin embraced him, held him there until Jason's sobs quieted, and the moon began to slide behind Mars Hill.

*   *   *

Jason drove Moony to the airport on Friday. Most of his things already had been shipped from San Francisco to Bowdoin College, but Moony had to return to Kamensic Village and the Loomises, to gather her clothes and books for school and make all the awkward explanations and arrangements on her own. Friends and relations in New York had been told that Ariel was undergoing some kind of experimental therapy, an excuse they bought as easily as they'd bought most of Ariel's other strange ideas. Now Moony didn't want to talk to anyone else on the phone. She didn't want to talk to anyone at all, except for Jason.

"It's kind of on the way to Brunswick," he explained when Diana protested his driving Moony. "Besides, Diana, if you took her she'd end up crying the whole way. This way I can keep her intact at least until the airport."

Diana gave in, finally. No one suggested that Ariel drive.

"Look down when the plane flies over Mars Hill," Ariel said, hugging her daughter by the car. "We'll be looking for you."

Moony nodded, her mouth tight, and kissed her mother. "You be okay," she whispered, the words lost in Ariel's tangled hair.

"I'll be okay," Ariel said, smiling.

Behind them Jason and Martin embraced. "If you're still here I'll be up Columbus Weekend," said Jason. "Maybe sooner if I run out of money."

Martin shook his head. "If you run out of money you better go see your mother."

It was only twenty minutes to the airport. "Don't wait," Moony said to Jason, as the same woman who had taken her ticket loaded her bags onto the little Beechcraft. "I mean it. If you do I'll cry and I'll kill you."

Jason nodded. "Righto. We don't want any bad publicity. 'Noted Queer Activist's Son Slain by Girlfriend at Local Airport. Wind Shear Is Blamed.'"

Moony hugged him, drew away to study his face. "I'll call you in the morning."

He shook his head. "Tonight. When you get home. So I'll know you got in safely. 'Cause it's dangerous out there." He made an awful face, then leaned over to kiss her. "Ciao, Moony."

"Ciao, Jason."

She could feel him watching her as she clambered into the little plane, but she didn't look back. Instead she smiled tentatively at the few other passengers—a businessman with a tie loose around his neck, two middleaged women with L.L. Bean shopping bags—and settled into a seat by the window.

During takeoff she leaned over to see if she could spot Jason. For an instant she had a flash of his car, like a crimson leaf blowing south through the darkening green of pines and maples. Then it was gone.

Trailers of mist whipped across the little window. Moony shivered, drew her sweatshirt tight around her chest. She felt that beneath her everything she had ever known was shrinking, disappearing, swallowed by golden light; but somehow it was okay. As the Beechcraft banked over Penobscot Bay she pressed her face close against the glass, waiting for the gap in the clouds that would give her a last glimpse of the gray and white cottages tumbling down Mars Hill, the wind-riven pier where her mother and Martin and all the rest stood staring up into the early autumn sky, tiny as fairy people in a child's book. For an instant it seemed that something hung over them, a golden cloud like a September haze. But then the blinding sun made her glance away. When she looked down again the golden haze was gone. But the others were still there, waving and calling out soundlessly until the plane finally turned south and bore her away, away from summer and its silent visitors—her mother's cancer, Martin's virus, the Light Children and Their hoard of stolen sufferings—away, away, away from them all, and back to the welcoming world.

From the start I had a somewhat uncanny feeling about this story, just as I did with "The Have-Nots;" though it took much longer to write. Mars Hill was inspired by an actual spiritualist community a few miles up the road from where I live in Maine. I often drove by it but never went in for a psychic reading until well after the story appeared. The place was pretty much as I had imagined it to be, though there were no golden phantoms around the day I visited.

People I loved had died of breast cancer and AIDS, and that was the impetus for the story, along with a strange song by Fred Frith called "The Welcome" (which was "Mars Hill's" original title). When I wrote this, it was pure wish fulfillment; protease inhibitors had not been recognized as the crucial treatment they've become for AIDS and breast cancer had yet to make an appearance on the front page of the *New York Times Magazine*. This story is about the cure we all pray for. And it's about hope, which is what keeps us going when there is no cure in sight. But mostly it's about keeping on, whether or not we want to, in a world where hope sometimes seems like another diminishing natural resource.

The Erl-King

The kinkajou had been missing for two days now. Haley feared it was dead, killed by one of the neighborhood dogs or by a fox or wildcat in the woods. Linette was certain it was alive; she even knew where it was.

"Kingdom Come," she announced, pointing a long lazy hand in the direction of the neighboring estate. She dropped her hand and sipped at a mug of tepid tea, twisting so she wouldn't spill it as she rocked back and forth. It was Linette's turn to lie in the hammock. She did so with feckless grace, legs tangled in her long peasant skirt, dark hair spilled across the faded canvas. She had more practice at it than Haley, this being Linette's house and Linette's overgrown yard bordering the woods of spindly young pines and birches that separated them from Kingdom Come. Haley frowned, leaned against the oak tree, and pushed her friend desultorily with one foot.

"Then why doesn't your mother call them or something?" Haley loved the kinkajou and justifiably feared the worst. With her friend exotic pets came and went, just as did odd visitors to the tumbledown cottage where Linette lived with her mother, Aurora. Most of the animals were presents from Linette's father, an elderly Broadway producer whose successes paid for the rented cottage and Linette's occasional artistic endeavors (flute lessons, sitar lessons, an incomplete course in airbrushing) as well as the bottles of Tanqueray that lined Aurora's bedroom. And, of course, the animals. An iguana whose skin peeled like mildewed wallpaper, finally lost (and never found) in the drafty dark basement where the girls held annual Hallowe'en seances. An intimidatingly large Moluccan cockatoo that escaped into the trees, terrorizing Kingdom Come's previous owner and his garden-party guests by shrieking at them in Gaelic from the wisteria. Finches and fire weavers small enough to hold in your fist. A quartet of tiny goats, Haley's favorites until the kinkajou.

The cockatoo started to smell worse and worse, until one day it flopped to the bottom of its wrought-iron cage and died. The finches escaped when Linette left the door to their bamboo cage open. The goats ran off into the woods surrounding Lake Muscanth. They were rumored to be living there still. But this summer Haley had come over every day to make certain the kinkajou had enough to eat, that Linette's cats weren't terrorizing it; that Aurora didn't try to feed it crème de menthe as she had the capuchin monkey that had fleetingly resided in her room.

"I don't know," Linette said. She shut her eyes, balancing her mug on her stomach. A drop of tea spilled onto her cotton blouse, another faint petal among faded ink stains and the ghostly impression of eyes left by an abortive attempt at batik. "I think Mom knows the guy who lives there now, she doesn't like him or something. I'll ask my father next time."

Haley prodded the hammock with the toe of her sneaker. "It's almost my turn. Then we should go over there. It'll die if it gets cold at night."

Linette smiled without opening her eyes. "Nah. It's still summer," she said, and yawned.

Haley frowned. She moved her back up and down against the bole of the oak tree, scratching where a scab had formed after their outing to Mandrake Island to look for the goats. It was early August, nearing the end of their last summer before starting high school, the time Aurora had named "the summer before the dark."

"My poor little girls," Aurora had mourned a few months earlier. It had been only June then, the days still cool enough that the City's wealthy fled each weekend to Kamensic Village to hide among the woods and wetlands in their Victorian follies. Aurora was perched with Haley and Linette on an ivied slope above the road, watching the southbound Sunday exodus of limousines and Porsches and Mercedes. "Soon you'll be gone."

"Jeez, Mom," laughed Linette. A plume of ivy tethered her long hair back from her face. Aurora reached to tug it with one unsteady hand. The other clasped a plastic cup full of gin. "No one's going anywhere, I'm going to Fox Lane,"—that was the public high school—"you heard what Dad said. Right, Haley?"

Haley had nodded and stroked the kinkajou sleeping in her lap. It never did anything but sleep, or open its golden eyes to half-wakefulness oh, so briefly before finding another lap or cushion to curl into. It reminded her of Linette in that, her friend's heavy lazy eyes always ready to shut, her legs quick to curl around pillows or hammock cushions or Haley's own battle-scarred knees. "Right," said Haley, and she had cupped her palm around the soft warm globe of the kinkajou's head.

Now the hammock creaked noisily as Linette turned onto her stomach, dropping her mug into the long grass. Haley started, looked down to see her hands hollowed as though holding something. If the kinkajou died she'd never speak to Linette again. Her heart beat faster at the thought.

"I think we should go over. If you think it's there. *And*—" Haley grabbed the ropes restraining the hammock, yanked them back and forth so that Linette shrieked, her hair caught between hempen braids—"it's—*my*—turn—*now.*"

They snuck out that night. The sky had turned pale green, the same shade as the crystal globe wherein three ivory-bellied frogs floated, atop a crippled table. To keep the table from falling Haley had propped a broom handle beneath it for a fourth leg—although she hated the frogs, bloated things with prescient yellow eyes. Some nights when she slept over they broke her sleep with their song, high-pitched trilling that disturbed neither Linette snoring in the other bed nor Aurora drinking broodingly in her tiny shed-roofed wing of the cottage. It was uncanny, almost frightening sometimes, how nothing ever disturbed them: not dying pets nor utilities cut off for lack of payment nor unexpected visits from Aurora's small circle of friends, People from the Factory Days she called them. Rejuvenated junkies or pop stars with new careers, or wasted beauties like Aurora Dawn herself. All of them seemingly forever banned from the real world, the adult world Haley's parents and family inhabited, magically free as Linette herself was to sample odd-tasting liqueurs and curious religious notions and lost arts in their dank corners of the City or the shelter of some wealthier friend's up-county retreat. Sleepy-eyed from dope or taut from amphetamines, they lay around the cottage with Haley and Linette, offering sips of their drinks, advice about popular musicians and contraceptives. Their hair was streaked with gray now, or dyed garish mauve or blue or green. They wore high leather boots and clothes inlaid with feathers or mirrors, and had names that sounded like the names of expensive perfumes: Liatris, Coppelia, Electric Velvet. Sometimes Haley felt that she had wandered into a fairy tale, or a movie. *Beauty and the Beast* perhaps, or *The Dark Crystal*. Of course it would be one of Linette's favorites; Linette had more imagination and sensitivity than Haley. The kind of movie Haley would choose to wander into would have fast cars and gunshots in the distance, not aging refugees from another decade passed out next to the fireplace.

She thought of that now, passing the globe of frogs. They went from the eerie interior dusk of the cottage into the strangely aqueous air outside. Despite the warmth of the late summer evening Haley shivered as she gazed back at the cottage. The tiny bungalow might have stood there unchanged for five hundred years, for a thousand. No warm yellow light spilled from the windows as it did at her own house. There was no smell of dinner cooking, no television chattering. Aurora seldom cooked, Linette never. There was no TV. Only the frogs hovering in their silver world, and the faintest cusp of a new moon like a leaf cast upon the surface of the sky.

The main house of the neighboring estate stood upon a broad slope of lawn overlooking the woods. Massive oaks and sycamores studded the grounds, and formal gardens that had been more carefully tended by the mansion's previous owner, a New York fashion designer recently dead. At the foot of the long drive a post bore the placard on which was writ in spidery silver letters KINGDOM COME.

In an upstairs room Lie Vagal perched upon a windowsill. He stared out at the same young moon that watched Haley and Linette as they made their way through the woods. Had Lie known where to look he might have seen them as well; but he was watching the kinkajou sleeping in his lap.

It had appeared at breakfast two days earlier. Lie sat with his grandmother on the south terrace, eating Froot Loops and reading the morning mail, *The Wall Street Journal,* and a quarterly royalty statement from BMI. His grandmother stared balefully into a bowl of bran flakes, as though discerning there unpleasant intimations of the future.

"Did you take your medicine, Gram?" asked Lie. A leaf fell from an overhanging branch into his coffee cup. He fished it out before Gram could see it as another dire portent.

"Did you take yours, Elijah?" snapped Gram. She finished the bran flakes and reached for her own coffee, black and laced with chicory. She was eighty-four years old and had outlived all of her other relatives and many of Lie's friends. "I know you didn't yester-day."

Lie shrugged. Another leaf dropped to the table, followed by a hail of bark and twigs. He peered up into the greenery, then pointed.

"Look," he said. "A squirrel or cat or something."

His grandmother squinted, shaking her head peevishly. "I can't see a thing."

The shaking branches parted to show something brown attached to a slender limb. Honey-colored, too big for a squirrel, it clung to a branch that dipped lower and lower, spattering them with more debris. Lie moved his coffee cup and had started to his feet when it fell, landing on top of the latest issue of *New Musical Express.*

For a moment he thought the fall had killed it. It just lay there, legs and long tail curled as though it had been a doodlebug playing dead. Then slowly it opened its eyes, regarded him with a muzzy golden gaze, and yawned, unfurling a tongue so brightly pink it might have been lipsticked. Lie laughed.

"It fell asleep in the tree! It's a—a what-you-call-it, a sloth."

His grandmother shook her head, pushing her glasses onto her nose. "That's not a sloth. They have grass growing on them."

Lie stretched a finger and tentatively stroked its tail. The animal ignored him, closing its eyes once more and folding its paws upon its glossy breast. Around its neck someone had placed a collar, the sort of leather-and-rhinestone ornament old ladies deployed on poodles. Gingerly Lie turned it, until he found a small heart-shaped tab of metal.

KINKAJOU
My name is Valentine
764–0007

"Huh," he said. "I'll be damned. I bet it belongs to those girls next door." Gram sniffed and collected the plates. Next to Lie's coffee mug, the compartmented container holding a week's worth of his medication was still full.

The animal did nothing but sleep and eat. Lie called a pet store in the City and learned that kinkajous ate insects and honey and bananas. He fed it Froot Loops, yogurt, and granola, a moth he caught one evening in the bedroom. Tonight it slept once more, and he stroked it, murmuring to himself. He still hadn't called the number on the collar.

From here he could just make out the cottage, a white blur through dark leaves and tangled brush. It was his cottage, really; a long time ago the estate gardener had lived there. The fashion designer had been friends with the present tenant in the City long ago. For the last fourteen years the place had been leased to Aurora Dawn. When he'd learned that, Lie Vagal had given a short laugh, one that the realtor had mistaken for displeasure.

"We could evict her," she'd said anxiously. "Really, she's no trouble, just the town drunk, but once you'd taken possession—"

"I wouldn't *dream* of it." Lie laughed again, shaking his head but not explaining. "Imagine, having Aurora Dawn for a neighbor again . . ."

His accountant had suggested selling the cottage, it would be worth a small fortune now, or else turning it into a studio or guest house. But Lie knew that the truth was, his accountant didn't want

Lie to start hanging around with Aurora again. Trouble; all the sur-
vivors from those days were trouble.

That might have been why Lie didn't call the number on the
collar. He hadn't seen Aurora in fifteen years, although he had often
glimpsed the girls playing in the woods. More than once he'd
started to go meet them, introduce himself, bring them back to the
house. He was lonely here. The visitors who still showed up at
Aurora's door at four A.M. used to bang around Lie's place in the
City. But that was long ago, before what Lie thought of as The Crash
and what *Rolling Stone* had termed "the long tragic slide into madness of the one-time *force majeur* of underground rock and roll."
And his agent and his lawyer wouldn't think much of him luring
children to his woodland lair.

He sighed. Sensing some shift in the summer air, his melancholy perhaps, the sleeping kinkajou sighed as well, and trembled
where it lay curled between his thighs. Lie lifted his head to gaze
out the open window.

Outside the night lay still and deep over woods and lawns and
the little dreaming cottage. A Maxfield Parrish scene, stars spangled
across an ultramarine sky, twinkling bit of moon, there at the edge
of the grass a trio of cottontails feeding peacefully amidst the dandelions. He had first been drawn to the place because it looked like
this, like one of the paintings he collected. "Kiddie stuff," his agent
sniffed; "fairy tale porn." Parrish and Rackham and Nielsen and
Clarke. Tenniel prints of Alice's trial. The DuFevre painting of the
Erl-King that had been the cover of Lie Vagal's second, phenome-
nally successful album. For the first two weeks after moving he had
done nothing but pace the labyrinthine hallways, planning where
they all would hang, this picture by this window, that one near
another. All day, all night he paced; and always alone.

Because he was afraid his agent or Gram or one of the doctors
would find out the truth about Kingdom Come, the reason he had
really bought the place. He had noticed it the first time the realtor
had shown the house. She'd commented on the number of windows there were—

"South-facing, too, the place is a hundred years old but it really
functions as passive solar with all these windows. That flagstone
floor in the green room acts as a heat sink—"

She nattered on, but Lie said nothing. He couldn't believe that she didn't notice. No one did, not Gram or his agent or the small legion of people brought in from Stamford who cleaned the place before he moved in.

It was the windows, of course. They always came to the windows first.

The first time he'd seen them had been in Marrakech, nearly sixteen years ago. A window shaped like a downturned heart, looking out onto a sky so blue it seemed to drip; and outside, framed within the window's heavy white curves, Lie saw the crouching figure of a young man, bent over some object that caught the sun and flared so that he'd had to look away. When he'd turned back the young man was staring up in amazement as reddish smoke like dust roiled from the shining object. As Lie watched the smoke began to take the shape of an immense man. At that point the joint he held burned Lie's fingers and he shouted, as much from panic as pain. When he looked out again the figures were gone.

Since then he'd seen them many times. Different figures, but always familiar, always fleeting, and brightly colored as the tiny people inside a marzipan egg. Sinbad and the Roc; the little mermaid and her sisters; a brave little figure carrying a belt engraved with the words SEVEN AT A BLOW. The steadfast tin soldier and a Christmas tree soon gone to cinders; dogs with eyes as big as teacups, as big as soup plates, as big as millstones. On tour in Paris, London, Munich, L.A., they were always there, as likely (or unlikely) to appear in a hotel room overlooking a dingy alley as within the crystal mullions of some heiress's bedroom. He had never questioned their presence, not after that first shout of surprise. They were the people, *his* people; the only ones he could trust in what was fast becoming a harsh and bewildering world.

It was just a few weeks after the first vision in Marrakech that he went to that fateful party; and a few months after that came the staggering success of *The Erl-King*. And then The Crash, and all the rest of it. He had a confused memory of those years. Even now, when he recalled that time it was as a movie with too much crosscutting and no dialogue. An endless series of women (and men) rolling from his bed; dark glimpses of himself in the studio cutting *Baba Yaga* and *The Singing Bone;* a few overlit sequences with surging crowds screaming soundlessly beneath a narrow stage. During those years his visions of the people changed. At first his psychiatrist was very interested in hearing about them. And so for a few months that was all he'd talk about, until he could see her growing impatient. That was the last time he brought them up to anyone.

But he wished he'd been able to talk to someone about them; about how different they were since The Crash. In the beginning he'd always noticed only how beautiful they were, how like his memories of all those stories from his childhood. The little mermaid gazing adoringly up at her prince; the two children in the cottage made of gingerbread and gumdrops; the girl in her glass coffin awakened by a kiss. It was only after The Crash that he remembered the *other* parts of the tales, the parts that in childhood had made it impossible for him to sleep some nights and which now, perversely, returned to haunt his dreams. The witch shrieking inside the stove as she was burned to death. The wicked queen forced to dance in the red-hot iron shoes until she died. The little mermaid's prince turning from her to marry another, and the mermaid changed to sea foam as punishment for his indifference.

But since he'd been at Kingdom Come these unnerving glimpses of the people had diminished. They were still there, but all was as it had been at the very first, myriad lovely creatures flitting through the garden like moths at twilight. He thought that maybe it was going off his medication that did it; and so the full prescription bottles were hoarded in a box in his room, hidden from Gram's eyes.

That was how he made sure the people remained at Kingdom Come. Just like in Marrakech: they were in the windows. Each one opened onto a different spectral scene, visual echoes of the fantastic paintings that graced the walls. The bathroom overlooked a twilit ballroom; the kitchen a black dwarf's cave. The dining room's high casements opened onto the Glass Hill. From a tiny window in the third-floor linen closet he could see a juniper tree, and once a flute of pale bone sent its eerie song pulsing through the library.

"You hear that, Gram?" he had gasped. But of course she heard nothing; she was practically deaf.

Lately it seemed that they came more easily, more often. He would feel an itching at the corner of his eyes, Tinkerbell's pixie dust, the Sandman's seed. Then he would turn, and the placid expanse of new-mown lawn would suddenly be transformed into gnarled spooky trees beneath a grinning moon, rabbits holding hands, the grass frosted with dew that held the impressions of many dancing feet. He knew there were others he didn't see, wolves and witches and bones that danced. And the most terrible one of all—the Erl-King, the one he'd met at the party; the one who somehow had set all this in motion and then disappeared. It was Lie's worst fear that someday he would come back.

Now suddenly the view in front of him changed. Lie started forward. The kinkajou slid from his lap like a bolt of silk to lie at his feet, still drowsing. From the trees waltzed a girl, pale in the misty light. She wore a skirt that fetched just above her bare feet, a white blouse that set off a tangle of long dark hair. Stepping onto the lawn she paused, turned back and called into the woods. He could hear her voice but not her words. A child's voice, although the skirt billowed about long legs and he could see where her breasts swelled within the white blouse.

Ah, he thought, and tried to name her. Jorinda, Gretel, Ashputtel?

But then someone else crashed through the brake of saplings. Another girl, taller and wearing jeans and a halter top, swatting at her bare arms. He could hear what *she* was saying; she was swearing loudly while the first girl tried to hush her. He laughed, nudged the kinkajou on the floor. When it didn't respond he bent to pick it up and went downstairs.

"I don't think anyone's home," Haley said. She stood a few feet from the haven of the birch grove, feeling very conspicuous surrounded by all this open lawn. She killed another mosquito and scratched her arm. "Maybe we should just call, or ask your mother. If she knows this guy."

"She doesn't like him," Linette replied dreamily. A faint mist rose in little eddies about them. She lifted her skirts and did a pirouette, her bare feet leaving darker impressions on the gray lawn. "And it would be even cooler if no one was there, we could go in and find Valentine and look around. Like a haunted house."

"Like breaking and entering," Haley said darkly, but she followed her friend tiptoeing up the slope. The dewy grass was cool, the air warm and smelling of something sweet, oranges or maybe some kind of incense wafting down from the immense stone mansion.

They walked up the lawn, Linette leading the way. Dew soaked the hem of her skirt and the cuffs of Haley's jeans. At the top of the slope stood the great main house, a mock-Tudor fantasy of stone and stucco and oak beams. Waves of ivy and cream-colored roses spilled from the upper eaves; toppling ramparts of hollyhocks grew against the lower story. From here Haley could see only a single light downstairs, a dim green glow from behind curtains of ivy. Upstairs, diamond-paned windows had been pushed open, forcing the vegetation to give way and hang in limp streamers, some of them almost to the ground. The scent of turned earth mingled with that of smoke and oranges.

"Should we go to the front door?" Haley asked. Seeing the back of the house close up like this unnerved her, the smell of things decaying and the darkened mansion's *déshabillé*. Like seeing her grandmother once without her false teeth: she wanted to turn away and give the house a chance to pull itself together.

Linette stopped to scratch her foot. "Nah. It'll be easier to just walk in if we go this way. If nobody's home." She straightened and peered back in the direction they'd come. Haley turned with her. The breeze felt good in her face. She could smell the distant dampness of Lake Muscanth, hear the croak of frogs and the rustling of leaves where deer stepped to water's edge to drink. When the girls turned back to the big house each took a step forward. Then they gasped, Linette pawing at the air for Haley's hand.

"Someone's there!"

Haley nodded. She squeezed Linette's fingers and then drew forward.

They had only looked away for an instant. But it had been long enough for lights to go on inside and out, so that now the girls blinked in the glare of spotlights. Someone had thrown open a set of French doors opening onto a sort of patio decorated with tubs of geraniums and very old wicker porch furniture, the wicker sprung in threatening and dangerous patterns. Against the brilliance the hollyhocks loomed black and crimson. A trailing length of white curtain blew from the French doors onto the patio. Haley giggled nervously, and heard Linette breathing hard behind her.

Someone stepped outside, a small figure not much taller than Haley. He held something in his arms, and cocked his head in a way that was, if not exactly welcoming, at least neutral enough to indicate that they should come closer.

Haley swallowed and looked away. She wondered if it would be too stupid just to run back to the cottage. But behind her Linette had frozen. On her face was the same look she had when caught passing notes in class, a look that meant it would be up to Haley, as usual, to get them out of this.

"Hum," Haley said, clearing her throat. The man didn't move. She shrugged, trying to think of something to say.

"Come on up," a voice rang out; a rather high voice with the twangy undercurrent of a Texas accent. It was such a cheerful voice, as though they were expected guests, that for a moment she didn't associate it with the stranger on the patio. "It's okay, you're looking for your pet, right?"

Behind her Linette gasped again, in relief. Then Haley was left behind as her friend raced up the hill, holding up her skirts and glancing back, laughing.

"Come on! He's got Valentine—"

Haley followed her, walking deliberately slowly. Of a sudden she felt odd. The too-bright lights on a patio smelling of earth and mandarin oranges; the white curtain blowing in and out; the welcoming stranger holding Valentine. It all made her dizzy, fairly breathless with anticipation; but frightened, too. For a long moment she stood there, trying to catch her breath. Then she hurried after her friend.

When she got to the top Linette was holding the kinkajou, crooning over it the way Haley usually did. Linette herself hadn't given it this much attention since its arrival last spring. Haley stopped, panting, next to a wicker chair, and bent to scratch her ankle. When she looked up again the stranger was staring at her.

"Hello," he said. Haley smiled shyly and shrugged, then glanced at Linette.

"Hey! You got him back! I told you he was here—"

Linette smiled, settled onto a wicker loveseat with Valentine curled among the folds of her skirt. "Thanks," she said softly, glancing up at the man. "He found him two days ago, he said. This is Haley—"

The man said hello again, still smiling. He was short, and wore a black T-shirt and loose white trousers, like hospital pants only cut from some fancy cloth. He had long black hair, thinning back from his forehead but still thick enough to pull into a ponytail. He reminded her of someone; she couldn't think who. His hands were crossed on his chest and he nodded at Haley, as though he knew what she was thinking.

"You're sisters," he said; then when Linette giggled shook his head, laughing. "No, of course, that's dumb: you're just friends, right? Best friends, I see you all the time together."

Haley couldn't think of anything to say, so she stepped closer to Linette and stroked the kinkajou's head. She wondered what happened now: if they stayed here on the porch with the stranger, or took Valentine and went home, or—

But what happened next was that a very old lady appeared in the French doors that led inside. She moved quickly, as though if she slowed down even for an instant she would be overtaken by one of the things that overtake old people, arthritis maybe, or sleep; and she swatted impatiently at the white curtains blowing in and out.

"Elijah," she said accusingly. She wore a green polyester blouse and pants patterned with enormous orange poppies, and fashionable eyeglasses with very large green frames. Her white hair was carefully styled. As she stood in the doorway her gaze flicked from Linette and the kinkajou to the stranger, then back to Linette. And Haley saw something cross the old woman's face as she looked at her friend, and then at the man again: an expression of pure alarm, terror almost. Then the woman turned and looked at Haley for the first time. She shook her head earnestly and continued to stare at Haley with very bright eyes, as though they knew each other from somewhere, or as though she had quickly sized up the situation and decided Haley was the only other person here with any common sense, which seemed precisely the kind of thing this old lady might think. "I'm Elijah's grandmother," she said at last, and very quickly crossed the patio to stand beside the stranger.

"Hi," said Linette, looking up from beneath waves of dark hair.

The man smiled, glancing at the old lady. His hand moved very slightly toward Linette's head, as though he might stroke her hair. Haley desperately wanted to scratch her ankle again, but was suddenly embarrassed lest anyone see her. The old lady continued to stare at her, and Haley finally coughed.

"I'm Haley," she said, then added, "Linette's friend." As though the lady knew who Linette was.

But maybe she did, because she nodded very slightly, glancing again at Linette and then at the man she had said was her grandson. "Well," she said. Her voice was strong and a little shrill, and she too had a Texas accent. "Come on in, girls. *Elijah.* I put some water on for tea."

Now this is too weird, thought Haley. The old lady strode back across the patio and held aside the white curtains, waiting for them to follow her indoors. Linette stood, cradling the kinkajou and murmuring to it. She caught Haley's eye and smiled triumphantly. Then she followed the old lady, her skirt rustling about her legs. That left Haley and the man still standing by the wicker furniture.

"Come on in, Haley," he said to her softly. He extended one hand toward the door, a very long slender hand for such a short man. Around his wrist he wore a number of thin silver- and gold-colored bracelets. There came again that overpowering scent of oranges and fresh earth, and something else, too, a smoky musk like incense. Haley blinked and steadied herself by touching the edge of one wicker chair. "It's okay, Haley—"

Is it? she wondered. She looked behind her, down the hill to where the cottage lay sleeping. If she yelled would Aurora hear her? Would anyone? Because she was certain now that something was happening, maybe had already happened and it was just taking a while (as usual) to catch up with Haley. From the woods edging Lake Muscanth came the yapping of the fox again, and the wind brought her the smell of water. For a moment she shut her eyes and pretended she was there, safe with the frogs and foxes.

But even with her eyes closed she could feel the man staring at her with that intent dark gaze. It occurred to Haley then that the only reason he wanted her to come was that he was afraid Linette would go if Haley left. A wave of desolation swept over her, to think she was unwanted, that even here and now it was as it always was:

Linette chosen first for teams, for dances, for secrets, and Haley waiting, waiting.

"Haley."

The man touched her hand, a gesture so tentative that for a moment she wasn't even sure it was him: it might have been the breeze, or a leaf falling against her wrist. She looked up and his eyes were pleading, but also apologetic; as though he really believed it wouldn't be the same without her. And she knew that expression—now who stared at her just like that, who was it he looked like?

It was only after she had followed him across the patio, stooping to brush the grass from her bare feet as she stepped over the threshold into Kingdom Come, that she realized he reminded her of Linette.

The tea was Earl Grey, the same kind they drank in Linette's kitchen. But this kitchen was huge: the whole cottage could practically have fit inside it. For all that it was a reassuring place, with all the normal kitchen things where they should be—microwave, refrigerator, ticking cat clock with its tail slicing back and forth, back and forth.

"Cream and sugar?"

The old lady's hands shook as she put the little bowl on the table. Behind her Lie Vagal grinned, opened a cabinet and took out a golden jar.

"I bet she likes *honey*," he pronounced, setting the jar in front of Linette.

She giggled delightedly. "How did you know?"

"Yeah, how did you know?" echoed Haley, frowning a little. In Linette's lap the kinkajou uncurled and yawned, and Linette dropped a spoonful of honey into its mouth. The old lady watched tight-lipped. Behind her glasses her eyes sought Haley's, but the girl looked away, shy and uneasy.

"Just a feeling I had, just a lucky guess," Lie Vagal sang. He took a steaming mug from the table, ignored his grandmother when she pointed meaningfully at the pill bottle beside it. "Now, would you girls like to tour the rest of the house?"

It was an amazing place. There were chairs of brass and ebony, chairs of antlers, chairs of neon tubes. Incense burners shaped like snakes and elephants sent up wisps of sweet smoke. From the living room wall gaped demonic masks, and a hideous stick figure that looked like something that Haley, shuddering, recalled from *Uncle Wiggly*. There was a glass ball that sent out runners of light when you touched it, and a jukebox that played a song about the Sandman.

And everywhere were the paintings. Not exactly what you would expect to find in a place like this: paintings that illustrated fairy tales. Puss in Boots and the Three Billy Goats Gruff. Aladdin and the Monkey King and the Moon saying goodnight. Famous paintings, some of them—Haley recognized scenes from books she'd loved as a child, and framed animation cells from *Pinocchio* and *Snow White* and *Cinderella*.

These were parceled out among the other wonders. A man-high tank seething with piranhas. A room filled with nothing but old record albums, thousands of them. A wall of gold and platinum records and framed clippings from *Rolling Stone* and *NME* and *New York Rocker*. And in the library a series of Andy Warhol silk-screens of a young man with very long hair, alternately colored green and blue, dated 1972.

Linette was entranced by the fairy-tale paintings. She walked right past the Warhol prints to peruse a watercolor of a tiny child and a sparrow, and dreamily traced the edge of its frame. Lie Vagal stared after her, curling a lock of his hair around one finger. Haley lingered in front of the Warhol prints and chewed her thumb thoughtfully.

After a long moment she turned to him and said, "I know who you are. You're, like, this old rock star. Lie Vagal. You had some album that my babysitter liked when I was little."

He smiled and turned from watching Linette. "Yeah, that's me."

Haley rubbed her lower lip, staring at the Warhol prints. "You must've been really famous, to get him to do those paintings. What was that album called? The Mountain King?"

"*The Erl-King.*" He stepped to an ornate ormulu desk adrift with papers. He shuffled through them, finally withdrew a glossy pamphlet. "Let's see—"

He turned back to Haley and handed it to her. A CD catalog,

opened to a page headed ROCK AND ROLL ARCHIVES and filled with reproductions of album cover art. He pointed to one, reduced like the others to the size of a postage stamp. The illustration was of a midnight landscape speared by lightning. In the foreground loomed a hooded figure, in the background tiny specks that might have been other figures or trees or merely errors in the printing process. *The Erl-King,* read the legend that ran beneath the picture.

"Huh," said Haley. She glanced up to call Linette, but her friend had wandered into the adjoining room. She could glimpse her standing at the shadowed foot of a set of stairs winding up to the next story. "Awesome," Haley murmured, turning toward Lie Vagal. When he said nothing she awkwardly dropped the catalog onto a chair.

"Let's go upstairs," he said, already heading after Linette. Haley shrugged and followed him, glancing back once at the faces staring from the library wall.

Up here it was more like someone had just moved in. Their footsteps sounded louder, and the air smelled of fresh paint. There were boxes and bags piled against the walls. Amplifiers and speakers and other sound equipment loomed from corners, trailing cables and coils of wire. Only the paintings had been attended to, neatly hung in the corridors and beside windows. Haley thought it was weird, the way they were beside all the windows: not where you usually hung pictures. There were mirrors like that, too, beside or between windows, so that sometimes the darkness threw back the night, sometimes her own pale and surprised face.

They found Linette at the end of the long hallway. There was a door there, closed, an ornate antique door that had obviously come from somewhere else. It was of dark wood, carved with hundreds of tiny figures, animals and people and trees, and inlaid with tiny mirrors and bits of glass. Linette stood staring at it, her back to them. From her tangled hair peeked the kinkajou, blinking sleepily as Haley came up behind her.

"Hey," she began. Beside her Lie Vagal smiled and rubbed his forehead.

Without turning Linette asked, "Where does it go?"

"My bedroom," said Lie as he slipped between them. "Would you like to come in?"

No, thought Haley.

"Sure," said Linette. Lie Vagal nodded and opened the door. They followed him inside, blinking as they strove to see in the dimness.

"This is my inner sanctum." He stood there grinning, his long hair falling into his face. "You're the only people who've ever been in it, really, except for me. My grandmother won't come inside."

At first she thought the room was merely dark, and waited for him to switch a light on. But after a moment Haley realized there *were* lights on. And she understood why the grandmother didn't like it. The entire room was painted black, a glossy black like marble. It wasn't a very big room, surely not the one originally intended to be the master bedroom. There were no windows. An oriental carpet covered the floor with purple and blue and scarlet blooms. Against one wall a narrow bed was pushed—such a small bed, a child's bed almost—and on the floor stood something like a tall brass lamp, with snaky tubes running from it.

"Wow," breathed Linette. "A hookah."

"A what?" demanded Haley; but no one paid any attention. Linette walked around, examining the hookah, the paintings on the walls, a bookshelf filled with volumes in old leather bindings. In a corner Lie Vagal rustled with something. After a moment the ceiling became spangled with lights, tiny white Christmas-tree lights strung from corner to corner like stars.

"There!" he said proudly. "Isn't that nice?"

Linette looked up and laughed, then returned to poring over a very old book with a red cover. Haley sidled up beside her. She had to squint to see what Linette was looking at—a garishly tinted illustration in faded red and blue and yellow. The colors oozed from between the lines, and there was a crushed silverfish at the bottom of the page. The picture showed a little boy screaming while a long-legged man armed with a pair of enormous scissors snipped off his thumbs.

"Yuck!" Haley stared open-mouthed, then abruptly walked away. She drew up in front of a carved wooden statue of a troll, child-sized. Its wooden eyes were painted white, with neither pupil nor iris. "Man, this is kind of a creepy bedroom."

From across the room Lie Vagal regarded her, amused. "That's what Gram says." He pointed at the volume in Linette's hands. "I collect old children's books. That's *Struwwelpeter.* German. It means Slovenly Peter."

Linette turned the page. "I love all these pictures and stuff. But isn't it kind of dark in here?" She closed the book and wandered to the far end of the room where Haley stared at a large painting. "I mean, there's no windows or anything."

He shrugged. "I don't know. Maybe. I like it like this."

Linette crossed the room to stand beside Haley in front of the painting. It was a huge canvas, very old, in an elaborate gilt frame. Thousands of fine cracks ran through it. Haley was amazed it hadn't fallen to pieces years ago. A lamp on top of the frame illuminated it, a little too well for Haley's taste. It took her a moment to realize that she had seen it before.

"That's the cover of your album—"

He had come up behind them and stood there, reaching to chuck the kinkajou under the chin. "That's right," he said softly. "The Erl-King."

It scared her. The hooded figure in the foreground hunched towards a tiny form in the distance, its outstretched arms ending in hands like claws. There was a smear of white to indicate its face, and two dark smudges for eyes, as though someone had gouged the paint with his thumbs. In the background the smaller figure seemed to be fleeing on horseback. A bolt of lightning shot the whole scene with splinters of blue light, so that she could just barely make out that the rider held a smaller figure in his lap. Black clouds scudded across the sky, and on the horizon reared a great house with windows glowing yellow and red. Somehow Haley knew the rider would not reach the house in time.

Linette grimaced. On her shoulder the kinkajou had fallen asleep again. She untangled its paws from her hair and asked, "The Erl-King? What's that?"

Lie Vagal took a step closer to her.

"—'Oh, father! My father! And dost
     thou not see?
The Erl-King and his daughter are
     waiting for me?'

—'Now shame thee, my dearest! Tis
fear makes thee blind
Thou seest the dark willows which
wave in the wind.'"

He stopped. Linette shivered, glanced aside at Haley. "Wow. That's creepy—you really like all this creepy stuff . . ."

Haley swallowed and tried to look unimpressed. "That was a *song?*"

He shook his head. "It's a poem, actually. I just ripped off the words, that's all." He hummed softly. Haley vaguely recognized the tune and guessed it must be from his album.

"'Oh, father, my father,'" he sang, and reached to take Linette's hand. She joined him shyly, and the kinkajou drooped from her shoulder across her back.

"Lie!"

The voice made the girls jump. Linette clutched at Lie. The kinkajou squealed unhappily.

"Gram." Lie's voice sounded somewhere between reproach and disappointment as he turned to face her. She stood in the doorway, weaving a little and with one hand on the doorframe to steady herself.

"It's late. I think those girls should go home now."

Linette giggled, embarrassed, and said, "Oh, we don't have—"

"Yeah, I guess so," Haley broke in, and sidled toward the door. Lie Vagal stared after her, then turned to Linette.

"Why don't you come back tomorrow, if you want to see more of the house? Then it won't get too late." He winked at Haley. "And Gram is here, so your parents shouldn't have to worry."

Haley reddened. "They don't care," she lied. "It's just, it's kind of late and all."

"Right, that's right," said the old lady. She waited for them all to pass out of the room, Lie pausing to unplug the Christmas-tree lights, and then followed them downstairs.

On the outside patio the girls halted, unsure how to say goodbye.

"Thank you," Haley said at last. She looked at the old lady. "For the tea."

"Yeah, thanks," echoed Linette. She looked over at Lie Vagal standing in the doorway. The backlight made of him a black shadow, the edges of his hair touched with gold. He nodded to her, said nothing. But as they made their way back down the moonlit hill his voice called after them with soft urgency.

"Come back," he said.

It was two more days before Haley returned to Linette's. After dinner she rode her bike up the long rutted dirt drive, dodging cabbage butterflies and locusts and looking sideways at Kingdom Come perched upon its emerald hill. Even before she reached the cottage she knew Linette wasn't there.

"Haley. Come on in."

Aurora stood in the doorway, her cigarette leaving a long blue arabesque in the still air as she beckoned Haley. The girl leaned her bike against the broken stalks of sunflowers and delphiniums pushing against the house and followed Aurora.

Inside was cool and dark, the flagstones' chill biting through the soles of Haley's sneakers. She wondered how Aurora could stand to walk barefoot, but she did: her feet small and dirty, toenails buffed bright pink. She wore a short black cotton tunic that hitched up around her narrow hips. Some days it doubled as nightgown and daywear; Haley guessed this was one of those days.

"Tea?"

Haley nodded, perching on an old ladderback chair in the kitchen and pretending interest in an ancient issue of *Dairy Goat* magazine. Aurora walked a little unsteadily from counter to sink to stove, finally handing Haley her cup and then sinking into an overstuffed armchair near the window. From Aurora's mug the smell of juniper cut through the bergamot-scented kitchen. She sipped her gin and regarded Haley with slitted eyes.

"So. You met Lie Vagal."

Haley shrugged and stared out the window. "He had Valentine," she said at last.

"He still does—the damn thing ran back over yesterday. Linette went after it last night and didn't come back."

Haley felt a stab of betrayal. She hid her face behind her steaming mug. "Oh," was all she said.

"You'll have to go get her, Haley. She won't come back for me, so it's up to you." Aurora tried to make her voice light, but Haley recognized the strained desperate note in it. She looked at Aurora and frowned.

You're her mother, you bring her back, she thought, but said, "She'll be back. I'll go over there."

Aurora shook her head. She still wore her hair past her shoulders and straight as a needle; no longer blonde, it fell in streaked gray and black lines across her face. "She won't," she said, and took a long sip at her mug. "He's got her now and he won't want to give her back." Her voice trembled and tears blurred the kohl around her eyelids.

Haley bit her lip. She was used to this. Sometimes when Aurora was drunk, she and Linette carried her to bed, covering her with the worn flannel comforter and making sure her cigarettes and matches were out of sight. Linette acted embarrassed, but Haley didn't mind, just as she didn't mind doing the dishes sometimes or making grilled cheese sandwiches or French toast for them all, or riding her bike down to Schelling's Market to get more ice when they ran out. She reached across to the counter and dipped another golden thread of honey into her tea.

"Haley. I want to show you something."

The girl waited as Aurora weaved down the narrow passage into her bedroom. She could hear drawers being thrown open and shut, and finally the heavy thud of the trunk by the bed being opened. In a few minutes Aurora returned, carrying an oversized book.

"Did I ever show you this?"

She padded into the umber darkness of the living room, with its frayed kilims and cracked sitar like some huge shattered gourd leaning against the stuccoed wall. Haley followed, settling beside her. By the door the frogs hung with splayed feet in their sullen globe, their pale bellies turned to amber by the setting sun. On the floor in front of Haley glowed a rhomboid of yellow light. Aurora set the book within that space and turned to Haley. "Have I shown you this?" she asked again, a little anxiously.

"No," Haley lied. She had in fact seen the scrapbook about a dozen times over the years—the pink plastic cover with its peeling Day-Glo flowers hiding newspaper clippings and magazine pages soft as fur beneath her fingers as Aurora pushed it towards her.

"He's in there," Aurora said thickly. Haley glanced up and saw that the woman's eyes were bright red behind their smeared rings of kohl. Tangled in her thin fine hair were hoop earrings that reached nearly to her shoulder, and on one side of her neck, where a love bite might be, a tattoo no bigger than a thumbprint showed an Egyptian Eye of Horus. "Lie Vagal—him and all the rest of them—"

Aurora started flipping through the stiff plastic pages, too fast for Haley to catch more than a glimpse of the photos and articles spilling out. Once she paused, fumbling in the pocket of her tunic until she found her cigarettes.

YOUTHQUAKER! the caption read. Beside it was a black-and-white picture of a girl with long white-blonde hair and enormous, heavily kohled eyes. She was standing with her back arched, wearing a sort of bikini made of playing cards. MODEL AURORA DAWN, BRIGHTEST NEW LIGHT IN POP ARTIST'S SUPERSTAR HEAVEN.

"Wow," Haley breathed. She never got tired of the scrapbooks: it was like watching a silent movie, with Aurora's husky voice intoning the perils that befell the feckless heroine.

"That's not it," Aurora said, almost to herself, and began skipping pages again. More photos of herself, and then others—men with hair long and lush as Aurora's; heavy women smoking cigars; twin girls no older than Haley and Linette, leaning on a naked man's back while another man in a doctor's white coat jabbed them with an absurdly long hypodermic needle. Aurora at an art gallery. Aurora on the cover of *Interview* magazine. Aurora and a radiant woman with shuttered eyes and long, long fishnet-clad legs—the woman was really a man, a transvestite Aurora said; but there was no way you could tell by looking at him. As she flashed through the pictures Aurora began to name them, bursts of cigarette smoke hovering above the pages.

"Fairy Pagan. She's dead.

"Joey Face. He's dead.

"Marletta. She's dead.

"Precious Bane. She's dead.

"The Wanton Hussy. She's dead."

And so on, for pages and pages, dozens of fading images, boys in leather and ostrich plumes, girls in miniskirts prancing across the backs of stuffed elephants at F.A.O. Schwartz or screaming deliriously as fountains of champagne spewed from tables in the back rooms of bars.

"Miss Clancy deWolff. She's dead.

"Dianthus Queen. She's dead.

"Markey French. He's dead."

Until finally the clippings grew smaller and narrower, the pictures smudged and hard to make out beneath curls of disintegrating newsprint—banks of flowers, mostly, and stiff faces with eyes closed beneath poised coffin lids, and one photo Haley wished she'd never seen (but yet again she didn't close her eyes in time) of a woman jackknifed across the top of a convertible in front of the Chelsea Hotel, her head thrown back so that you could see where it had been sheared from her neck neatly as with a razor blade.

"Dead. Dead. Dead," Aurora sang, her finger stabbing at them until flecks of paper flew up into the smoke like ashes; and then suddenly the book ended and Aurora closed it with a soft heavy sound.

"They're all dead," she said thickly; just in case Haley hadn't gotten the point.

The girl leaned back, coughing into the sleeve of her T-shirt. "What happened?" she asked, her voice hoarse. She knew the answers, of course: drugs, mostly, or suicide. One had been recent enough that she could recall reading about it in the *Daily News*.

"What *happened*?" Aurora's eyes glittered. Her hands rested on the scrapbook as on a Ouija board, fingers writhing as though tracing someone's name. "They sold their souls. Every one of them. And they're all dead now. Edie, Candy, Nico, Jackie, Andrea, even Andy. Every single one. They thought it was a joke, but look at it—"

A tiny cloud of dust as she pounded the scrapbook. Haley stared at it and then at Aurora. She wondered unhappily if Linette would be back soon; wondered, somewhat shamefully because for the first time, exactly what had happened last night at Kingdom Come.

"Do you see what I mean, Haley? Do you understand now?" Aurora brushed the girl's face with her finger. Her touch was ice cold and stank of nicotine.

Haley swallowed. "N-no," she said, trying not to flinch. "I mean, I thought they all, like, OD'd or something."

Aurora nodded excitedly. "They did! *Of course* they did—but that was afterward—that was how they *paid*—"

Paid. Selling souls. Aurora and her weird friends talked like that sometimes. Haley bit her lip and tried to look thoughtful. "So they, like, sold their souls to the devil?"

"Of course!" Aurora croaked triumphantly. "How else would they have ever got where they did? Superstars! Rich and famous! And for what reason? None of them had any talent—*none* of them—but they ended up on TV, and in *Vogue*, and in the movies— how else could they have done it?"

She leaned forward until Haley could smell her sickly berry-scented lipstick mingled with the gin. "They all thought they were getting such a great deal, but look how it ended—famous for fifteen minutes, then *pffftttt!*"

"Wow," Haley said again. She had no idea, really, what Aurora was talking about. Some of these people she'd heard of, in magazines or from Aurora and her friends, but mostly their names were meaningless. A bunch of nobodies that nobody but Aurora had ever even cared about.

She glanced down at the scrapbook and felt a small sharp chill beneath her breast. Quickly she glanced up again at Aurora: her ruined face, her eyes; that tattoo like a faded brand upon her neck. A sudden insight made her go *hmm* beneath her breath—

Because maybe that was the point; maybe Aurora wasn't so crazy, and these people really *had* been famous once. But now for some strange reason no one remembered any of them at all; and now they were all dead. Maybe they really were all under some sort of curse. When she looked up Aurora nodded, slowly, as though she could read her thoughts.

"It was at a party. At the Factory," she began in her scorched voice. "We were celebrating the opening of *Scag*—that was the first movie to get real national distribution, it won the Silver Palm at Cannes that year. It was a fabulous party, I remember there was this huge Lalique bowl filled with cocaine and in the bathroom Doctor Bob was giving everyone a pop—

"About three A.M. most of the press hounds had left, and a lot of the neophytes were just too wasted and had passed out or gone on to Max's. But Candy was still there, and Liatris, and Jackie and Lie Vagal—all the core people—and I was sitting by the door, I really was in better shape than most of them, or I thought I was, but then I looked up and there is this *guy* there I've never seen before. And, like, people wandered in and out of there all the time, that was no big deal, but I was sitting right by the door with Jackie, I mean it was sort of a joke, we'd been asking to see people's invitations, turning away the offal, but I swear I never saw this guy come in. Later Jackie said *she'd* seen him come in through the fire escape; but I think she was lying. Anyway, it was weird.

"And so I must have nodded out for a while, because all of a sudden I jerk up and look around and here's this guy with everyone huddled around him, bending over and laughing like he's telling fortunes or something. He kind of looked like that, too, like a gypsy—not that everyone didn't look like that in those days, but with him it wasn't so much like an act. I mean, he had this long curly black hair and these gold earrings, and high suede boots and velvet pants, all black and red and purple, but with him it was like maybe he had *always* dressed like that. He was handsome, but in a creepy sort of way. His eyes were set very close together and his eyebrows grew together over his nose—that's the mark of a warlock, eyebrows like that—and he had this very neat British accent. They always went crazy over anyone with a British accent.

"So obviously I had been missing something, passed out by the door, and so I got up and staggered over to see what was going on. At first I thought he was collecting autographs. He had this very nice leather-bound book, like an autograph book, and everyone was writing in it. And I thought, God, how tacky. But then it struck me as being weird, because a lot of those people—not Candy, she'd sign *anything*—but a lot of the others, they wouldn't be caught dead doing anything so bourgeois as signing autographs. But here just about everybody was passing this pen around—a nice gold Cross pen, I remember that—even Andy, and I thought, Well, this I got to see.

"So I edged my way in, and that's when I saw they *were* signing their names. But it wasn't an autograph book at all. It wasn't like anything I'd ever seen before. There was something printed on every page, in this fabulous gold and green lettering, but very official-looking, like when you see an old-fashioned decree of some sort. And they were all signing their names on every page. Just like in a cartoon, you know, 'Sign here!'. And, I mean, everyone had done it—Lie Vagal had just finished and when the man saw me coming over he held the book up and flipped through it real fast, so I could see their signatures . . ."

Haley leaned forward on her knees, heedless now of the smoke and Aurora's huge eyes staring fixedly at the empty air.

"What was it?" the girl breathed. "Was it—?"

"It was *their souls*." Aurora hissed the last word, stubbing out her cigarette in her empty mug. "Most of them, anyway—because, *get it,* who would ever want *their* souls? It was a standard contract—souls, sanity, first-born children. They all thought it was a joke—but look what happened." She pointed at the scrapbook as though the irrefutable proof lay there.

Haley swallowed. "Did you—did *you* sign?"

Aurora shook her head and laughed bitterly. "Are you crazy? Would I be here now if I had? No, I didn't, and a few others didn't—Viva, Liatris and Coppelia, David Watts. We're about all that's left, now—except for one or two who haven't paid up . . ."

And she turned and gazed out the window, to where the overgrown apple trees leaned heavily and spilled their burden of green fruit onto the stone wall that separated them from Kingdom Come.

"Lie Vagal," Haley said at last. Her voice sounded hoarse as Aurora's own. "So he signed it, too."

Aurora said nothing, only sat there staring, her yellow hands clutching the thin fabric of her tunic. Haley was about to repeat herself, when the woman began to hum, softly and out of key. Haley had heard that song before—just days ago, where was it? and then the words spilled out in Aurora's throaty contralto:

> "—'Why trembles my darling? Why
> shrinks she with fear?'
> —'Oh, father! My father! The Erl-King
> is near!
> 'The Erl-King, with his crown and his
> hands long and white!'

    —'Thine eyes are deceived by the
    vapors of night.'"

"That song!" exclaimed Haley. "He was singing it—"

Aurora nodded without looking at her. *"The Erl-King,"* she said. "He recorded it just a few months later . . ."

Her gaze dropped abruptly to the book at her knees. She ran her fingers along its edge, then as though with long practice opened it to a page towards the back. "There he is," she murmured, and traced the outlines of a black-and-white photo, neatly pressed beneath its sheath of yellowing plastic.

It was Lie Vagal. His hair was longer, and black as a cat's. He wore high leather boots, and the picture had been posed in a way to make him look taller than he really was. But what made Haley feel sick and frightened was that he was wearing makeup—his face powdered dead white, his eyes livid behind pools of mascara and kohl, his mouth a scarlet blossom. And it wasn't that it made him look like a woman (though it did).

It was that he looked exactly like Linette.

Shaking her head, she turned towards Aurora, talking so fast her teeth chattered. "You—does she—does he—does he know?"

Aurora stared down at the photograph and shook her head. "I don't think so. No one does. I mean, people might have suspected, I'm sure they talked, but—it was so long ago, they all forgot. Except for *him,* of course—"

In the air between them loomed suddenly the image of the man in black and red and purple, heavy gold rings winking from his ears. Haley's head pounded and she felt as though the floor reeled beneath her. In the hazy air the shining figure bowed its head, light gleaming from the unbroken ebony line that ran above its eyes. She seemed to hear a voice hissing to her, and feel cold sharp nails pressing tiny half-moons into the flesh of her arm. But before she could cry out the image was gone. There was only the still dank room, and Aurora saying.

". . . for a long time thought he would die, for sure—all those drugs—and then of course he went crazy; but then I realized he wouldn't have made that kind of deal. Lie was sharp, you see; he *did* have some talent, he didn't need this sort of—of *thing* to make him happen. And Lie sure wasn't a fool. Even if he thought it was a joke, he was terrified of dying, terrified of losing his mind—he'd already had that incident in Marrakech—and so that left the other option; and since he never knew, I never told him; well, it must have seemed a safe deal to make . . ."

A deal. Haley's stomach tumbled as Aurora's words came back to her—*A standard contract—souls, sanity, first-born children.* "But how—" she stammered.

"It's time." Aurora's hollow voice echoed through the chilly room. "It's time, is all. Whatever it was that Lie wanted, he got; and now it's time to pay up."

Suddenly she stood, her foot knocking the photo album so that it skidded across the flagstones, and tottered back into the kitchen. Haley could hear the clatter of glassware as she poured herself more gin. Silently the girl crept across the floor and stared for another moment at the photo of Lie Vagal. Then she went outside.

She thought of riding her bike to Kingdom Come, but absurd fears—she had visions of bony hands snaking out of the earth and snatching the wheels as she passed—made her walk instead. She clambered over the stone wall, grimacing at the smell of rotting apples. The unnatural chill of Linette's house had made her forget the relentless late-August heat and breathless air out here, no cooler for all that the sun had set and left a sky colored like the inside of a mussel shell. From the distant lake came the desultory thump of bullfrogs. When she jumped from the wall to the ground a windfall popped beneath her foot, spattering her with vinegary muck. Haley swore to herself and hurried up the hill.

Beneath the ultramarine sky the trees stood absolutely still, each moored to its small circle of shadow. Walking between them made Haley's eyes hurt, going from that eerie dusk to sudden darkness and then back into the twilight. She felt sick, from the heat and from what she had heard. It was crazy, of course, Aurora was always crazy; but Linette *hadn't* come back, and it had been such a creepy place, all those pictures, and the old lady, and Lie Vagal himself skittering through the halls and laughing . . .

Haley took a deep breath, balled up her T-shirt to wipe the

sweat from between her breasts. It was crazy, that's all; but still she'd find Linette and bring her home.

On one side of the narrow bed Linette lay fast asleep, snoring quietly, her hair spun across her cheeks in a shadowy lace. She still wore the pale blue peasant's dress she'd had on the night before, its hem now spattered with candle wax and wine. Lie leaned over her until he could smell it, the faint unwashed musk of sweat and cotton and some cheap drugstore perfume, and over all of it the scent of marijuana. The sticky end of a joint was on the edge of the bedside table, beside an empty bottle of wine. Lie grinned, remembering the girl's awkwardness in smoking the joint. She'd had little enough trouble managing the wine. Aurora's daughter, no doubt about that.

They'd spent most of the day in bed, stoned and asleep; most of the last evening as well, though there were patches of time he couldn't recall. He remembered his grandmother's fury when midnight rolled around and she'd come into the bedroom to discover the girl still with him, and all around them smoke and empty bottles. There'd been some kind of argument then with Gram, Linette shrinking into a corner with her kinkajou; and after that more of their laughing and creeping down hallways. Lie showed her all his paintings. He tried to show her the people, but for some reason they weren't there, not even the three bears drowsing in the little eyebrow window in the attic half-bath. Finally, long after midnight, they'd fallen asleep, Lie's fingers tangled in Linette's long hair, chaste as kittens. His medication had long since leached away most sexual desire. Even before The Crash, he'd always been uncomfortable with the young girls who waited backstage for him after a show, or somehow found their way into the recording studio. That was why Gram's accusations had infuriated him—

"She's a friend, she's just a *friend*—can't I have any friends at all? Can't I?" he'd raged, but of course Gram hadn't understood, she never had. Afterwards had come that long silent night, with the lovely flushed girl asleep in his arms, and outside the hot hollow wind beating at the walls.

Now the girl beside him stirred. Gently Lie ran a finger along her cheekbone and smiled as she frowned in her sleep. She had her mother's huge eyes, her mother's fine bones and milky skin, but none of that hardness he associated with Aurora Dawn. It was so strange, to think that a few days ago he had never met this child; might never have raised the courage to meet her, and now he didn't want to let her go home. Probably it was just his loneliness; that and her beauty, her resemblance to all those shining creatures who had peopled his dreams and visions for so long. He leaned down until his lips grazed hers, then slipped from the bed.

He crossed the room slowly, reluctant to let himself come fully awake. But in the doorway he started.

"Shit!"

Across the walls and ceiling of the hall huge shadows flapped and dove. A buzzing filled the air, the sound of tiny feet pounding against the floor. Something grazed his cheek and he cried out, slapping his face and drawing his hand away sticky and damp. When he gazed at his palm he saw a smear of yellow and the powdery shards of wings.

The hall was full of insects. June bugs and katydids, beetles and lacewings and a Prometheus moth as big as his two hands, all of them flying crazily around the lights blooming on the ceiling and along the walls. Someone had opened all the windows; he had never bothered to put the screens in. He swatted furiously at the air, wiped his hand against the wall and frowned, trying to remember if he'd opened them; then thought of Gram. The heat bothered her more than it did him—odd, considering her seventy-odd years in Port Arthur—but she'd refused his offers to have air conditioning installed. He walked down the corridor, batting at clouds of tiny white moths like flies. He wondered idly where Gram had been all day. It was strange that she wouldn't have looked in on him; but then he couldn't remember much of their argument. Maybe she'd been so mad she took to her own room out of spite. It wouldn't be the first time.

He paused in front of a Kay Nielsen etching from *Snow White*. Inside its simple white frame the picture showed the wicked queen, her face a crimson *O* as she staggered across a ballroom floor, her feet encased in red-hot iron slippers. He averted his eyes and stared out the window. The sun had set in a wash of green and deep blue;

in the east the sky glowed pale gold where the moon was rising. It was ungodly hot, so hot that on the lawn the crickets and katydids cried out only every minute or so, as though in pain. Sighing, he raised his arms, pulling his long hair back from his bare shoulders so that the breath of breeze from the window might cool his neck.

It was too hot to do anything; too hot even to lie in bed, unless sleep had claimed you. For the first time he wished the estate had a pool; then remembered the Jacuzzi. He'd never used it, but there was a skylight in there where he'd once glimpsed a horse like a meteor skimming across the midnight sky. They could take a cool bath, fill the tub with ice cubes. Maybe Gram could be prevailed upon to make some lemonade, or he thought there was still a bottle of champagne in the fridge, a housewarming gift from the realtor. Grinning, he turned and paced back down the hall, lacewings forming an iridescent halo about his head. He didn't turn to see the small figure framed within one of the windows, a fair-haired girl in jeans and T-shirt scuffing determinedly up the hill towards his home; nor did he notice the shadow that darkened another casement, as though someone had hung a heavy curtain there to blot out the sight of the moon.

Outside the evening had deepened. The first stars appeared, not shining so much as glowing through the hazy air, tiny buds of silver showing between the unmoving branches above Haley's head. Where the trees ended Haley hesitated, her hand upon the smooth trunk of a young birch. She felt suddenly and strangely reluctant to go further. Before her, atop its sweep of deep green, Kingdom Come glittered like some spectral toy: spotlights streaming onto the patio, orange and yellow and white gleaming from the window casements, spangled nets of silver and gold spilling from some of the upstairs windows, where presumably Lie Vagal had strung more of his Christmas lights. On the patio the French doors had been flung open. The white curtains hung like loose rope to the ground. In spite of her fears Haley's neck prickled at the sight: it needed only people there moving in the golden light, people and music . . .

As though in answer to her thought a sudden shriek echoed down the hill, so loud and sudden in the twilight that she started and turned to bolt. But almost immediately the shriek grew softer, resolved itself into music—someone had turned on a stereo too loudly and then adjusted the volume. Haley slapped the birch tree, embarrassed at her reaction, and started across the lawn.

As she walked slowly up the hill she recognized the music. Of course, that song again, the one Aurora had been singing a little earlier. She couldn't make out any words, only the wail of synthesizers and a man's voice, surprisingly deep. Beneath her feet the lawn felt brittle, the grass breaking at her steps and releasing an acrid dusty smell. For some reason it felt cooler here away from the trees. Her T-shirt hung heavy and damp against her skin, her jeans chafed against her bare ankles. Once she stopped and looked back, to see if she could make out Linette's cottage behind its scrim of greenery; but it was gone. There were only the trees, still and ominous beneath a sky blurred with stars.

She turned and went on up the hill. She was close enough now that she could smell that odd odor that pervaded Kingdom Come, oranges and freshly turned earth. The music pealed clear and sweet, an insidious melody that ran counterpoint to the singer's ominous phrasing. She *could* hear the words now, although the singer's voice had dropped to a childish whisper—

> —"'Oh, Father! My father! And dost
>   thou not hear
> 'What words the Erl-King whispers low
>   in mine ear?'
> —'Now hush thee, my darling, thy
>   terrors appease.
> 'Thou hearest the branches where
>   murmurs the breeze.'"

A few yards in front of her the patio began. She was hurrying across this last stretch of lawn when something made her stop. She waited, trying to figure out if she'd heard some warning sound—a cry from Linette, Aurora shrieking for more ice. Then very slowly she raised her head and gazed up at the house.

There was someone there. In one of the upstairs windows, gazing down upon the lawn and watching her. He was absolutely unmoving, like a cardboard dummy propped against the sill. It looked like he had been watching her forever. With a dull sense of dread she wondered why she hadn't noticed him before. It wasn't Lie Vagal, she knew that; nor could it have been Linette or Gram. So tall it seemed that he must stoop to gaze out at her, his face enormous, perhaps twice the size of a normal man's and a deathly yellow color. Two huge pale eyes stared fixedly at her. His mouth was slightly ajar. That face hung as though in a fog of black, and drawn up against his breast were his hands, knotted together like an old man's—huge hands like a clutch of parsnips, waxy and swollen. Even from here she could see the soft glint of the spangled lights upon his fingernails, and the triangular point of his tongue like an adder's head darting between his lips.

For an instant she fell into a crouch, thinking to flee to the cottage. But the thought of turning her back upon that figure was too much for her. Instead Haley began to run towards the patio. Once she glanced up: and yes, it was still there, it had not moved, its eyes had not wavered from watching her; only it seemed its mouth might have opened a little more, as though it was panting.

Gasping, she nearly fell onto the flagstone patio. On the glass tables the remains of this morning's breakfast sat in congealed pools on bright blue plates. A skein of insects rose and trailed her as she ran through the doors.

"Linette!"

She clapped her hand to her mouth. Of course it would have seen where she entered; but this place was enormous, surely she could find Linette and they could run, or hide—

But the room was so full of the echo of that insistent music that no one could have heard her call out. She waited for several heartbeats, then went on.

She passed all the rooms they had toured just days before. In the corridors the incense burners were dead and cold. The piranhas roiled frantically in their tank, and the neon sculptures hissed like something burning. In one room hung dozens of framed covers of *Interview* magazine, empty-eyed faces staring down at her. It seemed now that she recognized them, could almost have named them if Aurora had been there to prompt her—

Fairy Pagan, Dianthus Queen, Markey French . . .

As her feet whispered across the heavy carpet she could hear them breathing behind her, *dead, dead, dead.*

She ended up in the kitchen. On the wall the cat-clock ticked loudly. There was a smell of scorched coffee. Without thinking she crossed the room and switched off the automatic coffee maker, its glass carafe burned black and empty. A loaf of bread lay open on a counter, and a half-empty bottle of wine. Haley swallowed: her mouth tasted foul. She grabbed the wine bottle and gulped a mouthful, warm and sour; then, coughing, found the way upstairs.

Lie pranced back to the bedroom, singing to himself. He felt giddy, the way he did sometimes after a long while without his medication. By the door he turned and flicked at several buttons on the stereo, grimacing when the music howled and quickly turning the levels down. No way she could have slept through *that.* He pulled his hair back and did a few little dance steps, the rush of pure feeling coming over him like speed.

> "'If you will, oh, my darling, then with
>   me go away,
> My daughter shall tend you so fair and
>   so gay . . .'"

He twirled so that the cuffs of his loose trousers ballooned about his ankles. "Come, darling, rise and shine, time for little kinkajous to have their milk and honey—" he sang. And stopped.

The bed was empty. On the side table a cigarette—she had taken to cadging cigarettes from him—burned in a little brass tray, a scant half-inch of ash at its head.

"Linette?"

He whirled and went to the door, looked up and down the hall. He would have seen her if she'd gone out, but where could she have gone? Quickly he paced to the bathroom, pushing the door open as he called her name. She would have had to pass him to get there; but the room was empty.

"Linette!"

He hurried back to the room, this time flinging the door wide as he entered. Nothing. The room was too small to hide anyone. There wasn't even a closet. He walked inside, kicking at empty cigarette packs and clothes, one of Linette's sandals, a dangling silver earring. "Linette! Come on, let's go downstairs—"

At the far wall he stopped, staring at the huge canvas that hung there. From the speakers behind him the music swelled, his own voice echoing his shouts.

> "'My father! My father! Oh, hold me
>   now fast!
> He pulls me, he hurts, and will have
>   me at last—'"

Lie's hands began to shake. He swayed a little to one side, swiping at the air as though something had brushed his cheek.

The Erl-King was gone. The painting still hung in its accustomed place in its heavy gilt frame. But instead of the menacing figure in the foreground and the tiny fleeing horse behind it, there was nothing. The yellow lights within the darkly silhouetted house had been extinguished. And where the hooded figure had reared with its extended claws, the canvas was blackened and charred. A hawk-moth was trapped there, its furled antennae broken, its wings shivered to fragments of mica and dust.

"*Linette.*"

From the hallway came a dull crash, as though something had fallen down the stairs. He fled the room while the fairy music ground on behind him.

In the hall he stopped, panting. The insects moved slowly through the air, brushing against his face with their cool wings. He could still hear the music, although now it seemed another voice had joined his own, chanting words he couldn't understand. As he listened he realized this voice did not come from the speakers behind him but from somewhere else—from down the corridor, where he could now see a dark shape moving within one of the windows overlooking the lawn.

"Linette," he whispered.

He began to walk, heedless of the tiny things that writhed beneath his bare feet. For some reason he still couldn't make out the figure waiting at the end of the hallway: the closer he came to it the more insubstantial it seemed, the more difficult it was to see through the cloud of winged creatures that surrounded his face. Then his foot brushed against something heavy and soft. Dazed, he shook his head and glanced down. After a moment he stooped to see what lay there.

It was the kinkajou. Curled to form a perfect circle, its paws drawn protectively about its elfin face. When he stroked it he could feel the tightness beneath the soft fur, the small legs and long tail already stiff.

"Linette," he said again; but this time the name was cut off as Lie staggered to his feet. The kinkajou slid with a gentle thump to the floor.

At the end of the hallway he could see it, quite clearly now, its huge head weaving back and forth as it chanted a wordless monotone. Behind it a slender figure crouched in a pool of pale blue cloth and moaned softly.

"Leave her," Lie choked; but he knew it couldn't hear him. He started to turn, to run the other way back to his bedroom. He tripped once and with a cry kicked aside the kinkajou. Behind him the low moaning had stopped, although he could still hear that glottal voice humming to itself. He stumbled on for another few feet; and then he made the mistake of looking back.

The curved staircase was darker than Haley remembered. Halfway up she nearly fell when she stepped on a glass. It shattered beneath her foot; she felt a soft prick where a shard cut her ankle. Kicking it aside, she went more carefully, holding her breath as she tried to hear anything above that music. Surely the grandmother at least would be about? She paused where the staircase turned, reaching to wipe the blood from her ankle, then with one hand on the paneled wall crept up the next few steps.

That was where she found Gram. At the curve in the stairwell light spilled from the top of the hallway. Something was sprawled across the steps, a filigree of white etched across her face. Beneath Haley's foot something cracked. When she put her hand down she felt the rounded corner of a pair of eyeglasses, the jagged spar where she had broken them.

"Gram," the girl whispered.

She had never seen anyone dead before. One arm flung up and backwards, as though it had stuck to the wall as she fell; her dress raked above her knees so that Haley could see where the blood had pooled onto the next riser, like a shadowy footstep. Her eyes were closed but her mouth was half-open, so that the girl could see how her false teeth had come loose and hung above her lower lip. In the breathless air of the passageway she had a heavy sickly odor, like dead carnations. Haley gagged and leaned back against the wall, closing her eyes and moaning softly.

But she couldn't stay like that. And she couldn't leave, not with Linette up there somewhere; even if that horrible figure was waiting for her. It was crazy: through her mind raced all the movies she had ever seen that were just like this, some idiot kid going up a dark stairway or into the basement where the killer waited, and the audience shrieking *No!;* but still she couldn't go back.

The hardest part was stepping over the corpse, trying not to actually *touch* it. She had to stretch across three steps, and then she almost fell but scrabbled frantically at the wall until she caught her balance. After that she ran the rest of the way until she reached the top.

Before her stretched the hallway. It seemed to be lit by some kind of moving light, like a strobe or mirror ball; but then she realized that was because of all the moths bashing against the myriad lamps strung across the ceiling. She took a step, her heart thudding so hard she thought she might faint. There was the doorway to Lie Vagal's bedroom; there all the open windows, and beside them the paintings.

She walked on tiptoe, her sneakers melting into the thick carpeting. At the open doorway she stopped, her breath catching in her throat. But when she looked inside there was no one there. A cigarette burned in an ashtray next to the bed. By the door Lie Vagal's stereo blinked with tiny red and green lights. The music went on, a ringing music like a calliope or glass harp. She continued down the hall.

She passed the first window, then a painting; then another window and another painting. She didn't know what made her stop to look at this one; but when she did her hands grew icy despite the cloying heat.

The picture was empty. A little brass plate at the bottom of the frame read *The Snow Queen;* but the soft wash of watercolors showed only pale blue ice, a sickle moon like a tear on the heavy paper. Stumbling, she turned to look at the frame behind her. *La Belle et La Bête,* it read: an old photograph, a film still, but where two figures had stood beneath an ornate candelabra there was only a whitish blur, as though the negative had been damaged.

She went to the next picture, and the next. They were all the same. Each landscape was empty, as though waiting for the artist to carefully place the principals between glass mountain and glass coffin, silver slippers and seven-league boots. From one to the other Haley paced, never stopping except to pause momentarily before those skeletal frames.

And now she saw that she was coming to the end of the corridor. There on the right was the window where she had seen that ghastly figure; and there beneath it, crouched on the floor like some immense animal or fallen beam, was a hulking shadow. Its head and shoulders were bent as though it fed upon something. She could hear it, a sound like a kitten lapping, but so loud that it drowned out even the muted wail of Lie Vagal's music.

She stopped, one hand touching the windowsill beside her. A few yards ahead of her the creature grunted and hissed; and now she could see that there was something pinned beneath it. At first she thought it was the kinkajou. She was stepping backwards, starting to turn to run, when very slowly the great creature lifted its head to gaze at her.

It was the same tallowy face she had glimpsed in the window. Its mouth was open so that she could see its teeth, pointed and dulled like a dog's, and the damp smear across its chin. It seemed to have no eyes, only huge ruined holes where they once had been; and above them stretched an unbroken ridge of black where its eyebrows grew straight and thick as quills. As she stared it moved its hands, huge clumsy hands like a clutch of rotting fruit. Beneath it she could glimpse a white face, and dark hair like a scarf fluttering above where her throat had been torn out.

"Linette!"

Haley heard her own voice screaming. Even much later after the ambulances came she could still hear her friend's name; and another sound that drowned out the sirens: a man singing, wailing almost, crying for his daughter.

Haley started school several weeks late. Her parents decided not to send her to Fox Lane after all, but to a parochial school in Goldens Bridge. She didn't know anyone there and at first didn't care to, but her status as a sort-of celebrity was hard to shake. Her parents had refused to allow Haley to appear on television, but Aurora Dawn had shown up nightly for a good three weeks, pathetically eager to talk about her daughter's murder and Lie Vagal's apparent suicide. She mentioned Haley's name every time.

The nuns and lay people who taught at the high school were gentle and understanding. Counselors had coached the other students in how to behave with someone who had undergone a trauma like that, seeing her best friend murdered and horribly mutilated by the man who turned out to be her father. There was the usual talk about satanic influences in rock music, and Lie Vagal's posthumous career actually was quite promising. Haley herself gradually grew to like her new place in the adolescent scheme of things, half-martyr and half-witch. She even tried out for the school play, and got a small part in it; but that wasn't until the spring.

With apologies to Johann Wolfgang von Goethe

———

Another story set in Kamensic, reflecting my fascination with Andy Warhol's Factory. Like most of my work, there are numerous real-life touchpoints here, although the Erl-King himself isn't one of them. It was a finalist for the World Fantasy Award, and in an odd perambulation, prefigures my novel *Black Light*.

Justice

The gods always come. They will come down
from their machines, and some they will save,
others they will lift forcibly, abruptly
by the middle; and when they bring some order
they will retire. And then this one will do one thing,
that one another; and in time the others
will do their things. And we will start over again.

—C.P. Cavafy, "Intervention of the Gods"

I was in a Holiday Inn halfway between Joy and Sulphur, Oklahoma, when the call came about the mutilations.

"Janet? It's Pete." Peter Green, head of features at *OUR* magazine back in New York.

"What's the matter?" I said wearily. I'd just left Lyman, my photographer, back in the motel bar with a tableful of empty beer bottles and my share of the bill. I was already in bed and had almost not answered the phone. Now it was too late.

"Moira killed the Bradford story."

I snorted. "The hell she did."

Clink of ice in a glass: it was an hour later back in New York and two days before the weekly went to press. Pete would be at home, trying desperately to tie up all the loose ends before Moira McCain (*OUR* magazine was *her* magazine) started phoning him with the last-minute changes that had given Pete a heart attack last year, at the age of thirty-eight. "Too much fallout from the White's piece."

A month earlier I'd done a story on the mass murderer who'd rampaged through a White's Cafeteria in Dime Box, singling out women and children as targets for his AK–47. Turned out his estranged wife had tried to get a restraining order against him; she was meeting her mother at the cafeteria for lunch that day. A few weeks afterward there'd been another shooting spree. Same town, different restaurant chain, chillingly similar M.O.—girlfriend dumps guy, guy goes berserk, nine people end up dead. Now all the tabloids and networks were catching flack for over-publicizing the killings. Seven families had filed suit against a tabloid program that had presented the first killer—Jimmie Mac Lasswell, an overweight teenage boy—as a sensitive loner. Unbelievably, eight weeks later both killers were still at large. Not even sighted anywhere, which seemed impossible, given the scope of the publicity the killings had received. "Legal says put any kind of killer feature on hold till we find out how many of those suits are going to trial. That means Bradford. Moira's already called and canceled your interview."

"Son of a *bitch*."

I'd been working on this story for six months, contacting all the principals, writing to Billy Bradford in prison. This was my third visit to Oklahoma: I was finally going to interview him face-to-face. The story was slated to run next week.

"I know, Janet. I'm sorry." And he was, too. Pete hated Moira more than any of us, and he'd helped arrange any number of my meetings with Bradford's family and attorneys. Billy Bradford was a forty-two-year-old truck driver who had sexually abused his fourteen-year-old stepdaughter. When she'd threatened to go to her school guidance counselor with the story, he'd killed her. What made the story gruesomely irresistible, though, was the fact that Bradford was an amateur taxidermist who had then stuffed his stepdaughter and hidden her body at his Lake Murray hunting camp. PSYCHODADDY! the *New York Post* had called him, and everyone got a lot of mileage out of the Norman Bates connection.

But now the story was dead, and I was furious. "So what the hell am I supposed to do here in Bumfuck?"

A long pause. More ice rattled on Pete's end of the line. I knew something bad was coming.

"Actually, there's another story out there Moira wants you to cover."

"Oh, yeah? What?" I spat. "It's too early for the high school football championships."

"It's, uh—well, it's sort of a ritual thing. A—well, shit, Janet. It's a cattle mutilation."

"A *cattle mutilation?* Are you crazy?"

"Janet, look, we've got to have something—"

"What is this, I'm being punished? I won six fucking awards last year, you tell her that! I'm not dicking around with some UFO bull-shit—"

"Janet, listen to me. It's not like that, it's—" He sighed. "Look, I don't know what it is. Apparently Lyman was talking to her earlier today—this is *after* she killed the Bradford piece—and he mentioned hearing something on the radio down there about some cattle mutilations, and since you're both already out there Moira figured maybe you could get a story out of it. Lyman's got the details."

"Lyman's gonna have more than details," I snarled; but that was it. The Bradford story was dead. If Legal was worked up about it, Moira would never override their counsel. I could be in a room with Elvis Presley and the Pope and John Hinckley, and Moira would be whining with her lawyers over lunch at La Bernadine and refuse to run the story.

"Call me tomorrow. Lyman knows where this ranch is—" Lyman was from Oklahoma City, by way of a degree in Classics at Yale and a Hollywood apprenticeship—"hell, he's probably *related* to them—"

"Right. Later."

I clicked off and flopped back into bed.

Cattle mutilations. I should have switched from beer to tequila.

*   *   *

Lyman did know where the ranch was—a few hours outside of Gene Autry, an hour or so from the Texas border and about sixty miles from where we'd been staying.

"I'll meet you there," he said after giving me directions. Already his accent had kicked back in, and he'd resurrected a pair of ancient Tony Lama cowboy boots that he wore beneath his ninety-dollar jeans. "No later than noon, I swear."

He'd made plans to meet some distant cousin for a late breakfast somewhere on the way—

"Great barbecue, Janet, wish you'd join us—"

But I was too pissed to make small talk with Lyman and Don Ray. Instead I told Lyman I'd drop him off, and Don Ray would drive him down to find me in Gene Autry.

But Lyman was still determined that I salvage something from the trip. "Listen here, Janet, if you go about four miles past Sulphur you can get off the Interstate onto old Route 77. It'll take you right where we're going, and it's a real pretty road. I *know* you never got off the Interstate when you were here before. Route 77 goes through the Arbuckle Mountains and Turner Falls. And right before you hit the Interstate again there's a place called Val's Barbecue. Check it out for lunch."

He squeezed my arm and piled out of the rental car, weighted with cameras—he'd prove to the hick cousin that he was a real New York photographer now. And so I drove off, heading south for Gene Autry.

It took a while for Route 77 to get pretty. There was none of that Dustbowl ambiance I'd been expecting when I'd first come out here to meet with Bradford's wife. A lot of Oklahoma looked just like everywhere else now: McDonald's, franchised bars with stupid names, endless lots selling RVs and fancy pickup trucks. But after half an hour or so the landscape changed. The franchises dried up; the tacky ranch houses with over-watered lawns gave way to tiny dogtrot bungalows silvered with age, surrounded by rusting cars and oil wells long since run dry. Behind these stretched what remained of the great prairie—most of it given over to grazing lands now, but oddly empty of cattle or any other signs of cultivation. The sky was pale blue and dizzyingly immense above those endless green-gold plains, though on the southern horizon black clouds stretched as far as I could see, and spikes of lightning played in the distance. I fiddled with the radio till I found George Jones singing "He Stopped Loving Her Today."

"Well, shit," I said out loud. Maybe cattle mutilations weren't such a bad thing after all.

After about an hour I saw my first sign for the Arbuckle Mountains. A few miles further and I passed a grimy motel, with a hand-lettered cardboard sign dangling from its neon pilasters. NOW! AMERICAN OWNED, it read. Another mile and I saw another sign, this one for the local football team. A crude caricature of an Indian in full headdress, his face scarlet and mouth wide open to show white pointed teeth. In one hand he held a tomahawk, in the other a scalp. The sign proclaimed HOME OF THE SAVAGES. I began to wish I'd waited to come with Lyman.

A few miles out of town, the road started to climb. It narrowed until it was barely wide enough to let two pickups pass, but then I'd only seen three or four cars all morning. To either side white out-croppings of stone appeared, tufted with long brittle grass. Above me the blue sky had been overtaken by the storm front moving up from the south, and spates of rain slashed across the windshield now and again. I glanced down at the map on the seat beside me and decided to get off at the next exit for the Interstate, Turner Falls or not.

Suddenly, without warning the road ahead of me twisted, one hairpin turn after another. The map fell to the floor while I cursed and slowed to a crawl. To either side sheer walls of stone rose, only six or seven feet high but enough to block out any view and much of the yellowish light. Then the last turn ended, seeming to leave me hanging in the air. The radio reception crackled and inexplicably died. I glanced in the rearview mirror to make sure there was no one behind me and eased the car to the side of the road.

I was atop a jagged hill overlooking a vista out of ancient Britain. An expanse of hills that looked as though they had been formed by huge hands crumpling the land together and then gently pulling it apart again. Some of the valleys between these hills formed nearly perfect Vs, their clefts so sharp and steep that no sun seemed to penetrate them. It was like a child's drawing of mountains, although compared to real mountains back east, these were barely tall enough to pass for hills. What made it so creepy were the stones.

There were thousands of them; thousands upon thousands. Pale gray and bleached white, like the tips of shark's teeth protruding from the earth, and arranged in perfect lines, row after row, that dipped and rose as the hills did, until they disappeared upon the horizon. Between them the long prairie grasses grew sparsely, as though sown upon grave mounds. There were no trees, no shrubs, nothing except for the grass and stones. It was impossible to imagine who could have put them there—a task so immense and mindless it seemed beyond human comprehension—but so orderly was the progression it seemed unimaginable that it could be some natural formation.

I pulled my hair back with my bandanna and got out. The wind beat against me, hot and damp, and I could hear the grasses whispering as they bent across the rocks. On another morning, with clear sky overhead and wildflowers nodding between the rows of limestone, it might have been an exhilarating sight. That day I found it nearly unbearable. I hurried back into the car and cranked up the a/c. Ten minutes later I was on the Interstate.

Having circumvented Lyman's directions, it took me a little longer to find the Lauren ranch. The Arbuckle Mountains disappeared as quickly as they had appeared, and soon I was back on the unbroken flatlands, with cottonwood and mesquite along the roadside beneath signs for Stuckey's and Burger King. Finally I saw signs for Gene Autry, and a few miles later turned down a rutted gravel fire road that ran past tumbledown barns and a single rusting oil well. I was relieved when I saw three pickups pulled over to the side of the road. I checked my face in the mirror, rubbing my damp palms on my jeans and combing my hair back neatly. Too late I wondered if I should have worn a skirt—out here women still dressed like *women*. Not like they did in Texas, where housewives shopping at the H.E.B. all looked like *Dallas* extras; but I'd learned to be careful about how I looked, even for a cattle mutilation.

A hundred yards from the road four men were standing around a dark form sprawled on the ground. I crawled over the barbed wire fence, glad I'd worn my own (new) cowboy boots. Overhead buzzards circled. The heavy wind carried an oppressively sweet smell. The men knotted together, talking with heads downturned beneath their Stetsons and glancing at me sideways. The fourth walked toward me.

"I'm Janet Margolis from *OUR* magazine," I said, holding out my hand. He took it gingerly, nodding. "Thank you for seeing us. My photographer should be here soon."

"Well. I'm Hank Lauren." He cleared his throat uneasily. "This's my land here, some of my men."

I followed him to where the others stood upwind of the first carcass. A few feet behind it was another, and next to that a third. As I approached the men grew silent. One lit a cigarette and tossed the match so that it dropped onto one of the dead animals. Beside me Hank Lauren's feet fell heavily on the stony ground.

I stopped to gaze at the first body, then looked up at him in surprise.

"They're not cows."

He shook his head. "No ma'am. They're wild boars. Least I think they are. Agricultural Extension Office is checking, make sure nobody had some hogs escape the last few days."

"Javelinas," one of the other men explained. When I looked up at him he glanced away, but went on as though talking to the air. "That's a sort of wild pig we got around here. Sometimes they breed with the other kind. These're the biggest ones I ever seen." A shuffle and a murmur of agreement from the others. Hank coughed and waited while I stooped to look more closely.

It was a horrible sight, whatever it had been. An ugly thing to begin with, larger than any pig I'd ever seen, not that I'd seen many. Big enough for a man to ride on, if he could straddle its wide back. It was covered with coarse black hair, rising in a high bristly peak up its spine. Around its neck paler fur, nearly white, formed a collar. I took out my tape recorder and clicked it on.

"What'd you say this animal was called?"

"Javelina," the man answered loudly.

"Peccary," another said, stepping forward to nudge one of its stiff forelegs with his boot. "Collared peccary, that's what the Extension Office calls 'em. Down along the Mexican border they call 'em javelinas."

"Peccary," I repeated into the recorder, adding, "This is one big pig."

From the road echoed the sound of a car rattling along, and I looked back to see a big white Cadillac pull over. After a minute Lyman stumbled out, freighted with gear. He turned to shout thanks as the Cadillac roared away, then picked his way over the fence.

"Take a look at this, Lyman." I waved him over, trying not to grimace as a hot rank wave rose from the carcass at my feet. The men started talking among themselves again as Hank Lauren and Lyman shook hands. "I've never seen an animal this ugly in my life."

"Looks like someone didn't think it was ugly enough." Lyman swung out one of his cameras and started shooting. He squinted up at the sun, pewter-colored through the clouds, then back at the animal's face. "Damn, you all had one sick puppy out here, do that to a damn pig. I'm sorry, Janet," he added in a lower voice. "I shouldn't have made you come out here by yourself."

I frowned, but Lyman only turned back to his shoot. It wasn't until I crouched beside him to examine the thing's head that I saw what he meant. What I had thought to be the peccary's natural, if ugly, visage, was actually the result of some ghoulishly skillful work. The skin had been sliced into roseate petals around the eyes and folded back. Its ears were gone, and flies and gnats crawled in and out of the exposed white tubes that fed into its skull. Its lips were gone, too, so that the tusks and worn yellowed teeth looked enormous and raw, stained with blood and dirt-pocked.

"Jesus," I muttered. I stood, wiping the sweat from my palms, and glanced over at Lauren and his men. They said nothing, fastidiously ignoring me. I walked to the next carcass.

The other bodies were the same. "Mutilation of a ritual, probably sexual nature," I spoke into the recorder. "Damn, this is really sick—" I coughed and detailed some of the more obvious atrocities.

Hank Lauren was near enough to hear what I was saying: out of the corner of my eye I could see him nodding. I looked away, unaccustomedly embarrassed. How often did one use words like *castration, sodomy, coprophagy* when referring to a pig? Over the last few years I'd learned how to deal with such horrors when associated with women or children—you turned it into righteous outrage, and that turned into money in the pages of *OUR* magazine—but still, I'd never been there to see the bodies uncovered. The sight of those grotesque, pathetic corpses, coupled with the stench of excrement and putrefication made me feel faint. I switched off my recorder, surreptitiously covered my mouth and took a few deep breaths. I didn't want Lyman to see how this was affecting me. Then I stepped away to join Hank Lauren.

"So this happened last night?"

He shook his head. "Night before. Found them yesterday morning. Vet came out to do an autopsy said it happened that night."

"What do they think it was? Dogs?"

He snorted. "No *dog* could do that. No coyote either. Somebody with a razor—you ever see a dog do *that?*" He pointed at one of the carcasses, its violation grotesquely evident from where we stood.

"So what do they suspect?"

He shrugged but said nothing. One of the other men, the one who'd been smoking, coughed and said, "Something like this happened few weeks ago down in Ladonia. That's Texas, though."

Murmurs. "Last year there was something about it, some place in Colorado," another man put in. "These mutilations. Saw it on *Current Affair,*" he added, turning to his boss. "You remember I told you 'bout that?"

I nodded and looked at Hank expectantly, my thumb on the recorder button. He was staring at the buzzards wheeling patiently in the sky. "What do you think, Hank? I mean, anything strange going on around here—cults, stuff like that? Kids listening to weird music?" I didn't usually ask leading questions, but sometimes— with men especially—you had to keep probing before you finally hit a vein.

"Around here we don't go in for that kinder thing." It was one of the other men who answered. He'd been frowning, watching Lyman race through two rolls of film. Now the ground crackled beneath his heavy boots as he walked to join Hank and me with that slightly bowlegged gait. "Church is a big deal out here. Kids don't go in for that satanic music. Ones who do move on out."

The other men nodded. Lyman glanced over at me and winked.

"So nothing that might explain this?" My voice sounded a little desperate. I had visions of the rest of the day blown at the

Agricultural Extension Office, trying vainly to come up with some kind of hook for this damn story. "No kind of revenge angle, cattle rustling, anything like that?"

"Don't nobody rustle wild hogs," Hank remarked. The others laughed.

"Well, shit," I muttered, switching off the recorder. The stench from the corpses was starting to overwhelm me. The afternoon air was warm and humid, and clouds of blowflies were erupting from swellings in the pigs' bellies and their raw faces. "Lyman—?"

Lyman had moved out to focus on the four cattlemen, the bloated carcasses in the foreground. The smoker lit another cigarette, cupping cracked hands around a match. He looked up and said, "Hank, what about that business with your sister and Brownen?"

Hank Lauren didn't say anything, but after a moment he nodded. I tried not to look too eager, but fixed him with a quizzical look.

"Your sister?"

Hank Lauren breathed in noisily, raising his head to stare up at the sun raising a gray blister in the clouds. "Don't have a damn thing to do with this," he said.

"I just meant it's been in all the papers, Hank," the first man countered, and Hank sighed. I armed myself with the recorder again.

"Just some problems with her and her ex," he said wearily. "Locked him up on account he beat up on her and my nephew. But they let him out, some kind of restraining order. I testified, I heard that s.o.b. threaten t'kill her and the boy. He's a sorry bastard. Got arrested for dealing drugs, too. Well, they let him out anyway. He started calling her and now he's disappeared. Sue's about ready to leave town, she's so scared he'll come some night'n cut her throat."

"So you think this might be some kind of sick vengeance he's taking on your sister?"

He shrugged, glanced at his watch. His eyes when he raised them again were dull. "Well, I sure hope not." He dug his heel into the dirt and tilted his chin toward the pickups leaning at the roadside. "You got to excuse us, but we've got a few things to take care of this afternoon."

We shook hands and Lyman took some more pictures of Lauren and his crew. I got addresses and a few telephone numbers, and promised them the article would be out within the next week or two. Lyman and I watched the trucks leave, firing one after another and spurting off in a haze of dust and gravel.

"Well," I said as we headed to the car. "That was certainly a disgusting waste of time."

Lyman shrugged his equipment from one shoulder to the other. "What was that about his brother-in-law? Sounds like your kind of thing."

I kicked up a cloud of gritty dust, grimacing as we met the barbed-wire fence again. "It's only my kind of thing if he kills his ex-wife and shows up on national news. God, this is a depressing place."

"Well, we're done now. I booked us out tomorrow at eleven. So we can head to Oklahoma City tonight and get a hotel, or wait till morning."

He threw his stuff into the car and leaned against the trunk.

"For god's sake, let's get out of here." I glanced back at the carcasses. A buzzard had landed beside one, hopping about it like an excited kid, finally pouncing on a long ribbon of flesh and tugging at it. "Ugh."

"We-ell—" Lyman eased around to the driver's seat, shading his eyes and looking wistfully into the distance.

"Oh, come on, Lyman!" I yanked my door open, exasperated. "What in it? See Rock City? Best Little Whorehouse in Gene Autry?"

"Nooo . . ." He started the car and we jounced down the road. "Just there's this great place for barbecue up by the Arbuckle Reservoir. Indian territory but not too far from here. Only thing is, it's only open for dinner. But there used to be a pretty good motel—"

I was too dispirited to argue. "Sure, sure. Whatever. You drive, you feed me, whatever you want. Just make sure this time tomorrow I'm home. Okay?"

We found a dusty little motel and checked in. I made a few phone calls about Lauren's brother-in-law. I found his ex in the phone book. She hadn't bothered to change the number, but I'd long since ceased to be surprised by what women wouldn't do to avoid an abusive s.o.b. She was polite enough but didn't want to talk to me; I left the number of the motel in case she changed her mind. Then I called the local constable. According to him, yes, George Brownen had been released; no, there wasn't anything special they could do to protect his ex-wife, and the whole thing was probably being blown way out of proportion.

"Right," I said, dropping the phone in disgust and kicking back onto the bed. These things were always blown out of proportion, the proportions usually made up of some poor woman's face slammed against the wall, or blown to pieces inside a mobile home out by the Piggly Wiggly. But the hell with it. I tried to tell myself it was just a job.

I slept for a while. When I woke I showered, played back my tape and made a few notes, then buzzed Lyman's room. Out: no doubt soaking up more local color, or tracking down another cousin. I changed into jeans and a T-shirt and headed for the motel bar.

The motel sat on a sand-colored hillside, a few miles off Route 77 and with an impressive view of the Arbuckle Mountains rolled out like sepia corduroy to the east. A rusted sign advertising some defunct waterslide clapped loudly in the parking lot. Beneath the westering sun gleamed a tiny swimming pool half-full of overchlorinated water, the chemical smell so strong it made my eyes tear. I glanced vainly around for Lyman, crossed the parking lot, and stopped.

A single other car was parked in the lot, around the corner from our room. Not a car, actually. An RV, a mid-sized late-model leviathan with fake wood trim and darkened windows, identical to a million other RVs holding up traffic from Bar Harbor to Yosemite.

Only I recognized this one. I couldn't figure out how, or from where, but I'd seen it before. I stood staring at it, wiping the sweat from my upper lip and wishing I'd worn my sunglasses. All I had was a vague remembrance of unease, the name and the sight of that van making me distinctly uncomfortable. I walked past it slowly, and as I approached fierce barking broke out from inside. The vehicle shimmied slightly, as a dog—make that dogs—threw themselves against the side; and *that* was familiar, too. A flicker of shadow against one of the windows, then a thump and furious snarling as they leaped against the windows again.

"Huh." I paused, listening as the dogs grew more and more

frantic. From the sound of it they were big: no retirees with fluffy cockapoos here. The RV was big enough to house half-a-dozen Dobermans. And whoever owned the van wasn't putting hygiene at a premium—it smelled like the worst kind of puppy mill, with a lingering fecal odor of rotting meat and straw. Still I stood there, until finally I decided this was stupid. I probably *had* seen it before, parked at the motel in Oklahoma City, or even at the Holiday Inn. According to Lyman, the Arbuckle Mountains were supposed to be some big vacation spot. No real mystery.

But I couldn't shake the feeling that the RV was out of context, here; that wherever I'd seen it before, and heard those dogs, it hadn't been on this trip. At last I turned and went inside. The barking didn't cease until the bar door closed behind me.

The bar was one of those places where frigid air conditioning and near-darkness pass for atmosphere. The same Muzak piped into the motel's tiny coffeeshop echoed here, and the paltry clientele seemed to consist of motel employees getting off the three P.M. shift. I found a corner as far from the speakers as possible and sat there nursing a Pearl beer and squinting at the local paper. It was a weekly, nothing there about the animal mutilations yet, but the police blotter said that Susan Brownen, of Pauls Valley, had filed a complaint against her former husband. Seemed he'd tried to set her trailer on fire and, when that didn't work, totalled her car. George Brownen I assumed was still at large. There was also a long feature on someone celebrating her one-hundredth birthday in the Sulphur Rest Home, and a recipe for Frito Pie that used pickled okra. I finished my beer and decided to call Lyman again. Then I saw her.

She was at the bar, that's how I'd missed her before; but now she was turned toward me and smiling as the bartender shoved a mixed drink and a Pearl longneck in front of her. She slipped some money on the counter, took the drinks, and headed for my table.

"Janet Margolis, right?"

I nodded, frowning. "I *knew* I recognized that RV from somewhere. I'm sorry, I don't remember your name—"

She sat down, waving her hand self-deprecatingly as she slid the longneck to me. "Please! How could you? Irene Kirk—"

We shook hands and I thanked her for the beer. She pulled one leg up under her, smoothing the folds of an expensive pleated silk skirt. "We've got to stop meeting like this," she said, her eyes narrowing as she laughed and squeezed a lime into her glass. I nodded, leaning back in my chair as I sipped my beer.

Irene Kirk. I had been covering the trial of Douglas "Buddy" Grogan a year before, the story that had gotten me a Pulitzer nomination—the first ever for *OUR* magazine. It was a horrible experience, because the details of the case were horrible. Another estranged husband, this one granted visitation rights to his three-year-old son. After a year of threatening his ex-wife, then begging her to reconcile with him, one weekend when the little boy was visiting, Buddy Grogan had called her on the telephone and, as she listened and pleaded with him on the other end, shot the child. What made the whole thing almost unbearable, though, was that she had the whole thing on tape—she'd been recording her phone calls since he'd begun threatening her. And it wasn't the sort of thing you got used to hearing, even if you wrote for a tabloid that was trying to tart up its image for a more politically correct decade.

Irene Kirk had been there. She was a lawyer, the kind of feminist the newspapers always described as "ardent" rather than "militant." She lived in Chicago, but traveled all over the country doing *pro bono* work for rape crisis centers and abortion clinics and the like. She was a sort of camp follower of cases of this sort. Since the Grogan trial I'd heard of others running into her, at Congressional hearings, celebrity rape trials, shelters for the abused and homeless. But she wasn't exactly an ambulance chaser. For one thing, she obviously didn't need to work for a living. Small and delicate, with skin like white silk and inky hair pulled into a chignon, even here in the middle of nowhere she wore the kind of clothes you usually only saw on models in the European editions of tony women's magazines. And at the Grogan trial she spent a lot of time talking to women outside the courtroom—friends of Grogan's wife, women from local shelters, women who seemed to have stories not too different from the one I was covering, except they hadn't ended tragically—yet. Every morning she cruised around the courthouse until she found a parking space for her leviathan RV, and I'd wondered what a woman like that—with her sueded silk suits, smelling of

Opium and ylang-ylang shampoo—was doing with a van full of snarling dogs. Protection, I finally decided; *I* sure wouldn't want to mess with them.

During the course of the trial we'd spoken several times, mostly to shake our heads over the shameful state of affairs between men and women these days. Eight months later we would have had more to talk about: during a routine transfer to a federal penitentiary, Buddy Grogan somehow had escaped, aided by an unknown woman. He hadn't been heard from since. But that was still a ways off. When the trial ended Irene Kirk gave me her business card, but that was right before I got mugged by a couple of innocent-looking vegan types near Tompkins Square Park and lost my Filofax.

"I was very impressed by the way you handled the White's story," she said. She took a sip of her drink and glanced up at me through slitted black eyes. "It's amazing, isn't it, the way we just keep on going? One thing after another, and still we just can't quit."

I winced, tried to hide my expression behind my beer bottle. I remembered now why I'd been unhappy to see that van outside—Kirk's outspoken but somehow coy insistence that "we" were in this together, that together we formed some heroic bulwark for the victims we exploited, I with my articles, she in some subtler way I couldn't quite get a handle on. "It's my job," I said dryly. "I *can't* quit. Baby needs shoes, you know." I have my reasons for what I do—everybody does—but I'd be damned if I'd share them with Irene Kirk.

"Oh, I didn't mean you and me *individually.*" Kirk's cultivated voice was soft, but her eyes glittered in the dimness. "I mean all of us. Women. These terrible things happen but we just keep going on. We just keep fighting."

That last mouthful of beer turned sour in my mouth. I grimaced and looked around the room, as though seeking someone in the empty corners. "Yeah, well."

I thought of the photos I'd seen from the White's massacre: a mother hunched over the crumpled body of her daughter, a grandmother hugging a tiny limp figure, her face so raw with grief it no longer looked human. *Those* women sure hadn't been fighting. And then unbidden the images from that afternoon rose up in front of me: the bloated blackened carcasses slung out on the gravel, their eyes swollen with larvae and dust. When I looked up again Irene Kirk was still staring at me with those intent black eyes, her expression somewhere between concern and disdain. I suddenly wanted to leave.

"Well, it's all in the capable hands of the State of Oklahoma now." I tried to keep my voice light. "So I guess we just have to keep believing that justice will be done."

"Justice." She laughed, a small hard sound like pebbles clattering in a bowl, and leaned forward to stare into her half-empty glass. "The famous feminist reporter for *OUR* magazine still believes in justice."

The disdain in her voice was my cue to leave. I slid my chair back from the table and rose, giving her a blank smile. "I've got to go meet my photographer. Thanks again for the beer."

"I'll go with you." A slithering sound as the long folds of her skirt slipped down her legs. I shrugged, the smile frozen on my face, and headed for the door.

Outside the sun was dipping below the flattened edge of the prairie. The sawtoothed ridge of the Arbuckle Mountains cut a violet line against the bright sky. When I looked across the lot at Lyman's room I was relieved to see that the curtains had been drawn against the sunset.

"Well," I said again with forced cheerfulness—feeling ungrateful, somehow, and guilty for feeling so. "Nice seeing you again."

"Why are you here?"

The way she said it put an accusatory spin on the question, but when I looked at her she only smiled, her steps slowing as we approached her RV. For some reason I felt like lying. Instead I shrugged and said, "I was covering the Bradford case. But they pulled the story, so we're going back tomorrow."

"Mmm."

I turned to squint at the sun, then glanced back at her. She had an absent, almost dreamy look on her face, as though the name *Bradford* made her think of distant places—white beaches veined with blue water, an empty shoal beneath a midsummer sky. My earlier disgust returned. I whirled around, walking backwards across the empty lot, and called, "Have a good trip—thanks again for the drink—"

She raised a hand to me, her slight figure unnaturally black against the molten sunset. After a moment she turned and headed toward her van. As she approached it I heard again the frantic barking of the dogs inside. Then I was rapping on Lyman's door, falling inside with absurd relief as it swung open and the cool air flowed over my face.

Lyman's barbecue joint turned out to be small and crowded, run by a small woman named Vera who didn't crack a smile at Lyman's praise and left a handful of mintscented toothpicks beside our plates when she dropped the check. But the barbecue was good, lean and dry and smoky, with a vinegary sauce on the side—Texas-style barbecue, not the sweet soppy mess you get in New York. I asked him about the strange stones I'd seen along the old road.

"Dragon's teeth," he said. He lifted another piece of barbecue on his fork and eyed it dreamily. "That's what they call 'em out here. They're famous, geologically speaking. Arbuckle Mountains are one of the oldest places in the world, after the Black Hills and Olduvai Gorge."

I took a pull of my beer. "Dragon's teeth?"

"Sure. You know—Cadmus sowing dragon's teeth and an army springing up. It's in Aeschylus."

I snorted. "Lyman, you're the only person in this whole damn state ever even heard of Aeschylus."

After we ate he tried to talk me into going to some dive for a beer, but I was exhausted and too aware that the next day I'd be struggling to come up with some kind of story out of a few dead pigs.

"I'll put in for an eight o'clock wakeup call," he said as we stretched and yawned in the darkened parking lot. Overhead the day's clouds had blown on. There was a thin brittle moon and a few brilliant stars that made it seem like the air should be cool and brisk, instead of heavy and smelling of dust.

"Make it seven-thirty. I want to get out of here."

I saluted him and headed for my room, stopped after a few steps to look across the lot. Two other cars were parked beneath the yellow streetlights. I could hear a television shrieking from inside one of the rooms near mine. And Irene Kirk's RV was gone. I walked slowly past where it had been parked earlier and went inside.

It was a while before I could fall asleep. I felt like the whole day had been wasted; like months had been wasted, chasing another grim story and then having to bail out at the last minute. I knew it was absurd, that my coverage of the Bradford case was nothing more than another cheap tabloid hustling to cash in on misery in the Dust Belt. All my pieces were like that, but the process of writing them up and then seeing them in print somehow defused the stories of some of their horror, for me at least. It was like sticking around till the end of some particularly gruesome movie to read every line of the credits, reassuring myself that it was all nothing more than a string of sophisticated special effects and calculated screenwriting. Only with Bradford, of course, there were no credits; at least not until the TV movie appeared.

I finally dozed off, the distant grumble of trucks on the Interstate a comforting background roar. I was dreaming about pigs, pork barbecue, and beer, when the phone rang for my wakeup call.

"Mrs. Margolis?" A woman's twangy voice, like something you'd hear on a Bible call-in show. I groaned, feeling like I'd only been asleep for a few minutes, and rolled over, fumbling on the night table for my alarm clock. "Mrs. Margolis, is that you?"

I started to snap that I was *Mrs.* Nobody when the woman went on, "This is Sue Brownen. You called me today, n'I, I—"

I sat bolt upright, the clock in my hand. I *had* only been asleep for a few minutes. "Yes!" I said, a little breathlessly. I knocked aside a water glass, looking for my tape recorder, a notebook, anything. "Sue, of course, right. What's going on?"

"George—my husband, George—well, he called me tonight." In the background I could hear a child crying, another woman's comforting voice. "He says I don't meet him at Jojo's he's coming after me."

She stopped, her voice thick. I found a pen, scribbled *Jojo's* on the back of my hand. "You've called the police, right?" I was on my feet now, grabbing my jeans and crumpled T-shirt from the chair where I'd slung them. "And you're not alone, you're not at home, are you? You're not someplace he can find you?"

"No'm, I'm at—" The voice in the background suddenly rang

out shrilly, and Sue Brownen choked, "I'm somewhere safe. But I just thought—well, I been thinking about it, I thought maybe you could write this up, you said maybe you could pay me—"

I got an address, a post office box in Pauls Valley. She wouldn't tell me where she was now, but I made her promise to call me early in the morning, before I checked out. When I hung up I was already dressed.

It was crazy, getting all hyped up over some routine wife-beating case, but I needed some damn angle for that story. It was after eleven. I had no idea what time the bars closed here, but I figured on a weeknight I was probably pushing the limit at midnight. Outside I paused at Lyman's door. His room was dark, the shades still drawn. I thought of waking him up, but then Lyman hated going on any kind of location shoot where he might run into trouble. Although the odds were I'd end up cruising some dead bar with nothing to show for it but an interrupted night's sleep. I stopped at the motel desk, got directions to Jojo's, and left.

Returning from the Lauren Ranch we'd passed several small buildings at the edge of town. One right next to the other, each long and narrow beneath its corrugated tin roof. Names were painted on their fronts—BLACK CAT, ACAPULCO, JOJOS—but only the last was open. A number of pickups were parked in front, more of a clientele than I thought the tiny place could hold. When I drove past I saw men gathered before the crooked screened entry. Not the sort of men I'd want to tangle with alone; not the sort of place most women would go into, with or without an escort. I turned the car around in front of a boarded-up Sinclair station and made another pass, this time pulling into the lot of the shuttered roadhouse next door. I parked in front of the crude drawing of a black cat, shut off the motor, and waited.

There wasn't a lot of traffic in and out of Jojo's. The small group remained in front of the door, maybe because there wasn't room inside; but after about ten minutes two uniformed men came out. The rest of the little crowd parted, shuffling and adjusting their gimme caps as they passed, calling out greetings and laughing. The two cops crossed the crowded lot to another pickup, this one silvery blue and with a light on top, and leaned against it for a few more minutes, laughing and smoking cigarettes. Finally they slung their booted feet into the truck and drove off, the men by the door raising chins or hands in muted farewell.

So that was the local justice department. I sat in the car another five minutes, barely resisting the urge to lock myself in. I lived on the Lower East Side, I saw worse than this buying the *New York Times* every morning; but still my heart was pounding. *Stupid, Janet, stupid,* I kept thinking; I should have brought Lyman. But at last I got out and walked over to Jojo's.

No one said a word as I passed. One guy tipped the bill of his cap, and that was it. Inside was dim, lit by red bulbs the color of whorish lipstick. Smoke curled above the floor and a sound system blared a song I hated. It was crowded; I saw two women in booths toward the back, but their appearance didn't reassure me any. Behind the painted plywood bar a tall dark-skinned man yanked beers from a styrofoam cooler and slid them to his customers. The men moved aside as I approached, watching me coldly.

"I'm looking for George Brownen," I said. I pushed a ten dollar bill across the sticky counter. "He been here yet?"

The man looked suspiciously at the bill, finally set a Miller bottle atop it and pulled it toward him. "He's gone," he said shortly. He kept his eye on the bill but still didn't touch it.

"How long ago?"

The bartender turned pointedly to serve another customer. I waited, trying not to lose my temper or my nerve. Still he ignored me, finally crouching to attend to some business behind the plywood counter. A few more minutes passed.

"Sheriff lookin' for him, too," a voice announced beside me. I looked up to see a weathered man in a faded Harley T-shirt. He lit a cigarette, holding the pack out to me and then sticking it back in his pocket. He raised his chin to indicate the bartender. "He ain't gonna tell you nothin'."

Another man poked his head over the first's, staring at me appraisingly. "Brownen just left with another gal, young lady. But maybe I can help you."

I smiled tightly, shaking my head, and looked back for the bartender.

"Yessir, he sure did. 'Nother yankee," the first man was saying. "Hey Jo, you bringin' in tourists these days?"

Scattered laughter. The bartender stood and looked at me with dangerous red eyes. I nodded once, turned, and fled.

The crowd at the door let me pass again, though this time their voices followed me as I walked back to my car. I did my best not to run, once inside I hit the autolock and sat for a moment trying to compose myself. After a minute or two the faces in front of the roadhouse had all turned away.

Still, I didn't want to sit there, and I sure didn't want anyone to follow me. When I started the car I drove behind the Black Cat, hoping to find a way out; and that was where I saw them.

She had changed her clothes. Now she wore tight jeans and a red blouse, and cowboy boots—surprisingly worn-looking boots, even in the cracked circle of blue light from the single streetlamp I could see how old those boots were, a working man's boots, not some rich urban lawyer's. They were leaning against her RV, arms crossed in front of their chests, talking. Once she threw her head back and laughed, and the man looked at her, confused, before he laughed, too. He was tall and good-looking, with dark hair and a neatly trimmed beard. He glanced at my car as I drove by, but Irene Kirk didn't even look up. I knew without a doubt in my mind that he was George Brownen.

Abandoned railroad tracks crisscrossed behind the roadhouses. Next to them stood a burned-out warehouse with the rusted logo RED CHIEF flapping from a pole. I shut the engine, killed the lights and sat, watching Kirk and Brownen, trying to imagine what they were saying. Was she doing some kind of research, pretending to be one of her hard-luck clients? Or did she just have a taste for rough trade? The thought made me grimace, and I slid down in my seat so there'd be no way they could see me.

Only a few more minutes passed before she slapped the front of her van and started for the door. Brownen waited, called something and pointed across the lot. I knew he was trying to get her to follow him to his truck. But Irene only laughed, slinging her slight frame up into the driver's seat and leaning over to open the other door. Brownen waited another moment, until she turned on the headlights. Then he walked slowly to the RV and climbed inside. Very faintly I could hear barking, and then that was swallowed by the van's engine and the crunch of flying gravel as the RV pulled away.

I followed them. I knew it was crazy but I felt reckless and pumped up after my visit to Jojo's. Plus there was nothing to worry about, really; there was no way they could recognize me, cruising a safe distance behind them, and back inside my car I felt invulnerable. I don't know what I was thinking—probably nothing more than some misplaced voyeurism, or maybe a hope that they might stop somewhere and I could see where Brownen lived.

A rusted double-wide trailer on the outskirts of this failing oil town . . .

That would be how I'd write it up; but they didn't go to Brownen's place. They headed north, toward the Interstate and the mountains, then turned onto a gravel road that ran parallel to the highway. I slowed until there was a good distance between us; it was easy to keep them in sight. There was no other traffic. After a few minutes we were in open country again.

They drove for a long time. I rolled down the window to catch the night wind, heavy with the smell of wild sage and the ubiquitous taint of petroleum. I didn't turn on the radio, from some faint ridiculous fear that they might somehow hear it.

Overhead the moon was setting, bright as a streetlamp. The stars looked white and surprisingly solid, like salt spilled on a black table. As I drove the land slowly began to rise around me, gentle hills at first, hiding the rolling farmlands and the dull orange glow on the horizon that marked Ardmore to the south. The air streaming through the window was warm and sweet. I was composing my article in my head, thinking how Lyman had enough grisly photos that we wouldn't need much text. Far ahead of me the RV's taillights jounced and swam, twin meteors burning across the darkness.

I don't know when I realized that we were back among the stones. On some unconscious level it must have registered—I'd been climbing steadily for a long time, the prairie somewhere in the soft darkness behind me. But suddenly I jerked upright, as though I had drifted asleep at the wheel.

I hadn't: it was just that it was a shock, to look out the window and suddenly see them like that. In the moonlight they looked more like tombstones than ever. No, not tombstones, really, but something worse, infinitely more ancient and incomprehensible: barrows, menhirs, buried ossuaries. Lyman's comment about dragon's teeth didn't seem so stupid now. I stared out the window at those meticulous rows of bleached sharp spines, and wondered if it was true, if those stones were as ancient as he'd said.

When I looked up again a moment later I thought I'd lost the RV. In front of me the cracked road twisted until it disappeared in the blackness. The van's lights were gone. I had a jolt of panic, then sighted it: it had turned off to the right and parked. It sat on a high ridge overlooking the lines of stones, its rounded bulk silhouetted against the moon on the edge of the world.

Absurdly, I still wanted to follow them. If they'd been watching at all they must have seen the car behind them; still, I cut my lights and pulled to the side of the road to park. I was in one of those tiny deep clefts poked into the strata of limestone and scrub. No one could see me, although they might notice that my car had abruptly disappeared. I waited a long time, striving to hear something above the soft hissing of the wind in thorny brush and the staccato cries of a nightjar.

I finally got out of the car. The air felt cooler here. Something scrabbled at my feet and I looked down to see a hairy spider, nearly big as my hand, crouch in a pocket of dust. I turned and began to walk quickly up the rise.

In a few minutes I could hear voices, surprisingly close. As I reached the top of the little hill I crouched down, until I was half walking, half crawling through loose scree and underbrush. When I reached the top I kept my head down, hidden behind a patch of thorns.

I was close enough that I could have thrown a stone and hit the side of the RV. Another sheer drop separated us, a sort of drywash gully. The ridge where they were parked was a little lower than where I crouched. Between us marched three rows of stones, sharp and even as a sawblade. I heard faint music—Irene must have put the radio on—and their voices, soft, rising now and then to laughter.

They were walking around the van. Irene kicked idly at stones. The wind carried the acrid smell of cigarette smoke from where Brownen followed her. I tried to hear what they were saying, caught Irene pronouncing something that sounded like "wife" and then Brownen's laughter. I peered through the brush and saw that she was carrying something in one hand. At first I thought it was a whip, but then I saw it was a stick, something slender and pliable like a forsythia wand. When she slapped it against her thigh it made a whining sound.

That sound and the thought of a whip suddenly reminded me of the dogs. I swore under my breath, squatting back on my heels. And as though the same idea had come to her, Irene headed for the back of her van. She walked slowly, almost unthinkingly; but somehow I knew that this was calculated. She'd meant all along to let those dogs out. It was the reason she'd come here; and suddenly I was afraid.

For a moment she stood in front of the door, staring at where Brownen stood with his shoulders hunched, looking at his feet and smoking. Behind her the moon hung like a silver basket. The jagged hills with their lines of stones marched on, seemingly forever, the stones dead-white against the gray earth and somber sky. Still Irene Kirk waited and watched Brownen. She didn't stand there hesitantly. It was more like she was thinking, trying to make up her mind about something. Then, with one sure motion she threw the door open.

I had thought the dogs would bound out, snarling or barking. Instead at first their heads and front paws appeared. There were two of them, sniffing and whining and clawing at the air. Big dogs, not as large as mastiffs but with that same clumsy bulk, their heads looking swollen compared to the rest of them. I heard Irene's voice, soothing yet also commanding. Brownen looked up. There was no way for me to tell if he was afraid, but then he dragged on his cigarette and ground it out, shoved his hands in his jeans pockets and looked quickly from Irene to her animals.

The whining grew louder. The dogs still remained at the edge of the van, crouched like puppies afraid to make the little jump to the ground. And then I realized they *were* afraid. When Irene took a step toward them their whining grew louder and they fell over each other, trying to race back into the van; but then she raised that slender wand and called something. Her voice was clear and loud, but I had no idea what she said.

The dogs did, though. At the sound of her voice they stopped. When she repeated the command they turned and leaped from the cab, their great forms flowing to the ground like black syrup poured from a jug. Big as they were they looked scared. Even from where I crouched I could see their ribs, the swollen joints of their legs, and the silvery glint where one still wore a cruel collar around his neck. Sudden panic overcame me: what if they scented me and attacked? But running would only make it worse, so I bellied down against the coarse ground, praying the wind wouldn't turn and bring my scent to them.

And the dogs seemed to want to run. They started to race across the narrow ridge, but once again Irene shouted a command, her switch slashing through the air. As though they'd been shot the dogs dropped, burying their muzzles between their front paws like puppies. Irene turned her back to them and walked toward Brownen.

She walked right up to him, until her hands touched his sides. He drew his arms up to hold her, but I saw how his eyes were on the dogs. Then she thrust her pelvis against his, ran her hands along his thighs and up his arms, until he looked down at her. His head dipped; moonlight sliced a gray furrow across his scalp. I could no longer make out Irene's face beneath his; and that was when she raised her hand.

The slender switch she held hung in the air for a moment. When it dropped I could hear its whistling, so that I thought he'd cry out as it struck his shoulder. But he didn't; he only looked up in surprise. He started to draw away from her, puzzled, his mouth opening to say something. He never did.

As smoothly as the dogs had poured from the back of the van, Brownen fell to his knees. For an instant I lost sight of him, thought I was looking at another of the stony cusps stretching across the hills. Then I saw him; saw what he was becoming.

A wail cut across the hillside. I thought it was Brownen at first, but it was one of the dogs. At Irene's feet a dark form writhed, man-size but the wrong shape. In her hand the switch remained, half-raised as though she might strike him again. The shape twisted, as though struggling to get up. I heard a guttural sound, a sort of grunting. My stomach contracted; I thought of running back to my car but that would mean standing, and if I stood there would be no way of pretending that I hadn't seen what had become of Brownen. In another moment it was too late, anyway.

Irene Kirk stepped back. As her shadow fell away the figure at her feet squirmed one last time, tried to rear onto his hind legs and finally rolled onto all fours. It was an animal. A pig: a boar, one of the things I'd seen that afternoon, slaughtered on the Lauren ranch. In the moonlight it looked immense and black, its grizzled collar of fur seeming to cast a sheen upon the ground beneath it. It had tusks, not large but still vicious-looking, and surprisingly dainty feet ending in small pointed hooves. There was no man where Brownen had stood a moment before; nothing but the javelina and Irene Kirk, and crouched a few yards away her two dogs.

My eyes burned. I covered my mouth with one hand, retching, somehow kept from getting sick. I heard a high-pitched sound, something screeching; when I looked up the javelina had darted across the ridge, heading toward the car.

"Jimmie Mac! Buddy!" Irene's voice was clear and loud, almost laughing. She raised her wand, pointed at the boar scrabbling through the brush and yelled something I couldn't make out. I raised myself another inch, in time to see the two dogs burst from their crouch and take off after the javelina.

Within seconds they had it down, within the shadow of the RV. Their snarls and the peccary's screams ripped the still air. I could hear its hooves raining against the metal side of the van, the dogs' snarling giving way to frightened squeals. The sharp odor of shit came to me suddenly, and a musky smell. Then it was quiet, except for low whimpering.

I let my breath out, so loudly I was sure they'd hear me. But the dogs didn't move. They wriggled belly-down against the ground, as though trying to back away from the carcass in front of them. A few feet away Irene watched, her arms lowered now, her stick twitching against her thigh. Then she walked slowly to the animals.

The dogs groaned and whined at her approach, writhing as though chained to the wheels of the van. When she reached them her arm shot up. I thought she would strike them, but instead she brought the switch down upon the javelina's corpse. The moon glinted off the slender wand as though it were a knife; and then it seemed it *was* a knife. Because where she struck the carcass slivers of flesh spun into the air, like a full-blown rose slashed by a child's hand. Ears, lips, nose; gleaming ribbons falling around her feet like leaves. She was laughing, a sweet pure sound, while at her feet the dogs moaned and clawed their muzzles with bloody paws.

I couldn't bear any more. Before I could stop myself I was on my feet and bolting, my feet sliding through the loose scree and dust swirling up all around me. Only a few yards away was my car. I jumped over a pointed tooth of stone, thought almost that I had made it; but then I was screaming, falling beneath some great weight onto the rocky ground.

"Janet."

The weight was gone. Above me something blotted out the sky, and there was warmth and wet all around me. Then I heard kicking, and the dark shape whimpered and fell away. I threw my arm protectively across my face, groaning as I tried to sit up.

"Janet," the voice repeated. I could see her now, arms crossed, a line creasing her forehead where a scratch was drawn as though with red ink. "What are you doing here?" Her tone was disbelieving, but also a little amused, as though I were a disappointing student who had suddenly proved to have some faint spark of intelligence.

I said nothing, tried to back away from her. A dog lay at either side of her legs; in between I saw her boots, the worn creased leather now bloodstained and covered with a scruff of dirt. Blinking I looked up again. Her eyes were cold, but she smiled very slightly.

"I have to go now," she said. I flinched as she raised her arms, but she only yawned.

Behind her the sky had faded to the color of an oyster shell. The moon was gone and now only the stars remained, pale flecks like bits of stone chipped from the ground beneath me. In the ashen light Irene suddenly looked very old: not like an old woman but truly ancient, like a carven image, some cycladic figure risen from among the stones. I thought of Lyman talking about dragon's teeth; of an ancient Greek hero sowing an army from broken stones.

And suddenly I remembered something. An absurd image, thrown back from some movie I'd seen as a child decades before. One of those grim bright Technicolor epics where toga-clad heros fought hydras and one-eyed giants, and sweating men groaned and yelled as they strove against the oars of a trireme. A woman on a white beach, a sea like blue ink spilling behind where she stood smiling at an assembly of shipwrecked men. Then her hands swept up, one of them holding an elaborately carved wand. In front of her the sand whipped up in a shimmering wall. When it subsided the men were gone, and she was surrounded by pink grunting pigs and snarling German shepherds that were stand-ins for wolves. She raised her arms and the wolves turned upon the swine, howling. I could almost remember her name, it was almost familiar . . .

"Goodbye, Janet."

Irene Kirk knelt, bending over one of the dogs; and it came back to me.

Not Kirk. *Circe.*

I struggled to pronounce it, then saw how she held her switch, so tightly her fingers were white.

"Time's up, Buddy," she said softly. Her other hand grasped the dog by its collar, and I saw where something pale fluttered, a piece of tattered cloth wrapped around the leather. There was something printed on it; but before I could focus her hand moved, so swiftly the switch became a shining blur. The dog made a gasping sound, gave a single convulsive shake. When her hands drew back I saw where its throat had been cut, a deep black line across the folds of loose skin where blood quickly pooled over the paler knobs of trachea and bone. Frantically I pushed myself away from it, heedless of the other dog whining beside its mistress.

As quickly as she'd slashed its throat the woman stood. She took a step toward her van, then stopped. She glanced down at me, her eyes black as though hollowed in stone.

"Don't think about it too much," she said, her mouth curving slightly. Then she stooped and with one swift motion flicked the collar from the dead animal's neck. "Or—"

Her smile widened as she finished ironically, "Think of it as *justice.*"

She tossed the collar and I shrank back as it landed almost in my lap. There was enough dawn light now that I could see that the scrap of cloth wrapped around the leather had been torn from some kind of uniform. I could make out the faint letters beneath the crust of dirt and blood.

D.L. GROGAN, it read, US PENITENTIARY 54779909.

I watched her walk away. When she called "Jimmie Mac!" the remaining dog stumbled to its feet and followed her, its shadow humping between the lines of stone brightening in the sunrise. Then they stood at the rear of the van, the woman holding the door while the dog whined and groveled at her feet. I stood and staggered to my car, glancing over my shoulder to see if they were watching, but neither one looked back at me.

———

Like "The Bacchae," this was another story that annoyed readers, this time in *Fantasy & Science Fiction*. I wrote "Justice" in a blind red rage, after reading an article about a support group called Parents of Murdered Children. A man of my acquaintance read it in manuscript and was so enraged by it that he didn't talk to me for two days. The Oklahoma setting of "Justice" is real; so were the murders committed by the men who merit Circe's justice.

Dionysus Dendrites

I see him only in bright dreams:
white face laughing, crouching in the crook
of an oak with thrashing leaves. It seems
he waits patiently, the years to him a blink, a look
(glancing; no haste for those hands that reach
for mine) to see if I have wakened since last we met.
Breathlessly I beg him, "Speak to me, teach
me the words that act as passkeys, the quiet
song that soothes the Dog; name the place where I
can cross the narrow river, enter the forest, climb
that tree to join you."

He laughs at the lie they taught me:
Of course I will cross that black water, in time.

And then I wake.
The leaves fade. The vivid eyes grow dim.

I pull the curtains fast against the dawn,
and turn to wait for him

———

This is about the Boy in the Tree, the demonic figure I've
been dreaming about since I was seventeen. In Boetia, in
ancient Greece, Dionysus was called Dendrites, "the one in
the tree."

The Have-Nots

Now you know Eddie Rule came and took that baby girl three days after she was born.

Actually, his mother took her, Nora Margaret. That was his mother's name, not the girl's. Marched right into that hospital room, Loretta said the nurse was checking her stitches Down There and Nora Margaret marched right in anyway, didn't give a tinker's damn.

I'm taking that baby, she said.

Pardon me? said the nurse. She didn't know Nora Margaret Rule from a hole in the ground.

Excuse *us,* she told the nurse, I think you better go now.

The hell you will, said Loretta; at least now that's what she says she said, but I knew Loretta since fourth grade and she never said a swear in her life 'til she met Eddie Rule, and let me tell you, he was such a goddamn son of a bitch, pardon my French, I would of swore, too.

Now, Alice Jean honey, let me explain something. That shade is just all wrong for you. You're a Summer Rose, remember, you got that blonde hair and blue eyes, you just *have* to go with the Love

That Pink. That's the wonder of Mary Rose Cosmetics, everyone gets their own special coordinated color. I think the Salmon Joy is for Erika here, now see the difference?

I thought you would.

Now I'm sorry, I got distracted. But Loretta says now she should of told Nora Margaret off like that, anyhow, swears or not, and I wish she had.

We're married, Loretta said. Ask that nurse, she saw it, Mr. Proctor came down and did it before the baby came. The nurse was gone by then but Loretta showed me the license, it was real all right, she's still got it at home. They wanted to see it for the movie.

Well, you ain't married no more, says Nora Margaret. Loretta told me later, she was surprised a rich lady'd talk like that, but I told her Nora Margaret Rule had no more schooling than my dog King, she just married a rich man is all. Anyway she flaps some thing in front of Loretta's face, Loretta practically went into hysterics then and they called the doctor in. She got them to annex the marriage—

Pardon?

Oh. Well, whatever. Annul it, then, she went to court and had them fix it somehow, said 'cause her son is a Catholic and there was no priest it wasn't a real marriage. Loretta said if you're a Christian how come you're taking my baby and I'm gonna call the police.

Catholic, not Christian, Nora Margaret says, and don't waste your breath, Miss Missy.

Loretta says, It's *Missus*, and Nora Margaret says, Not anymore it ain't. And you know she really did, she took that little baby practically out of her mama's arms and took it away. Paid somebody to adopt it in Richmond and that was the last Loretta saw of it.

Erika, honey, I swear that color takes ten years off your life. Not that you need it. I swear. Alice Jean, don't you think so? I love it that we can compare like this, friends at home. That's why I love Mary Rose Cosmetics, I can come right here to your house with everything and then later, in the middle of the night, you change your mind, why next day I can come right back and you can exchange that Salmon Joy for anything you like.

That Touch of Teal is *very* popular this year, Erika, you just go right ahead and try it. Kind of smudge it around your eyelid like that. There. I sold one to Suzanne Masters last week, she had that

Dinner Dance at the Club to go to and it just matched her dress. I told her if I keep going like this, I'm gonna have that Mary Rose Cadillac by the end of summer and drive my kids to school in it.

I haven't forgotten I'm telling about Loretta's Cadillac, Alice Jean. You get too impatient. Let me give you a facial massage and masque, you got that hot water there, Erika? All right. Now this only takes a few minutes but I swear you will feel like a new woman. You need to relax more, Alice Jean.

There. Isn't that nice? I think it smells like that shampoo they use at Fashion Flair.

So that was, what, Nineteen fifty-six? Nineteen fifty-six. Loretta got out of the hospital and I got her a job at the Blue Moon. Now I swear to god every small town and every city I ever lived in had a diner called the Blue Moon. But it wasn't a bad place to work, just not what you'd want to do after you were married for three days to a Catholic whose rude mama came into the hospital and stole your baby and then gave it to a chiropractor and his wife in Richmond. Plus Nora Margaret said she was gonna change the baby's name—

Her name is Eloise, Loretta shouted. Eloise LeMay Rule.

Not anymore it ain't, Nora Margaret yelled back.

So she's gone forever, Eloise or whatever her name was. Eddie Rule is gone, too, his father sent him off to college, some place where they take people even if you got kicked out of high school without graduating and your mother's the kind of person says ain't. But let me tell you, it's an ill wind blows no one any good, 'cause Loretta hasn't seen him since then and that's the best thing ever happened to her. Good riddance to bad rubbish and I mean that. But of course she didn't feel like that then—

I love him, Terry! she'd tell me, and I'd say, Sure, honey, you love him, but he's gone now and don't do you any good to moon over him. We all thought it best not to bring up the baby at all. Nowadays they wouldn't do that, they'd have her going to some kind of Group, like now Loretta's been going to AA, some place where they'd all talk about having their babies taken away. Like when Noreen was on Oprah, they had all these people claimed to have seen him since he died—

Well, all right, Alice Jean, I *am* getting to it. Let me put some more warm water there—

Well, I'm sorry, was that too hot? I'm sorry, honey, I surely am. Erika, see if there's any ice there, will you?

All right. So we're at work one day, this is still at the Blue Moon, and *he* comes in. The Colonel was with him, we recognized the Colonel first 'cause of he's wearing this big hat, but let me tell you, it didn't take us more than a New York second to recognize him. He was famous then but it wasn't like later, he could still walk around like a regular person.

My god he's a handsome man, said Loretta. Sweet Jesus he sure is.

Yup, I said. I was Manageress-in-Training so I had to be more professional, though that was a dead-end job, too. Doing this Mary Rose thing is the best thing ever happened to me, god strike me if that isn't the truth. Erika, if you're still interested you let me know, 'cause I get extra points for signing up new people and it all goes towards the You-Know-What.

The one they had you wouldn't believe. One of the other girls saw it and told us, Look outside, and we did and there it was. Looked like it took up the whole parking lot, and that was before they opened the Piggly Wiggly next door.

Holy cow, said Loretta. That's the biggest goddamn Cadillac I ever saw. Pardon my French, I told you she started talking like that after Eddie. But she was right, it *was* a big car—but you all've seen it, least you saw it the way Loretta had it. Sure you have, oh, Erika honey, thank you—

Alice Jean, I *am* telling it! Here, put this ice there and see if that helps. If it swells up Mary Rose makes this Aloe Vera Nutrifying Lotion, Kenny Junior sunburned himself caddying after school last week and I gave him some and he said it really helped.

So they come in and sit down, I started to give them the booth in the back corner 'cause I thought, well, they're famous, maybe they'd like some privacy, but the Colonel said, No ma'am, we're on vacation, and then *he* said, Put us right here in the front window, it'll be good for business!

Which was just like him, because he meant it to be nice. He always was a nice man and good to his mother, I tell Kenny Junior he should pay attention to that. So anyway I sat them there and since I was in charge I had Loretta serve them. We were all feeling sorry for her, she just had that dinky little Half-Moon trailer to live in and some people in town thought she was just Bad Luck back in those days, she hadn't had a real date since Eddie left. Though she was really nice looking, she hadn't started drinking yet, not much at least, we used to have rum and Cokes sometimes after work but nobody thought anything of it back then.

The Colonel ordered a ribeye steak sandwich and he got fried chicken. Loretta says she doesn't remember, she was so nervous, but I remember. I told the director for the TV movie exactly what they had and even showed her how to set the platter. Just pay me my consulting fee, I told her.

I was only joking, Alice Jean. They're not really going to pay me for it.

Here's that Nutrifying Lotion. It doesn't smell as nice as the other but it sure feels good, doesn't it?

You're welcome, honey. I'm sure sorry about burning you like that.

Well, he said it was the best fried chicken he ever had, and as you know if you read that book his wife wrote about him after he was dead, that man loved fried chicken better than Saint John loved the Lord, even after he got to be so famous he had to have it sent up to him in disguise from Popeye's. And really Loretta did a real nice job, she brought the Colonel extra ketchup without him asking and extra napkins for the fried chicken, because it *was* a little greasy, but good, and she was so cute in that pink uniform and all that when they left he gave her his car. Just like that.

Brand-new Cadillac. They just walked downtown to Don Thomas's dealership and bought another one. Drove by and waved to us on their way out of town.

Well, Loretta just about fainted. He kissed her cheek and the Colonel shook her hand and took a picture. Later Hal Morehead from the *Reporter Dispatch* came and took another picture of her and the car, and WINY made the next day Loretta Dooley Day and played "Hound Dog" and "Love Me Tender" about sixty-three million times, I thought I was going to throw up if I heard that song one more time but it did get the point across. And of course Loretta had to learn to drive, but by then people were starting to show more interest and think maybe she wasn't bad luck after all, the absolute reverse in fact. Don Thomas came over, to see what model

Cadillac it was this waitress got tipped with, and after a while he and Loretta started seeing each other. And I got promoted to Manager Full-Time. It was all good for business at the Blue Moon, I can tell you that.

But eventually it all settled down. She was still working at the Blue Moon, 'cause of course it was just a *car*, it wasn't like he gave her a million dollars or something. But she'd drive to work every day and park it out front, and people'd stop by just to see it, and then of course they'd come in to see *her*, and most of the time they'd have something to eat. I always recommended the fried chicken.

After a while Loretta stopped seeing Don Thomas. She found out he wasn't actually divorced from his wife after all, just separated, and his wife told him she was pregnant and Loretta put two and two together and told him he better find somewhere else to eat fried chicken, if he knew what was good for him. It was around then she got this weird idea for finding her daughter again.

Erika, I really do like the way he did your hair this time. Those red streaks really show off your eyes. With that color eye shadow you look like that actress in *Working Girl*. Doesn't she, Alice Jean? You know, what's-her-name's daughter. Kim Novak. The one married to what's-his-name.

Whoever.

So look at this, Loretta tells me one day at work. She'd been off for two days and drove in but I was in the back checking on the freezer 'cause the freon tube seized up, so I didn't see her drive up. Come on out, I want to show you something.

Well, okay, I said. Just a minute; and then I went outside.

And you know, she had just ruined that car.

It was sky-blue and black, that car, I swear it was the prettiest thing on earth. The TV movie director, she wanted to make it pink but I told her, Come on, you think a man like that would drive a *pink* car? Back then you wouldn't be caught dead in a pink car, less you were a fairy.

Pardon me, can't say that anymore. I mean a gay. But *you* know what I mean, right Alice Jean? Back then regular people did *not* drive pink cars around. This one was sky-blue.

Look at this, Erika—Mojave Turquoise! Since you're a Spring

Rose you can wear that. Try this tester here. Alice Jean, that blusher takes ten years off your life, I am serious.

Did I tell you what she did?

All right. What she did was this: she spent that whole weekend off putting stuff on her car. I mean, *stuff*—old headlights painted green and blue and orange, rocking horses she took off their rockers and painted like carousel animals, Barbie dolls, you name it. All these old antennas she got at the dump and covered in foil and colored paper and stuck all over the car like—well, like these antennas stuck all over the car. There was even this Virgin Mary thing she put where a hood ornament would go, I think that was because of Eddie being a Catholic and having the marriage canceled. I mean, it looked *awful*. And I said, Loretta honey, what in god's name have you done to your car?

She got kind of defensive. What do you mean? she said.

What do I *mean*? I said. I *mean* why have you made the car that beautiful man gave you look like it belongs in Ripley's Believe It or Not?

It's *my* car, she said. She was mad but she also looked like she might cry. And I already was one girl short because Jocelyn Reny's son Peter, the older one who's at Fort Bragg now, had unexpectedly fallen off the roof of their house and broken his arm and she had to take him to the hospital. So I couldn't afford for Loretta to go home because she was crying because I insulted her car, which looked like a blind person had decorated it.

So I said, Well, it's very interesting Loretta, that's all. It's very unusual.

She smiled then and walked over to it. She'd put a bicycle wheel over the front grill, and stuck these little Troll dolls all around the edge of the wheel so it looked like a wheel with all these Troll things sticking on it. I mean, how she drove that car to work without getting arrested I don't know.

Thank you, she said. She started braiding one of the Trolls' hair. She was always good at things like that. Probably she should of gone to the Academy of Beauty and studied Cosmetology. That's another reason it was so sad about her little girl.

Really, I said. It's very interesting.

I had to think about the customers.

Thank you, she said again, and she adjusted another part of the front, where she had stuck these Rat Fink key chains and a flamingo like we have in our front yard. Thank you, Terry. I put a lot of work into it.

I didn't know what else to say, but I had to say something so we could end this conversation and get back to work. So I said, Well, they're sure gonna see you coming, Loretta, that's for sure.

I know, she said. That's what I want. That's the whole point. And she patted it like it was something she had just won on "Let's Make a Deal" instead of a car you wouldn't want to see clowns climbing out of at the Fork Union Fair.

She said, People'll see me coming and they'll talk about me, and everyone'll know who is in this car. Even if they've never been to this town, even if they're a complete and total stranger, they'll hear about me and know how to find me.

Then without another word she turned around and went inside, like nothing unusual had happened at all.

Well, I'll tell you, everyone in the tri-state area pretty well *did* know who owned that car already, because even though it had been a couple years now since she got it Loretta was sort of the town drunk and people knew her 'cause of that. And let's face it, a sky-blue Cadillac that the most famous man in the world gave you as a tip, who could forget about *that*? I mean, some people had forgotten, but then they recognized her for the other reason, so one way or the other Loretta Dooley was not exactly sneaking around Black Spot, Virginia, without somebody knowing about it. So I didn't get why she wanted people to see it was her driving this car that looked like a King Kone on wheels, unless she wanted to give them the chance to see her coming from about three miles away and stay home if they wanted to.

Later I understood better, how she had this kind of daydream that someday her daughter would figure out who her real mother was and start looking for her. And I guess in Loretta's mind somehow her daughter would hear about the story of what happened and come to Black Spot to find her. And then of course once she was here she'd hear about the lady with this famous car, which on top of everything else now it looks like Woolworth's blew up on it. And so that way she'd be able to find her mama. It was kind of a sad thing, to think Loretta had this crazy old idea and thought junking up her nice car would help things along. But I didn't have time to discuss Loretta's problems right then.

Although to tell you the truth, it did seem to cheer her up some. She was lonely a lot, and sort of quiet. Some people thought she was stuck up, because of the Cadillac, but it wasn't that. It was that Nora Margaret Rule took her baby girl and gave her to perfect strangers when she was only three days old. Up until then Loretta was fine as frog hair. And afterwards, well, she wasn't mean or anything. I mean, she was always nice to the customers and me and everybody, it's not like she was *ever* mean. But you could just sort of tell that maybe she felt like the only good thing that was ever going to happen to her already had, and let's face it, living in a rented Half-Moon trailer down on Delbarton and slinging hash at the Blue Moon is not what anyone wants to spend the rest of their life doing, even if you do own a famous Cadillac.

Which, incidentally, by this time was worth about zero money. All that junk she stuck on it weighed it down, and of course kids started trying to pull off the Rat Fink key chains and the baby dolls, and the antennas got snagged on branches and broke off. And to tell you the absolute truth, Loretta's driving wasn't all that great to begin with, so you can just imagine how that poor car looked after a few years.

He would roll over in his grave if he could see what you've done to his nice car, I told her once.

I'd be surprised there was room in his grave for him to turn in, Loretta said. She never forgave him for getting fat and running around on his wife and those other nasty things. Truth was, I think she never forgave him for not coming back and getting her and taking her the hell out of Black Spot.

Besides, why should he care, she sniffled. He never really gave a shit about me. It was just a publicity stunt, like Don said.

She really started crying then. He did tell her that once, Don Thomas did. I thought it was a real mean thing for him to say to her. Loretta is a *very* sensitive person.

Oh, honey, that's not true, I told her. I was trying to fix that damn freezer again and she'd stayed late, to keep me company and also 'cause her license had been suspended and she didn't want

Sergeant Merdeck to see her driving. She thought in the dark he wouldn't be able to tell it was her but there was no way you could sneak that thing around, no way. Plus she'd had a few. I didn't say anything, but I could tell.

What?

Well, Alice Jean, all I can say is, if anyone ever had a good reason to drink, it was Loretta Dooley. I know some people do it just for fun. I cut back except for cookouts and parties sometimes. It just *ruins* your skin.

Why, thank you, Erika. I got it last quarter, for being Mary Rose's Most Improved Salesperson in the Southern Mid-Atlantic Area. Ken Senior gave me the gold chain for our anniversary, so it's sort of double special. The Mary Rose Cadillac is the same color, only kind of darker, sort of more purple. It's got whitewalls, too. I could have the first one in the Southern Mid-Atlantic, if I get it.

Doesn't that Aloe Vera feel nice, Alice Jean? I keep it in the fridge—makes it sort of a treat to get burned!

Anyway, as I was saying, Loretta was pretty upset that night. I guess it had just all sort of gotten her depressed. It was right after they shut down the Merriam Brick Plant in Petrol, and at the Blue Moon everybody's hours were cut back, not that we were making any money to begin with. That was when I first started thinking about working for myself. Plus her landlord had given her notice, they were developing that part of Delbarton and he just figured he'd cash in, I guess. But I was only trying to be nice to her, cheer her up.

It's not true, Loretta, I told her. I think he really meant it to be a nice thing. I think he truly appreciated the service you gave him.

Well, you are wrong, Terry Westerburgh, she said. You are wrong, 'cause he just did not give a shit, about me or anyone else. Her eyes got this kind of look sometimes when she was drinking, like if you were made of paper they would just burn you up. She crumpled her Dixie cup and threw it on the floor and said, There are two kinds of people in this world, the Haves and the Have-Nots. And I am a Have-Not, and you know what *he* was.

Well, I got sort of P.O.'d then. I mean, here I was on my hands and knees, trying to fix that damn refrigerator, and it wasn't like Ken didn't have to work nights at Big Jim's Barbeque just so we'd get by, and here she was throwing Dixie cups on the floor like she was the Queen of Sheba.

Now you listen to me, *Miss* Dooley, I said. I was pretty aggravated. He worked for everything he ever got, that man did, he was poor as dirt when he started and until the day he died he never forgot where he came from. *That's* why he gave you that car. But you just go ahead and listen to Don Thomas if you want and see where it gets you.

I see where it got me, she said, too mad herself by now to even care who it was she was talking to, Number One, her oldest friend Terry Westerburgh, Number Two, her boss. It got me a shitty job I can't even work enough hours to make my rent, if I had a place to rent, which I don't.

Well, then you just see if you can find another place where you'll be happier, Miss Potty-mouth, I said, and I slammed the refrigerator shut and stomped out.

I was so mad. I shouldn't have to put up with that kind of talk. That was when I decided I was going to really have my own business someday, not work for some person who owns a diner. Sort of the first step towards working for Mary Rose Cosmetics, only of course I didn't know that then.

Erika honey, I know you would love it. You can set your own hours, sleep late as you want, plus you get all your makeup free! And you-know-who would like *that!*

But you know I felt terrible about five minutes after yelling at her. I went into the back room, but she was gone. I heard her leaving, that poor old car scraping along the ground like some dog that got run over. It's funny but I even had started to like that car in a way. I mean it really *did* get your attention. The kids loved it. We got so we'd save old toys, dolls and things, and parts from Ken's Buick and the lawnmower, and I'd bring them over and give them to Loretta and they'd all end up on her car. She had this giant Mr. Potato Head she put on the roof and these colored tennis balls she stuck on all the antennas and really, it was a hoot. Plus her nephew had rigged up some kind of lights that blinked all around the rearview window and Jocelyn's son Peter gave her this funny moose horn she could honk. It was really from the football team but none of us was supposed to know that.

I went outside but it was too late. I really felt terrible. Like Ann Landers says, you should always make your words sweet, 'cause you never know when you'll have to eat them. If I had to eat my words right then I would have thrown up. And so right then I decided to quit the Blue Moon. If it was making me into this mean unkind person, well then it wasn't the job for me.

Alice Jean, you should kind of dab that Aloe Vera stuff off now, I think, honey, otherwise your pores turn a funny color. Here, use this—these are specially formulated for removing deep-down dirt and grime. Doesn't it smell refreshing!

Okay, this is the good part now. So Loretta is gone, and I felt real bad. I felt guilty, too, because I knew she'd had a few and all I could think of was her and her famous car going off the bridge into the reservoir. I thought of calling Bud Merdeck but then I thought, well, Loretta's not going to feel any better spending the night in the drunk tank, so I decided I'd go after her. She was supposed to get all moved out the next day, she was supposed to have started packing stuff that night. Her sister was going to let her stay with her until she found another place. And you know, she really was in a tight spot, because where are you going to find a decent place to live on what you make working fifteen hours a week at the Blue Moon?

So I got in my car and drove to her house. It was dark by then, and a bad night. It had been raining off and on and now it had finally stopped but it was so foggy, I drove with my low beams on the whole way. Once I even slowed down and opened the window and stuck my head out, 'cause I couldn't see otherwise.

You know where she used to live. Where those Hunters Glen condos are now. That used to be all fields, just these three mobile homes that Gus Brinzer used to rent out. Loretta had the nicest one but that's not saying much. After they sold them they found out the Hell's Angels used one of the others to make LSD in.

Well, I finally got there, but there was nobody home. I would've let myself in but when I peeked in the windows I saw all these boxes, and stuff thrown around everywhere, and—well, to tell you the truth, it was a terrible mess. I mean, it looked like the Hell's Angels had been living *there*. And I knew then, things were worse with Loretta than I'd known. I mean, here she was, my oldest friend plus I was her supervisor, but I just had no idea. If I'd known I would've done something, she had a lot of friends, really, but I just had no idea at all.

So I waited outside. There was a kind of metal stairs in front of the trailer but that was broken so I sat on my car. I was there for a long time. It was cold, the fog was real damp and just sank into you after a while. I was starting to worry, too; I mean I was starting to get so worried I was afraid I'd start to scream, thinking of all the horrible things that might've happened to Loretta and I was nasty to her. I was just getting ready to let myself in and call Ken, when I heard somebody walking down the road.

I turned around and it was her. She looked awful, like when you see movies and there's people been in a car wreck. There was no blood or anything but she was wet and her hair was wet and she had mud on her face and oh, I just screamed and ran over and started hugging her.

Loretta, thank god you're all right! What happened?

She made a noise like she was embarrassed and then she started to cry.

I wrecked it, she said. I put my arms around her, I didn't even care I had already changed out of my uniform. She said, I went down Lee Highway and rolled it into the reservoir.

Oh, my god! I said. You could have killed yourself, Loretta!

I know, she said. I had to swim out. It's in there so deep they'll never get it out. She really started crying then.

Why'd you do *that?* I said and started crying, too, but I stopped. I only had one clean tissue left, and I gave it to her.

Because it doesn't matter, she said. My whole life and nothing matters. I live *here*—she bent and picked up a rock and threw it and broke a window, I heard it—in this *dump,* and now I don't even live here anymore. I had a husband and a baby for three days, and twenty-seven years ago someone famous gave me a goddamn Cadillac as a tip, and that's it. That's my whole life. That's it, Terry. My whole life is right there.

Well, you know I wished I could of said something to her, but she was right. That was her whole life, right there.

I just wish I could've kept my baby, she said. She was crying so I could hardly hear what she said. If they'd of left me my baby girl I would've felt like I had something. Like you have Ken and Little Kenny. I would have had Eloise.

I started crying again then, too. I mean, god! It was just so *sad.* So then we sat for a little while but we didn't say anything. It was all just too depressing.

But after a while I started to think, Well, we have got to do something, we can't sit here all night in the mud, and I thought maybe I'd call Ken and see was it okay if Loretta came back with me and could stay at our house. I was just thinking of standing up and asking Loretta was it okay if I went inside to use the phone, when we heard it. It had started raining again, a little, and we had sat on that broken step in front of the trailer, 'cause there's an awning there.

Loretta stood up first. Oh, my god, she said. Shit.

I listened and stood, too. Shit, I said.

It was her car. That was obvious, I mean you couldn't mistake that car for anything else in the world. It sounded like it was having trouble getting over the last hill, where it was always overgrown and muddy anyway. And you figure a car that was in the bottom of the reservoir, it probably wouldn't run too well.

Shit, Loretta said again. That's it.

I knew just what she meant. I was thinking that Bud Merdeck had found it somehow and gotten Lynnwood Gentry to tow it out, and now how was Loretta going to pay for it, not to mention they could have arrested her, probably, for rolling a car into the reservoir on purpose. Especially that car.

And then it made this grinding nose, and suddenly it popped over the rise. The headlights were on, at least one of them was. The wheel that used to have the Trolls on it and now had this Big Bird sort of tied to it was all bent up and the antennas were all mashed together. Whoever was driving it tried to honk the moose horn but it hardly made a noise at all. It was just about the saddest car you ever saw.

Loretta and I looked at each other and she rubbed at her face, trying to get some of the mud off.

We better go see who it is, I whispered. If it's Lynnwood I'll call Ken and he'll talk to him.

Thank you, Terry, she said. She knew that was my way of making up with her.

We started walking to the car, slowly because of the rain and it was sloppy going. The car had stopped at the edge of the drive and waited with the motor running. It didn't sound too good either. Maybe better than you'd expect, but it was pretty sad, to think that car had come to this. As we walked up to it the door on the passenger side popped open.

Hello? It was this woman's voice, nobody we knew.

Hi, I said. I stopped, wondering if maybe Lynnwood brought along his girlfriend Donna. He stays at the shop all night sometimes and on weekends she usually keeps him company.

But it wasn't Donna. It wasn't anybody that I recognized at all. This short woman, with dyed blonde hair. She stepped out of the car, jumping over the water. She had on nice clothes, not expensive or designer clothes but like a secretary's clothes, like she hadn't changed from work yet. She had a nice smile, and nice eyes—I know you wouldn't think you'd notice something like that in the dark but I did, I have a good eye for things like that. Mary Rose says that a great saleswoman needs an eye for detail.

Are you—? The woman started to say something, then she turned around and leaned back into the car, liked she was asking the driver something. Then she turned around again and said, Is one of you Loretta Dooley?

That's me, said Loretta. She had this squinched-up tone. I knew she was nervous they were going to ask, Have you been drinking?

Instead the girl says, My name is Noreen Marcus.

Marcus? Loretta says.

That's right, says the girl. She glances back at the car, sort of nervously, but then it was like whoever was inside told her it was okay, so she goes on.

Noreen Marcus. My parents are Lowell and Angeline Marcus, in Richmond. I hitchhiked here. This man gave me a ride out by the reservoir. I'm your daughter.

My daughter? Loretta says, and *I'm* saying, Your *who?*

Ye-es—

And the girl stepped forward, holding up her skirt so it wouldn't get wet, and then she looked up, and it was like for the first time she got a good look at Loretta in the headlight. 'Cause she suddenly gave this scream and started laughing, and dropped her purse in the water and ran across and I started running, too, next to Loretta, only then at the last minute I stopped because I thought, Now wait a minute, this is something very special going on here between Loretta and this young woman who is her daughter, and so I stayed and waited a little while until they calmed down.

Well, Alice Jean, I knew it was her because she had Eddie Rule's eyes and his smile. He may have been a poor father but he did have a nice smile.

And so for a little while there was some crying and laughing and you can just imagine how we all felt. And all the while that old car just sat there, though whoever was inside turned the motor off after a while and smoked a cigarette. There was no radio in it but you could hear him sort of humming to himself.

And finally Loretta said, Well, for god's sakes let's go inside, we're getting soaked.

Well, wait a minute while I get my bag, said Noreen.

She went back to the car and stuck her head in and said something to whoever was in there.

Okay, now this is when I got goosebumps.

Because I couldn't hear what he was saying—it was too far away, and it wasn't like I wanted to eavesdrop or anything. I guess I sort of expected it must be old Eddie Rule inside. But now I could definitely hear his voice, and it wasn't Eddie Rule's voice at all. It was—

Well, *you* know whose voice it was.

Loretta knew, too. She stood by me with her arms crossed, shivering, and when she heard him she turned to me and opened her mouth and for a minute there I thought she was going to faint.

Oh, my god, she said, oh, my *god*—

Thank you for the ride, I heard Noreen yelling at him, and I could just barely make out his voice saying something back to her, goodbye I guess, something like that. Then she pulled this suitcase out of the car and stood back while it backed up.

Loretta! I said, elbowing her and then pulling her to me. Loretta, hurry up! Tell him thank you—

And she yelled, Thank you, thank you! and then she started running after the car, yelling and waving like she was crazy. Which we all were by then, all of us yelling and waving at him and laughing like we'd known each other all this time, when it'd really only been, like, five minutes. And the car just kept backing up 'til it got over the top of the hill, and then I guess he turned it around and drove off. And that was the last time anybody ever saw Loretta's famous Cadillac.

Afterwards we went inside and kind of dried off and then on the way to my house we stopped at Big Jim's and got a half-dozen Specials and went home. The Specials were so Ken Senior wouldn't be too mad about me being out so late.

And so that's how it happened. Next day of course the story got out, because there is no way, just no way, you can keep something like that a secret. Noreen says she thinks it was just a coincidence, she says everybody out here in Black Spot looks like him and who could tell the difference? Plus she said if it was really him wouldn't he have been in a fancy limousine, not some crazy fixed-up car her real mother drove into the reservoir.

But *I* said, Well, that's how you know it was really him. 'Cause it's like Loretta said, there's the Haves and there's the Have-Nots, and if you're a Have-Not you never forget what it's like to be poor and on your own. I mean how could he have sung "Heartbreak Hotel" otherwise? Noreen said, Well, I still have my doubts, but when she and her mama went on Oprah they played it up for all they could, I can tell you that. And like the TV movie director says, it doesn't really matter, does it? Because it's such a good story.

And I mean there's Noreen reunited with Loretta to prove it, not to mention how would you ever get a car like that out of the reservoir, *plus* where is that car now, I ask you? Because I saw it, too, and I hadn't had a thing to drink.

What do I think? Well, Erika honey, I guess it's just one of those things. Strange things happen sometimes and you just got to take the good with the bad, is all. But you won't hear me complaining about how it all turned out, not as long as business stays this good and I get that new Mary Rose Cadillac in the fall, no ma'am.

———

I always felt like I couldn't take any credit for this, the strangest single thing that's ever happened to me as a writer. I woke up one Saturday morning when I was alone at home with my daughter Callie, then about a year old. I put on Wall of Voodoo's *Happy Planet* and started listening to the song "Elvis Bought Dora a Cadillac," and then "The Have-Nots," by X. And all of a sudden, I heard this woman's voice talking in my head: "Now you know Eddie Rule came and took that baby girl . . ."

Well, when the King calls, you can bet that I listen. So I put Callie in the playpen, sat down and wrote this story in one sitting, finishing it at ten that night. (I remembered to feed and change the baby, too.) The next day I reread the story, corrected a few punctuation marks and sent it off to Gardner Dozois at *Asimov's,* who *accepted* it.

If only writing were always like that.

When I lived in D.C., there was a man who drove a car like Loretta's. For years I wondered what the deal was with this guy, and then one day someone told me that he had a grownup daughter he'd never met, but he thought that maybe she might see his decked-out vehicle and somehow figure out that he was her real father. Damned if it didn't work, too.

In the Month
of Athyr

In the month of Athyr Leucis fell asleep.

—C.P. Cavafy, "In the Month of Athyr"

The argala came to live with them on the last day of Mestris, when Paul was fifteen. High summer, it would have been by the old Solar calendar; but in the HORUS station it was dusk, as it always was. The older boys were poring over an illustrated manual of sexual positions by the sputtering light of a lumiere filched from Father Dorothy's cache behind the galley refrigerator. Since Paul was the youngest he had been appointed to act as guard. He crouched beside the refrigerator, shivering in his pajamas, and cursed under his breath. He had always been the youngest, always would be the youngest. There had been no children born on the station since Father Dorothy arrived to be the new tutor. In a few months, Father Dorothy had converted Teichman Station's few remaining women to the Mysteries of Lysis. Father Dorothy was a *galli,* a eunuch who had made the ultimate sacrifice to the Great

Mother during one of the high holy days Below. The Mysteries of Lysis was a relatively new cult. Its adherents believed that only by reversing traditional gender roles could the sexes make peace after their long centuries of open hostility. These reversals were enacted literally, often to the consternation of non-believing children and parents.

On the stations, it was easier for such unusual sects and controversial ideas to gain a toehold. The current ruling Ascendancy embraced a cult of rather recent vintage, a form of religious fundamentalism that was a cunning synthesis of the more extreme elements of several popular and ancient faiths. For instance, the Ascendants encouraged female infanticide among certain populations, including the easily monitored network of facilities that comprised the Human Orbital Research Units in Space, or HORUS. Because of recent advances in bioengineering, the Ascendants believed that women, long known to be psychologically mutable and physically unstable, might also soon be unnecessary. Thus were the heavily reviled feminist visionaries of earlier centuries unhappily vindicated. Thus the absence of girl children on Teichman, as well as the rift between the few remaining women and their husbands.

To the five young boys who were his students, Father Dorothy's devotion to the Mysteries was inspiring in its intensity. Their parents were also affected; Father Dorothy believed in encouraging discussions of certain controversial gender policies. Since his arrival, relations between men and women had grown even more strained. Paul's mother was now a man, and his father had taken to spending most of his days in the station's neural sauna, letting its wash of endorphins slowly erode his once-fine intellect to a soft soppy blur. The argala was to change all that.

"Pathori," hissed Claude Illo, tossing an empty salt-pod at Paul's head. "Pathori, come here!"

Paul rubbed his nose and squinted. A few feet away Claude and the others, the twins Reuben and Romulus and the beautiful Ira Claire, crouched over the box of exotic poses.

"Pathori, come *here!*"

Claude's voice cracked. Ira giggled; a moment later Paul winced as he heard Claude smack him.

"I *mean* it," Claude warned. Paul sighed, flicked the saltpod in Ira's direction and scuttled after it.

"Look at this," Claude whispered. He grabbed Paul by the neck and forced his head down until his nose was a scant inch away from the hologravures. The top image was of a woman, strictly forbidden. She was naked, which made it doubly forbidden; and with a man, and smiling. It was that smile that made the picture particularly damning; according to Father Dorothy, a woman in such a posture would never enjoy being there. The woman in the gravure turned her face, tossing back hair that was long and impossibly blonde. For an instant Paul glimpsed the man sitting next to her. He was smiling, too, but wearing the crimson leathers of an Ascendant Aviator. Like the woman, he had the ruddy cheeks and even teeth Paul associated with antique photographs or tapes. The figures began to move suggestively. Paul's head really *should* explode, now, just like Father Dorothy had warned. He started to look away, embarrassed and aroused, when behind him Claude swore—

"—move, damn it, it's Dorothy!—"

But it was too late.

"Boys . . ."

Father Dorothy's voice rang out, a hoarse tenor. Paul looked up and saw him, clad as always in salt-and-pepper tweeds, his long gray hair pulled back through a copper loop. "It's late, you shouldn't be here."

They were safe: their tutor was distracted. Paul looked beyond him, past the long sweep of the galley's gleaming equipment to where a tall figure stood in the shadows. Claude swept the box of hologravures beneath a stove and stood, kicking Paul and Ira and gesturing for the twins to follow him.

"Sorry, Father," he grunted, gazing at his feet. Beside him Paul tried not to stare at whoever it was that stood at the end of the narrow corridor.

"Go along, then," said Father Dorothy, waving his hands in the direction of the boys' dormitory. As they hurried past him, Paul could smell the sandalwood soap Father Dorothy had specially imported from his home Below, the only luxury he allowed himself. And Paul smelled something else, something strange. The scent made him stop. He looked over his shoulder and saw the figure still standing at the end of the galley, as though afraid to enter while the boys were there. Now that they seemed to be gone the figure began to walk towards Father Dorothy, picking its feet up with exaggerated delicacy. Paul stared, entranced.

"Move it, Pathori," Claude called to him; but Paul shook his head and stayed where he was. Father Dorothy had his back to them. One hand was outstretched to the figure. Despite its size—it was taller than Paul, taller than Father Dorothy—there was something fragile and childlike about it. Thin and slightly stooped, with wispy yellow hair like feathers falling onto curved thin shoulders, frail arms crossed across its chest and legs that were so long and frail that he could see why it walked in that awkward tippy-toe manner: if it fell its legs would snap like chopsticks. It smelled like nothing else on Teichman Station, sweet and powdery and warm. Once, Paul thought, his mother had smelled like that, before she went to stay in the women's quarters. But this thing looked nothing like his mother. As he stared, it slowly lifted its face, until he could see its enormous eyes fixed on him: caramel-colored eyes threaded with gold and black, staring at him with a gaze that was utterly adoring and absolutely witless.

"Paul, come *on!*"

Ira tugged at him until he turned away and stumbled after the others to the dormitory. For a long time afterwards he lay awake, trying to ignore the laughter and muffled sounds coming from the other beds; recalling the creature's golden eyes, its walk, its smell.

At tutorial the next day Father Dorothy said nothing of finding the boys in the galley, nor did he mention his strange companion. Paul yawned behind the time-softened covers of an ancient linguistics text, waiting for Romulus to finish with the monitor so he could begin his lesson. In the front of the room, beneath flickering lamps that cast gray shadows on the dusty floor, Father Dorothy patiently went over a hermeneutics lesson with Ira, who was too stupid to follow his father into the bioengineering corps, but whose beauty and placid nature guaranteed him a place in the Izakowa priesthood on Miyako Station. Paul stared over his textbook at Ira with his corkscrew curls and dusky skin. He thought of the creature in the galley—its awkwardness, its pallor; the way it had stared at him. But mostly he tried to remember how it smelled. Because on

Teichman Station—where they had been breathing the same air for seventeen years, and where even the most common herbs and spices, cinnamon, garlic, pepper, were no longer imported because of the expense to the station's dwindling group of researchers—on Teichman Station everything smelled the same. Everything smelled of despair.

"Father Dorothy."

Paul looked up. A server, one of the few that remained in working order, lurched into the little room, its wheels scraping against the door. Claude snickered and glanced sideways at Paul: the server belonged to Paul's mother, although after her conversion she had declared it shared property amongst all the station women. "Father Dorothy, KlausMaria Dalven asks that her son be sent to her quarters. She wishes to speak with him."

Father Dorothy looked up from the monitor cradled in his hand. He smiled wryly at the ancient server and looked back at Paul.

"Go ahead," he said. Ira gazed enviously as Paul shut his book and slid it into his desk, then followed the server to the women's quarters.

His mother and the other women lived at the far end of the Solar Walk, the only part of Teichman where one could see outside into space and realize that they were, indeed, orbiting the moon and not stuck in some cramped Airbus outside of New Delhi or one of the other quarantined areas Below. The server rolled along a few feet ahead of him, murmuring to itself in an earnest monotone. Paul followed, staring at his feet as a woman passed him. When he heard her leave the Walk he lifted his head and looked outside. A pale glowing smear above one end of the Walk was possibly the moon, more likely one of the station's malfunctioning satellite beacons. The windows were so streaked with dirt that for all Paul knew he might be looking at Earth, or some dingy canister of waste deployed from the galley. He paused to step over to one of the windows. A year before Claude had drawn an obscene figure in the dust along the edge, facing the men's side of the Walk. Paul grinned to himself: it was still there.

"Paul, KlausMaria Dalven asks that you come to her quarters. She wishes to speak with you," the server repeated in its droning voice. Paul sighed and turned from the window. A minute later he crossed the invisible line that separated the rest of Teichman from the women's quarters.

The air was much fresher here—his mother said that came from thinking peaceful thoughts—and the walls were painted a very deep green, which seemed an odd choice of colors but had a soothing effect nonetheless. Someone had painted stars and a crescent moon upon the arched ceiling. Paul had never seen the moon look like that, or stars. His mother explained they were images of power and not meant to resemble the dull shapes one saw on the navgrids.

"Hello, Paul," a woman called softly. Marija Kerényi, who had briefly consorted with his father after Paul's mother had left him. Then, she had been small and pretty, soft-spoken but laughing easily. Just the sort of pliant woman Fritz Pathori liked. But in the space of a few years she had had two children, both girls. This was during an earlier phase of his father's work on the parthogenetic breeders, when human reproductive tissue was too costly to import from Below. Marija never forgave Paul's father for what happened to her daughters. She was still small and pretty, but her expression had sharpened almost to the point of cunning, her hair had grown very long and was pulled back in the same manner as Father Dorothy's. "Your mother is in the Attis Arcade."

"Um, thanks," Paul mumbled. He had half-turned to leave when his mother's throaty voice echoed down the hallway. "Marija, is that him? Send him back—"

"Go ahead, Paul," Marija urged. She laughed as he hurried past her. For an instant her hand touched the top of his thigh, and he nearly stumbled as she stroked him. Her fingers flicked at his trousers and she turned away disdainfully.

His mother stood in a doorway. "Paul, darling. Are you thirsty? Would you like some tea?"

Her voice was deeper than it had been before, *when she was really my mother,* he thought; before the hormonal injections and implants; before Father Dorothy. He still could not help but think of her as *she,* despite her masculine appearance, her throaty voice. "Or—you don't like tea, how about betel?"

"No, thanks."

She looked down at him. Her face was sharper than it had been. Her chin seemed too strong, with its blue shadows fading into her unshaven jaw. She still looked like a woman, but a distinctly mannish one. Seeing her Paul wanted to cry.

"Nothing?" she said, then shrugged and walked inside. He followed her into the arcade.

She didn't look out of place here, as she so often had back in the family chambers. The arcade was a circular room, with a very high ceiling; his mother was very tall. Below, her family had been descended from aristocratic North Africans whose women prided themselves on their exaggerated height and the purity of their yellow eyes and ebony skin. Paul took after his father, small and fair-skinned, but with his mother's long-fingered hands and a shyness that in KlausMaria was often mistaken for *hauteur.* In their family chambers she had had to stoop, so as not to seem taller than her husband. Here she flopped back comfortably on the sand-covered floor, motioning for Paul to join her.

"Well, *I'm* having some tea. Mawu—"

That was the name she'd given the server after they'd moved to the women's quarters. While he was growing up, Paul had called it Bunny. The robot rolled into the arcade, grinding against the wall and sending up a little puff of rust. "Tea for me and my boy. Sweetened, please."

Paul stood awkwardly, looking around in vain for a chair. Finally he sat down on the floor near his mother, stretching out his legs and brushing sand from his trousers.

"So," he said, clearing his throat. "Hi."

KlausMaria smiled. *"Hi."*

They said nothing else for several minutes. Paul squirmed, trying to keep sand from seeping into his clothes. His mother sat calmly, smiling, until the server returned with tea in small soggy cups already starting to disintegrate. It hadn't been properly mixed. Sipping his, bits of powder got stuck between Paul's teeth.

"Your father has brought an argala here," KlausMaria announced. Her voice was so loud that Paul started, choking on a mouthful of tea and coughing until his eyes watered. His mother only stared at him coolly. "Yesterday. There wasn't supposed to be a drop until Athyr, god knows how he arranged it. Father Dorothy told me. They had him escort it on board, afraid of what would happen if one of the men got hold of it. A sex slave. Absolutely disgusting."

She leaned forward, her long beautiful fingers drumming on the floor. Specks of sand flew in all directions, stinging Paul's cheeks. "Oh," he said, trying to give the sound a rounded adult tone, regretful or disapproving. *So that's what it was,* he thought, and his heart beat faster.

"I wish to god I'd never come here," KlausMaria whispered. "I wish—"

She stopped, her voice rasping into the breathy drone of the air filters. Paul nodded, staring at the floor, letting sand run between his fingers. They sat again in silence. Finally he mumbled, "I didn't know."

His mother let her breath out in a long wheeze; it smelled of betel and bergamot-scented tea powder. "I know." She leaned close to him, her hand on his knee. For a moment it was like when he was younger, before his father had begun working on the Breeders, before Father Dorothy came. "That's why I wanted to tell you, before you heard from—well, from anyone else. Because—well, shit."

She gave a sharp laugh—a real laugh—and Paul smiled, relieved. "It's pathetic, really," she said. Her hand dropped from his knee to the floor and scooped up fistfuls of fine power. "Here he was, this brilliant beautiful man. It's destroyed him, the work he's done. I wish you could have known him before, Below—"

She sighed again and reached for her tea, sipped it silently. "But that was before the last Ascension. Those bastards. Too late now. For your father, at least. But Paul," and she leaned forward again and took his hand. "I've made arrangements for you to go to school Below. In Tangier. My mother will pay for it, it's all taken care of. In a few months. It'll be fall then, in Tangier, it will be exciting for you . . ."

Her voice drifted off, as though she spoke to herself or a server. "An argala. I will go mad."

She sighed and seemed to lose interest in her son, instead staring fixedly at the sand running between her fingers. Paul waited for several more minutes, to see if anything else was forthcoming, but his mother said nothing more. Finally the boy stood, inclined his head to kiss her cheek, and turned to go.

"Paul," his mother called as he hesitated in the doorway.

He turned back: she made the gesture of blessing that the followers of Lysis affected, drawing an exaggerated *S* in the air and blinking rapidly. "Promise me you won't go near it. If he wants you to. Promise."

Paul shrugged. "Sure."

She stared at him, tight-lipped. Then, "Goodbye," she said, and returned to her meditations in the Arcade.

That night in the dormitory he crept to Claude's bunk while the older boy was asleep and carefully felt beneath his mattress, until he found the stack of pamphlets hidden there. The second one he pulled out was the one he wanted. He shoved the others back and fled to his bunk.

He had a nearly new lumiere hidden under his pillow. He withdrew it and shook it until watery yellow light spilled across the pages in front of him. Poor-quality color images, but definitely taken from life. They showed creatures much like the one he had seen the night before. Some were no bigger than children, with tiny pointed breasts and enormous eyes and brilliant red mouths. Others were as tall and slender as the one he had glimpsed. In one of the pictures an argala actually coupled with a naked man, but the rest showed them posing provocatively. They all had the same feathery yellow hair, the same wide mindless eyes and air of utter passivity. In some of the pictures Paul could see their wings, bedraggled and straw-colored. There was nothing even remotely sexually exciting about them.

Paul could only assume this was something he might feel differently about, someday. After all, his father had been happy with his mother once, although that of course was before Paul was born, before his father began his work on the Breeders Project. The first generations of geneslaves had been developed a century earlier on Earth. Originally they had been designed to toil in the lunar colonies and on Earth's vast hydrofarms. But the reactionary gender policies of the current Ascendant administration suggested that there were other uses to which the geneslaves might be put.

Fritz Pathori had been a brilliant geneticist, with impressive ties to the present administration. Below, he had developed the prototype for the argala, a gormless creature that the Ascendants hoped would make human prostitution obsolete—though it was not the act itself the Ascendants objected to, so much as the active involvement of women. And at first the women had welcomed the argalæ. But that was before the femicides; before the success of the argalæ led Fritz Pathori to develop the first Breeders.

He had been an ethical man, once. Even now, Paul knew that it was the pressures of conscience that drove his father to the neural sauna. Because now, of course, his father could not stop the course of his research. He had tried, years before. That was how they had ended up exiled to Teichman Station, where Pathori and his staff had for many years lived in a state of house arrest, part of the dismal constellation of space stations drifting through the heavens and falling wearily and irretrievably into madness and decay.

A shaft of light flicked through the dormitory and settled upon Paul's head. The boy dove beneath the covers, shoving the pamphlet into the crack between bedstand and mattress.

"Paul." Father Dorothy's whispered voice was surprised, shaming without being angry. The boy let his breath out and peered up at his tutor, clad in an elegant gray kimono, his long iron-colored hair unbound and falling to his shoulders. "What are you doing? What do you have there—"

His hand went unerringly to where Paul had hidden the pamphlet. The shaft of light danced across the yellowed pages, and the pamphlet disappeared into a kimono pocket.

"Mmm." His tutor sounded upset. "Tomorrow I want to see you before class. Don't forget."

His face burning, Paul listened as the man's footsteps padded away again. A minute later he gave a muffled cry as someone jumped on top of him.

"You idiot! Now he *knows*—"

And much of the rest of the night was given over to the plebeian torments of Claude.

He knew he looked terrible the next morning, when, still rubbing his eyes, he shuffled into Father Dorothy's chamber.

"Oh, dear." The tutor shook his head and smiled ruefully. "Not much sleep, I would imagine. Claude?"

Paul nodded.

"Would you like some coffee?"

Paul started to refuse politely, then saw that Father Dorothy had what looked like real coffee, in a small metal tin stamped with Arabic letters in gold and brown. "Yes, please," he nodded, and watched entranced as the tutor scooped it into a silver salver and poured boiling water over it.

"Now then," Father Dorothy said a few minutes later. He indicated a chair, its cushions ballooning over its metal arms, and Paul sank gratefully into it, cupping his bowl of coffee. "This is all about the argala, isn't it?"

Paul sighed. "Yes."

"I thought so." Father Dorothy sipped his coffee and glanced at the gravure of Father Sofia, founder of the Mysteries, staring myopically from the curved wall. "I imagine your mother is rather distressed—?"

"I guess so. I mean, she seems angry, but she always seems angry."

Father Dorothy sighed. "This exile is particularly difficult for a person as brilliant as your mother. And this—" he pointed delicately at the pamphlet, sitting like an uninvited guest on a chair of its own. "This argala must be very hard for KlausMaria to take. I find it disturbing and rather sad, but considering your father's part in developing these—things—my guess would be that your mother finds it, um, *repellent*—?"

Paul was still staring at the pamphlet; it lay open at one of the pages he hadn't yet gotten to the night before. "Uh—um, oh, yes, yes, she's pretty mad," he mumbled hastily, when he saw Father Dorothy staring at him.

The tutor swallowed the rest of his coffee. Then he stood and paced to the chair where the pamphlet lay, picked it up and thumbed through it dismissively, though not without a certain curiosity.

"You know it's not a real woman, right? That's part of what's *wrong* with it, Paul—not what's wrong with the thing itself, but with the act, with—well, *everything*. It's a geneslave, it can't enter into any sort of—relations—with anyone of its own free will. It's a— well, it's like a machine, except of course it's *alive*. But it has no thoughts of its own. They're like children, you see, only incapable of thought, or language. Although of course we have no idea what other things they *can* do—strangle us in our sleep or drive us mad. They're incapable of ever learning, or loving. They can't suffer or feel pain or, well, *anything*—"

Father Dorothy's face had grown red, not from embarrassment, as Paul first thought, but from anger—real fury, the boy saw, and he sank back into his chair, a little afraid himself now.

"—institutionalized rape, it's exactly what Sofia said would happen, why she said we should start to protect ourselves—"

Paul shook his head. "But—wouldn't it, I mean wouldn't it be easier? For women: if they used the geneslaves, then they'd leave the women alone . . ."

Father Dorothy held the pamphlet open, to a picture showing an argala with its head thrown back. His face as he turned to Paul was still angry, but disappointed now as well. And Paul realized there was something he had missed, some lesson he had failed to learn during all these years of Father Dorothy's tutelage.

"That's right," his tutor said softly. He looked down at the pamphlet between his fingers, the slightly soiled image with its gasping mouth and huge, empty eyes. He looked sad, and Paul's eyes flickered down from Father Dorothy's face to that of the argala in the picture. It looked very little like the one he had seen, really; but suddenly he was flooded with yearning, an overwhelming desire to see it again, to touch it and breathe again that warm scent, that smell of blue water and real sand and warm flesh pressed against cool cotton. The thought of seeing it excited him, and even though he knew Father Dorothy couldn't see anything (Paul was wearing one of his father's old robes, much too too big for him), Father Dorothy must have understood, because in the next instant the pamphlet was out of sight, squirrelled into a cubbyhole of his ancient steel desk.

"That's enough, then," he said roughly. And gazing at his tormented face Paul thought of what the man had done, to become an initiate into the Mysteries; and he knew then that he would never be able to understand anything his tutor wanted him to learn.

*   *   *

"It's in there now, with your father! I saw it go in—"

Ira's face was flushed, his hair tangled from running. Claude and Paul sat together on Claude's bunk poring over another pamphlet, a temporary truce having been effected by this new shared interest.

"My father?" Paul said stupidly. He felt flushed, and cross at Ira for interrupting his reverie.

"The argala! It's in there with him now. If we go we can listen at the door—everyone else is still at dinner."

Claude closed the pamphlet and slipped it beneath his pillow. He nodded, slowly, then reached out and touched Ira's curls. "Let's go, then," he said.

Fritz Pathori's quarters were on the research deck. The boys reached them by climbing the spiral stairs leading up to the second level, speaking in whispers even though there was little chance of anyone seeing them there, or caring if they did. Midway up the steps Paul could see his father's chambers, across the open area that had once held several anaglyphic sculptures. The sculptures had long since been destroyed, in one of the nearly ritualized bouts of violence that periodically swept through the station. Now his father's balcony commanded a view of a narrow concrete space, swept clean of rubble but nonetheless hung about with a vague odor of neglect and disrepair.

When they reached the hallway leading to the chief geneticist's room the boys grew quiet.

"You never come up here?" Claude asked. For once there was no mockery in his voice.

Paul shrugged. "Sometimes. Not in a while, though."

"I'd be here all the time," Ira whispered. He looked the most impressed, stooping to rub the worn but still lush carpeting and then tilting his head to flash a quick smile at himself in the polished metal walls.

"My father is always busy," said Paul. He stopped in front of the door to his father's chambers, smooth and polished as the walls, marked only by the small onyx inlay with his father's name engraved upon it. He tried to remember the last time he'd been here—early autime, or perhaps it had been as long ago as last Mestris.

"Can you hear anything?" Claude pushed Ira aside and pressed close to the door. Paul felt a dart of alarm.

"I do," whispered Ira excitedly. "I hear them—listen—"

They crouched at the door, Paul in the middle. He *could* hear something, very faintly. Voices: his father's, and something like an echo of it, soft and soothing. His father was groaning—Paul's heart clenched in his chest but he felt no embarrassment, nothing but a kind of icy disdain—and the other voice was cooing, an almost perfect echo of the deeper tone, but two octaves higher. Paul pressed closer to the wall, feeling the cool metal against his cheek.

For several more minutes they listened, Paul silent and impassive, Claude snickering and making jerking motions with his hands, Ira with pale blue eyes growing wide. Then suddenly it was quiet behind the door. Paul looked up, startled: there had been no terminal cries, none of the effusive sounds he had heard were associated with this sort of thing. Only a silence that was oddly furtive and sad, falling as it did upon three pairs of disappointed ears.

"What happened?" Ira looked distressed. "Are they all right?"

"Of course they're all right," Claude hissed. He started to his feet, tugging Ira after him. "They're finished, is all—come on, let's get out of here—"

Claude ran down the hall with Ira behind him. Paul remained crouched beside the door, ignoring the other boys as they waved for him to follow.

And then before he could move the door opened. He looked up and through it and saw his father at the far end of the room, standing with his back to the door. From the spiral stairs Claude's voice echoed furiously.

Paul staggered to his feet. He was just turning to flee when something moved from the room into the hall, cutting off his view of his father; something that stood teetering on absurdly long legs, a confused expression on its face. The door slid closed behind it, and he was alone with the argala.

"Oh," he whispered, and shrank against the wall.

"*O,*" the argala murmured.

Its voice was like its scent, warm yet somehow diffuse. If the hallway had been dark, it would have been difficult to tell where the sound came from. But it was not dark, and Paul couldn't take his eyes from it.

"It's all right," he whispered. Tentatively he reached for it. The argala stepped towards him, its frail arms raised in an embrace. He started, then slowly let it enfold him. Its voice echoed his own, childlike and trusting.

It was irresistible, the smell and shape of it, the touch of its wispy hair upon his cheeks. He opened his eyes and for the first time got a good look at its face, so close to his that he drew back a little to see it better. A face that was somehow, indefinably, female. Like a child's drawing of a woman: enormous eyes surrounded by lashes that were spare but thick and straight. A round mouth, tangerine-colored, like something one would want to eat. Hair that was more like feathers curled about its face. Paul took a tendril between his fingers, pulled it to his cheek and stroked his chin with agonizing slowness.

His mother had told him once that the argalæ were engineered from human women and birds, storks or cranes the boy thought, or maybe some kind of white duck. Paul had thought this absurd, but now it seemed it could be true—the creature's hair looked and felt more like long downy filaments than human hair, or fur. And there was something birdlike about the way it felt in his arms: fragile but at the same time tensile, and strong, as though its bones were lighter than human bones, filled with air or even some other element. Paul had never seen a real bird. He knew they were supposed to be lovely, avatars of physical beauty of a certain type, and that their power of flight imbued them with a kind of miraculous appeal, at least to people Below. His mother said people thought that way about women once. Perhaps some of them still did.

He could not imagine any bird, anything at all, more beautiful or miraculous than this geneslave.

Even as he held it to his breast, its presence woke in him a terrible longing, a yearning for something he could scarcely fathom— open skies, the feel of running water beneath his bare feet. Images flooded his mind, things he had only ever seen in files of old movies. Small houses made of wood, clouds skidding across a sky the color of Ira Claire's eyes, cream-colored flowers climbing a trellis beside a green field. As the pictures fled across his mind's eye his heart pounded: *where did they come from?* Sensations spilled into him, as though they had been contained in too shallow a vessel and had nowhere else to pour but into whomever the thing touched. And then those first images slid away, the white porch and cracked concrete and saline taste—bitter yet comforting—of tears running into his mouth. Instead he felt dizzy. He reached out and his hands struck at the air feebly. Something seemed to move at his feet. He looked down and saw ripples like water, and something tiny and bright moving there. A feeling stabbed at him, a hunger so sharp it was like love; and suddenly he saw clearly what the thing was—a tiny creature like a scarlet salamander, creeping across a mossy bank. But before he could stoop to savage it with his beak (*his beak?*), with a sickening rush the floor beneath him dropped, and there was only sky, white and gray, and wind raking at his face; and above all else that smell, filling his nostrils like pollen: the smell of water, of freedom.

Then it was gone. He fell back against the wall, gasping. When he opened his eyes he felt nauseated, but that passed almost immediately. He focused on the argala staring at him, its eyes wide and golden and with the same adoring gaze it had fixed on him before. Behind it his father stood in the open doorway to his room.

"Paul," he exclaimed brightly. He skinned a hand across his forehead and smiled, showing where he'd lost a tooth since the last time they'd met. "You found it—I wondered where it went. Come on, you!—"

He reached for the argala and it went to him, easily. "Turned around and it was gone!" His father shook his head, still grinning, and hugged the argala to his side. He was naked, not even a towel draped around him. Paul looked away. From his father's even, somewhat muffled, tone he could tell that he'd recently come from the neural sauna. "They told me not to let it out of my sight, said it would go sniffing after anyone, and they were right . . ."

As suddenly as he'd appeared he was gone, the metal door flowing shut behind him. For one last instant Paul could see the argala, turning its glowing eyes from his father to himself and back again, lovely and gormless as one of those simulacrums that directed travelers in the HORUS by-ports. Then it was only his own reflection that he stared at, and Claude's voice that he heard calling softly but insistently from the foot of the spiral stairs.

He had planned to wait after class the following morning, to ask Father Dorothy what he knew about it, how a mindless creature could project such a powerful and seemingly effortless torrent of images and sensations; but he could tell from his tutor's cool smile that somehow he had gotten word of their spying. Ira, probably. He was well-meaning but tactless, and Father Dorothy's favorite. Some whispered conference during their private session; and now Father Dorothy's usual expression, of perpetual disappointment tempered with ennui, was shaded with a sharper anger.

So *that* was pointless. Paul could scarcely keep still during class, fidgeting behind his desiccated textbooks, hardly glancing at the monitor's ruby scroll of words and numerals when his turn came to use it. He did take a few minutes to sneak to the back of the room. There a huge and indescribably ancient wooden bookcase held a very few, mostly useless volumes—*Reader's Digest Complete Do-It-Yourself Manual, Robert's Rules of Order, The Ascent of Woman.* He pulled out a natural history text so old that its contents had long since acquired the status of myth.

Argala, Paul read, after flipping past *Apteryx, Aquilegia, Archer, Areca,* each page releasing its whiff of Earth, mildew and silverfish and trees turned to dust. *Adjutant bird: Giant Indian Stork, living primarily in wetlands and feeding upon crustaceans and small amphibians. Status, endangered; perhaps extinct.* There was no illustration.

"Hey, Pathori." Claude bent over his shoulder, pretending to ask a question. Paul ignored him and turned the pages, skipping *Boreal Squid* and *(Bruijn's) Echidna,* pausing to glance at the garishly colored *Nebalia Shrimp* and the shining damp skin of the Newt, *Amphibian: A kind of eft (Juvenile salamander).* Finally he found the Stork, a simple illustration beside it.

Tall stately wading bird of family *Ciconiidae,* the best-known species pure white except for black wing tips, long reddish bill, and red feet, and in the nursery the pretended bringer of babies and good fortune.

". . . you hear me?" Claude whispered hoarsely, pinching is ear. Paul closed the book and pushed it away. Without a word he returned to his desk, Claude following him. Father Dorothy raised his head, then went back to explaining the subtleties of written poetry to Ira Claire. Paul settled into his seat. Behind him Claude stood and waited for their tutor to resume his recitation. In a moment Father Dorothy's boyish voice echoed back to them—

. . . I make out a few words—	. . . "SORROW,"
then again "TEARS,"	and "WE HIS FRIENDS MOURN."
It seems to me that Leucis	must have been dearly beloved . . ."

Paul started as Claude shook him, and the older boy repeated, "I have an idea—I bet he just leaves it alone, when he's not in the room. We could get in there, maybe, and sneak it out. . . "

Paul shrugged. He had been thinking the same thing himself; thinking how he would never have the nerve to do it alone. He glanced up at Father Dorothy.

If he looks at me now, he thought, *I won't do it; I'll talk to him later and figure out something else . . .*

Behind him Claude hissed and elbowed him sharply. Paul waited, willing their tutor to look up; but the man's head pressed closer to his lovely student as he recited yet another elegiac fragment, wasted on the hopeless Ira—

"A poet said, 'That music is beloved
that cannot be sounded.'
And I think that the choicest life
is the life that cannot be lived."

"Paul!"

Paul turned and looked at Claude. "We could go when the rest are at dinner again," the older boy said. He too gazed at Ira and Father Dorothy, but with loathing. "All right?"

"All right," Paul agreed miserably, and lowered his head when Father Dorothy cast him a disapproving stare.

*   *   *

Trudging up the steps behind Claude, Paul looked back at the narrow plaza where the sculptures had been. They had passed three people on their way here, a man and two women; the women striding in that defiant way they had, almost swaggering, Paul thought. It was not until they turned the corner that he realized the man had been his mother, and she had not acknowledged him, had not seen him at all.

He sighed and looked down into the abandoned courtyard. Something glittered there, like a fleck of bright dust swimming across his vision. He paused, his hand sliding along the cool brass banister.

On the concrete floor he thought he saw something red, like a discarded blossom. But there were no flowers on Teichman. He felt again that rush of emotion that had come when he embraced the argala, a desire somehow tangled with the smell of brackish water and the sight of a tiny salamander squirming on a mossy bank. But when he leaned over the banister there was nothing there. It must have been a trick of the light, or perhaps a scrap of paper or other debris blow by the air filters. He straightened and started back up the stairs.

That was when he saw the argala. Framed on the open balcony in his father's room, looking down upon the little courtyard. It looked strange from this distance and this angle: less like a woman and more like the somber figure that had illustrated the Stork in the natural history book. Its foot rested on the edge of the balcony, so it seemed that it had only one leg, and the way its head was tilted he saw only the narrow raised crown, nearly bald because its wispy hair had been pulled back. From here it looked too bony, hardly female at all. A small flood of nausea raced through him. For the first time it struck him that this really *was* an alien creature. Another of the Ascendants' monstrous toys, like the mouthless hydrapithecenes that tended the Pacific hydrofarms, or the pallid bloated forms floating in vats on the research deck of Teichman Station, countless fetuses tethered to them by transparent umbilical cords. And now he had seen and touched one of those monsters. He shuddered and turned away, hurrying after Claude.

But once he stood in the hallway his nausea and anger faded. There was that scent again, lulling him into seeing calm blue water and myriad shapes, garnet salamanders and frogs like candied fruit drifting across the floor. He stumbled into Claude, the older boy swearing and drawing a hand across his face.

"Shit! What's that smell?—" But the older boy's tone was not unpleasant, only befuddled and slightly dreamy.

"The thing," said Paul. They stood before the door to his father's room. "The argala . . ."

Claude nodded, swaying a little, his dark hair hiding his face. Paul had an awful flash of his father opening the door and Claude seeing him as Paul had, naked and doped, with that idiot smile and a tooth missing. But then surely the argala would not have been out on the balcony by itself? He reached for the door and very gently pushed it.

"Here we go," Claude announced as the door slid open. In a moment they stood safely inside.

"God, this is a mess." Claude looked around admiringly. He flicked at a stack of 'files teetering on the edge of a table, grimaced at the puff of dust that rose around his finger. "Ugh. Doesn't he have a server?"

"I guess not." Paul stepped gingerly around heaps of clothes, clean and filthy piled separately, and eyed with distaste a clutter of empty morpha tubes and wine jellies in a corner. A monitor flickered on a table, rows of numerals and gravid shapes tracing the progress of the Breeders Project.

"*Not,*" a voice trilled. On the balcony the argala did not turn, but its bright tone, the way its vestigial wings shivered, seemed to indicate some kind of greeting.

"All right. Let's see it—"

Claude shoved past him, grinning. Paul looked over and for a second the argala's expression was not so much idiotic as tranquil; as though instead of a gritty balcony overlooking shattered concrete, it saw what he had imagined before, water and wriggling live things.

"*Unh.*"

Claude's tone abruptly changed. Paul couldn't help but look: the tenor of the other boy's lust was so intense it sounded like pain.

He had his arms around the argala and was thrusting at it, his trousers askew. In his embrace the creature stood with its head thrown back, its cries so rhapsodic that Paul groaned himself and turned away.

In a minute it was over. Claude staggered back, pulling at his clothes and looking around almost frantically for Paul.

"God, that was incredible, that was the *best*—"

Like what could you compare it to, you idiot? Paul leaned against the table with the monitor and tapped a few keys angrily, hoping he'd screw up something; but the scroll continued uninterrupted. Claude walked, dazed, to a chair and slouched into it, scooped up a half-full wine jelly from the floor and sucked at it hungrily.

"Go on, Pathori, you don't want to miss *that!*" Claude laughed delightedly, and looked at the argala. "God, it's amazing, isn't it? What a beauty." His eyes were dewy as he shook his head. "What a fucking thing."

Without answering Paul crossed the room to the balcony. The argala seemed to have forgotten all about them. It stood with one leg drawn up, staring down at the empty courtyard, its topaz eyes glittering. As he drew near to it its smell overwhelmed him, a muskier scent now, almost fetid, like water that had stood too long in an open storage vessel. He felt infuriated by its utter passivity, but somehow excited, too. Before he knew what he was doing he had grabbed it, just as Claude had, and pulled it to him so that its bland child's face looked up at him rapturously.

Afterwards he wept, and beside him the argala crooned, mimicking his sobs. He could dimly hear Claude saying something about leaving, then his friend's voice rising and finally the snick of the door sliding open and shut. He grit his teeth and willed his tears to stop. The argala nestled against him, silent now. His fingers drifted through its thin hair, ran down its back to feel its wings, the bones like metal struts beneath the breath of down. What could a bird possibly know about what he was feeling? he thought fiercely. Let alone a monster like this. A real woman would talk to you, afterwards.

To *complain,* he imagined his father saying.

. . . *never enjoyed it, ever,* his mother's voice echoed back, and Father Dorothy's intoned, *That's what's wrong with it, it's like a machine.*

He pulled the argala closer to him and shut his eyes, inhaling deeply. A wash of yellow that he knew must be sunlight: then he saw that ghostly image of a house again, heard faint cries of laughter. Because it was a woman, too, of course; otherwise how could it recall a house, and children? but then the house broke up into motes of light without color, and he felt the touch of that other, alien mind, delicate and keen as a bird's long bill, probing at his own.

"Well! Good afternoon, good afternoon . . ."

He jumped. His father swayed in the doorway, grinning. "Found my little friend again. Well, come in, come in."

Paul let go of the argala and took a few unsteady steps. "Dad— I'm sorry, I—"

"God, no. Stop." His father waved, knocking a bottle to the floor. "Stay, why don't you. A minute."

But Paul had a horrible flash, saw the argala taken again, the third time in what, half an hour? He shook his head and hurried to the door, face down.

"I can't, Dad. I'm sorry—I was just going by, that's all—"

"Sure, sure." His father beamed. Without looking he pulled a wine jelly from a shelf and squeezed it into his mouth. "Come by when you have more time, Paul. Glad to see you."

He started to cross to where the argala gazed at him, its huge eyes glowing. Paul ran from the room, the door closing behind him with a muted sigh.

At breakfast the next morning he was surprised to find his mother and Father Dorothy sitting in the twins' usual seats.

"We were talking about your going to school in Tangier," his mother announced, her deep voice a little too loud for the cramped dining hall as she turned back to Father Dorothy. "We could never meet the quotas, of course, but Mother pulled some strings, and—"

Paul sat next to her. Across the table, Claude and Ira and the twins were gulping down the rest of their breakfast. Claude mumbled a goodbye and stood to leave, Ira behind him.

"See you later, Father," Ira said, smiling. Father Dorothy waved.

"When?" said Paul.

"In a few weeks. It's nearly Athyr now"—that was what they called this cycle—". . . which means it's July down there. The next drop is on the Fortieth."

He didn't pay much attention to the rest of it. There was no point: his mother and Father Dorothy had already decided everything, as they always did. He wondered how his father had ever been able to get the argala here at all.

A hand clamped his shoulder and Paul looked up.

"—must go now," Father Dorothy was saying as he motioned for a server to clean up. "Class starts in a few minutes. Walk with me, Paul?"

He shook his mother's hand and left her nodding politely as the next shift of diners filed into the little room.

"You've been with it," the tutor said after a few minutes. They took the long way to the classroom, past the cylinders where vats of nutriment were stored and wastewater recycled, past the spiral stairs that led to his father's chamber. Where the hallway forked Father Dorothy hesitated, then went to the left, towards the women's quarters. "I could tell, you know—it has a—"

He inhaled, then made a delicate grimace. "It has a smell."

They turned and entered the Solar Walk. Paul remained at his side, biting his lip and feeling an unexpected anger churning inside him.

"I like the way it smells," he said, and waited for Father Dorothy to look grim. Instead his tutor paused in front of the window. "I love it."

He thought Father Dorothy would retort sharply; but instead he only raised his hands and pressed them against the window. Outside two of the HORUS repair units floated past, on their interminable and futile rounds. When it seemed the silence would go on forever, his tutor said, "It can't love you. You know that. It's an abomination—an animal—"

"Not really," Paul replied, but weakly.

Father Dorothy flexed his hands dismissively. "It can't love you. It's a geneslave. How could it love anything?"

His tone was not angry but questioning, as though he really thought Paul might have an answer. And for a moment Paul thought of explaining to him: about how it felt, how it seemed like it was showing him things—the sky, the house, the little creatures crawling in the moss—things that perhaps it *did* feel something for. But before he could say anything Father Dorothy turned and began striding back in the direction they'd come. Paul hurried after him in silence.

As they turned down the last hallway, Father Dorothy said, "It's an ethical matter, really. Like having intercourse with a child, or someone who's mentally deficient. It can't respond, it's incapable of anything—"

"But I love it," Paul repeated stubbornly.

"Aren't you listening to me?" Father Dorothy did sound angry, now. "*It* can't love *you.*" His voice rose shrilly. "How could something like *that* tell you that it *loved* you!? And *you* can't love it—god, how could you love *anything,* you're only a boy!" He stopped in the doorway and looked down at him, then shook his head, in pity or disgust Paul couldn't tell. "Get in there," Father Dorothy said at last, and gently pushed him through the door.

He waited until the others were asleep before slipping from his bunk and heading back to his father's quarters. The lights had dimmed to simulate night; other than that there was no difference, in the way anything looked or smelled or sounded. He walked through the violet corridors with one hand on the cool metal wall, as though he was afraid of falling.

They were leaving just as he reached the top of the spiral stairs. He saw his father first, then two others, other researchers from the Breeders Project. They were laughing softly, and his father threw his arms around one man's shoulders and murmured something that made the other man shake his head and grin. They wore loose robes open in the front and headed in the opposite direction, towards the neural sauna. They didn't see the boy pressed against the wall, watching as they turned the corner and disappeared.

He waited for a long time. He wanted to cry, tried to make himself cry; but he couldn't. Beneath his anger and shame and sadness there was still too much of that other feeling, the anticipation and arousal and inchoate tenderness that he only knew one word for, and Father Dorothy thought that was absurd. So he waited until he couldn't stand it anymore, and went inside.

His father had made some feeble attempt to clean the place up. The clothing had been put away, and table tops and chairs cleared of papers. Fine white ash sifted across the floor, and there was a musty smell of tobacco beneath the stronger odors of semen and wine jelly. The argala's scent ran through all of it like a fresh wind.

He left the door open behind him, no longer caring if someone found him there or not. He ran his hands across his eyes and looked around for the argala.

It was standing where it usually did, poised on the balcony with its back to him. He took a step, stopped. He thought he could hear something, a very faint sound like humming; but then it was gone. He craned his neck to see what it was the creature looked at but saw nothing; only that phantom flicker of red in the corner of his eye, like a mote of ruby dust. He began walking again, softly, when the argala turned to look at him.

Its eyes were wide and fervent as ever, its tangerine mouth spun into that same adoring smile; but even as he started for it, his arms reaching to embrace it, it turned from him and jumped.

For an instant it hung in the air and he could imagine it flying, could almost imagine that perhaps it thought its wings would carry it across the courtyard or safely to the ground. But in that instant he caught sight of its eyes, and they were not a bird's eyes but a woman's; and she was not flying but falling.

He must have cried out, screamed for help. Then he just hung over the balcony, staring down at where it lay motionless. He kept hoping that maybe it would move again but it did not, only lay there twisted and still.

But as he stared at it it changed. It had been a pale creature to begin with. Now what little color it had was leached away, as though it were bleeding into the concrete; but really there was hardly any blood. Its feathers grew limp, like fronds plucked from the water, their gold fading to a gray that was all but colorless. Its head was turned sideways, its great wide eye open and staring up. As he watched the golden orb slowly dulled to yellow and then a dirty white. When someone finally came to drag it away its feathers trailed behind it in the dust. Then nothing remained of it at all except for the faintest breath of ancient summers hanging in the stale air.

*   *   *

For several days he wouldn't speak to anyone, not even responding to Claude's cruelties or his father's ineffectual attempts at kindness. His mother made a few calls to Tangier and, somehow, the drop was changed to an earlier date in Athyr. On the afternoon he was to leave they all gathered, awkwardly, in the dormitory. Father Dorothy seemed sad that he was going, but also relieved. The twins tried to get him to promise to write, and Ira cried. But, still without speaking, Paul left the room and walked down to the courtyard.

No one had even bothered to clean it. A tiny curl of blood stained the concrete a rusty color, and he found a feather, more like a furry yellowish thread than anything else, stuck to the wall. He took the feather and stared at it, brought it to his face and inhaled. There was nothing.

He turned to leave, then halted. At the corner of his eye something moved. He looked back and saw a spot on the ground directly beneath his father's balcony. Shoving the feather into his pocket he walked slowly to investigate.

In the dust something tiny wriggled, a fluid arabesque as long as his finger. Crouching on his heels, he bent over and cupped it in his palm. A shape like an elongated tear of blood, only with two bright black dots that were its eyes and, beside each of those, two perfect flecks of gold.

An eft, he thought, recognizing it from the natural history book and from the argala's vision. A juvenile salamander.

Giant Indian stork, feeding upon crustaceans and small amphibians.

He raised it to his face, feeling it like a drop of water slithering through his fingers. When he sniffed it it smelled, very faintly, of mud.

There was no way it could have gotten here. Animals never got through by-port customs, and besides, were there even things like this still alive, Below? He didn't know.

But then how did it get here?

A miracle, he thought, and heard Father Dorothy's derisive voice—*How could something like that tell you that it loved you?* For the first time since the argala's death, the rage and despair that had clenched inside him uncoiled. He moved his hand, to see it better, and with one finger stroked its back. Beneath its skin, scarlet and translucent, its ribs moved rapidly in and out, in and out, so fine and frail they might have been drawn with a hair.

An eft.

He knew it would not live for very long—what could he feed it, how could he keep it?—but somehow the argala had survived, for a little while at least, and even then the manner of its dying had been a miracle of sorts. Paul stood, his hands folding over the tiny creature, and with his head bowed—though none of them would really see, or understand, what it was he carried—he walked up the stairs and through the hallway and back into the dormitory where his bags waited, past the other boys, past his mother and father and Father Dorothy, not saying anything, not even looking at them; holding close against his chest a secret, a miracle, a salamander.

———

I don't write much science fiction, and have always found it particularly difficult in the short story format; this takes place in the same universe as my first three novels. I had read Connie Willis's "All My Darling Daughters" and was taken with the idea of setting a tale on a space station. Bill McKibben's *The End of Nature* was still very much on my mind; thus the little red salamander at story's end.

Engels Unaware

"It's a pretty ritzy office," the agent at Kahn Temps warned Rebecca, staring pointedly at Rebecca's uneven hem where the faint glint of a staple hinted at what was holding the worn skirt together at the knees. "I don't know why they don't just hire a permanent receptionist. Don't want to pay for benefits, I guess. But it's your assignment if you want it."

"Thanks," squeaked Rebecca, promising herself that she'd pay off her credit-card bills and start from scratch, really save some money this time and clear her credit rating.

"Fine. You start Monday." The agent's glance slipped from the frayed skirt to a run that began just below Rebecca's knee and arrowed to the curled edge of her old loafer. Rebecca knew the look. She cleared her throat and smiled, tugging furtively at the loose pocket of nylon behind her knee as she fidgeted in her seat. The agent wrote the name and address of Lorimer Brothers on a little pink business card, then handed it to Rebecca.

"Thanks," said Rebecca, coughing as she stood and lined her left foot behind the right, so the agent wouldn't notice the broken heel curled like a blackened sliver of dried beef. "I have to run now.

Shopping." She smiled brightly. When the agent turned to answer the phone she fled.

On Monday she didn't feel so good about the new skirt. It didn't actually go with last season's gaucho jacket, and her old pumps were the wrong color: écru when they really should have been toast. The skirt had cost her one hundred and seventeen dollars, even on sale at Glumball's; but sale items couldn't be returned, and besides she'd had to charge something or they were going to close out her account. Now she stood too long in the lobby of the vast corporate office building, squinting at her reflection in the black marble walls and wondering why she hadn't bought the moleskin cardigan. By the time she got to the eighty-seventh floor she was late.

"This is your station," barked a woman in a fire-engine red Italian suit. She pointed to a slab of polished gray marble surrounded by a low smoked glass wall, the whole thing facing the hallway; Rebecca's head suddenly felt very light. She rested her hand on the edge of the dark glass wall to steady herself. It was so cold, its edge so sharp that she gasped and snatched her hand away, checking her fingers for blood. The office manager pursed her lips and took a tissue from her wallet, then wiped the offending glimmer of Rebecca's fingerprint from the glass.

"I assume you've worked the Magister telephone system before?" The office manager coughed discreetly, dropping the tissue into a steel cylinder. Rebecca followed her into the workstation and nodded, lying.

"But maybe you'd better go over it with me to make sure," she said, settling into an ergonomic chair shaped like a tiny velvet S. The office manager regarded her with wide surprised eyes, then shook her head.

"I've never actually used it. I'll see if I can send Victor out after he's got my coffee." She smoothed the narrow band of scarlet leather across the top of her thighs, shrugged and returned to her office.

It took Rebecca a week to learn the phone system. For the most part, her duties began and ended with answering the phone and screening visitors. Occasionally a secretary would hand her something to type. Then she'd get to use the tiny word processor, with its printer that hummed as it spat the neat pages onto her marble desktop. She could see through the smoked glass wall to the banks of elevator doors in the corridor, and straight across the wall to the glass elevator that slid up and down the outside of the building like a silvery water spider on emerald cables.

Only one other office occupied this level, its door catty-corner to Rebecca's station. If she positioned herself just right she could see everyone who came and went there, too. Not that the other office had many clients; certainly not as many as the young and stylish firm of Lorimer Brothers.

"What do they *do?*" Rebecca finally got up the courage to ask one of the secretaries, after she'd stayed late the previous evening copying out a complex tiramísu recipe for her.

"Who's that?" The secretary scanned the recipe, tapping her fingernail against her lower lip so that it left a faint half-moon in her lipstick.

"That other office. The World Business Forum."

"Hmmm? Oh—*them?*" She tilted her chin towards the door and slid the recipe into her portfolio. "Nothing, actually. Just a bunch of retired businessmen. Dinosaurs who couldn't keep up with the times. They rent the office space and play 'corporation.' Kind of sad, really. Like all these old guys who used to be important and now they can't quit, even though they're retired. No one ever really talks to any of them."

Rebecca talked to one of them. Every evening when she left the office she took the glass elevator downstairs, floating along the outside of the great steel and marble tower and watching the flickering spans of lights in the financial district, like an earthbound aurora. It was a languorous descent, and for this reason the brokers and analysts and accountants used the interior express elevators, whose doors barely hushed shut on the eighty-seventh floor before they gaped open upon the glossy lobby. So each night Rebecca rode down alone, imagining herself sole witness to the city's silent shimmering display.

Until the evening she met Mr. Lancaster. Office talk had been of rain, although Rebecca never saw a window to check for herself. She dashed from her console into the corridor, wrapping a vinyl scarf around her head and wishing she'd bought an umbrella last week instead of charging those gila-lizard print gaiters at Frothingale's. At the end of the hallway the glass elevator glistened and shuddered in the rain. Rebecca tugged her scarf tight, shivering at the thought of seven blocks of storm before she reached the subway. And so, her head bowed and swathed in cerise vinyl, she didn't even see the old man rushing into the glass elevator until she smacked into him.

"Oh, god, I'm sorry!" squealed Rebecca, unraveling her scarf to peer crestfallen at an elderly gentleman catching his breath beside her. "I didn't even see—no one ever rides this one—Gee, I'm sorry." She stood awkwardly, the vinyl scarf falling in crackling ribbons as the elevator door sighed shut.

"That's quite all right," the old man coughed, smoothing an immaculate fawn-colored trenchcoat and drawing a large white handkerchief from a pocket to dab at his cheeks. He replaced the handkerchief and slid a pair of glasses from another pocket, placed them on his nose and regarded Rebecca thoughtfully. "Are you lost, my dear?"

Rebecca fumbled to stuff her scarf into her purse. "No—I, uh, I work here."

The man tilted his head to stare at her above the rims of his spectacles. "Here?" His tone was somewhat doubtful.

Rebecca flushed, fingering a hole where she'd lost a button on her coat. "A temp—I'm a temporary. A receptionist."

"Ah." He removed the glasses, nodding slightly, as though relieved. "Forgive my curiosity. We don't socialize much with our neighbors here. I didn't recognize you." And he smiled. "I am Hugh Lancaster, of the World Business Forum."

"Rebecca Strunk." Rebecca pumped his hand earnestly. "Of Kahn Temps Inc."

"Ah," Mr. Lancaster repeated, absently this time, and he leaned forward to touch the elevator controls. "Lobby, Miss Strunk?"

"Yes, thanks." She let her breath out in a wheeze and tried to stand up straight. Rain battered the heavy glass walls as the elevator began to slip down the side of the building. Rebecca cleared her throat. "No one ever takes this one, you know. You're the only person I've ever seen in it besides me."

Mr. Lancaster adjusted the fleece-lined collar of his trenchcoat and smiled. "I prefer my own company at the end of a busy day. As I imagine you must as well, Miss Strunk."

Rebecca nodded eagerly, delighted at being addressed as *Miss Strunk*. "Oh, yes, Mr. Lancaster! It's such a nice view—" And she turned to press her cheek against the cold glass and stare out at the steel canyons awash with reflected light.

Mr. Lancaster looked at her more closely for this unguarded moment, noting the broken heel and missing button, as well as the dangling slip that Rebecca herself had yet to discover. Then he took a step closer to the glass wall, nodding as he surveyed the shining frieze of scarlet and amber lights that wove through the somber canyons below. "It is a lovely view," he agreed. "I often wonder why no one else travels this way to see it."

Rebecca shook her head. "They all say it's too slow," she murmured, rubbing her cheek to dispel the chill.

"A shame," remarked Mr. Lancaster. "When I work into the evenings, I always ride down alone. But now I hope to occasionally have company." And he smiled gently as the elevator finally settled into the lobby, and waited for Rebecca to step out of the elevator before following her.

"Shall I hail you a cab?" he asked as they poised at the main entrance, among the gleaming crowds shaking raincoats and umbrellas onto the slick marble floor.

Rebecca shook her head hastily, wrapping the scarf around her neck. "Uh—no thanks, a—um—a friend is picking me up." She smiled brightly, then impulsively stuck out her hand. "Very nice to meet you, Mr. Lancaster."

"Likewise, Miss Strunk," replied the old man, and his warm gloved hand shook her bare cold one. "Have a pleasant evening."

"Oh, I *will*," Rebecca assured him. "See you soon, Mr. Lancaster." And she shoved her way through the crowds into the stormswept night.

She did not see him soon, although she watched for him through the glass walls of the Lorimer Brothers office and even worked late in hopes of meeting him in the elevator again. Sometimes she saw other elderly men entering or leaving the World Business Forum office, all of them impeccably attired in expensive but unfashion-able suits. None of them ever rode the glass elevator with her, and none of them greeted her as Miss Strunk.

One afternoon the copier in her office broke. A vast machine that took up most of a large room, it exhaled manuscripts and charts and reports along with the fumes of dry ink and expensive rag paper. When it died, gasping out a final stream of crumpled papers with a vindictive wheeze, panicky secretaries raced to pile papers atop Rebecca's desk.

"You can type, right?" the office manager demanded, reshuffling the stack in front of Rebecca so that her own work was on top.

Rebecca nodded, dazed. "But not all this—I can't possibly do fifteen copies of all this—"

"Then see if *they've* got a copier!" snapped the office manager, raking her nails across the sheaf of papers so that they left faint razor lines pointing in the direction of the office next door. "I've got a French-wrap manicure scheduled for three and *I need that report ASAP.*"

After the office manager stormed off Rebecca pulled a comb through her hair, wincing at the curls that snarled the plastic teeth. She shouldn't have tried the home perm. Now her hair was falling out, and the home cello-color kit she'd charged at The Body Electric had stained her dry curls a jaundiced yellow. Hastily she ran a tube of *Oh! de Bris* lip emulsifier over her mouth, then gathered the stack of papers into her arms.

A very small brass plate identified the World Business Forum office. There was no doorbell; no internal security system intercom. Rebecca hesitated before rapping at the polished oaken door. After a moment she knocked again, and this time heard the creak of a chair being pushed across the floor, then the muted thud of footsteps.

"Yes?" An unfamiliar man's voice, quivering with age and suspi-cion.

"It's Rebecca, from next door," said Rebecca, coughing in embarrassment. "I—um, our copier broke—do you think I could use yours for just a minute please?"

"Hold on." Scrabbling and clinking; the whirr of bolts being drawn. Then a wizened face popped out. "May I help you?"

Rebecca stepped back, startled, and dropped several reports. "The copier," she repeated breathlessly, stooping to retrieve the papers and spilling more in the process. "Please—is Mr. Lancaster in?"

The man swung the door inwards, shaking his head. "No, he's not here today. I really don't see how I can help you—"

"It's just that they gave me all this—" Rebecca exclaimed help-lessly, stumbling into the office after him. *"Oh."* She straightened and fell silent.

Dark oaken paneling covered high walls, glistening with lemon oil that scented the room faintly. Burgundy wing chairs, their leather veined and cracked with age, circled a long and intricately carven table. There was a small but ornate desk adorned with mar-ble pen-holders and an ancient Royal Upright typewriter, black and gleaming and segmented like a scorpion. An elephant's-foot waste-basket filled with papers stood beside the desk.

"I think there might be some carbon paper," the man was saying brusquely as he marched to the desk. He began to pull open tiny drawers and rummage through pigeonholes adrift with pencils and pen-nibs. "We haven't hired a girl yet and I really don't know what's here—"

"Oh," Rebecca repeated as she clutched her papers to her chest, staring at the gilded arabesques of an Art Nouveau floor lamp, the bronze bookends shaped like inscrutable sphinxes. With some relief she noted a Magister phone deck in its case on the floor.

"Have you—are you very busy here?"

"Hmm. I know we ordered some," muttered the old man, glanc-ing up as he clinked together several bottles of Indian ink. "Well, I guess not. No—er, not quite busy. This is a slow time of year for us." With a muffled groan he straightened and Rebecca grimaced sympathetically.

"I'm sorry—I didn't mean for you—thank you anyway."

The man nodded, rubbing his bald head and then adjusting his cufflinks—which were, Rebecca noted with some amazement, of exquisitely wrought gold, and shaped like the heads of the sphinxes atop the beveled-glass bookcase.

"I'm sorry I can't help you," he said gruffly, and with a slight nod motioned her towards the door. "But I must get back to my work now. Goodbye."

"'Bye," chimed Rebecca, turning to wave. But the door had

already clicked shut behind her, leaving only the musky fragrance of old leather and lemon oil in the chilly hallway.

Autumn shuddered into winter and still she remained at the firm. Meanwhile, Lorimer Brothers got involved in the successful buy-outs of a large avionics manufacturer and the Paddy O'Furniture chain of deluxe wicker ware. Senior staff members were rewarded with a sky trip to Vail. The office manager's secretary hired his own secretary. And more and more often Rebecca worked late, hand-addressing Christmas cards and typing up invitation lists for holiday gatherings that never included her.

One such evening found her there past nine o'clock. All day the Nuzak endlessly intoned market returns, futures information, industrial averages. Now it finally fell silent. From back offices wafted the faint ticking of sleepless analysts' fingers upon keyboards. She heard the fax keening to itself; the dry chatter of the telex machine chewing through reels of newsprint. After several hours Banzai Sushi-Togo delivered a plastic laminate tray of sashimi for the analysts and VPs. Rebecca smiled wanly as the leather-clad courier left, trailing the scent of wasabi and shaved bonito, and wished she'd brought an extra can of tuna fish. Once or twice the telephone rang and she took messages. She addressed more Christmas cards and read the latest issue of SEXFAX! She dozed.

And jerked awake, the edge of the console raking her wrist as she shook her head. Shouting. Certain she'd been caught sleeping again, she whirled and snagged her ankle in the stirrup of the ergonomic chair as she stumbled to her feet.

There was no one in the front office. Rebecca blinked and rubbed her eyes, wincing as the charcoal mascara left smears across her hand. Muffled thuds and moans from the back offices signaled that the analysts and VPs were taking a break from research and performing their plastimetrix exercises. That was all. Rebecca turned back to her console, relieved.

And heard it again. Deep chanting tones, masculine, wordless, throbbing with obscene portent. They echoed dully from the hallway, and with a start Rebecca realized the ominous voices came from the World Business Forum.

Football? she wondered, but it was Tuesday night. Warily she crept from her console.

That was when she saw the smoke curling from beneath the door of the World Business Forum office. For a long moment she just stared, watching the gray-green plumes rising from the aubergine carpet to form a heavy viscous curtain that severed her view of the corridor. Not until she actually smelled the smoke did she stir. An acrid yet cloying scent, redolent of funerals and the wrong sort of poster shops. With a muted shriek Rebecca dashed into the hallway.

"Mr. Lancaster! Mr. Lancaster! Are you okay?" she choked, pounding on the door. Smoke slid down her throat like pungent oil. "Mr. Lancaster!"

Abruptly the door swung open. Coughing, Rebecca wiped tears from her eyes to focus on the pinched shape of the frail old man she had seen last time.

"Yes?" he hissed, waving the smoke from his cheeks with an irritated flourish. "What is it now?"

Rebecca stared dumbfounded. Then came a small sound, like the turning of a key in a lock, and Mr. Lancaster stepped from the haze, smiling gently.

"My dear Miss Strunk!" he murmured, and clapped his hand upon the other man's shoulder. "I beg your pardon, Edmund . . ."

Glowering, the first man stalked back into the murky office. Mr. Lancaster produced a huge linen handkerchief and waved it, dispersing most of the smoke. "You must forgive us, Miss Strunk," he said. From a hidden pocket in his somber gray suit he withdrew a tiny scissors and a cigar bound with silver filigree. "The proverbial gathering of the Old Boy Network in a smoke-filled room." With a wry smile he sheared the end from the cigar.

"Ohhh," Rebecca breathed in relief. "I was so afraid—I thought the smoke—I thought there was a fire."

Mr. Lancaster replaced the scissors, pursing his lips. "How thoughtful of you to think of us," he said gently, placing one hand upon Rebecca's shoulder to steer her towards her own office. "Although—heaven forbid!—should there ever be a *real* fire, certainly you should think of your own safety, and call the fire department."

Crestfallen, Rebecca nodded and bit her lip. "I panicked," she admitted.

"Don't fret, Miss Strunk," continued Mr. Lancaster, pausing in his office's doorway. "People panic over less important things all the time. Perhaps you are over-tired." He peered thoughtfully at her wide pale face and reddened eyes, pinched to slits by fatigue. "It's late. Why don't you go home now?"

"Oh, I will. Soon," sighed Rebecca, then smiled. "Good night, Mr. Lancaster."

Next morning she overslept. She arrived thirty minutes late to discover a new mound of invitations to be addressed, printed on mock papyrus with the Lorimer Brothers hologram. There was also a memo revoking extra holiday leave for all non-essential personnel. Sighing, Rebecca settled at her console and began sifting through her morning's work.

She didn't even hear the Engels enter the office. A slight cough made her jump, dropping her alphabetized stack of cards. When she looked up they stood before her desk, stark and stunning as twin pillars of gold.

"Ah—can I help you?" Rebecca stammered, stumbling to her feet and ripping her stockings on the console.

The woman regarded her coldly. "We are here to see the Vice Presidents." Her crimson lips parted to reveal teeth so glitteringly white that Rebecca didn't even notice they were bared in a snarl rather than a smile. "Will you tell them we are here?"

"Uh—n-no one without an appointment," stuttered Rebecca. In the halogen lights the woman's hair flamed in a brilliant golden nimbus around her face. Blinking, Rebecca turned to stare at the man beside her. He did not smile, but his azure eyes gazed at Rebecca caressingly. When he licked his lips she slid limply back into her chair.

"Tell them the Engels are here," he purred, glancing down at a scrawled note on her desk. "*Rebecca.*"

"The Engels," she repeated, looking at them with a glazed expression.

"Myself and my sister," the man explained, flicking an atom of dust from the lapel of his caracal overcoat. "Our card." He whisked a tiny placard from an onyx case and placed it before her. Then he smiled and, taking his sister's arm, glanced conspiratorially at Rebecca.

"This way?" He raised an eyebrow rakishly, pointing to the back offices with a kid-gloved hand. *"Rebecca?"*

Rebecca nodded rapidly, still too dazed to speak, and watched the pair stride past. Their briefcases bumped together with a kiss of exotic leathers: distressed ostrich and moray eelskin. Rebecca wondered if the metal clasps and hinges glowing so lustrously could possibly be real gold and platinum.

"Gee," she whispered when they had disappeared, and only then realized her intercom was buzzing.

"This is Rebecca," she answered breathlessly, but the caller was already gone. When she looked up the office manager was marching down the hall towards her.

"Who the hell was that?" she demanded, snatching the business card but holding it so that Rebecca could read as well.

Grædig & Avaratia Engel
Futures Speculation

"Oh," the office manager said knowingly. *"Europeans."* Then she glared at Rebecca. "But *no one* comes in without an appointment. I see I'll just have to do your job for you." She spun about, her chrome heel grinding into the carpet, and called back warningly, "Your six-month review is coming soon, Rebecca." Then she stalked into the back office.

Rebecca waited anxiously for the office manager to return, Engels in tow. An hour passed; nothing. When she tried to patch phone calls to the VPs their secretaries flashed DO NOT DISTURB signals back to Rebecca's console. Several times admiring laughter echoed from the offices, and once a brittle burst of applause startled Rebecca as she hunched over her mound of invitations.

At lunchtime she finally heard doors opening in the back, and after a few minutes the Engels entered the reception area once more—this time surrounded by excited VPs and analysts. The office manager trailed several feet behind them, her yearning gaze fixed upon Grædig Engel's caracal topcoat.

"Will you please make a luncheon reservation for thirteen at

Priazzi Inferno?" a VP commanded Rebecca, then turned to pump Avaratia Engel's hand.

"This is an extraordinary piece of work," the VP beamed, waving a portfolio bound in glossy black sharkskin. "And I just can't tell you how fortuitous it is that you approached us first, Ms Engel—"

"I believe you mean *fortunate,*" Grædig Engel corrected him, deflecting a yawn with his long pale fingers. "And I regret that my sister and I will be unable to join you for lunch—"

"But you must!" cried another Vice President, covetously eyeing Grædig Engel's attaché case. "They serve the most superb blowfish *rillettes!*"

Avaratia wrinkled her nose in distaste, stooping to whisk a chamois glove across the instep of one gavial boot. "I'm afraid we have another appointment this afternoon," she said, tossing her mane of golden hair. "Perhaps another time."

The Vice President looked crushed. Smiling, Avaratia took her brother's arm. Rebecca stared entranced at the curve of her neck, the warm reflection cast upon her throat by the heavy gold chain nestling there. For a moment the two stood poised, Avaratia gazing out into the corridor, Grædig beside her a lupine shadow hidden within the folds of his caracal coat, cashmere scarf coiled about his neck. Then, with slight bows to the staff crowding the reception area, the Engels turned and strode down the hall.

A breathless instant, so still that Rebecca could hear the creak of Avaratia's boots, the rustle of her brother's coat. Then—

"Did you see his *ring?*"

"—guarantees return at three-hundred percent if we strike this week!"

"—dyed, *has* to be—"

"—calling Chicago right now before this gets loose—"

"—would *die* for that suit, just *die* for it!"

The office manager swept from the group and leaned over the console, her face flushed. "Not a word!" she hissed to Rebecca. "I'll be back by three—"

Everyone took a long lunch that afternoon, except for Rebecca. They began straggling back into the office after four, the VPs rosy-cheeked from their lunch at Priazzi Inferno, the brokers and analysts laden with shopping bags and hatboxes, hand-marbled

Venetian pencil-cases and gilt panniers of chocolate-glazed nasturtium blossoms.

It was too much for her. Rebecca nearly tripped as she ran out of the office at five and raced into the first express elevator that stopped on her floor.

She arrived home hours later, after charging a nutria-rimmed *faux* Chanel suit and a three-hundred-dollar silk moiré evening burnoose from Bedouin Outfitters. Among the stack of bills at the door of her efficiency was a disconnect notice from the telephone company. Rebecca burst into tears.

In the weeks following, the office telephone wailed nonstop. Rebecca's ears rang with its shrieks long after she left. Every evening the entire staff worked until midnight, feverishly following recommendations the Engels phoned almost hourly. The *Wall Street Journal* did a front-page piece on the firm. Lorimer Brothers had a second phone system installed to handle all the new client calls.

After the Engels' next visit the VPs flew to Val d'Isere and the Pyrenées for a weekend of skiing. Three of the female analysts threw political correctness to the winds and bought full-length lynx-belly coats and sashayed into work on Monday morning, giggling like parochial schoolgirls skipping Mass. The office manager began scheduling crushed-pearl defoliating body scrubs during her lunch hours. Even Rebecca found herself visiting The Body Electric for placenta hair-wraps and an electrolytic platinum rinse that left her with chemical burns over most of her scalp.

Lorimer Brothers' clients began to do business with the Engels as well. Rebecca screened referrals every day, and once spoke to a television reporter regarding the siblings' cyclonic influence upon the street. She even saw the Engels leaving the World Business Forum early one morning, Avaratia and Grædig shaking hands with Mr. Lancaster in the doorway.

As Christmas grew nearer Rebecca guiltily surveyed the heaps of unworn new clothes beside her futon, the designer bath linens and vicuña napkins still in their original packing. She swore not to charge another thing before she started her Christmas shopping, and wondered if her grandmother would enjoy the Valencia oranges poached in Armagnac she'd ordered for herself from Rabelaisian Delights. Each evening she spent in darkness now, since they had cut off her electricity. But the efficiency looked nice lit by hand-dipped beeswax candles. And she didn't feel so bad when she saw the collection notices that had begun to arrive at Lorimer Brothers for various staff members.

A week before Christmas it snowed. Rebecca slogged to work, ruining her new silk spring-weight trenchcoat and wondering again why she hadn't bought an umbrella, or maybe a down parka. Or warm boots, or gloves. In the glittering lobby she threaded her way through the crowd to the glass elevator. It had been weeks since she'd taken it; but she wanted to see the snow from above. When the door opened she laughed, delighted.

"Mr. Lancaster!"

The old man stepped gingerly into the lobby, staring at her puzzled.

"Miss Strunk!" he exclaimed, drawing back a little. "I didn't recognize you."

"It's my hair," Rebecca said ruefully. "It fell out after the last conditioning treatment."

Mr. Lancaster nodded sympathetically, then peered at her more closely. "Something else though, too," he murmured, and shook his head knowingly. "Ah, well, it's a busy season, and we all have lots to do before the big day." He smiled, tipping his hat. "I hope to see you before the holidays, Miss Strunk. Goodbye."

"Goodbye, Mr. Lancaster." Waving, she stepped backwards into the elevator, catching a heel in the door and tearing it from her new mock-ocelot pumps.

The office manager sat rigidly at Rebecca's console when she arrived. "Chicago's just notified us of a major loss on the Skam account," she said curtly. "I've been ordered to start making staff cutbacks. Tomorrow will be your last day."

"But—" stammered Rebecca, clutching her broken heel as she dripped on the aubergine carpet.

"Sorry. I called your agency. They said contact them after New Year's for possible new assignments."

"Possible!" exclaimed Rebecca.

"I haven't got *time* for this now," the office manager shrilled.

"Things are crazy enough this morning—" And she stormed into the back offices.

Rebecca stared after her in shock, then through tearing eyes glanced at her empty desk. No messages. No assignments. Someone had switched off the Nuzak. Even the phones were oddly silent. And then—

"Get me Sheared Young & Lamb!" a voice boomed from her intercom. *"Now!"*

Rebecca jumped, then placed the call. Afterward she leaned back, curious. From the back offices drifted strained whispers. An analyst fled through the reception area in tears. Suddenly the Nuzak barked back on—

"London Exchange plummeting to oh point nine seven four—"

And then the intercom started buzzing.

"I want Avaratia Engel—"

"Get me Grædig!"

"The Engels!"

At the Engels' number an answering machine played the opening notes of Pachelbel's Canon in D before requesting a message. After Rebecca had called several times she could no longer get through. Their line remained busy for the rest of the morning.

She stopped taking messages for the Vice Presidents and analysts and brokers. "They're unavailable," Rebecca told anxious callers until she was hoarse. Two more analysts fled the office, one of them carrying a large box from which dangled computer cables. A hysterical VP ordered Rebecca to phone his ex-wife, burst into tears and hung up before she could place the call.

"New York plummeting to a record oh oh three seven oh six oh points—" the Nuzak droned.

"Cancel my one-thirty at L'Ordure," the Office Manager ordered Rebecca over the intercom.

Rebecca started getting nervous.

She hung up on a man from the *Tokyo Times* and canceled seventeen lunches and one American Express Titanium Account. She was thinking about leaving early when through the door staggered a young woman in a disheveled sueded-silk suit.

"I want to see my broker," she commanded Rebecca, gripping the console's edge so tightly that blood seamed the cracks between her fingers.

"I'm sorry, he's unavailable right now," Rebecca gulped.

"He recommended the Engels to me. I want to see him *now*," the woman repeated, her palms streaking the glass with crimson.

"I'm sorry, no one can see you right now. You can leave a business card with me and I'll be happy to—" Rebecca started, when the woman yanked a Blush Micron Uzi from her pocket and pointed it at the ceiling.

"*Here's* my business card!" she shrieked. Glass shattered as she emptied a cartridge and ran towards the back offices. Rebecca fainted.

But came to a moment later when the office manager stumbled past, blood staining her mango lambswool coatdress a sullen purple.

"*No one without an appointment,*" she gasped, and staggered into the hallway.

Rebecca raised herself to her knees, then quickly ducked beneath the console as a tattoo of bullets shuddered through the walls. Muffled screams from the back offices; an answering volley of gunfire. She heard a soft spurt of sound, like a bulb blowing. Then a louder explosion shook the suite. Glancing up she saw smoke trailing from beneath the keys of her tiny word processor. A moment later it burst into flames.

Rebecca lurched to her feet, heedless of the shrieks and thuds raging behind her. Smoke seeped into the reception area. Gagging she fumbled for the telephone, punched in the emergency code and listened: a recording. Several figures reeled past her, coughing and weeping. Silently a VP settled on the sofa in the reception area, staring bemused at a small perfect hole in her thigh before stretching out as though to nap. Rebecca watched, frozen. Not until a fleeing analyst knocked against her as he raced for the door did she stir.

Behind her flames tore through the office, their roar nearly drowning the wail of smoke detectors and the clack of circuit breakers. The halogen lights guttered and went out. Screams rent the fire-lit rooms, and Rebecca fled blindly towards the door, choking as she stepped over bodies and burning heaps of paper.

In the corridor emergency lights flickered hellishly through the haze. A recorded message urged workers to be calm and use the fire stairs. Rebecca huddled against the wall, wiping her streaming eyes as she vainly tried to locate the stairwell. Knots of people clawed past her, moaning as they stumbled in front of the express elevators. Pale fingers stabbed at the elevator buttons. A door opened; inside she glimpsed a twisted mass of bodies gasping and screaming as they fled the upper stories. Then the doors slid shut and the elevator plunged down once more. Sobbing, Rebecca wrenched her eyes away.

At the end of the hallway glowed the glass elevator, its empty crystal booth spangled with reflected flames. Rebecca floundered towards it, inching past the crowd still futilely pounding at the express elevator doors. Someone kicked her to the floor. Rebecca crept the rest of the way, breathing through her sleeve. The carpet scorched her knees; her stockings melted in fiery tatters about her legs. Chemical fumes mingled with the smells of charred wood and hot steel. With a gasp she stood, flung herself against the glass door and pounded the button with her fist. With a soft chime the door slid open and Rebecca staggered into the tiny chamber. As the door shut behind her she glimpsed livid faces pressed against the steaming glass, mouths twisted and gasping soundlessly. Crying, Rebecca stabbed buttons over and over and over, until slowly the elevator began to descend. Then she leaned exhausted against the wall and stared spellbound at the scene outside.

Flames engulfed the financial district. From steel towers erupted sheets of gold as entire stories blazed like immense glass furnaces. Rebecca covered her ears against their gleeful roar, but she could not look away. She cowered against the wall, watching in horror as she passed flaming windows where black figures seethed behind molten glass, fighting to break through. Until the glass elevator itself trembled as one window exploded, and shrieking Rebecca covered her eyes to blot out the brilliant parhelion that sent scattered sparks and burning shadows plummeting to the street below.

When she looked up again the elevator had stalled. Trembling she reached for the control panel, but with a cry snatched her hand back: the metal buttons were too hot to touch. Whimpering she turned back to the glass wall. And saw them.

Silhouetted in a great arched window, side by side they stood and watched the inferno all around them. As she stared transfixed, Rebecca could see their clothes burning away in glittering ribbons of gold and black, but still they waited, unmoving, wreathed in flames until it seemed that vast burning wings sprang from their shoulders and fanned the glowing air.

Then one of them stirred. Very slowly she turned her head, as if seeking a small sound, her unblinking gaze sweeping across broken windows and shattered stone until it struck the small glass cell. And pinned Rebecca there, so that she dropped to her knees, whining softly in her throat as she read the names written across their brows in streaming letters—

Avaratia and Grædig.

Greed and Avarice.

Crying out, Rebecca had started to her feet when with a groan of emerald cables the elevator shuddered and dropped once more. She fell back against the wall. When she turned and desperately sought them again, the shining figures were gone.

With a grating clang the elevator stopped. The inner doors remained shut, but the outer set chimed and opened smoothly onto the building's courtyard. Freezing wind slashed through Rebecca's thin blouse as she stumbled onto the sidewalk.

Everywhere the knell of sirens rent the air. Black-helmeted figures raced through the street from hydrant to hydrant, and spumes of water froze as they dragged huge coils behind them. Ambulances and police cars choked the alleys. In a daze Rebecca wandered along the curb, heedless of slush soaking her burned legs.

At the corner she stopped, leaned against a broken traffic light that blinked madly from green to red. Cold numbed her fingers, and she drew her shaking hands to her face to warm them. A dark and narrow side street stretched beside her. As she stood trying to catch her breath, she saw twin headlights piercing the gloom. They grew nearer, and Rebecca stared dully as a long dove-gray limousine pulled up to her corner. Its smoky black window reflected her face, scorched raw and blackened with soot. Very slowly the window slid down.

"Miss Strunk!" a gentle voice exclaimed, soft with concern. Trembling, Rebecca stepped towards the car. Through the open window she glimpsed two figures, tall and golden-haired, clad in thick furs. They were smiling and toasting each other with long-stemmed crystal flutes. But next to the window sat another figure, smaller, white-haired, and his warm hands enveloped hers as he drew her to the opening door.

"My dear Miss Strunk," he murmured as he drew her in and the door hissed shut behind her. "Would you like a new job?"

My yuppie-bashing Black Monday story, this was written while I was working as an office slave for various D.C. temporary agencies. Can you tell?

The Bacchae

She got into the elevator with him, the young woman from down the hall, the one he'd last seen at the annual Coop Meeting a week before. Around her shoulders hung something soft that brushed his cheek as Gordon moved aside to let her in: a fur cape, or pelt, or no, something else. The flayed skin of an animal, an animal that when she shouldered past him to the corner of the elevator proved to be her Rottweiler, Leopold. He could smell it now: the honey-eyed stench of uncured flesh, a pink and scarlet veil still clinging to the pelt's ragged fringe of coarse black hair. It had left a crimson streak down the back of her skirt, and stippled her legs with pink rosettes.

Gordon got off at the next floor and ran all the way down the hall. When he got into his own apartment he locked and chained the door behind him. For several minutes he stood there panting, squinting out the peephole until he saw her turn the corner and head for her door. It still clung to her shoulders, stiff front legs jouncing against the breast of her boiled-wool suit jacket. After the door closed behind her Gordon walked into the kitchen, poured himself a shot of Jameson's, and stood there until the trembling stopped.

Later, after he had changed and poured himself several more glasses of whisky, he saw on the news that the notorious Debbie DeLucia had been found not guilty of the murder of the young man she claimed had assaulted her in a parking garage one evening that summer. The young man had been beaten severely about face and chest with one of Ms. DeLucia's high-heeled shoes. When he was found by the parking lot attendant most of his hair was missing. Gordon switched off the television when it displayed photographs of these unpleasantries followed by shots of a throng of cheering women outside the courthouse. That evening he had difficulty falling asleep.

He woke in the middle of the night. Moonlight flooded the room, so brilliant it showed up the tiny pointed feathers poking through his down comforter. Rubbing his eyes Gordon sat up, tugged the comforter around his shoulders against the room's chill. He peered out at a full moon, not silver nor even the sallow gold he had seen on summer nights but a color he had never glimpsed in the sky before, a fiery bronze tinged with red.

"Jeez," Gordon said to himself, awed. He wondered if this had something to do with the solar shields tearing, the immense satellite-borne sails of mylar and solex that had been set adrift in the atmosphere to protect the cities and farmlands from ultraviolet radiation. But you weren't supposed to be able to see the shields. Certainly Gordon had never noticed any difference in the sky, although his friend Olivia claimed she could tell they were there. Women were more sensitive to these things than men, she had told him with an accusing look. There was a luminous quality to city light that had formerly been sooty and gray at best, and the air now had a russet tinge. Wonderful for outdoor setups—Olivia was a noted food photographer—or would be save for the odd bleeding of colors that appeared during developing, winesap apples touched with violet, a glass of Semillon shot with sparks of emerald, the parchment crust of an aged camembert taking on an unappetizing salmon glow.

It would be the same change in the light that made the moon bleed, Gordon decided. And now he had noticed it, even though he wasn't supposed to be sensitive to these things. What did that mean, he wondered? Maybe it was better not to notice, or to pretend he had seen nothing, no sanguine moon, no spectral colors in a photograph of a basket of eggs. Strange and sometimes awful things happened to men these days. Gordon had heard of some of these on television, but other tales came from friends, male friends. Near escapes recounted in low voices at the gym or club, random acts of violence spurred by innocent offers of help in carrying groceries, the act of holding a door open suddenly seen as threatening. Women friends, even relatives, sisters and daughters refusing to accompany family on trips to the city. An exodus of wives and children to the suburbs, from the suburbs to the shrinking belts of countryside ringing the megalopolis. And then, husbands and fathers disappearing during weekend visits with the family in exile. Impassive accounts by the next of kin of mislaid directions, trees where there had never been trees before. Evidence of wild animals, wildcats or coyotes perhaps, where nothing larger than a squirrel had been sighted in fifty years.

Gordon laughed at these tales at first. Until now. He pulled a feather from the bed-ticking and stroked his chin thoughtfully before tossing it away. It floated down, a breath of tawny mist. Gordon determinedly pulled the covers over his head and went back to sleep.

He was reading the paper in the kitchen next morning, a detailed account of Ms. DeLucia's trial and a new atrocity. Three women returning late from a nightclub had been harassed by a group of teenage boys, some of them very young. It was one of the young ones the women had killed, turning on the boys with a ferocity the newspaper described as "demonic." Gordon turned to the section that promised full photographic coverage and shuddered. Hastily he put aside the paper and crossed the room to get a second cup of coffee. How could a woman, even three women, be strong enough to do that? He recalled his neighbor down the hall. Christ. He'd take the fire stairs from now on, rather than risk seeing her again. He let his breath out in a low whistle and stirred another spoonful of white powder into his cup.

As he turned to go back to the table he noticed the MESSAGE light blinking on his answering machine. Odd. He hadn't heard the phone ring during the night. He sipped his coffee and played back the tape.

At first he thought there was nothing there. Dead silence, a wrong number. Then he heard faint sounds, a shrill creaking that he recognized as crickets, a katydid's resolute twang, and then the piercing, distant wail of a whippoorwill. It went on for several minutes, all the way to the end of the message tape. Nothing but night sounds, insects and a whippoorwill, once a sharp yapping that, faint as it was, Gordon knew was not a dog but a fox. Then abrupt silence as the tape ended. Gordon started, spilling coffee on his cuff, and swearing rewound the tape while he went to change shirts.

Afterward he played it back. He could hear wind in the trees, leaves pattering as though struck by a soft rain. Had Olivia spent the night in the country? No: they had plans for tonight, and there was no country within a day's drive in any direction from here. She wouldn't have left town on a major shoot without letting him know. He puzzled over it for a long while, playing back the gentle pavane of wind and tiny chiming voices, trying to discern something else there, breathing or muted laughter or a screen door banging shut, anything that might hint at a caller. But there was nothing, nothing but crickets and whippoorwills and a solitary vixen barking at the moon. Finally he left for work.

It was the sort of radiant autumn day when even financial analysts wax rapturous over the color of the sky—in this case a startling electric blue, so deep and glowing Gordon fancied it might leave his fingers damp if he reached to touch it, like wet canvas. He skipped his lunchtime heave at the gym. Instead he walked down to Lafayette Park, filling his pockets with the polished fruit of horse-chestnuts and wondering why it was the leaves no longer turned colors in the fall, only darkened to sear crisps and then clogged the sewers when they fell, a dirty brown porridge.

In the park he sat on a bench. There he ate a stale ersatz croissant and shied chestnuts at the fearless squirrels. A young woman with two small children stood in the middle of a circle of dun-colored grass, sowing crusts of bread among a throng of bobbing pigeons. One of the children pensively chewed a white crescent.

She squealed when a dappled white bird flew up at her face, dropped the bread as her mother laughed and took the children's hands, leading them back to the bench across from Gordon's. He smiled, conspiratorially tossed the remains of his lunch onto the grass, and watched it disappear beneath a mass of iridescent feathers.

A shadow sped across the ground. For an instant it blotted out the sun and Gordon looked up, startled. He had an impression of something immense, immense and dark and moving very quickly through the bright clear air. He recalled his night-time thoughts, had a delirious flash of insight: it was one of the shields torn loose, a ragged gonfalon of Science's floundering army. The little girl shrieked, not in fear but pure excitement. Gordon stood, ready to run for help; saw the woman, the children's mother, standing opposite him pointing at the grass and shouting something. Beside her the two children watched motionless, the little girl clutching a heel of bread.

In the midst of the feeding pigeons a great bird had landed, mahogany wings beating the air as its brazen feathers flashed and it stabbed, snakelike, at the smaller fowl. Its head was perfectly white, the beak curved and as long as Gordon's hand. Again and again that beak gleamed as it struck ferociously, sending up a cloud of feathers gray and pink and brown as the other birds scattered, wings beating feebly as they tried to escape. As Gordon watched blood pied the snowy feathers of the eagle's neck and breast until it was dappled white and red, then a deeper russet. Finally it glowed deep crimson. Still it would not stop its killing. And it seemed the pigeons could not flee, only fill the air with more urgent twittering and, gradually, silence. No matter how their wings flailed it was as though they were stuck in bird-lime, or one of those fine nets used to protect winter shrubs.

Suddenly the eagle halted, raised its wings protectively over the limp and thrashing forms about its feet. Gordon felt his throat constrict. He had jammed his hands in his pockets and now closed them about the chestnuts there, as though to use them as weapons. Across the grass the woman stood very still. The wind lifted her hair across her face like a banner. She did not brush it away, only stared through it to where the eagle waited, not eating, not moving, its baleful golden eye gazing down at the fluttering ruin of feather and bone.

As her mother stared the little girl broke away, ran to the edge of the ruddy circle where the eagle stood. It had lifted one clawed foot, thick with feathers, and shook it. The girl stopped and gazed at the sanguine bird. Carelessly she tossed away her heel of bread, wiped her hand and bent to pluck a bloodied feather from the ground. She stared at it, marveling, then pensively touched it to her face and hand. It left a rosy smear across one cheek and wrist and she laughed in delight. She glanced around, first at her mother and brother, then at Gordon.

The eyes she turned to him were ice-blue, wondering but fearless; and absolutely, ruthlessly indifferent.

He told Olivia about it that evening.

"I don't see what's so weird," she said, annoyed. It was intermission of the play they had come to see: Euripides' "The Bacchae" in a new translation. Gordon was unpleasantly conscious of how few men there were at the performance, the audience mostly composed of women in couples or small groups, even a few mothers with children, boys and girls who surely were much too young for this sort of thing. He and Olivia stood outside on the theater balcony overlooking the river. "Eagles kill things, that's what they're made for."

"But here? In the middle of the city? I mean, where did it come from? I thought they were extinct."

All about them people strolled beneath the sulfurous crimelights, smoking cigarettes, pulling coats tight against the wind, exclaiming at the full moon. Olivia leaned against the railing and stared up at the sky, smiling slightly. She wore ostrich cowboy boots with steel toes and tapped them rhythmically against the cement balcony. "I think you just don't like it when things don't go as you expect them to. Even if it's the way things really are supposed to be. Like an eagle killing pigeons."

He snorted but said nothing. Beside him Olivia tossed her hair back. Thick and lustrous darkbrown hair, like a caracal's pelt, hair that for years had been unfashionably long. Though lately it seemed that more women wore it the way she did, loose and long and artlessly tangled. As she pulled a lock away from her throat he saw something there, a mark upon her shoulder like a bruise or scrape.

"What's that?" he wondered, moving the collar of her jacket so he could see better.

She smiled, arching her neck. "Do you like it?"

He touched her shoulder, wincing. "Jesus, what the hell did you do? Doesn't it hurt?"

"A little." She shrugged, turned so that the jaundiced spotlight struck her shoulder and he could see better. A pattern of small incisions had been sliced into her skin, forming the shape of a crescent, or perhaps a grin. Blood still oozed from a few of the cuts. In the others ink or colored powder had been rubbed so that the little moon, if that's what it was, took on the livid shading of a bruise or orchid: violet, verdigris, citron yellow. From each crescent tip hung a gold ring smaller than a teardrop.

"But why?" He suddenly wanted to tear off her jacket and blouse, search the rest of her to see what other scarifications might be hiding here. "Why?"

Olivia smiled, stared out at the river moving in slow streaks of black and orange beneath the sullen moon. "A melted tiger," she said softly.

"What?" The electronic ping of bells signaled the end of intermission. Gordon grasped her elbow, overwhelmed by an abrupt and unfathomable fear. He recalled the moon last night, not crescent but swollen and blood-tinged as the scar on her shoulder. "What did you say?"

A woman passing them turned to stare in disapproval at his shrill voice. Olivia slipped from him as though he were a stranger crowding a subway door. "Come on," she said gently, brushing her hair from her face. She flashed him a smile as she adjusted her blouse to hide the scar. "We'll miss the second act." He followed her without another word.

After the show they walked down by the river. Gordon couldn't shake a burgeoning uneasiness, a feeling he might have called terror were it not that the word seemed one he couldn't apply to his own life, this measured round of clocks and stocks and evenings on the town. But he didn't want to say anything to Olivia, didn't want to upset her; more than anything he didn't want to upset her.

She was flushed with excitement, smoking cigarette after cigarette and tossing each little brand into the moonlit water snaking sluggishly beside them.

"Wonderful, just wonderful! The *Post* really did it justice, for a change." She stooped to pluck something from the mucky shadows and grimaced in distaste. "Christ. Their fucking beer cans—"

She glared at Gordon as though he had tossed it there. Smiling wanly he took it from her hand and carried it in apology. "I don't know," he began, and stopped. They had almost reached the Memorial Bridge. A path curved up through the tangled grasses toward the roadway, a path choked with dying goldenrod and stunted asters and Queen Anne's Lace that he suspected should not be such a luminous white, almost greenish in the moonlight. Shreds of something silver clung to the stunted limbs of lowgrowing shrubs. The way they fluttered in the cold wind made him think again of the atmospheric shields giving way, leaving the embarrened earth beneath them vulnerable and soft as the inner skin of some smooth green fruit. He squinted, trying to see exactly what it was that trembled from the branches. His companion sighed loudly and pointedly where she waited on the path ahead of him. Gordon turned from the shrubs and walked more quickly to join her.

"We should probably get up on the street," he said a little defensively.

Olivia made a small sound showing annoyance. "I'm tired of goddam streets. It's so peaceful here . . ."

He nodded and walked on beside her. A little ways ahead of them the bridge reared overhead, the ancient iron fretwork shedding green and russet flakes like old bark. Its crumbling concrete piers were lost in the blackness beneath the great struts and supports. The river disappeared and then materialized on the other side, black and gold and crimson, the moon's reflection a shimmering arrow across its surface. Gordon shivered a little. It reminded him of the stage set they had just left, all stark blacks and browns and greens. Following a new fashion for realism in the theater there had been a great deal of stage blood that had fairly swallowed the monolithic pillars and bound the proscenium with bright ribbons.

"I thought it was sort of gruesome," he said at last. He walked slowly now, reluctant to reach the bridge. In his hand the beer can felt gritty and cold, and he thought of tossing it away. "I mean the way the king's own mother killed him. Ugh." The scene had been very explicit. Even though warned by the *Post* critic Gordon had been taken aback. He had to close his eyes once. And then he couldn't block out their voices, the sound of knife ripping flesh (and how had they done that so convincingly?), the women chanting *Evohe! evohe!,* which afterwards Olivia explained as roughly meaning "O ecstasy" or words to that effect. When he asked her how she knew that she gave him a cross look and lit another cigarette.

No wonder the play was so seldom revived. "Don't you think we should go back? I mean, it's not very safe here at night."

"Huh." Olivia had stopped a few feet back. He turned and saw that she didn't seem to have heard him. She squatted at the river's edge, staring intently at something in the water.

"What is it?" He stood behind her, trying to see. The water smelled rank, not the brackish reek of rotting weeds and rich mud but a chemical smell that made his nostrils burn. The ruddy light glinted off Olivia's hair, touched her steel boot-tips with bronze. In the water in front of her a fish swam lethargically on its side, sides striped with scales of brown and yellow. Its mouth gaped open and closed and its gills showed an alarming color, bright pink like the inside of a wound.

"Ah," Olivia was murmuring. She put her hand into the water and lifted the fish upon it. It curled delicately within her palm, its fins stretching open like a butterfly warming to the sun as the water dripped heavily from her fingers. It took him a moment to realize it had no eyes.

"Poor thing," he said; then added, "I don't think you should touch it, Olivia. I mean, there's something wrong with it—"

"Of course there's something wrong with it," Olivia spat, so vehemently that he stepped backward. The mud smelled of ammonia where his heels slipped through it. "It's dying, poisoned, everything's been poisoned—"

"Well, then for Christ's sake drop it, Olivia, what's the sense in *playing* with it—"

Hissing angrily she slid her hand back through the water. The fish vanished beneath the surface and floated up again a foot away, fins fluttering pathetically. Olivia wiped her hand on her trousers, heedless of the dark stain left upon the silk.

"I wasn't playing with it," she announced coldly, shaking her head so that her jacket slipped to one side and he glimpsed the gold rings glinting from her shoulder. "You don't care, do you, you don't even notice anymore what's happened. There'd be nothing left at all if it was up to people like you—"

He swore in aggravation as she stormed off in the direction of the bridge, then hurried after her. Muck covered his shoes and he stumbled upon another cache of beer cans. When he looked up again he saw Olivia standing at the edge of the bridge's shadow, hands clenched at her sides as she confronted two tall figures.

"Oh, fuck," Gordon breathed. He felt sick with apprehension but hurried on, finally ran to stand beside her. "Hey!" he said loudly, pulling at Olivia's arm.

She stood motionless. One of the men held something small and dark at his side, a gun, the other wore a tan trenchcoat and looked calmly back and forth, as though preparing to cross a busy street. Before Gordon could take another breath the second man was shoving at his chest. Gordon shouted and struck at him, his hand flailing harmlessly against the man's coat. His other hand tightened around the beer can and he felt a sudden warm rush of pain as the metal sliced through his palm. He glanced down at his hand, saw blood streaming down his wrist and staining the white cuffs of his shirt. He stared in disbelief, heard a thudding sound and then a moan. Then running, stones rattling down the grassy slope.

The man in the trenchcoat was gone. The other, the man with the gun, lay on the ground at river's edge. Olivia was kicking him in the head, over and over, her boots scraping through the mud and gravel when they missed him and sending up a spume of gritty water. The gun was nowhere to be seen. Olivia paused for an instant. Gordon could hear her breathing heavily, saw her wipe her hands upon her trousers as she had when she freed the dying perch. "Olivia," he whispered. She grunted to herself, not hearing him, not looking; and suddenly he was terrified that she *would* look and see him there watching her. He stepped backwards, and as he did so she glanced up. For an instant she was silhouetted against the glimmering water, her white face spattered with mud, hair a coppery nimbus about her shoulders. Behind her the moon shone brilliantly, and on the opposite shore he could see the glittering lights of the distant airfield. It did not seem that she saw him at all. After a moment she looked down and began to kick again, more powerfully, and this time she would bring her heel back down across the man's back until Gordon could hear a crackling sound. He looked on, paralyzed, his good hand squeezing tighter and tighter about the wrist of his bleeding hand as she went on and on and on. One of her steel boot-tips tore through his shoulder and the man screamed. Gordon could see one side of his face caved in like a broken gourd, dark and shining as though water pooled in its ragged hollows. Olivia bent and lifted something dark and heavy from the shallow water. Gordon made a whining noise in his throat and ran away, up the hill to where the crimelights cast wavering shadows through the weeds. Behind him he heard a dull crash and then silence.

A crowd had gathered in front of his apartment building when he finally got there. He shoved a bill at the cab driver and stumbled from the car. "Oh, no," he said out loud as the cab drove off, certain the crowd had something to do with Olivia and the man by the river: policemen, reporters, ambulances.

But it didn't have anything to do with that after all. There was music, cheerful music pouring from a player set inside one of the ground floor windows. Suddenly Gordon remembered talk of this at the Coop meeting last week: a party, an opportunity for the tenants to get to know one another. It had been his neighbor's idea, the one with the dog. Someone had strung Christmas lights from another window, and several people had set up barbecues on the gray front lawn. Flames leaped from the grills, making the shadows dance so it was impossible to determine how many people were actually milling about. Quite a few, Gordon thought. He smelled roasting meat, bitter woodsmoke with the unpleasant reek of paint in it—were they burning *furniture?*—and a strange sweetish scent, herbs or perhaps marijuana. The pain in his hand had dulled to a steady throbbing. When he looked down he closed his eyes for a few seconds and grit his teeth. There was so much blood.

"Hi!" a voice cried. He opened his eyes to see the woman from down the hall. She was no longer wearing her Rottweiler, nor the expensively tailored suits she usually favored. Instead she wore faded jeans and the kind of extravagantly beaded and embroidered tunic Gordon associated with his parents' youth. These and the many jingling chains and jewels that hung from her ears and about her wrists and ankles (she was barefoot, in spite of the cool evening) gave her a gypsy air. In the firelight he could see that her face *sans* makeup was childishly freckled. She looked very young and very happy.

"Mm, hi," Gordon mumbled, moving his bloodsoaked arm from her sight. "A block party." He tried to keep his tone polite but uninterested as he pushed through the crowd of laughing people, but the young woman followed him, grinning.

"Isn't it great? You should come down, bring something to throw on the grill or something to drink, we're running out of hooch—"

She laughed, raising a heavy crystal wineglass and gulping from it something that was a deep purplish color and slightly viscous, certainly not wine. When she lowered the goblet he saw there was a small crack along its rim. This had cut the girl's upper lip which spun a slender filament of blood down across her chin. She didn't notice and threw her arm around his shoulders. "Promise you'll come back, mmmm? We need more guys so we can *dance* and stuff, there's just never enough guys anymore—"

She whirled away drunkenly, swinging her arms out like a giddy spinning child. Whether purposely or not the goblet flew from her hand and shattered on the broken concrete sidewalk. A cheer went up from the crowd. Someone turned the music up louder. A number of people by the glowing braziers seemed to be dancing as the girl was, drunkenly, merrily, arms outstretched and hair flying. Gordon heard the tinkling report of another glass breaking, then another; then the sharper crash of what might have been a window. He put his face down and fairly ran through the swarm to the front door, which had been propped open with an old stump overgrown with curling ivy. The neatly lettered sign warning against strangers and open doors had been yanked from the doorframe and lay in a twisted mass on the steps inside. Gordon kicked it aside and fled down the hall to the firestairs.

There were people in the stairwell, sitting or lying on the steps in drunken twos and threes. One couple had shed their clothes and stood grunting and heaving in the darkened corner near the fire extinguisher. Gordon averted his eyes, stepping carefully among the others. A small pile of twigs had been ignited on the floor and sweet-smelling smoke trailed upward through the dimness. And other things were scattered upon the steps: branches of fir-trees scenting the air with balsam, sheaves of goldenrod, empty wine bottles. One of these clattered underfoot, nearly tripping him. Gordon looked over his shoulder to see it roll downstairs, bumping the head of a woman passed out near the bottom and then spinning across the floor, finally coming to rest beside the couple in the corner. No one noticed it; no one noticed Gordon as he flung open the door to the fifth floor and ran to his apartment.

He walked numbly through the kitchen. The answering machine blinked. Mechanically he reset it as he passed, paused between the kitchen and living room as the tape began. A sound of wind filled the room, wind and the rustle of many feet in dead leaves. Gordon swallowed, pressed his shaking hands together as the tape played on behind him. The wind grew louder, then softer, swelled and whispered. And all the while he heard beneath the faint staticky recording the ceaseless passage of many feet, and sometimes voices, murmurous and laughing, eerie and wild as the wind itself. The tape ended. The apartment was silent save for the dull insistent clicking of the answering machine begging to be switched off, that and the muffled sound of laughter from outside.

Gordon stepped warily into the next room. He had forgotten to leave a light on. But it was not dark: moonlight flooded the space, glimmering across the dark wooden floor, making the shadowed bulk of armchairs and sofa and electronic equipment seem black and strange and ominous. On the sill of the picture window that covered an entire wall the moonlight gleamed upon one of his treasures, a fish of handblown Venetian glass, hundreds of years old. Its mauve and violet swirls glowed in the milky light, its gaping mouth and crystalline eyes reminding him of the perch he had seen earlier, eyeless, dying. He stepped across the living room and stood there at the window staring down at the glass fish. And suddenly his head hurt, his chest felt heavy and cold. Looking at the glass fish he was filled with a dull puzzling ache, as though he were trying to remember a dream. He pondered how he had come to have such a thing, why it was that this marvel of spun glass and pastel coloring had ever meant more to him than a blind perch struggling through the poisonous river. His hand traced the delicate filigree of its spines. They felt cold, burning cold in the cloudy light spilling through the window.

There was a knock at the door. Gordon started, as though he had been asleep, then crossed the darkened room. Through the peephole he saw Olivia, her hair atangle, a streak of black across one cheek. Her expression was oddly calm and untroubled in the carmine glare of the EXIT light. He tightened his hand about the doorknob, biting his lip against the pain that shot up through his arm as he did so. He wondered dully how she had gotten into the building, then remembered the chaos outside. Anyone could come in; even a woman who had seemingly just kicked a man to death by the polluted river. Perhaps it was like this all across the city, perhaps doors that had been locked since the riots had this evening suddenly sprung open.

"Gordon," Olivia commanded, her voice muffled by the heavy door that separated them. He was not surprised to feel the knob twist beneath his throbbing palm, or see the door swing inward to bump against his toe. Olivia slipped in, and with her a breath of incense-smelling smoke, the muted clamor of voices and laughter and pulsing music.

"Where'd you go?" she asked, smiling. He noticed that behind her the door had not quite closed. He reached to pull it shut but before he could grasp it she took him by the hand, the one that hurt. Grunting softly with pain he turned from the door to follow her into the living room.

"What's happening?" he whispered. "Olivia, what is it?" Without speaking she pulled him to the floor beside her, still smiling. She pulled his jacket from him, then his shoes and trousers and finally his bloodstained shirt. He reached to remove her blouse but Olivia pushed him away ungently, so that he cried out. As she moved above him his hand began to bleed again, leaving dark petals across her blouse and arms. The pain was so intense that he moaned, tried in vain to slow her but she only tightened her grip about his upper arm, tossing her hair back so that it formed a dark haze against the window's milky light. The blouse slipped from her shoulder and he could see the scars there, the little golden rings against her skin, drops of blood like rain flashing across her throat. Behind her the moon shone, bloated and sanguine. He could hear voices chanting counterpoint to the blood thudding in his temples. It took him a long time to catch his breath afterward. Olivia had bitten him on the shoulder, hard enough to bruise him. The pain coupled with that from his cut hand had suddenly made everything very intense, made him cry out loudly and then fall back hard against the cold floor as Olivia slipped from him. Now only the pain was left. He rubbed his shoulder ruefully. "Olivia? Are you angry?" he asked. She stood impassively in front of the window. The torn blouse had slipped from her shoulder. She had kicked her silk trousers beneath the sofa but pulled her boots back on, and moonlight glinted off the two wicked metal points. She seemed not to have heard him, so he repeated her name softly.

"Mmmm?" she said, distracted. She stared up at the sky, then leaned forward and opened the casement. Cold air flooded the room, and a brighter, colder light as well, as though the glass had ceased to filter out the lunar brilliance. Gordon shivered and groped for his shirt.

"Look at them," whispered Olivia. He got unsteadily to his feet and stood beside her, staring down at the sidewalk. Small figures capered across the broken tarmac, forms made threatening by the lurid glow of myriad bonfires that had sprung up across the dead gray lawn. He heard music, too, not music from the radio or stereo but a crude raw sound, thrumming and beating as of metal drums, voices howling and forming words he could not quite make out, an unknown name or phrase—

"*Evohe,*" whispered Olivia. The face she turned to him was white and merciless, her eyes inflamed. "*Evohe.*"

"What?" said Gordon. He stepped backwards and stumbled on one of his shoes. When he righted himself and looked up he saw

that there were other people in the room, other women, three four
six of them, even more it seemed, slipping silently through the door
that Olivia had left open behind her. They filled the small apartment with a cloying smell of smoke and burning hair, some of them
carrying smoking sticks, others leather pocketbooks or scorched
briefcases. He recognized many of them: though their hair was matted and wild, their clothes torn: dresses or suits ripped so that their
breasts were exposed and he could see where the flesh had been
raked by their own fingernails, leaving long wavering scars like signatures scratched in blood. Two of them were quite young and
naked and caressed each other laughing, turning to watch him with
sly feral eyes. Several of the older women had golden rings piercing
their breasts or the frail web of flesh between their fingers. One
traced a cut that ran down her thigh, then lifted her bloodied finger
to her lips as though imploring Gordon to keep a secret. He saw
another gray-haired woman whom he had greeted often at the
newsstand where they both purchased the *Wall Street Journal*. She
seemingly wore only a furtrimmed camel's-hair coat. Beneath its
soft folds Gordon glimpsed an undulating pattern of green and gray
and gold. As she approached him she let the coat fall away and he
saw a snake encircling her throat, writhing free to slide down
between her breasts and then to the floor at Gordon's feet. He
shouted and turned to flee.

Olivia was there, Olivia caught him and held him so tightly that
for a moment he imagined she was embracing him, imagined the
word she repeated was his name, spoken more and more loudly as
she held him until he felt the breath being crushed from within his
chest. But it was not his name, it was another name, a word like a
sigh, like the whisper of a thought coming louder and louder as the
others took it up and they were chanting now:

"Evohe, evohe . . ."

As he struggled with Olivia they fell upon him, the woman from
the newsstand, the girl from down the hall now naked and laughing
in a sort of grunting chuckle, the two young girls encircling him
with their slender cool arms and giggling as they kissed his cheeks
and nipped his ears. Fighting wildly he thrashed until his head was
free and he could see beyond them, see the open window behind
the writhing web of hair and arms and breasts, the moon blazing

now like a mad watchful eye above the burning canyons. He could see shreds of darkness falling from the sky, clouds or rain or wings, and he heard faintly beneath the shrieks and moans and panting voices the wail of sirens all across the city. Then he fell back once more beneath them.

There was a tinkling crash. He had a fleeting glimpse of something mauve and lavender skidding across the floor, then cried out as he rolled to one side and felt the glass shatter beneath him, the slivers of breath-spun fins and gills and tail slicing through his side. He saw Olivia, her face serene, her liquid eyes full of ardor as she turned to the girl beside her and took from her something that gleamed like silver in the moonlight, like pure and icy water, like a spar of broken glass. Gordon started to scream when she knelt between his thighs. Before he fainted he saw against the sky the bloodied fingers of eagle's wings, blotting out the face of a vast triumphant moon.

———

My attempt at writing a J.G. Ballard story. I did this after reading Bill McKibben's *The End of Nature*. Couldn't find a U.S. publisher so I sent it to *Interzone,* where David Pringle published it in 1991. "The Bacchae" proceeded to generate a bit of controversy, and *Interzone's* readers voted it the most hated story of the year. Another trope on ancient Greek myth, and one that prefigures *Waking the Moon.*

Snow on Sugar Mountain

When Andrew was seven, his mother turned into a fox. Snow freed the children from school at lunchtime, the bus skating down the hill to release cheering gangs at each sleety corner. Andrew got off last, nearly falling from the curb as he turned to wave goodbye to the driver. He ran to the front door of the house, battering at the screen and yelling, "Mom! Mom!" He tugged the scarf from his face, the better to peer through frost-clouded windows. Inside it looked dark; but he heard the television chattering to itself, heard the chimes of the old ship's clock counting half past one. She would be downstairs, then, doing the laundry. He dashed around the house, sliding on the iced flagstones.

"Mom . . . I'm home, it snowed, I'm—"

He saw the bird first. He thought it was the cardinal that had nested in the box tree last spring: a brilliant slash of crimson in the snow, like his own lost mitten. Andrew held his breath, teetering as he leaned forward to see.

A bluejay: no longer blue, scattered quills already gray and somber as tarnished silver, its pale crest quivering erect like an accusing finger. The snow beneath it glowed red as paint, and threads of steam rose from its mauled breast. Andrew tugged at his scarf, glancing across the white slope of lawn for the neighbor's cat.

That was when he saw the fox, mincing up the steps to the open back door. Its mouth drooped to show wet white teeth, the curved blade of the jay's wing hanging from its jaw. Andrew gasped. The fox mirrored his surprise, opening its mouth so that the wing fell and broke apart like the spinning seeds of a maple. For a moment they regarded each other, blue eyes and black. Then the fox stretched its forelegs as if yawning, stretched its mouth wide, too wide, until it seemed that its jaw would split like the broken quills. Andrew saw red gums and tongue, teeth like an ivory stair spiraling into black, black that was his mother's hair, his mother's eyes, his mother crouched naked, retching on the top step in the snow.

After that she had to show it to him. Not that day, not even that winter; but later, in the summer, when cardinals nested once more in the box tree and shrieking jays chased goldfinches from the birdbath.

"Someday you can have it, Andrew," she said as she drew her jewelry box from the kitchen hidey-hole. "When you're older. There's no one else," she added. His father had died before he was born. "And it's mine, anyway."

Inside the box were loops of pearls, jade turtles, a pendant made of butterfly's wings that formed a sunset and palm trees. And a small ugly thing, as long as her thumb and the same color: marbled cream, nut brown in the creases. At first he thought it was a bug. It was the locust year, and everywhere their husks stared at him from trees and cracks in the wall.

But it wasn't a locust. His mother placed it in his hand, and he held it right before his face. Some sort of stone, smooth as skin. Cool at first, after a few moments in his palm it grew warm, and he glanced at his mother for reassurance.

"Don't worry," she laughed wryly. "It won't bite." And she sipped her drink.

It was an animal, all slanted eyes and grinning mouth, paws tucked beneath its sharp chin like a dog playing Beg. A tiny hole had been drilled in the stone so that it could be tied onto a string.

"How does it work?" Andrew asked. His mother shook her head.

"Not yet," she said, swishing the ice in her glass. "It's mine still; but someday—someday I'll show you how." And she took the little carving and replaced it, and locked the jewelry box back in the hidey-hole.

That had been seven years ago. The bus that stopped at the foot of the hill would soon take Andrew to the public high school. Another locust summer was passing. The seven-year cicadas woke in the August night and crept from their split skins like a phantom army. The night they began to sing, Andrew woke to find his mother dead, bright pills spilling from one hand when he forced it open. In the other was the amulet, her palm blistered where she clenched the stone.

He refused the sedatives the doctor offered him, refused awkward offers of comfort from relatives and friends suddenly turned to strangers. At the wake he slouched before the casket, tearing petals from carnations. He nodded stiffly at his mother's sister when she arrived to take him to the funeral.

"Colin leaves for Brockport in three weeks," his aunt said later in the car. "When he goes, you can have the room to yourself. It's either that or the couch—"

"I don't care," Andrew replied. He didn't mean for his voice to sound so harsh. "I mean, it doesn't matter. Anywhere's okay. Really."

And it was, really.

Because the next day he was gone.

North of the city, in Kamensic Village, the cicadas formed heavy curtains of singing green and copper, covering oaks and beeches, houses and hedges and bicycles left out overnight. On Sugar Mountain they rippled across an ancient Volkswagen Beetle that hadn't moved in months. Their song was loud enough to wake the old astronaut in the middle of the night, and nearly drown out the sound of the telephone when it rang in the morning.

"I no longer do interviews," the old astronaut said wearily. He started to hang up. Then, "How the hell did you get this number, anyway?" he demanded; but the reporter was gone. Howell glared at Festus. The spaniel cringed, tail vibrating over the flagstones, and moaned softly. "You giving out this new number?" Howell croaked, and slapped his thigh. "Come on—"

The dog waddled over and lay his head upon the man's knee. Howell stroked the old bony skull, worn as flannel, and noted a hole in the knee of his pajamas.

Eleven o'clock and still not dressed. Christ, Festus, you should've said something.

He caught himself talking aloud and stood, gripping the mantel and waiting until his heart slowed. Sometimes now he didn't know if he was talking or thinking; if he had taken his medicine and slipped into the dreamy hold that hid him from the pain or if he was indeed dreaming. Once he had drifted, and thought he was addressing another class of eager children. He woke to find himself mumbling to an afternoon soap opera, Festus staring up at him intently. That day he put the television in a closet.

But later he dragged it back into the bedroom once more. The news helped remind him of things. Reminded him to call Lancaster, the oncologist; to call his son Peter, and the Kamensic Village Pharmacy.

"Festus," he whispered, hugging the dog close to his knee. "Oh, Festus." And when he finally glanced at the spaniel again was surprised to see the gentle sloping snout matted and dark with tears.

From the western Palisades, the radio tower blazed across the Hudson as Andrew left the city that dawn. He stood at the top of the road until the sun crept above the New York side, waiting until the beacon flashed and died. The first jet shimmered into sight over bridges linking the island to the foothills of the northern ranges. Andrew sighed. No tears left; but grief feathered his eyes so that the river swam, blurred and finally disappeared in the burst of sunrise. He turned and walked down the hill, faster and faster, past bus stops and parked cars, past the high school and the cemetery. Only when he reached the Parkway did he stop to catch his breath, then slowly crossed the road to the northbound lane.

Two rides brought him to Valhalla. He walked backward along the side of the road, shifting his backpack from shoulder to shoulder as he held his thumb out. A businessman in a BMW finally pulled over and unlocked the passenger door. He regarded Andrew with a sour expression.

"If you were my kid, I'd put your lights out," he growled as Andrew hopped in, grinning his best late-for-class smile. "But I'd wish a guy like me picked you up instead of some pervert."

"Thanks," Andrew nodded seriously. "I mean, you're right. I missed the last train out last night. I got to get to school."

The man stared straight ahead, then glanced at his watch. "I'm going to Manchester Hills. Where do you go to school?"

"John Jay."

"In Mount Lopac?"

"Kamensic Village."

The man nodded. "Is 684 close enough?"

Andrew shrugged. "Sure. Thanks a lot."

After several miles, they veered onto the highway's northern hook. Andrew sat forward in the seat, damp hands sticking to his knapsack as he watched for the exit sign. When he saw it he dropped his knapsack in nervous excitement. The businessman scowled.

"This is it . . . I mean, please, if it's okay—" The seat belt caught Andrew's sneaker as he grabbed the door handle. "Thanks—thanks a lot—"

"Next time don't miss the train," the man yelled as Andrew stumbled onto the road. Before he could slam the door shut, the lock clicked back into place. Andrew waved. The man lifted a finger in farewell, and the BMW roared north.

From the Parkway, Kamensic Village drifted into sight like a dream of distant towns. White steeples, stone walls, granite turrets rising from hills already rusted with the first of autumn. To the north the hills arched like a deer's long spine, melting golden into the Mohank Mountains. Andrew nodded slowly and shrugged the knapsack to his shoulder. He scuffed down the embankment to where a stream flowed townward. He followed it, stopping to drink and wash his face, slicking his hair back into a dark wave. Sunfish floated in the water above sandy nests, slipping fearlessly through his fingers when he tried to snatch them. His stomach ached from hunger, raw and cold as though he'd swallowed a handful of cinders. He thought of the stone around his neck. That smooth pellet under his tongue, and how easy it would be then to find food . . .

He swore softly, shaking damp hair from his eyes. Against his chest the amulet bounced, and he steadied it, grimacing, before heading upstream.

The bug-ridden sign swayed at the railroad station: KAMENSIC VILLAGE. Beneath it stood a single bench, straddled by the same kid Andrew remembered from childhood: misshapen helmet protecting his head, starry topaz eyes widening when he saw Andrew pass the station.

"Hey," the boy yelled, just as if he remembered Andrew from years back. "HEY."

"Hey, Buster." Andrew waved without stopping.

He passed the Kamensic Village Pharmacy, where Mr. Weinstein still doled out egg creams; Hayden's Delicatessen with its great vat of iced tea, lemons bobbing like toy turtles in the amber liquid. The library, open four days a week (CLOSED TODAY). That was where he had seen puppet shows, and heard an astronaut talk once, years ago when he and his mother still came up in the summer to rent the cottage. And, next to the library, the seventeenth-century court-house, now a museum.

"Fifty cents for students." The same old lady peered suspiciously at Andrew's damp hair and red-rimmed eyes. "Shouldn't you be in school?"

"Visiting," Andrew mumbled as she dropped the quarters into a little tin box. "I got relatives here."

He shook his head at her offer to walk him through the rooms. "I been here before," he explained. He tried to smile. "On vacation."

The courtroom smelled the same, of lemon polish and the old lady's Chanel No. 5. The Indian Display waited where it always had, in a whitewashed corner of the courtroom where dead bluebottles drifted like lapis beads. Andrew's chest tightened when he saw it. His hand closed around the amulet on its string.

A frayed map of the northern county starred with arrowheads indicated where the tribes had settled. Ax blades and skin scrapers marked their battles. A deer hide frayed with moth holes provided a backdrop for the dusty case. From beneath the doeskin winked a vole's skull.

At the bottom of the case rested a small printed board. Andrew leaned his head against the glass and closed his eyes, mouthing the words without reading them as he fingered the stone.

> . . . members of the Tankiteke tribe of
> the Wappinger Confederacy of Mohicans:
> Iroquois warriors of the Algonquin Nation . . .

When he opened his eyes they fixed upon an object at the bottom of the case: a carved gray stone in the image of a tiny animal with long eyes and smooth sharp teeth.

> Shaman's Tallsman [Animistic Figure]

> The Tankiteke believed their shamans could change shape
> at will and worshipped animal spirits.

From the narrow hallway leading to the front room came the creak of a door opening, the answering hiss of women's laughter.

"Some boy," Andrew heard the old lady reply. He bit his lip. "Said he had relatives, but I think he's just skipping school . . ."

Andrew glanced around the courtroom, looking for new exhibits, tools, books. There was nothing. No more artifacts; no other talisman. He slipped through a door leading to an anteroom and found there another door leading outside. Unlocked; there would be no locked doors in Kamensic Village. In the orchard behind the courthouse, he scooped up an early apple and ate it, wincing at the bitter flesh. Then he headed for the road that led to The Fallows.

In the dreams, Howell walked on the moon.

The air he breathed was the same stale air, redolent of urine and refrigeration, that had always filled the capsules. Yet he was conscious in the dreams that it tasted different on the moon, filtered through the spare silver ducts coiled on his back. Above him the sky loomed sable, so cold that his hands tingled inside heated gloves at the sight of it: as he had always known it would be, algid, black, speared with stars that pulsed and sang as they never did inside the capsule. He lifted his eyes then and saw the orbiter passing overhead. He raised one hand to wave, so slowly it seemed he might start to drift into the stark air in the pattern of that wave. And then the voice crackled in his ears, clipped words echoing phrases from memoranda and newscasts. His own voice, calling to Howell that it was time to return.

That was when he woke, shivering despite quilts and Festus snoring beside him. A long while he lay in bed, trying to recall the season—winter, surely, because of the fogged windows.

But no. Beneath the humming cough of air-conditioning, cicadas droned. Howell struggled to his feet.

Behind the bungalow the woods shimmered, birch and ancient oaks silvered by the moonlight streaming from the sky. Howell opened the casement and leaned out. Light and warmth spilled upon him as though the moonlight were warm milk, and he blinked and stretched his hands to catch it.

Years before, during the final two moon landings, Howell had been the man who waited inside the orbiter.

Long ago, before the actors and writers and wealthy children of the exurbs migrated to Kamensic Village, a colony of earnest socialists settled upon the scrubby shores of the gray water named Muscanth. Their utopia had shattered years before. The cozy stage and studios rotted and softly sank back into the fen. But the cottages remained, some of them still rented to summer visitors from the city. Andrew had to ask in Scotts Corners for directions—he hadn't been here since he was ten—and was surprised by how much longer it took to reach The Fallows on foot. No autos passed. Only a young girl in jeans and flannel shirt, riding a black horse, her braids flying as her mount cantered by him. Andrew laughed. She waved, grinning, before disappearing around a kink in the birchy lane.

With that sharp laugh, something fell from Andrew: as if grief could be contained in small cold breaths, and he had just exhaled. He noticed for the first time sweat streaking his chest, and unbuttoned his shirt. The shirt smelled stale and oily, as though it had absorbed the city's foul air, its grimy clouds of exhaust and factory smoke.

But here the sky gleamed slick and blue as a bunting's wing. Andrew laughed again, shook his head so that sky and leaves and scattering birds all flickered in a bright blink. And when he focused again upon the road, the path snaked *there:* just where he had left it four years ago, carefully cleared of curling ferns and moldering birch.

I'm here, he thought as he stepped shyly off the dirt road, glancing back to make certain no car or rider marked where he broke trail. In the distance glittered the lake. A cloud of red admiral butterflies rose from a crab-apple stump and skimmed beside him along the overgrown path Andrew ran, laughing. He was home.

The abandoned cottage had grown larger with decay and disuse. Ladders of nectarine fungi and staghorn lichen covered it from eaves to floor, and between this patchwork straggled owls' nests and the downy homes of deer mice.

The door did not give easily. It was unlocked, but swollen from snow and rain. Andrew had to fling himself full force against the timbers before they groaned and relented. Amber light streamed from chinks and cracks in the walls, enough light that ferns and pokeweed grew from clefts in the pine floor. Something scurried beneath the room's single chair. Andrew turned in time to see a deer mouse, still soft in its gray infant fur, disappear into the wall.

There had been other visitors as well. In the tiny bedroom, Andrew found fox scat and long rufous hairs clinging to the splintered cedar wall; by the front door, rabbit pellets. Mud daubers had plastered the kitchen with their fulvous cells. The linoleum was scattered with undigested feathers and the crushed spines of voles. He paced the cottage, yanking up pokeweed and tossing it into the corner, dragged the chair into the center of the room and sat there a long time. Finally, he took a deep breath, opened his knapsack and withdrew a bottle of gin pilfered from his mother's bureau, still nearly full. He took a swig, shut his eyes and waited for it to steam through his throat to his head.

"Don't do it drunk," his mother had warned him once—drunk herself, the two of them sipping Pink Squirrels from a lukewarm bottle in her bedroom. "You ever seen a drunk dog?"

"No," Andrew giggled.

"Well, it's like that, only worse. You can't walk straight. You can't smell anything. It's worse than plain drunk. I almost got hit by a car once, in Kamensic, when I was drunk." She lit a cigarette. "Stayed out a whole night that time, trying to find my way back . . ."

Andrew nodded, rubbing the little talisman to his lips.

"No," his mother said softly, and took it from him. She held it up to the gooseneck lamp. "Not yet."

She turned and stared at him fiercely, glittering eyes belying her slurred voice. "See, you can't stay that long. I almost did, that time . . ."

She took another sip. "Forget, I mean. You forget . . . fox or bear or deer, you forget . . ."

"Forget what?" Andrew wondered. The smoke made him cough, and he gulped his drink.

"What you are. That you're human. Not . . ."

She took his hand, her nails scratching his palm. "They used to forget. The Indians, the Tankiteke. That's what my grandfather said. There used to be more of these things—"

She rolled the stone between her palms. "And now they're all gone. You know why?"

Andrew shook his head.

"Because they forgot." His mother turned away. "Fox or what-ever—they forgot they once were human, and stayed forever, and died up there in the woods." And she fingered the stone as she did her wedding ring, eyes agleam with whiskey tears.

But that night Andrew lay long awake, staring at his Mets pen-nants as he listened to the traffic outside; and wondered why any-one would ever want to come back.

Howell woke before dawn, calling, "Festus! Morning." The spaniel snorted and stared at him blearily before sliding off the bed.

"Look," said Howell, pointing to where tall ferns at wood's edge had been crushed to a green mat. "They were here again last night."

Festus whined and ran from the room, nails tick-tocking upon the floor. Howell let him out the back door and watched the old dog snuffle at the deer brake, then crash into the brush. Some mornings Howell felt as if he might follow the dog on these noisy hunts once more. But each time, the dawn rush of light and heat trampled his strength as carelessly as deer broke the ferns. For a few minutes he breathed easily, the dank mountain air slipping like water down his throat, cold and tasting of granite. Then the coughing started. Howell gripped the door frame, shuddering until the tears came, chest racked as though something smashed his ribs to escape. He stumbled into the kitchen, fingers scrabbling across the counter until they clutched the inhaler. By the time he breathed easily again, sunlight gilded Sugar Mountain, and at the back door Festus scratched for entry, panting from his run.

The same morning found Andrew snoring on the cottage floor. The bottle of gin had toppled, soaking the heap of old newspapers where he lay pillowed. He woke slowly but to quick and violent conclusions when he tried to stand.

"Christ," he moaned, pausing in the doorway. The reek of gin made him sick. Afterward, he wiped his mouth on a wild grape leaf, then with surprising vigor smashed the bottle against a tree. Then he staggered downhill toward the stream.

Here the water flowed waist-deep. Andrew peeled off T-shirt and jeans and eased himself into the stream, swearing at the cold. A deep breath. Then he dunked himself, came up sputtering, and floated above the clear pebbled bottom, eyes shut against the shadows of trees and sky trembling overhead.

He settled on a narrow stone shelf above the stream, water rippling across his lap. His head buzzed between hunger and hangover. Beneath him minnows drifted like willow leaves. He dipped a hand to catch them. but they wriggled easily through his fingers. A feverish hunger came over him. He counted back three days since he'd eaten: the same evening he'd found his mother . . .

He blinked against the memory, blinked until the hazy air cleared and he could focus on the stream beneath him. Easing himself into the water, he knelt in the shallows and squinted at the rocks. Very slowly, he lifted one flat stone, then another. The third uncovered a crayfish, mottled brown against chocolate-colored gravel. Andrew bit his hand to stop it shaking, then slipped it beneath the surface. The crayfish shot backward, toward his ankles. Andrew positioned his feet to form a V, squatting to cut off its escape. He yelped triumphantly when he grabbed its tail.

"Son of a bitch!" Pincers nipped his thumb. He flung the crayfish onto the mossy bank, where it jerked and twitched. For a moment Andrew regarded it remorsefully. Then he took the same flat stone that had sheltered it and neatly cracked its head open.

Not much meat to suck from the claws. A thumb's worth (still quivering) within the tail, muddy and sweet as March rain. In the next hour he uncovered dozens more, until the bank was littered with empty carapaces, the mud starred with his handprints like a great raccoon's. Finally he stopped eating. The mess on the bank sickened him. He crawled to stream's edge and bit his lip, trying not to throw up. In the shadowy water he saw himself: much too thin, black hair straggling across his forehead, his slanted eyes shadowed by exhaustion. He wiped a thread of mud from his lip and leaned back. Against his chest the amulet bounced like a stray droplet, its filthy cord chafing his neck. He dried his face with his T-shirt, then pulled the string until the amulet dangled in front of him.

In the late summer light it gleamed eerily, swollen as a monarch's chrysalis. And like the lines of thorax, head, wings evident upon a pupae, the talisman bore faint markings. Eyes, teeth, paws; wings, fins, antlers, tail. Depending on how it caught the light, it was fox or stoat; flying squirrel or cougar or stag. The boy pinched the amulet between thumb and middle finger, drew it across his check. Warm. Within the nugget of stone he felt a dull buzzing like an entrapped hornet.

Andrew rubbed the talisman against his lips. His teeth vibrated as from a tiny drill. He shut his eyes, tightened his fingers about the stone, and slipped it beneath his tongue. For a second he felt it, a seed ripe to burst. Then nausea exploded inside him, pain so violent he screamed and collapsed onto the moss, clawing wildly at his head. Abruptly his shrieks stopped. He could not breathe. A rush of warm air filled his nostrils, fetid as pond water. He sneezed.

And opened his eyes to the muddy bank oozing between black and velvet paws.

*   *   *

Perhaps it was the years spent in cramped spaces—his knees drawn to his chest in capsule mock-ups; sleeping suspended in canvas sacks; eating upside down in metal rooms smaller than a refrigerator—perhaps the bungalow had actually seemed *spacious* when Howell decided to purchase it over his son's protests and his accountant's sighs.

"Plenty of room for what I need," he told his son. They were hanging pictures. NASA shots, *Life* magazine promos. The Avedon portrait of his wife, a former Miss Rio Grande, dead of cancer before the moon landing. "And fifty acres: most of the lakefront."

"Fifty acres most of it nowhere," Peter said snidely. He hated the country; hated the disappointment he felt that his father hadn't taken the penthouse in Manhattan. "No room here for anyone else, that's for sure."

That was how the old man liked it. The bungalow fit neatly into a tiny clearing between glacier-riven hills. A good snow cut him off from the village for days: the town's only plow saved Sugar Mountain and the abandoned lake colony for last. "The Astronaut don't mind," the driver always said.

Howell agreed. After early retirement he took his pension and retired, truly retired. No honorary university positions. No airline endorsements. His investments were few and careless. He corresponded with crackpots, authors researching astral landing fields in rain forests, a woman who claimed to receive alien broadcasts through her sunglasses, an institutionalized patient who signed his letters Rubber Man Lord of Jupiter. During a rare radio interview, Howell admitted to experimentation with hallucinogenic drugs and expressed surprising bitterness at the demise of the Apollo program, regret untempered by the intervening years. On spring afternoons he could be seen walking with his English cocker spaniel on the dirt roads through Kamensic. The village schoolchildren pointed him out proudly, although his picture was not in their books. Once a year he spoke to the fifth graders about the importance of the space program, shyly signing autographs on lunch bags afterwards: no, the Astronaut did not mind.

The old man sighed and walked to his desk. From his frayed shirt rose a skull barren of hair, raised blue veins like rivers on a relief globe. Agate blue eyes, dry as if all the dreams had been sucked from them, focused now on strange things. Battalions of pill bottles. Bright lesions on hands and feet. Machines more dreadful than anything NASA had devised for his training. The road from Sugar Mountain lay so far from his front door that he seldom walked there anymore.

The medicine quelled his coughing. In its place a heaviness in his chest and the drug's phantom mettle.

"I wish the goddamn car keys were here," he announced to Festus, pacing to the door. He was not supposed to drive alone. Peter had taken the keys, "for safety." "I wish my goddamn dog could drive."

Festus yawned and flopped onto the floor. Sighing, the astronaut settled onto the couch, took pen and notebook to write a letter. Within minutes he was asleep.

Andrew staggered from the sound: the bawl of air through the trees, the cicadas' song a steady thunder. From beneath the soil thrummed millipedes and hellgrammites, the ceaseless tick of insect legs upon fallen leaves. He shivered and shook a ruff of heavy fur. The sunlight stung his eyes and he blinked. The world was bound now in black and gray.

He sneezed. Warm currents of scent tickled his muzzle. So many kinds of dirt! Mud like cocoa, rich and bitter; sand fresh as sunlight; loam ripe with hidden worms. He stood on wobbly legs, took a few steps and stumbled on his clothes. Their rank smell assaulted him: detergent, sweat, city gravel and tarmac. He sneezed ferociously, then ambled to the streambed. He nosed a crayfish shell, licking it clean. Afterward he waded into the stream and lapped, long tongue flicking water into his eyes. A bound brought him to the high bank. He shook water from his fur and flung his head back, eyes shut, filled with a formidable wordless joy. From far away he heard low thunder; he tasted the approach of rain upon the breeze.

Something stirred in the thickets nearby. Without looking he knew it was a rabbit, smelled milk and acrid fear clinging to her. He raised his head, tested the air until he found her crouched at the base of a split birch. He crept forward, his belly grazing the dirt.

When he was scarcely a muzzle-length away, she spooked, hind legs spraying leaves in his face as she vaulted into the underbrush. He followed, slipping under grapevines and poison ivy, his dewclaws catching on burdock leaves.

The rabbit led him through a birch stand to a large clearing, where she bounded and disappeared into a burrow. He dug furiously at the hole, throwing up clouds of soft loam, stopping finally when he upturned a mass of black beetles clicking over a rock. Curious, he nudged the beetles, then licked up a mouthful and crunched them between his long teeth. The remaining insects scurried beneath the earth. Suddenly tired, he yawned, crawled inside a ring of overgrown ferns heavy with spores and lay there panting.

The air grew heavy with moisture. Thunder snarled in the distance. How could he ever have thought the woods silent? He heard constantly the steady beat, the hum of the turning day beneath his paws. Rain began to fall, and he crept deeper into the ferns until they covered him. He waited there until nightfall, licking rain from the fronds and cleaning the earth from between his footpads.

At dusk the rain stopped. Through slitted eyes he saw a stag step into the clearing and bend to lick rain from a cupped leaf, its tongue rasping against the grass. Nuthatches arrowed into the rhododendrons, and the bushes shuddered until they settled into sleep. He stretched, the hair on his back rustling as moisture pearled and rolled from his coat. In the damp air scents were acute: he tasted mist rising from the nearby swamp, smelled an eft beneath a rotting stump. Then the breeze shifted, brought a stronger scent to him: hot and milky, the young rabbit, motionless at the entrance of its burrow.

He cocked his ears to trace the faint wind stirring the rabbit's fur. He crouched and took a half step toward it, sprang as it bolted in a panic of flying fur and leaves. The rabbit leaped into the clearing, turned and tripped on a fallen branch. In that instant he was upon it, his paws hesitantly brushing its shuddering flank before he tore at its throat. The rabbit screamed. He rent skin and sinew, fur catching between his teeth, shearing strings of muscle as he growled and tugged at its jaw. It stopped kicking. Somewhere inside the fox, Andrew wanted to scream; but the fox tore at the rabbit's head, blood spurting from a crushed artery and staining his muzzle. The smell maddened him. He dragged the rabbit into the brush and fed, then dug a shallow hole and buried the carcass, nosing leaves over the warm bones.

He stepped into the clearing and stared through the tangle of trees and sky. The moon was full. Blood burned inside him; its smell stung his nostrils, scorched his tongue so that he craved water. An owl screeched. He started, leaping over the rank midden, and continued running through the birch clearing until he found the stream, dazzling with reflected moonlight. He stepped to the water's edge and dipped a tentative paw into the shallows, rearing back when the light scattered at his touch. He crossed the stream and wandered snuffling across the other bank. A smell arrested him: overwhelming, alien to this place. He stared at a pile of clothes strewn upon the moss, walked to them stiff-legged and sniffed. Beneath his tongue something small and rough itched like a blister. He shook his head and felt the string around his neck. He coughed, pawed his muzzle; buried his face in the T-shirt. The talisman dropped from between his jaws.

On the bank the boy knelt, coughing, one hand clutching the bloody talisman. He crawled to the stream and bowed there, cupping water in his hands and gulping frantically. Then he staggered backward, flopped onto the moss to stare exhausted at the sky. In a little while he slept uneasily, legs twitching as he stalked fleeing hares through a black and twisted forest.

Rain woke him the next morning, trickling into his nostrils and beneath his eyelids. Andrew snorted and sat up, wiping his eyes. The stream swelled with muddy whirlpools. He stared as the rain came down harder, slicing through the high canopy and striking him like small cold stones. Shivering, he grabbed his clothes and limped to the cottage. Inside he dried himself with his damp T-shirt, then stepped into the tiny bedroom. It was so narrow that when he extended his arms his fingertips grazed opposing walls. Here sagged an ancient iron-framed camp bed with flattened mattress, hard and lean as an old car seat. Groaning, he collapsed onto it, heedless of dead moths scattered across the cushion. His crumpled jeans made a moist pillow as he propped himself against the wall and stared at the ceiling.

He could come back here every day. It was dry, and if he pulled up all the pokeweed, swept out the dirt and fallen feathers, it would be home. He had the stream for water; a few warm clothes in his knapsack for winter. At night he could hunt and feed in the woods, changing back at dawn. During the day he'd sleep, maybe go to the library and look up survival books. No one would ever find him. He could hide forever here where the Tankiteke had hunted.

It didn't have to drive you crazy. If you didn't fight it, if you used it in the right places; if you didn't care about family or friends or school. He pulled fiercely at the string and held the amulet before his eyes.

They would never know. Ever: no one would ever know.

Howell's treatments stopped that winter. One evening Dr. Lancaster simply shook his head, slid the latest test results into the folder and closed it. The next morning he told Howell, "No more."

The astronaut went home to die.

As long as there was no snow, he could walk with Festus, brief forays down the dirt drive to check the mailbox. Some afternoons he'd wait there with the spaniel for the mail car to pull up.

"Some winter, Major Howell," the mailman announced as he handed him a stack of letters from the insurance company, vitamin wholesalers, the Yale hospital. "Think we'll ever get snow?"

Howell took the mail, shrugging, then looked at the cloudless sky. "Your guess is as good as mine. Better, probably."

They laughed, and the car crept down the hillside. Howell turned and called Festus from the woods. For a moment he paused, staring at the brilliant winter sky, the moon like a pale eye staring down upon the afternoon.

That night he dreamed of the sky, ice melting into clouds that scudded across a ghostly moon so close that when he raised his hands his fingers left marks upon its face, tiny craters blooming where he touched. When he awoke the next morning it was snowing.

The blizzard pounced on Kamensic Village, caught the hamlet as it drowsed after the long Christmas holidays. A brief and bitter autumn had given way to a snowless winter. Deer grew fat grazing upon frosty pastures. With no snow to challenge them, school-bus drivers grew complacent, then cranky, while children dreamed of brightly varnished toboggans and new skis still beribboned in frigid garages. In The Fallows a fox could find good hunting, warm holes to hide in; the door blew off an abandoned bungalow and leaves drifted in its corners, burying a vinyl knapsack.

Beneath a tumbledown stone wall, he'd found an abandoned burrow, just large enough to curl up in and sleep through the bitter days. He avoided the cottages now. The fetid scent of men still clinging to the forsaken structures frightened him, ripe as it was with some perplexing memory. He yawned and drew his paws under him, tail curving to cover his muzzle and warm the freezing air he breathed. Above him the wall hid the remains of the grouse he'd killed last night. The faint rotting smell comforted him, and he slept deeply.

He woke to silence: so utterly still that his hackles rose and he growled softly with unease. Even in the burrow he could always hear the soft stirrings of the world—wind in dead leaves, chick-adees fighting in the pines, the crack of branches breaking from the cold. Now he heard only a dull scratching. Stiff-legged he crept through the tunnel and emerged into the storm.

Stones had prevented snow from blocking the entrance to his den. He slunk through the narrow burrow and shook himself. Snow fell so fast that within moments his fur was thick with it. Everywhere branches had collapsed. Entire pines bowed toward the ground until they snapped, dark trunks quickly and silently buried. He buried his muzzle in the drift, then reared back, snarling. Abruptly he turned and leaped atop the stone wall. As he did so, he dislodged a heavy ledge of snow that fell behind him without a sound.

From the wall he tested the wind. Nothing. It blew his ruff back until he shivered beneath snow so thick that he could not shake himself dry. He slunk down, stumbling into a drift, and sniffed for the burrow entrance.

Gone. Displaced snow blocked the hole. He could smell noth-ing. Frantically he dug at the wall. More snow slid from the stones, and he jumped back, growling. From stone to stone he ran, pawing frenziedly, burying his muzzle as he tried to find a warm smell, the scent of frozen blood or spoor. Snow congealed between his pads, matting his legs so that he swam gracelessly through the shifting mass. Exhausted, he huddled at the base of the wall until cold gnawed at his chest. Then he staggered upward until he once again stood clear at the top. Bitter wind clamped his muzzle. His eyelids froze. Blindly he began to run along the wall's crest, slipping between rocks and panting.

The wall ended. A wind-riven hill sloped away from him, and he leaped, tumbled by the storm until the snow met him and he flailed whimpering through the endless drifts.

Howell sat before the window, watching the storm. The telephone lines linking him to the village sagged drearily in hoary crescents. He knew they would break as they did during every blizzard. He had already spoken to Peter, to Dr. Lancaster, to Mr. Schelling, the grocer, who wondered if he needed anything before the store closed. He could snap the lines himself now if he wanted. There was no one else to talk to.

He no longer cared. The heaviness in his lungs had spread these last few weeks until his entire chest felt ribbed in stone, his legs and arms so light in comparison they might be wings. He knew that one by one the elements of his body were leaving him. Only the pills gave him strength, and he refilled the plastic bottles often.

A little while ago he had taken a capsule, washing it down with a scant tumbler of scotch. He took a childish pleasure in violating his body now.

"Festus," he croaked, his hand ruffling the air at his side. Festus shambled over, tail vibrating. "Hey Festus, my good dog. My good bright dog."

Festus licked Howell's hand, licked his chops and whined hopefully.

"Dinner?" Howell said, surprised. "So early." Then wondered in alarm if he had fed the dog yesterday; if he had forgotten that as he had sometimes forgotten the mail, his clothes, his own meals. He stood uneasily, head thrumming, and went to the kitchen.

A moist crust still rimmed the dog's dish. There was water in his bowl. But when Howell opened the cabinet beneath the sink there were no cans there. The tall red Purina bag was empty.

"Oh, no," he murmured, then looked in the refrigerator. A few eggs; some frozen vegetables. There would be soup in the cupboard. "Festus, Christ, I'm sorry." Festus danced expectantly across the planked floor to wait at his dish.

Howell leaned against the sink and stared outside. Schelling's might still be open; if not, Isaac lived behind the store. There was gas in the car. Peter had returned the keys, reluctantly, but Howell hadn't driven in months. If he waited it might be two days before anyone called or checked Sugar Mountain. He rummaged through closets until he found boots and heavy parka, then shoved his inhaler into a pocket. He paused in the kitchen, wondering if he should bring the dog with him.

"I'll be back soon," he said at last, rumpling the spaniel's ears. Then he swallowed another pill.

Outside, flakes the size of his thumb swirled down and burst into hundreds of crystals upon his parka. The sky hung so low and dark that it seemed like nightfall. Howell had no idea what time it really was. He staggered to the car, kicking the door until snow fell from it and he could find the handle. He checked the back seat for shovel, sand, blankets. Then he started the engine. The car lurched forward.

He had heard the snowplow earlier, but the road was already buried once more. As the car drifted toward a high bank, Howell wondered why it was he had decided to go out, finally recalled Festus waiting hungrily at home.

In a few minutes he realized it was futile to steer toward one side of the road or the other. Instead he tried to keep a few feet between car and trees, and so avoid driving into the woods. Soon even this was difficult. Pines leaned where he had never seen trees. The stone walls that bounded the road had buckled into labyrinthine waves. Down the gentle slope inched the car, bluish spume flying behind it. The heater did not work. The windshield wipers stuck again. He reached out and cleared a tiny patch to see through the frigid black glass starred with soft explosions.

Through the clear spot, Howell saw only white and gray streaks. Smears left by his fingers on the glass froze and reflected the steady green and red lights of the dashboard. His hands dropped from the wheel, and he rubbed them together. The car glided onward.

Dreaming, he saw for an instant a calm frozen sea swelling beneath tiny windows, interior darkness broken by blinking panel lights while, outside, shone the azure bow of Earth. Then his forehead grazed the edge of the steering wheel, and he started, gently pressing the brake.

An animal plunged in front of the car, a golden blur like a summer stain upon the snow. It thudded against the bumper.

"Son of a bitch," murmured Howell.

The car stopped. As he stepped out he glanced behind him, shielding his eyes. Snow already filled the tracks snaking a scant hundred feet to the end of his drive. He pulled the hood tight about his face and turned.

In front of the car sprawled a naked boy, eyes closed as if asleep, skin steaming at the kiss of melting snow. Long black hair tangled with twigs; one fist raised to his lips. A drowsing child. The astronaut stooped and very gently touched his cheek. It was feverishly hot.

The boy moaned. Howell staggered against the bumper. The freezing pain jolted him. He stumbled to the door, reaching for the old Hudson's Bay blanket. Then he knelt beside the boy, head pounding, and wrapped him in the blanket. He tried to carry him: too heavy. Howell groaned, then dragged boy and blanket to the side of the car. For a moment he rested, wheezing, before heaving the boy into the passenger seat.

Afterward he couldn't remember driving back to the house. Festus met him at the door, barking joyfully. Staggering beneath the boy's weight, Howell kicked the door shut behind him, then kneeling placed the bundle on the floor.

"Festus, shh," he commanded.

The dog approached the boy, tail wagging. Then he stiffened and reared back snarling.

"Festus, shut up." Exhausted, Howell threw down his parka. He paused to stare at the blizzard still raging about the mountainside. "Festus, I'm throwing you out there if you don't shut up." He clapped and pointed toward the kitchen. "Go lie down."

Festus barked, but retreated to the kitchen.

Now what the hell is this? Howell ran his hands over his wet scalp and stared down at the boy. Melting snow dripped from the blanket to stain the wooden floor. Tentatively he stooped and pulled back a woolen corner.

In the room's ruddy light the boy looked even paler, his skin ashen. Grime streaked his chest. The hair on his legs and groin was stiff with dirt. Howell grimaced: the boy smelled like rotting meat.

He brushed matted hair from the thin face. "Jesus Christ, what have you been doing?" he murmured. Drugs? What drugs would make someone run naked through the snow? Wincing, Howell let the tangled locks slip from his hand.

The boy moaned and twisted his head. He bared his teeth, eyes still tightly shut, and cried softly. His hand drooped upon his chest, fingers falling open. In his palm lay a stone attached to a filthy string around his neck.

Howell crossed the room to a bay window. Here a window seat served as spare bed, fitted neatly into the embrasure. He opened a drawer beneath the seat and pulled out blankets, quickly smoothed the cushion and arranged pillows. Then he got towels and tried his best to dry the boy before wrapping him in a clean blanket and dragging him to the window. Grunting, he eased him onto the bed. He covered him first with a cotton comforter, then heaped on coarse woolen blankets until the boy snorted and turned onto his stomach. After a few minutes his breathing slowed. Howell sank into an armchair to watch him sleep.

From a white dream, Andrew moaned and thrashed, floundering through unyielding pastures that resolved into blankets tangled about his legs. He opened his eyes and lay very still, holding his breath in terror. The darkness held an awful secret. He whimpered as he tried to place it. Turning his head, he saw a shining patch above him, a pale moon in a cobalt sky. His eyes burned. Shrugging free of the comforter, he sat up. Through the window he glimpsed the forest, snowy fields blued by moonlight. Colors. He glanced down and, for the first time since autumn, saw his hands. Slowly he drew them to his throat until they touched the stone there. His fingers ached, and he flexed them until the soreness abated. New blood tingled in his palms. He sniffed tentatively: dust and stale wood smoke, his own sweat—and another's.

In an armchair slept an old man, mouth slightly ajar, his breathing so soft it scarcely stirred the air. At his feet lay a dog. It stared at Andrew and growled, a low ceaseless sound like humming bees.

"Hey," whispered the boy, his voice cracking. "Good dog."

The dog drew closer to the old man's feet. Andrew swung his legs over the bedside, gasping at the strain on forgotten muscles. As blankets slid to the floor, he noted, surprised, how the hair on his legs had grown thick and black.

Even without covers the room's warmth blanketed him, and he sighed with pleasure. Unsteadily, he crossed to a window, balancing himself with one hand against the wall. The snow had stopped. Through clouded glass he saw an untracked slope, a metal birdfeeder listing beneath its white dome. He reached for the talisman, remembering. Autumn days when he tugged wild grapes from brittle vines had given way to the long fat weeks of a winter without snow. Suddenly he wondered how long it had been—months? years?—and recalled his mother's words.

. . . they forgot . . . and stayed forever, and died up there in the woods . . .

Closing his eyes, he drew the amulet to his mouth and rubbed it against his lip, thinking, *Just for a little while, I could go again just for a little while . . .*

He had almost not come back. He shook his head, squeezing tears from shut eyes. Shuddering, he leaned forward until his forehead rested against the windowpane.

A house.

The talisman slipped from his hand to dangle around his neck once more. Andrew held his breath, listening. His heartbeat quickened from desire to fear.

Whose house?

Someone had brought him back. He faced the center of the room.

In the armchair slumped the old man, regarding Andrew with mild pale eyes. "Aren't you cold?" he croaked, and sat up. "I can get you a robe."

Embarrassed, Andrew sidled to the window seat and wrapped himself in the comforter, then hunched onto the mattress. "That's okay," he muttered, drawing his knees together. The words came out funny, and he repeated them, slowly.

Howell blinked, trying to clear his vision. "It's still night," he stated, and coughed. Festus whined, bumping against Howell's leg. The astronaut suddenly stared at Andrew more closely. "What the hell were you doing out there?"

Andrew shrugged. "Lost, I guess."

Howell snorted. "I guess so."

The boy waited for him to bring up parents, police; but the man only gazed at him thoughtfully. The man looked sick. Even in the dimness, Andrew made out lesions on his face and hands, the long skull taut with yellow skin.

"You here alone?" Andrew finally asked.

"The dog." Howell nudged the spaniel with his foot. "My dog, Festus. I'm Eugene Howell. Major Howell."

"Andrew," the boy said. A long silence before the man spoke again.

"You live here?"

"Yeah."

"Your parents live here?"

"No. They're dead. I mean, my mother just died. My father died a long time ago."

Howell rubbed his nose, squinting. "Well, you got someone you live with?"

"No. I live alone." He hesitated, then inclined his head toward the window. "In The Fallows."

"Huh." Howell peered at him more closely. "Were you—some kind of drugs? I found you out there—" He gestured at the window. "Butt naked. In a blizzard." He laughed hoarsely, then gazed point-edly at the boy. "I'm just curious, that's all. Stark naked in a snow-storm. Jesus Christ."

Andrew picked at a scab on his knee. "I'm not on drugs," he said at last. "I just got lost." Suddenly he looked up, beseeching. "I'll get out of your way. You don't have to do anything. Okay? Like you don't have to call anyone. I can just go back to my place."

Howell yawned and stood slowly. "Well, not tonight. When they clear the roads." He looked down at his feet, chagrined to see he still had his boots on. "I'm going to lie down for a little while. Still a few hours before morning."

He smiled wanly and shuffled toward the bedroom, Festus following him. In the kitchen he paused to get his inhaler, then stared with mild disbelief at the counter where an unopened sack of dog food and six cans of Alpo stood next to a half-filled grocery bag.

"Festus," he muttered, tearing open the sack. "I'll be damned. I forgot Pete brought this." He dumped food into the dog's bowl and glanced back at the boy staring puzzled into the kitchen.

"You can take a shower if you want," suggested Howell. "In there. Towels, a robe. Help yourself." Then he went to bed.

In the bathroom Andrew found bedpans, an empty oxygen tank, clean towels. He kicked his comforter outside the door, hesitated before retrieving it and folding it upon the sofa. Then he returned to the bathroom. Grimacing, he examined his reflection in the mirror. Dirt caked his pores. What might be scant stubble roughened his chin, but when he rubbed it, most came off onto his fingers in tiny black beads.

In the tub stood a white metal stool. Andrew settled on this and turned on the water. He squeezed handfuls of shampoo through his long hair until the water ran clear. Most of a bar of soap dissolved before be stepped out, the last of the hot water gurgling down the drain. On the door hung a thin green hospital robe, E. HOWELL printed on the collar in Magic Marker. Andrew flung this over his shoulders and stepped back into the living room.

Gray light flecked the windowpanes, enough light that finally he could explore the place. It was a small house, not much bigger than his abandoned cottage. Worn Navaho rugs covered flagstone floors in front of a stone fireplace, still heaped with dead ashes and the remains of a Christmas tree studded with blackened tinsel. Brass gaslight fixtures supported light bulbs and green glass shades. And everywhere about the room, pictures.

He could scarcely make out the cedar paneling beneath so many photographs. He crossed to the far wall stacked chest-high with tottering bookshelves. Above the shelves hung dozens of framed photos.

"Jeez." Andrew shivered a little as he tied the robe.

Photos of Earthrise, moonrise. The Crab Nebula. The moon. He edged along the wall, reading the captions beside the NASA logo on each print.

Mare Smythii. Crater Gambart. Crater Copernicus. Crater Descartes. Sea of Tranquillity.

At wall's end, beside the window, two heavy gold frames. The first held artwork from a *Time* magazine cover showing three helmeted men against a Peter Max galaxy: MEN OF THE YEAR: THE CREW OF APOLLO 18, printed in luminous letters. He blew dust from the glass and regarded the picture thoughtfully. Behind one of the men's faceplates, he recognized Howell's face.

The other frame held an oversized cover of *Look*, a matte photograph in stark black. In the upper corner floated the moon, pale and dreaming like an infant's face.

APOLLO 19: FAREWELL TO TRANQUILLITY.

Outside, the sun began to rise above Sugar Mountain. In the west glowed a three-quarter moon, fading as sunlight spilled down the mountainside. Andrew stood staring at it until his eyes ached, holding the moon there as long as he could. When it disappeared, he clambered back into bed.

When he woke later that morning, Andrew found Howell sitting in the same chair again, dozing with the dog Festus at his feet. Andrew straightened his robe and tried to slide quietly from bed. The dog barked. Howell blinked awake.

"Good morning," he yawned, and coughed. "The phone lines are down."

Andrew grinned with relief, then tried to look concerned. "How long before they're up again?"

Howell scratched his jaw, his nails rasping against white stubble. "Day or two, probably. You said you live alone?"

Andrew nodded, reaching gingerly to let Festus sniff his hand.

"So you don't need to call anyone." Howell rubbed the dog's back with a slippered foot. "He's usually pretty good with people," he said as Festus sniffed and then tentatively licked Andrew's hand. "That's good, Festus. You hungry—?"

He stumbled, forgetting the boy's name.

"Andrew," the boy said, scratching the dog's muzzle. "Good dog. Yeah, I guess I am."

Howell waved toward the kitchen. "Help yourself. My son brought over stuff the other day, on the counter in there. I don't eat much now." He coughed again and clutched the chair's arms until the coughing stopped. Andrew stood awkwardly in the center of the room.

"I have cancer," Howell said, fumbling in his robe's pockets until he found a pill bottle. Andrew stared a moment longer before going into the kitchen.

Inside the grocery bag he found wilted lettuce, several boxes of frozen dinners, now soft and damp, eggs and bread and a packet of spoiled hamburger meat. He sniffed this and his mouth watered, but when he opened the package the smell sickened him and he hastily tossed it into the trash. He settled on eggs, banging around until he found skillet and margarine. He ate them right out of the pan. After a hasty cleanup he returned to the living room.

"Help yourself to anything you want," said Howell. "I have clothes, too, if you want to get changed."

Andrew glanced down at his robe and shrugged. "Okay. Thanks." He wandered to the far wall and stared a moment at the photos again. "You're an astronaut," he said.

Howell nodded. "That's right."

"That must've been pretty cool." He pointed to the Men of the Year portrait. "Did you fly the shuttle?"

"Christ, no. That was after my time. We were Apollo. The moon missions."

Andrew remained by the wall, nodding absently. He wanted to leave, but how? He couldn't take off right away, leave this man wondering where he lived, how he'd get there in three feet of snow. He'd wait until tonight. Leave a note, the robe folded on a chair. He turned back to face Howell.

"That must've been interesting."

Howell stared at him blankly, then laughed. "Probably the most interesting thing *I* ever did," he gasped, choking as he grabbed his inhaler. Andrew watched alarmed as the astronaut sucked the mouthpiece. A faint acrid smell infused the room when Howell exhaled.

"Can't breathe," he whispered. Andrew stared at him and coughed nervously himself.

Howell sighed, the hissing of a broken bellows. "I wanted to go back. I was queued next time as commander." He tugged at the sleeves of his robe, pulling the cuffs over bony wrists. "They canceled it. The rest of the program. Like that." He tried to snap his fingers. They made a dry small sound. "Money. Then the rest. The explosion. You know."

Andrew nodded, rolling up his sleeves until they hung evenly. "I remember that."

Howell nodded. "Everybody does. But the moon. Do you remember that?"

Andrew shook his head.

"You forget it?" said Howell, incredulous.

"I wasn't born," said Andrew. He leaned against the wall, bumping a frame. "I'm only fourteen."

"Fourteen," repeated Howell. "And you never saw? In school, they never showed you?"

The boy shrugged. "The shuttle, I saw tapes of that. At school, maybe. I don't remember."

Howell stood, bumping the spaniel so that Festus grumbled noisily before settling back onto the floor. "Well, here then," he said, and shuffled to the bookcase. "I have it, here—"

He fingered impatiently through several small plastic cases until he found one with NASA's imprimatur. Fastidiously he wiped the plastic cover, blowing dust from the cracks before opening it and pawing the tape carefully.

In the corner a television perched on a shelf. Beneath it was a VCR, meticulously draped with a pillowcase. Howell removed the cloth, coughing with excitement. He switched the set on.

"Okay," he announced as the flickering test pattern resolved into the NASA logo. "Now sit back. You're going to see something. History."

"Right," said Andrew loudly, and rubbed his eyes.

Static. A black expanse: dead black, unbroken by stars. Then a curve intruding upon the lower edge of the screen, dirty gray and pocked with shadow.

The image shifted. Static snarled into a voice, crisply repeating numbers. A beep. Silence. Another beep. The left side of the screen now showed a dark mass, angular limbs scratching the sky.

"What's that?" asked Andrew. It was all out of focus, black and white, wavering like cheap animation.

"The lander," said Howell. "Lunar lander."

"Oh," said Andrew: the moon. "They're there already?"

Howell nodded impatiently. "Watch this."

The mass shuddered. The entire horizon dipped and righted itself. From a bright square within the lander something emerged clumsily like a tethered balloon, and descended the blurred pattern that must be steps. Andrew yawned, turning his head so the old man couldn't see. A voice answered commands. Garbled feedback abruptly silenced so that a single voice could be heard.

The figure bounced down, once, twice. The landscape bobbed with him. Andrew fidgeted, glancing at Howell. The old man's hands twisted in his lap as though strangling something, pulling at the hem of his robe. His eyes were riveted to the television. He was crying.

The boy quickly looked back at the screen. After another minute the tape ended. Angry hissing from the television. Andrew stood and turned down the volume, avoiding Howell's face.

"That's it, huh?" he remarked with hollow cheerfulness, hitting the rewind button.

Howell stared at him. "Did you see?"

Andrew sat back on his heels. "Yeah, sure. That's real interesting. The moon. Them landing on the moon."

"You never saw it before?"

He shook his head. "No. I like that stuff, though. Science fiction. You know."

"But this really happened."

Andrew nodded defensively. "I know. I mean, I don't remember, but I know it happened."

Howell coughed into a handkerchief, glaring at the boy. "Pretty boring to you, I guess." He stepped to the machine and removed the tape, shoving it back into its case. "No lights. Nothing exciting. Man lands on moon."

Embarrassed, Andrew stared at him. Howell returned his gaze fiercely, then sighed and rubbed the back of his neck.

"Who cares," he coughed; then looked suddenly, helplessly at the boy.

"That's all I ever wanted to do, you know. Fly. And walk on the moon."

"But you did. You went. You just told me." Andrew gestured at the walls, the photographs. "All this—" He hesitated. "*Stuff,* all this stuff you got here—"

Howell stroked the videotape, gnawed fingertips catching on its plastic lip, and shook his head, shameless of tears that fell now like a disappointed child's. Andrew stared, horrified, waiting for the old man to stop, to apologize. But he went on crying. Finally the boy stood and crossed the room, turned to shut the bathroom door behind him, ran the water so as not to hear or think of him out there: an old man with a dog at his ankles, rocking back and forth with an old videotape in his hand, heedless of the flickering empty screen before him.

Andrew made dinner that night, a couple of meals on plastic trays slid into the microwave. He ended up eating both of them.

"I'll bring in some wood tomorrow," he said, pausing in the kitchen doorway to hitch up his pants. Howell had insisted on him wearing something other than the old hospital robe. Andrew had rummaged around in a bureau until he found faded corduroy trousers and a flannel shirt, both too big for him. Even with the pants cuffed they flopped around his ankles, and he had to keep pushing back his sleeves as he ran the dinner plates under the tap. When he finished the dishes he poured Howell a glass of scotch and joined him in the other room. The old man sipped noisily as the two of them sat in front of the cold fireplace, Andrew pulling at his frayed shirt cuffs. In the kitchen he'd swallowed a mouthful of scotch when Howell wasn't looking. Now he wished he'd taken more.

"I could bring in some wood tonight, I guess," he said at last.

Howell shook his head. "Tomorrow'll be fine. I'll be going to bed soon anyway. I haven't had a fire here since Christmas. Peter built it." He gestured at the half-burned spruce. "As you can see. My son can't build a fire worth a tinker's damn."

Andrew pushed a long lock of hair from his eyes. "I don't know if I can either."

"That's okay. I'll teach you." Howell took another sip of scotch, placed the glass on the floor. Festus stood and flopped beside Andrew, mumbling contentedly. The boy scratched the dog's head. He wondered how soon Howell would go to sleep, and glanced at the back door before turning to the old man. In the dim light, Howell's cheeks glowed rosily, and he looked more like the man on the magazine cover. Andrew tugged at the dog's ears and leaned back in his chair.

"You got Man of the Year," he said at last.

"We all got Man of the Year. Peter was just a kid. Not impressed." Howell grimaced. "I guess it comes with the territory."

Andrew looked away. "I was impressed," he said after a moment. "I just didn't remember. They don't have any of that stuff now."

Howell nodded. For a few minutes they sat, the silence broken only by the battering of wind at the roof.

Then, "You're a runaway," said Howell.

Andrew stared fixedly at the dog at his feet. "Yeah."

Howell rubbed his chin. "Well, I guess that's not so bad. At least in Kamensic it's safe enough. You found one of the abandoned cabins down there."

Andrew sighed and locked his hands behind his head. "Yeah. We used to go there when I was a kid. My mother and I. Up until a few years ago." He tousled Festus's ears with elaborate casualness. "You gonna call the police?"

Howell peered at him. "Do you want me to?"

"No." The boy drew back his hand, and Festus yawned loudly. "There's no one to go to. My mom died last summer. She killed herself. My father died before I was born. Nobody cares."

"Nobody looked for you?"

Andrew shrugged. "Who's to look? My aunt, I guess. They have their own kids. I did okay."

Howell nodded. "Until the first snow." He coughed. "Well, you must be a damned resourceful kid, that's all I can say. I won't call the police. But I can't let you go back out there alone. It'll snow again, and I won't be around to find you."

Andrew shook his head. "Just leave me alone." He rubbed his

stinging eyes. "No one ever cared except her, and she—"

"That's okay," Howell said softly. He coughed again, then asked, "What happened to your father?"

"Dead. He disappeared one day. They never found him."

"The war?"

Andrew shook his head. "Up here—he was up here. Visiting. We had family. He—my mother said he died here in the woods." He stared at the floor, silent.

He wants to leave, thought Howell. In the dimness the boy looked very young. Howell recalled other nights, another boy. His heart ached so suddenly that he shuddered, gasping for breath. Andrew stood in alarm.

"Nothing—nothing—" Howell whispered, motioning him away. His head sank back onto his chest. After a few minutes he looked up. "Guess I'll go to bed now."

Andrew helped him into the bedroom. Not much bigger than the room in Andrew's abandoned cottage, but scrupulously neat, and almost all windows except for the wall behind the double bed. Howell slipped from his robe, leaving Andrew holding it awkwardly while the old man eased himself into bed, grunting from the effort.

"Just put it there—" Howell pointed to the door. Andrew hung the robe on a hook. He tried to avoid looking directly at Howell, but there was little else: the black windows, a bureau, a closet door. Above the bed a framed NASA photo of the moon. Andrew pretended interest in this and leaned over Howell to stare at it. In the white margin beneath the moon's gray curve someone had written in a calligraphic hand:

> Come on all you
> Lets get busy
> for the speedy trips
> to all Planets and
> back to earth again.

"Huh," said Andrew. Behind him, Festus shambled into the room and, grumbling, settled himself on a braided rug.

The old man winced, twisting to stare up at the photograph. "You like that?" he said.

"Sure," said Andrew, shrugging. "What's it mean? That poem or whatever. You write that?"

Howell smiled. He was so thin that it was hard to believe there was a body there beneath all the smooth quilts and blankets. "No, I didn't write that. I'll show you where it came from, though; tomorrow maybe. If you want. Remind me."

"Okay." Andrew waited: to see if Howell needed anything; to see if he would be dismissed. But the old man just lay there, eyes fluttering shut and then open again. Finally the boy said, "Good night," and left the room.

It took Andrew a long time to fall asleep that night. He sat on the window seat, staring out at the snow-covered fields as he fingered the amulet around his neck. He didn't know why he'd stayed this long. He should have left as soon as he could that morning, waited for the old man to fall asleep (he slept all day: he must be really sick, to sleep so much) and then crept out the back door and disappeared into the woods.

Even now . . . He pulled at the amulet, holding it so tightly it bit into the ball of his thumb. He should leave now.

But he didn't. The wrinkled white face staring up from the double bed reminded him of his mother in the coffin. He had never noticed how many lines were in her face; she really hadn't been that old. He wondered how long Howell had been sick. He remembered the astronaut he'd seen at the library that summer, a disappointment, really. Andrew had been expecting a spacesuit and something else: not ray guns, that would be dumb, but some kind of instruments, or moon rocks maybe. Instead there'd been an old man in Izod shirt and chinos talking about how the country had failed the space program. Andrew had fidgeted until his mother let him go outside.

It must have been the same man, he thought now. Major Howell, not really any more interesting now than he'd been then. He hadn't even walked on the moon. Andrew dropped the amulet onto his chest and pulled a blanket about his knees, stared out the window. Clouds drifted in front of the rising moon. At the edge of the woods there would be rabbit tracks, fox scat. A prickle of excitement ran through him at the thought, and he lay back upon the narrow bed. He would leave tomorrow, early, before Howell got up to let the dog out.

*   *   *

He didn't leave. He woke to Howell calling hoarsely from the bed-room. Andrew found him half-sitting on the side of the bed, his hand reaching pathetically for the nightstand where a glass of water had been knocked over, spilling pill bottles and inhalers and soggy tissues onto the floor.

"Could you—please—"

Andrew found Howell's inhaler and gave it to him. Then he straightened out the mess, put more water in the glass and watched as Howell took his pills, seven of them. He waited to see if Howell wanted anything else, then let Festus outside. When the boy returned to the bedroom, Howell was still sitting there, eyes shut as he breathed heavily through his nose. His eyes flickered open to stare at Andrew: a terrified expression that made the boy's heart tumble. But then he closed them again and just sat there.

Finally Andrew said, "I'll help you get dressed." Howell nodded without opening his eyes.

It didn't take Andrew long to help him into a flannel robe and slippers, and into the bathroom. Andrew swore silently and waited outside the door, listening to the groan of water in the taps, the old man's wheezing and shambling footsteps. Outside, Festus scratched at the back door and whined to be let in. Sighing, Andrew took care of the dog, went back to the bathroom and waited until Howell came out again.

"Thank you," the old man said. His voice was faint, and he trembled as he supported himself with one hand on the sink, the other against the door frame.

"It's okay, Major Howell," said Andrew. He took Howell's elbow and guided him into the living room. The old man was heavy, no matter that he was so thin; Andrew was terrified that he'd fall on the flagstone floor. "Here, sit here and I'll get you something. Break-fast?"

He made instant coffee and English muffins with scrambled eggs. The eggs were burned, but it didn't really matter: Howell took only a bite of the muffin and sipped at his tepid coffee. Andrew gave the rest to Festus. *He* would eat later, outside.

Afterward, as Howell sat dozing in the armchair by the fireplace,

Andrew made a fire. The room filled with smoke before he figured out how to open the damper, but after that it burned okay, and he brought in more wood. Then he took Festus outside for a walk. He wore Howell's parka and heavy black mittens with NASA stenciled on the cuffs. The sunlight on the snow made his eyes ache as he tried to see where Festus ran up the first slope of Sugar Mountain. He took off one glove, unzipped the neck of the parka and stuck his hand inside. The amulet was still there, safe against his chest. He stopped, hearing Festus crashing through the underbrush. Would the dog follow him? Probably not: he was an old dog, and Andrew knew how fast a fox could run, knew that even though he had never hunted this spot it would be easy to find his way to a safe haven.

Then the wind shifted, bringing with it the tang of wood smoke. Festus ambled out of the woods, shaking snow from his ears, and ran up to Andrew. The boy let the amulet drop back inside his flannel shirt and zipped up the parka. He turned and walked back to the house.

"Have a nice walk?" Howell's voice was still weak but his eyes shone brightly, and he smiled at the boy stomping the snow from boots too big for him.

"Oh, yeah, it was great." Andrew hung up the parka and snorted, then turning back to Howell tried to smile. "No, it was nice. Is all that your property back there?" He strode to the fireplace and crouched in front of it, feeding it twigs and another damp log.

"Just about all of it." Howell pulled a lap blanket up closer to his chin. "This side of Sugar Mountain and most of the lakefront."

"Wow." Andrew settled back, already sweating from the heat. "It's really nice back there by the lake. We used to go there in the summer, my mom and me. I love it up here."

Howell nodded. "I do, too. Did you live in the city?"

Andrew shook his head. "Yonkers. It sucks there now; like living in the Bronx." He opened the top button of his shirt and traced the string against his chest. "Once, when I was a kid, we heard an astronaut talk here. At the library. Was that you?"

Howell smiled. "Yup. I wondered if you might have been one of those kids, one of those times. So many kids, I must have talked to a thousand kids at the school here. You want to be an astronaut when you were little?"

"Nah." Andrew poked at the log, reached to pet Festus. "I never wanted to be anything, really. School's really boring, and like where I lived sucks, and . . ." He gestured at the fire, the room and the door leading outside. "The only thing I ever really liked was being up here, in the woods. Living in The Fallows this year, that was great."

"It's the only thing I liked, too. After I stopped working." Howell sighed and glanced over at the pictures covering the wall, the sagging bookcases. He had never really been good with kids. The times he had spoken at the school he'd had films to back him up, and later, videotapes and videodiscs. He had never been able to entertain his son here, or his friends, or the occasional visiting niece or nephew. The pictures were just pictures to them, not even colorful. The tapes were boring. When Peter and his friends were older, high school or college, sometimes Howell would show them the Nut File, a manila envelope crammed with letters from Rubber Man Lord of Jupiter and articles clipped from tabloids, a lifetime of NASA correspondence with cranks and earnest kooks who had developed faster-than-light drives in their garages. Peter and his friends had laughed at the letters, and Howell had laughed, too, reading them again. But none of his visitors had ever been touched, the way Howell had. None of them had ever wondered why a retired NASA astronaut would have a drawer full of letters from nuts.

"Andrew," he said softly; then, "Andrew," as loud as he could. The boy drew back guiltily from the fire. Festus started awake and stared up, alarmed.

"Sorry—"

Howell drew a clawed hand from beneath the blanket and waved it weakly. "No, no—that's all right—just . . ."

He coughed; it took him a minute to catch his breath. Andrew stood and waited next to him, staring back at the fire. "Okay, I'm okay now," Howell wheezed at last. "Just: remember last night? That picture with the poem?"

Andrew looked at him blankly.

"In my room—the moon, you wanted to know if I wrote it—"

The boy nodded. "Oh, yeah. The moon poem, right. Sure."

Howell smiled and pointed to the bookcase. "Well here, go look over there—"

Andrew watched him for a moment before turning to the bookcase and looking purposefully at the titles. Sighing, Festus moved closer to the old astronaut's feet. Howell stroked his back, regarding Andrew thoughtfully. He coughed, inclining his head toward the wall.

"Andrew." Howell took a long breath, then leaned forward, pointing. "That's it, there."

Beneath some magazines, Andrew found a narrow pamphlet bound with tape. "This?" he wondered. He removed it gingerly and blew dust from its cover.

Howell settled back in his chair. "Right. Bring it here. I want to show you something."

Andrew settled into the chair beside Howell. A paperbound notebook, gray with age. On the cover swirled meticulous writing in Greek characters, and beneath them the same hand, in English.

Return address:

Mr. Nicholas Margalis
116 Argau Dimitrou
Apt. No. 3
Salonika, Greece

"Read it," said Howell. "I found that in the NASA library. He sent it to Colonel Somebody right after the war. It floated around for forty years, sat in NASA's Nut File before I finally took it."

He paused. "I used to collect stuff like that. Letters from crackpots. People who thought they could fly. UFOs, moonmen. *Outer space.* I try to keep an open mind." He gestured at the little book in Andrew's hand. "I don't think anyone else has ever read that one. Go ahead."

Carefully Andrew opened the booklet. On lined paper tipsy block letters spelled PLANES, PLANETS, PLANS. Following this were pages of numerical equations, sketches, a crude drawing labeled THE AIR DIGGER ROCKET SHAPE.

"They're plans for a rocket ship," said Howell. He craned his neck so he could see.

"You're kidding." Andrew turned the brittle pages. "Did they build it?"

"Christ, no! I worked it out once. If you were to build the Margalis Planets Plane it would be seven miles long." He laughed silently.

Andrew turned to a page covered with zeros.

"Math," said Howell.

More calculations. Near the end Andrew read,

Forty years of continuous flying will cover the following space below, 40 years, 14,610 days, 216,000,000,000,000 × 14610—equals 3,155,750,000,000,000,000 miles. That is about the mean distance to the farthest of the Planets, Uranus.

Trillions, Quatrillions, Billions and Millions of miles all can be reached with this Plan.

Andrew shook his head. "This is so sad! He really thought it would fly?"

"They all thought they could fly," said Howell. "Read me the end."

"'Experimenting of thirty-five years with levers, and compounds of,'" read Andrew. "'I have had made a patent model of wooden material and proved a very successful work.

"'My Invention had been approved by every body in the last year 1944, 1946 in my native village Panorma, Crevens, Greece. Every body stated it will be a future great success in Mechanics.

"'Yours truly.'"

Andrew stopped abruptly.

"Go on," prodded Howell. "The end. The best part."

On the inside back cover, Andrew saw the same hand, somewhat shakier and in black ink.

I have written in these copy book about 1/1000 of what actually will take in building a real Rocket Shape Airo-Plane to make trips to the Planets.

There in the planets we will find Paradise, and the undiying water to drink so we never will die, and never be in distress.

Come on all you
Lets get busy
for the speedy trips
to all Planets and
back to earth again.

NICHOLAS S. MARGALIS
AUG 19 1946

Howell sat in silence. For a long moment Andrew stared at the manuscript, then glanced at the old man beside him. Howell was smiling now as he stared into the fire. As Andrew watched, his eyelids flickered, and then the old astronaut dozed, snoring softly along with the dog at his feet. Andrew waited. Howell did not wake. Finally the boy stood and poked at the glowing logs. When he turned back, the blanket had fallen from the old man's lap and onto the dog's back. Andrew picked it up and carefully draped it across Howell's knees.

For a moment he stood beside him. The old man smelled like carnations. Against his yellow skin broken capillaries bloomed blue and crimson. Andrew hesitated. Then he bowed his head until his lips grazed Howell's scalp. He turned away to replace the booklet on its shelf and went to bed.

That night the wind woke Howell. Cold gripped him as he sat up in bed, and his hand automatically reached for Festus. The dog was not beside him.

"Festus?" he called softly, then slid from bed, pulling on his robe and catching his breath before walking across the bedroom to the window.

A nearly full moon hung above the pine forest, dousing the snow so that it glowed silvery blue. Deer and rabbits had made tracks steeped in shadow at wood's edge. He stood gazing at the sky when a movement at the edge of the field caught him.

In the snow an animal jumped and rolled, its fur a fiery gleam against the whiteness. Howell gasped in delight: a fox, tossing the snow and crunching it between its black jaws. Then something else moved. The old man shook his head in disbelief.

"Festus."

Clumsily, sinking over his head in the drifts, the spaniel tumbled and rose beside the fox, the two of them playing in the moonlight. Clouds of white sparkled about them as the fox leaped gracefully to land beside the dog, rolling until it was only an auburn blur.

Howell held his breath, moving away from the window so that his shadow could not disturb them. Then he recalled the boy sleeping in the next room.

"Andrew," he whispered loudly, his hand against the wall to steady himself as he walked into the room. "Andrew, you have to see something."

The window seat was empty. The door leading outside swung open, banging against the wall in the frigid wind. Howell turned and walked toward the door, finally stopping and clinging to the frame as he stared outside.

In the snow lay a green hospital gown, blown several feet from the door. Bare footprints extended a few yards into the field. Howell followed them. Where the shadows of the house fell behind him, the footprints ended. Small pawprints marked the drifts, leading across the field to where the fox and dog played.

He lifted his head and stared at them. He saw where Festus's tracks ran off to the side of the house and then back to join the other's. As he watched, the animals abruptly stopped. Festus craned his head to look back at his master and then floundered joyfully through the drifts to meet him. Howell stepped forward. He stared from the tracks to the two animals, yelled in amazement and stood stark upright. Then stumbling he tried to run toward them. When Festus bounded against his knees the man staggered and fell. The world tilted from white to swirling darkness.

It was light when he came to. Beside him hunched the boy, his face red and tear streaked.

"Major Howell," he said. "Please—"

The old man sat up slowly, pulling the blankets around him. He stared for a moment at Andrew, then at the far door where the flagstones shone from melted snow.

"I saw it," he whispered. "What you did, I saw it."

Andrew shook his head. "Don't—You can't—"

Howell reached for his shoulder and squeezed it. "How does it work?"

Andrew stared at him, silent.

"How does it work?" Howell repeated excitedly. "How can you do it?"

The boy bit his lip. Howell's face was scarlet, his eyes feverishly bright. "I—it's this," Andrew said at last, pulling the amulet from his chest. "It was my mother's. I took it when she died."

His hands shaking, Howell gently took the stone between his fingers, rubbing the frayed string. "Magic," he said.

Andrew shivered despite the fire at his back. "It's from here. The Indians. The Tankiteke. There were lots, my mother said. Her grandfather found it when he was little. My father—" He ended brokenly.

Howell nodded in wonder. "It works," he said. "I saw it work."

Andrew swallowed and drew back a little, so that the amulet slipped from Howell's hand. "Like this," he explained, opening his mouth and slipping one finger beneath his tongue. "But you don't swallow it."

"I saw you," the old man repeated. "I saw you playing with my dog." He nodded at Festus, dozing in front of the fire. "Can you be anything?"

Andrew bit his lip before answering. "I think so. My mother said you just concentrate on it—on what you want. See—"

And he took it into his hand, held it out so that the firelight illuminated it. "It's like all these things in one. Look: it's got wings and horns and hooves."

"And that's how you hid from them." Howell slapped his knees. "No wonder they never found you."

Andrew nodded glumly.

"Well," Howell coughed. He sank back into the chair, eyes closed. He reached for Andrew, and the boy felt the old man's hand tighten about his own, cold and surprisingly strong. After a minute Howell opened his eyes. He looked from the flames to Andrew and held the boy's gaze for a long time, silent. Then,

"You could fly with something like that," he said. "You could fly again."

Andrew let his breath out in a long shudder. "That's right," he said finally beneath his breath. He turned away. "You could fly again, Major Howell."

Howell reached for the boy's hand again, his fingers clamping there like a metal hinge. "Thank you," he whispered. "I think I'll go to sleep now."

The following afternoon the plow came. Andrew heard it long before it reached Sugar Mountain, an eager roar like a great wave overtaking the snowbound bungalow. The phone was working, too; he heard Howell in the next room, talking between fits of coughing. A short time later a pickup bounced up the drive. Andrew stared in disbelief, then fled into the bathroom, locking the door behind him.

He heard several voices greeting Howell at the door, the thump of boots upon the flagstones.

"Thank you, Isaac," wheezed the astronaut. Andrew heard the others stomp into the kitchen. "I was out of everything." Andrew opened the door a crack and peered out, glaring at Festus when the dog scratched at it.

Howell motioned the visitors into the bedroom, shutting the door behind him. Andrew listened to their murmuring voices before storming back into the living room. He huddled out of sight on the window seat, staring outside until they left. After the pickup rattled back down the mountainside, he stalked into the kitchen to make dinner.

"I didn't tell them," Howell said mildly that evening as they sat before the fire.

Andrew glared at him but said nothing.

"They wouldn't be interested," Howell said. Every breath now shook him like a cold wind. "Andrew . . ."

The boy sat in silence, his hand tight around the amulet. Finally Howell stood, knocking over his glass of scotch. He started to bend to retrieve it when Andrew stopped him.

"No," he said hoarsely. "Not like that." He hesitated, then said, "You ever see a drunk dog?"

Howell stared at him, then nodded. "Yes."

"It's like that," said Andrew. "Only worse."

Festus followed them as they walked to the door, Andrew holding the old man's elbow. For a moment they hesitated. Then
Andrew shoved the door open, wincing at the icy wind that stirred
funnels of snow in the field.

"It's so cold," Howell whispered, shivering inside his flannel robe.

"It won't be so bad," said Andrew, helping him outside.

They stood in the field. Overhead the full moon bloomed as
Festus nosed after old footprints. Andrew stepped away from
Howell, then took the talisman from around his own neck.

"Like I told you," he said as he handed it to the old man.

Howell hesitated. "It'll work for me?"

Andrew clutched his arms, shivering. "I think so," he said, gazing at the amulet in the man's hand. "I think you can be whatever
you want."

Howell nodded and turned away. "Don't look," he whispered.

Andrew stared at his feet. A moment later the flannel robe blew
against his ankles. He heard a gasp and shut his eyes, willing away
the tears before opening them again.

In front of Andrew the air sparkled for an instant with eddies of
snow. Beside him, Festus whined, staring above his head. Andrew
looked up and saw a fluttering scrap like a leaf: a bat squeaking as
its wings beat feebly, then more powerfully, as if drawing strength
from the freezing wind. It circled the boy's head—once, twice—
then began to climb, higher and higher, until Andrew squinted to
see it in the moonlight.

"Major Howell!" he shouted. "Major Howell!"

To Howell the voice sounded like the clamor of vast and thundering bells. All the sky now sang to him as he flailed through the
air, rising above trees and roof and mountain. He heard the faint
buzzing of the stars, the sigh of snow in the trees fading as he flew
above the pines into the open sky.

And then he saw it: more vast than ever it had been from the
orbiter, so bright his eyes could not bear it. And the sound! like
the ocean, waves of air dashing against him, buffeting him as he
climbed, the roar and crash and peal of it as it pulled him upward.
His wings beat faster, the air sharp in his throat, thinning as the
darkness fell behind him and the noise swelled with the brightness,
light now everywhere, and sound, not silent or dead as they had

told him but thundering and burgeoning with heat, light, the vast eye opening like a volcano's core. His wings ceased beating and he drifted upward, all about him the glittering stars, the glorious clamor, the great and shining face of the moon, his moon at last: the moon.

Andrew spent the night pacing the little house, sitting for a few minutes on sofa or kitchen counter, avoiding the back door, avoiding the windows, avoiding Howell's bedroom. Festus followed him, whining. Finally, when the snow glimmered with first light, Andrew went outside to look for Howell.

It was Festus who found him after just a few minutes, in a shallow dell where ferns would grow in the spring and deer sleep on the bracken. Now snow had drifted where the old man lay. He was naked, and even from the lawn Andrew could tell he was dead. The boy turned and walked back to the house, got Howell's flannel robe and a blanket. He was shaking uncontrollably when he went back out.

Festus lay quietly beside the body, muzzle resting on his paws. Andrew couldn't move Howell to dress him: the body was rigid from the cold. So he gently placed the robe over the emaciated frame, tucked the blanket around him. Howell's eyes were closed now, and he had a quiet expression on his face. Not like Andrew's mother at all, really: except that one hand clutched something, a grimy bit of string trailing from it to twitch across the snow. Andrew knelt, shivering, and took one end of the string, tugged it. The amulet slid from Howell's hand.

Andrew stumbled to his feet and held it at arm's length, the little stone talisman twisting slowly. He looked up at the sky. In the west, above the cottage, the moon hung just above the horizon. Andrew turned to face the dark bulk of Sugar Mountain, its edges brightening where the sun was rising above Lake Muscanth. He pulled his arm back and threw the amulet as hard as he could into the woods. Festus raised his head to watch the boy. They both waited, listening; but there was no sound, nothing to show where it fell. Andrew wiped his hands on his pants and looked down at the astronaut again. He stooped and let the tip of one finger brush the old man's forehead. Then he went inside to call the police.

There were questions, and people from newspapers and TV, and Andrew's own family, overjoyed (he couldn't believe it, they all cried) to see him again. And eventually it was all straightened out.

There was a service at the old Congregational church in Kamensic Village near the museum. After the first thaw they buried Howell in the small local cemetery, beside the farmers and Revolutionary War dead. A codicil to his will left the dog Festus to the fourteen-year-old runaway discovered to have been living with the dying astronaut in his last days. The codicil forbade sale of the bungalow and Sugar Mountain, the property to revert to the boy upon his twentieth birthday. Howell's son protested this: Sugar Mountain was worth a fortune now, the land approved for subdivisions with two-acre zoning. But the court found the will to be valid, witnessed as it was by Isaac and Seymour Schelling, village grocers and public notaries.

When he finished school, Andrew moved into the cottage at Sugar Mountain. Festus was gone by then, buried where the deer still come to sleep in the bracken. There is another dog now, a youngish English cocker spaniel named Apollo. The ancient Volkswagen continues to rust in the driveway, next to a Volvo with plates that read NASA NYC. The plows and phone company attend to the cottage somewhat more reliably, and there is a second phone line as well, since Andrew needs to transmit things to the city and Washington nearly every day now, snow or not.

In summer he walks with the dog along the sleepy dirt road, marking where an owl has killed a vole, where vulpine tracks have been left in the soft mud by Lake Muscanth. And every June he visits the elementary school and shows the fifth graders a videotape from his private collection: views of the moon's surface filmed by Command Module Pilot Eugene Howell.

AUTHOR'S NOTE: Nicholas Margalis's manuscript is in the archives of the National Air & Space Museum, Smithsonian Institution.

In memory of Nancy Malawista and Brian Hart

This is probably the story I love most of all my short works. It received my favorite rejection letter of all time: the editor of *Weird Tales* turned it down because he found it "bizarre." *Wow,* I thought, I've written something that's too weird for *Weird Tales.*

Kamensic Village is the fictionalized version of the small town where I grew up in northern Westchester County; I first started writing stories set there when I was in high school. For a few years in college I worked off and on as a home health aide, and in 1977, when I was nineteen, I spent a week in that small town living with a woman who was dying of cancer. Her cottage became the dying astronaut's refuge on Sugar Mountain (and her dog, Apollo, became Festus). A few years later, the death of someone I knew triggered what has become a continuing struggle to understand suicide. "Snow on Sugar Mountain" was my first attempt to put this into writing (subsequent efforts include "Last Summer at Mars Hill" and most of my novels). It also hints at my lifelong secret love affair with the American space program. I discovered Nicholas Margalis's notebook when I was working at NASA; it was squirreled away in what the Records Management Division technically termed "The Nut Files." I cried when I read the notebook, and still keep a xeroxed copy on my desk. The original remains at the Smithsonian.

On the Town Route

I met the bearded lady the first day I rode with Cass on the town route. That sweltering afternoon I sprawled across my mattress on the floor. A few inches from my nose lay the crumpled notice of the revocation of my scholarship. Beside it a less formally worded letter indicated that in light of my recent lack of interest in the doings of The Fertile Mind Bookstore, my services there would no longer be needed, and would I please return the *Defries Incunabula* I had "borrowed" for my thesis immediately? From downstairs thumped the persistent bass line of the house band's demo tape. Then another, more insistent thudding began outside my room. I moaned and pulled my pillow onto my head. I ignored the pounding on the door, finally pretended to be asleep as Cass let himself in.

"Time to wake up," he announced, kneeling beside the mattress and sliding a popsicle down my back. "Time to go on the ice cream truck."

I moaned and burrowed deeper into the bed. "Ow—that hurts—"

"It's ice cream, Julie. It's supposed to hurt." Cass dug the popsicle into the nape of my neck, dripping pink ice and licking it from my skin between whispers. "Snap out of it, Jules. You been in here two whole weeks. Natalie at the bookstore's worried."

"Natalie at the bookstore fired me." I reached for a cigarette and twisted to face the window. "You better go, Cass. I have work to do."

"Huh." He bent to flick at the scholarship notice, glanced at yet another sordid billet: UNDERGRADUATE ACADEMIC SUSPENSION in bold red characters. Beneath them a humorlessly detailed list of transgressions. "You're not working on your thesis. You're not doing *anything*. You got to get out of here, Julie. You promised. You said you'd come with me on the truck and you haven't gone once since I started." He stalked to the door, kicking at a drift of unpaid bills, uncashed checks, unopened letters from my parents, unreturned phone messages from Cass Tyrone. "You don't come today, Julie, that's it. No more ice cream."

"No more Bomb Pops?" I asked plaintively.

"Nope." He sidled across the hall, idly nudging a beer bottle down the steps.

"No more Chump Bars?"

"Forget it. And no Sno-Cones, either. I'll save 'em for Little Eva." Reaching into his knapsack, he tossed me another popsicle and waited. I unpeeled it and licked it thoughtfully, applying it to my aching forehead. Then I stood up.

"Okay. I'm coming."

Outside, on the house's crumbling brick, someone had spray-painted *Dog Is Glove* and *You Are What You Smell*, along with some enthusiastic criticism of the house band written by Cass himself. A few steps farther and the truck stood in a vacant parking lot glittering with squashed beer cans and shattered bottles. Before I could climb in, Cass made me walk with him around the rusted machine. He patted the flaking metal signs and kicked the tires appraisingly. The truck settled ominously into the gravel at this attention and Cass sighed. "Damn. Hope we don't get another flat your first time out."

Once it had been a Good Humor truck. Ghostly letters still glowed balefully above a phantom ice cream bar, since painted over with the slogan *Jolly Times*. One side of the cab was plastered with ancient decals displaying mottled eclairs twisted into weird shapes and faded, poisonous colors. I grimaced, then clambered in after Cass.

As the engine wheezed, the ancient cab rattled like a box of marbles, empty pop bottles and freezer cartons rolling underfoot as I tried to clear a place to lean against the freezer. Cass lit a cigarette, dropping the match into a grape puddle.

"You ready?" he shouted, and the truck lurched forward. I braced myself against the freezer lid, my hands sticking to the cool metal. Cass glanced back and apologized. "Sorry about that. Left a Chump Bar there last night. First stop's Tandy Court."

The truck hurtled through the university town of Zion, past the college lawn and the student ghettos, past tiny churches where clots of the faithful stirred listlessly on brown lawns, fanning themselves with Sunday bulletins. Cass and I sucked popsicles to cool off, the sticks piling on the floor between us like chicken bones at a barbecue. Above the dashboard dangled a string of rusty bells. Occasionally Cass tugged at an old gray shoelace to ring them, frowning at the wan metallic gargle. He hunched over the steering column, like a rodeo clown clinging to that great ugly hulk. Then he whooped, jangled the bells, and gunned the motor.

The road narrowed to a silvery track stretching before us, churches and homes falling away as we left the town limits. About us began the slow steady erosion of village into farmland, farmland into open country, the furrows of plowed fields plunging into the ravines and ancient hollows of the Blue Ridge. We turned off the highway, bouncing across train tracks. I breathed the cloudy sweet scents of anthracite and honeysuckle and laughed, suddenly elated.

Below us perched a dozen trailer homes, strewn among stands of poplar and red oak like a doll village sprung from a sandbox. Old pickups and junked Chevys rusted side by side like Tonka Toys. The truck crept gingerly between ruts and boulders until we reached a little midden where an inflated Yogi Bear hung from a broom handle, revolving lazily in the breeze.

Cass shook his head, bemused. "Lot of toys on this route." He pointed to a shiny new trailer shell, its brown pocket of lawn vivid with red plastic tulips and spinning whirligigs. In the trailer's windows huddled small figures, brown and green and pink, staring out with shiny black eyes. More toys peered from other trailers as we crept by, rag dolls and inchworms abandoned in back lots. Only the pickups and motorcycles parked between Big Wheel bikes hinted that there might be adults somewhere.

"So where are all the kids?" I demanded, unwrapping a Neapolitan sandwich.

Cass halted the truck in a cul-de-sac. "Watch this."

The bells jingled, echoing against the mountainside until the hollow chimed. Silence, except for distant birdsong.

Then another sound began, a clamorous tide of screen doors slamming open and shut, door after door creaking, booming, hissing closed. Drawers banged, coins jingled. And the children came, big ones dragging smaller ones, toddlers dragging dolls, galloping dogs and kittens scampering beneath the stalled truck. Cass fell into his seat, grinning. "Ready to sell some ice cream?" He threw open the freezer drawers, nodding to the group outside.

"Here's the three Kims," he commented, hefting an unopened carton. Three girls in cut-offs and T-shirts squirmed to the side of the truck, eyeing me warily.

"Hi," whispered the prettiest girl, staring at Cass boldly enough to belie her soft voice. "Give me a ee-clair."

Cass winked as he reached into the freezer. "Eclair? That's a new one. Anything for your momma?"

She shook her head, clinked down two quarters and slipped away.

"What about you, Kim?" asked Cass. "Same thing?"

"Kim*berly*," lisped the second girl. She had protruding front teeth and a true harelip, her split upper lip glowing pink and wet as bubblegum when she smiled. "Fudgesicle."

He handed her a fudgesicle, and then the remaining children piled forward, yelling requests as I dredged ice cream from the freezer, frost billowing around me like steam. After the last child darted off, Cass wheeled the truck around and we plunged back up the road.

From one side of the mountain to the other I watched the same scene, an endless procession of children unwinding beneath the blinding sun. I felt sick from too many cigarettes and ice cream bars. My eyes ached; the landscape looked flat and bright, overexposed, the streams of children a timelapsed film: first the tiniest boys and girls, grinning and dirty as if freshly pulled from a garden.

Then their older brothers and sisters, feral creatures with slanted eyes yellowed in the sunlight, bare arms and legs sleek and golden as perch. Girls just past puberty, one with her mother's bra flapping loosely around her thin chest. An occasional boy, rude and bashful, a wad of chewing tobacco plumping his cheek. And finally another baby stumbling to the truck behind a mother ungraced by a gold ring, the two of them leaving naked footprints in the road.

"Wild girls," Cass said softly as we watched them run from the truck, to swing over fences or perch there for an instant, staring back at us with glittering eyes. "Like dragonflies," he murmured. I saw them as he did, shining creatures darting between the pines. A flicker in the trees and they were gone, their pretty husks crumbled in the sun.

Farther up and farther in we drove. The houses grew older, more scattered. There were no more telephone poles. The truck scaled tortuous roads so narrow I wondered how we'd get back down after dark. I stood beside the driver's seat, balancing myself so that I could watch the sun dance in and out of the distant mountaintops. In front of me Cass fidgeted in his seat, chainsmoking.

"Count and see if we got enough for a case of beer when we get back," he yelled over the droning motor.

My hands were stained in minutes, counting streaked pennies and quarters sticky with tar and gum and more lint than I cared to think about. I felt rather than saw the difference in one coin, so heavy I thought at first it was a silver dollar.

"What's this?"

I tossed it gingerly into my other hand, extending it to Cass. The face was worn to a dull moon, but letters still caught the afternoon light and flashed as Cass took it from me. "Look: it's not even in English."

He shut one eye and regarded it appraisingly. "Another one? She gives me those sometimes. It's real silver."

I took it back, weighed it in my fist. "They worth anything?"

"Worth their weight in silver," Cass replied brusquely, and he reddened. "I told Sam. But he wouldn't take 'em back," he added defensively. He bent to trace the characters on the coin with one finger. "They're Greek. And they're real, real old. I bring them to the stamp shop in Zion and the guy there gives me twenty bucks apiece. You can keep that one. I haven't seen any for awhile."

"I bet they're worth more than twenty bucks," I said, but Cass only shrugged.

"Not in Zion. And up here they're only worth fifty cents." And laughing he lit a cigarette.

"We're almost at the bearded lady's," he announced. "You'll meet Sam there. That's always my last stop. I found her place by mistake," he went on, pounding the dashboard for emphasis. "We're not even supposed to go *down* this road."

He pointed his cigarette at the dusty track winding before us, so narrow that branches poked through the windows, raking my arms as the truck crept down the hill.

"No one lives here. Just the kids, they're always around. Come to play with Little Eva. But I never see anyone in these houses," he mused, slowing the truck as it drifted past two dilapidated cottages, caved in upon themselves like an old man's gums. Cass yanked on the shoelace and the bells rang faintly.

From the shadowy verdure appeared a tiny white house, stark and precise as a child's drawing chalked against the woodlands. Here the dirt road straightened and the hill ended, as if too exhausted to go on. The truck, too, grated to a stop.

Behind the house stretched woods and fallow farmland, ochre clay, yellow flax fading into the silvery horizon where a distant silo wavered in the heat like a melting candle. From an unseen bog droned the resolute thud of a croaking bullfrog, the splash of a heron highstepping through the marsh. Shrill tuneless singing wafted from inside the house.

A kitten lay panting beneath the worn floorboards of a little porch, ignoring a white cabbage butterfly feebly beating its wings in the scant shade. The singing stopped abruptly and I heard a radio's blare.

"Watch," Cass whispered. He lit another cigarette and rang the bells. The kitten sprang from beneath the porch, craning to watch the front door.

One moment the doorway was black. The next a girl stood there, her hair a spiky orange nimbus flared about a white face. Barefoot, a dirty white nightgown flapping around legs golden with dust and feet stained brick red from the clay. She smiled and jigged up and down on her heels, glancing back at the house. The kitten ran to her, cuffing her ankle—I could have circled one of those ankles with my thumb and forefinger and slid a pencil between. Her thin arm lashed out and grabbed the kitten by its nape, dangling it absently like a pocketbook.

"Hi," called Cass, blowing a smoke ring out the window. "Little Eva."

The girl beamed, stepping towards the road, then stopped to squint back at the doorway. "She's real shy," Cass muttered. "Hey, Eva—"

He flourished a green and yellow popsicle shaped like a daisy. "I saved this for you. The three Kims wanted it but I told 'em, no way, this one's for Little Eva."

Giggling, she shuffled down the dirt walk, her feet slipping between paving stones and broken glass. I smiled, nodding reassuringly as she took the popsicle and squatted beside Cass on the truck's metal side-steps. He opened a can of grape pop and drained it in one pull, then tossed the empty into the back of the truck. "Where's your mom, Eva?"

"Right there." She pointed with her ice pop, dropping and retrieving it from the dirt in one motion. The kitten scrambled from her arms and disappeared in the jewelweed.

From the shadows of the doorway stepped a woman, small and fat as a bobwhite, wearing a baggy blue shift like a hospital gown. Long greasy hair was bunched in a clumsy ball at the back of her neck; long black hairs plastered her forehead. From her chin curled thick tufts of black hair, coarse as a billy goat's beard. A pair of glasses pinched her snub nose, thick-lensed glasses with cheap black plastic frames—standard county issue. Behind the grimy lenses her eyes glinted pale cloudy yellow. When she spoke, her voice creaked like burlap sacking and her head bobbed back and forth like a snake's. It was a whole minute before I realized she was blind.

"Little Eva," she yelled, her twang thick and muddy as a creek bottom. "Who's it?"

"Ice cream man," drawled Eva, and she poked her popsicle into the woman's hand. "He give me this. Get money from Sam."

Cass nodded slowly. "It's Cass Tyrone, Maidie." He thumped a heavy carton on the side of the truck. "I got you a box of eclairs here. That what you want?"

Her hands groped along the side of the truck, pouncing on the frost-rimed box. "Sam," she shrilled. "Ice cream man."

Someone else shuffled onto the porch then, wiping his hands on the front of a filthy union suit. Much older than Maidie, he wore only those greasy coveralls and a crudely drawn tattoo. He took very small steps to the edge of the porch—such small steps that I glanced down at his feet. Bare feet, grub white and hardly bigger than Little Eva's.

How he walked on those feet was a mystery. He was very fat, although there was something deflated about his girth, as though the weight had somewhere slipped from him, leaving soft folds and ripples of slack papery skin. His head and neck looked as though they'd been piped from pastry cream, ornate folds and dimples of white flesh nearly hiding his features. Even his tattoo was blurred and softened by time, as though it had shrunk with him, like the image on a deflated balloon. I turned my head to keep from laughing nervously. But the old man turned his head as well, so that I stared into a pair of vivid garter-blue eyes fringed with lashes black as beetles. I coughed, embarrassed. He smiled at me and I drew back, my skin prickling.

Such a beautiful smile! Perfect white teeth and lips a little too red, as though he'd been eating some overripe fruit. I thought of Ingrid Bergman—that serene glow, those liquid eyes with their black lashes fluttering beneath a shock of grimy white hair. He was irresistible. Shyly I smiled back, and in a very soft voice he said, "Hello, Ice Cream."

He was the ugliest man I had ever seen.

Cass nudged me, explaining, "That's what he calls me. 'Ice Cream.' Like you call a blacksmith Smith, or a gardener Gardner." I nodded doubtfully, but Sam smiled, tilting his head to Little Eva as he bent to tug her gently by the ear.

"You want a cigarette, Sam?" drawled Cass, handing him an Old Gold. Sam took it without a word.

"That's my girl, Sam." Cass sighed mournfully. "Julie Dean: she's awful mean. Maidie, that's my girl."

The bearded lady wagged her head, then thumped her hand on

the side of the truck, palm up, until I stuck my own hand out the window. She grabbed it and nearly yanked me out into the road.

"Maidie," I said loudly, wincing as I heard my fingers crackle in her grip. "I'm Julie."

She shook her head, staring eagerly at the roof of the truck. "I knowed all about you. He told me. He got this girl . . ." Her voice ebbed and she turned to Sam, wildly brandishing her box of eclairs as she shouted, "Take 'em, Sam! That Ice Cream's girl?"

Sam smiled apologetically as he enfolded the box in one great soft paw. "I don't know, Maidie," he told her, then whispered to me, "She don't see much people." He spoke so slowly, so gently, that I wondered if he was dim-witted; if he'd ever been off the mountain. Ice Cream," he murmured, and reached to stroke my hand. "Ice Cream, this your girl?"

Cass grabbed me, shaking me until my hair flew loose from my bandana and my jaw rattled. "This is her. The one and only. What you think, Sam?"

Sam stared at me. I saw a light flare and fade in his iris: the pupils pulsed like a pair of flexing black wings, then shrank to tiny points once more. I shrugged, then nodded uneasily.

"Julie," he whispered. "You his girl?"

I shook my head, stammering, and shrank from the window.

"Julie Dean. I'll remember," whispered Sam. He slid his hand over mine, his skin smooth and dry and cool as glass. "You know, Ice Cream is awful good to us."

"I thought everybody hated the ice cream man," I remarked, grinning.

Sam shook his head, shocked. "We *love* ice cream."

Cass grinned. "Hear that? They love me. Right, Maidie? Right, Eva?"

Maidie giggled sharply, tilting her head so that I saw the moles clustered beneath her chin, buried like dark thumbprints in that fleshy dewlap where the hairs grew thickest. I shuddered, thinking of cancers, those dark little fingers tickling her throat in the middle of the night. Little Eva laughed with her mother, clutching the truck's fender.

"Ice Cream!" she shrieked. "Give me ice cream!"

Cass beamed and scooped another popsicle from the freezer,

tossing it to her like a bear slapping a trout to shore. The kitten flashed from the grass, tumbling the pop in mid-air so it fell at Maidie's feet.

"I'll be by tomorrow," Cass called to Sam, and he started back into the truck. "You catch me then."

"I got money," Sam muttered. He wriggled his hand into a pocket, then opened his palm to display a handful of tarnished coins, age-blackened and feathered with verdigris. Cass scrutinized the coins, finally picked out three. Eva giggled, baring a mouthful of green-iced teeth.

"Okay," he said. "But I got to go now. Kiss, Little Eva?"

She fled tittering to the porch, pausing to spin and wave like one of those plastic whirligigs, bobbing goodbye before she skipped indoors. Cass started the truck and waved.

"So long, Maidie, Sam. Anything special tomorrow?"

Maidie yelled, "Eclairs," then waddled back to the porch. For another minute Sam lingered, stroking the rusted metal of the truck's headlights. "You'll be back?" he finally asked.

"Sure, Sam," Cass shouted above the motor. "Tomorrow."

Sam nodded, lifting his hand and opening it a single time in measured farewell. "Tomorrow," he repeated, and stepped back from the cloud of dirt and grass that erupted behind us. A minute later and they were gone from sight, hidden behind the oaks and serpentine road. Cass grinned like a dog, twisting in his seat to face me. "What'd you think?"

I lit a cigarette, staring at the fields streaming red and gold in the twilight, the tumbledown walls and rotting fenceposts. I waited a long time before answering him, and then I only said, "I thought it was sad," and tossed my cigarette across the road.

"Sad?" said Cass, puzzled. "You thought Little Eva was sad?"

"Christ, they're so poor. Like they haven't had a real meal in months."

"Sad?" he repeated. "Sad?" And he stomped the gas pedal. "I thought they'd make you happy."

"Cass!" I shook my head, kicking at an empty beer bottle. "You're *feeding* them."

"I don't give them anything," he protested. "They buy that ice cream."

"Cass, I saw you give him a box of eclairs."

He shook his head violently, jerking the wheel from side to side. "He bought that, Julie. He paid for it."

"Fifty cents for ten bucks worth of eclairs."

"What are you saying? Just what are you saying?" Cass demanded. "I sold him that ice cream." His face glowed bright pink, the stubble on his face a crimson fuzz. I hunched back against the freezer and looked away stubbornly.

"Look, Cass, I don't care what you do with your money—"

"Shut up. Just shut up. What the hell do you know? They don't need that ice cream. They *love* it. That's why I go there. Not like—" He stopped, furious, switching the radio on and then off again.

We rode in silence. It grew darker as we traced our way back down again. Night leaked like black water to fill the rims and ridges of the mountains. The first stars gleamed as the trees began to bow before a cool rising wind. I reached over to roll up the window, as much to shut out the night itself as the chill air; but the handle was broken. I rubbed my arms and wished I'd brought a sweater. Silently Cass groped beneath his seat with one hand, then tossed me a dirty sweatshirt. I pulled it on gratefully and leaned forward to kiss him.

"Am I your girl? Is that what you tell them?"

He shrugged and shifted gears. He drove with his face pressed right up to the gritty windshield, shoving his glasses against the bridge of his nose as if that might make his eyes strong enough to pierce the dark tunnel of pine and shivering aspen. "Damn," he muttered. "This place gets dark."

I nodded, huddling into his sweatshirt as I peered into the night. It was like day was something that could be peeled away, and now the black core of the mountain, the pith and marrow of it, throbbed here. I saw averted eyes, heard wings and the rustle of pokeweed where something loped alongside us for a few yards before veering off into the bracken. I stuck my head out the window and saw reflected in the scarlet taillights a fox, one black foreleg raised as he watched us pass.

Then came a long stretch where the road flattened out and stretched before us like a solid shaft of darkness flying into the heart of the country. Overhead, branches linked and flowers dangled against the windshield, laving us in their dreamy scent. Cass cut back the engine and the truck glided down this gentle slope, headlights guttering on rabbits that did not run, but stopped to regard us with gooseberry eyes from the roadside. I yawned and let my arms droop out the window.

"Poison ivy," warned Cass; but he did the same thing, sparks from his cigarette singeing sphinx moths and lacewings. Great white blossoms belled from the trees and I reached to grab a handful of flowers, yanking them through the window until the branch snapped and showered us with pollen and dew.

"Look," I gasped, breathless from the cold spray. "What are they?"

Cass poked sagely at his glasses, leaning over to inhale.

"Moonflowers," he announced.

"Really?" I lifted my face and shook the branch, spattering more dew on my sunburned cheeks. "They smell like heaven."

"Nah. I don't know what they are, really. White things—asphodel, moonflowers," he finished, yawning. "They do smell like—"

He choked on the word, twisting the wheel sharply. "Sweet Jesus . . ."

In the road before us crouched a child, her eyes incandescent in the highbeams. I shouted and lunged for the wheel, tearing it from Cass's hands. With a shearing sound the wheel spun free and the truck plowed forward.

There was no way we could avoid hitting her. The soft thump was almost a relief, the gentle slap of a great wave against a dinghy. The truck shuddered to a stop and Cass groaned, knocking me aside as he staggered through the door to land on his knees in the dirt. I followed and collapsed beside him.

She was dead, of course. A vivid russet bruise smeared her face from neck to shoulder, staining her torn T-shirt. At first I didn't recognize the face beneath the speckled dirt and blood. Then I noticed the tiny pink cleft above her teeth, the blood pooling there to trickle into her mouth. Cass dabbed at her chin with his shirt sleeve, halted and began to cry. His keening rose higher and higher until I covered my ears against his screams, too stunned to calm him. I didn't think to go for help. We knelt there a long time, and I dully brushed away the insects that landed on the child's face.

Behind us something moved. A silhouette cut off the headlights' beam. I stared at my hand splayed against the girl's clenched fist, afraid to turn and face the figure standing in the light. Instead I waited for the cry that would drown out Cass's voice: mother, father, searching sister.

But the voice was laconic, dull as dust. "What you crying for?"

I lifted my head and saw Maidie feeling her way along the front of the truck, balancing clumsily by grabbing the grill above one headlight. Cass stared at her and choked, clutching wildly at my knee. "She can't see," he gasped, and suddenly pushed at the girl's body. "Julie—"

Maidie stood in front of the truck, her blue shift glowing in the backlight. I stammered loudly, "Maidie—we got trouble—Kimberly— we hit her."

She stumbled towards us, smacking the grill and kicking violently at stones in her path. A rock bounded against the child's forehead and Cass gagged, drawing closer to me. I rose to my knees and reached to halt the blind woman.

"Maidie. You better go back . . ."

Then she was on her knees beside us, groping in the dirt until she grasped the crushed shoulder, the head lolling like an overripe peach. "Hurt that pore old head," she laughed, and her yellow eyes rolled behind glinting lenses. "Bang."

I drew back in disgust, then squeezed Cass's hand as I stood. "Don't leave," I warned him. "I'm getting help."

Maidie leaned over the child, brushing the girl's hair from her forehead. "Poor old head," she chortled. Then she spat on her fingers and rubbed the dirt from the girl's mouth, all the while staring blankly into the glaring headlights.

For a moment I hesitated, watching the gleam of light on her beard, the flash of her glasses like two bright coins. Then I turned to leave. Where the circle of light ended I paused, blinking as I tried to see where the road twisted. Behind me Cass hissed and Maidie giggled, the two sounds like a bird's call. I glanced back once again.

Between Cass and the bearded woman the child stirred, thrashing at the ground until she heaved herself upright to stare at them sleepy-eyed. She shook her head so that her hair shone in a blur of dust, the face beneath that mane a sticky mess of blood and dirt.

Then she stuck her finger in her mouth, blinking in the painful light, and asked doubtfully, "You the ice cream man?"

Cass nodded, dazed, pulled his glasses from his nose, put them back, stared from Maidie to the child once more. Then he laughed, hooting until the mountain rang, and I heard an owl's mournful reply. "Jesus, you scared me! Kim, you all right?"

"Kimberly," she murmured, rubbing her shoulder. She glanced at her bloody hand and wiped it on her shorts. "I sure fell," she said. "Can I have a Sno-Cone?"

Cass staggered to his feet and sprinted to the truck. From inside he tossed Sno-Cones, eclairs, a frozen Moon-Pie. A can of pop exploded on the ground in a cherry mist and he stopped, seeing me for the first time. He ran his hands through his hair. "Sno-Cone," he repeated.

"I just want an e-clair," Maidie called petulantly, and she pounded the road with her palm. "We got to get back, Kimberly." She lumbered to her feet and hobbled to the truck, the girl beside her scratching. Cass stepped down and put a Sno-Cone in each small hand, turned and handed Maidie an eclair. The bearded lady grabbed Kimberly by the neck and pushed her impatiently. "Take me home," she rasped, and Kimberly started to walk up the road, limping slightly. Maidie kicked the stones from her path as they plodded past me, trailing melting ice cream. At the edge of light they disappeared from view, the soft uneven pad of their feet fading into the pines.

From the doorway Cass squinted after them, and I stared at him, both of us silent. Cass trembled so that the cigarette he lit flew off into the darkness like a firefly. In the road melted a dozen Sno-Cones and eclairs, pooling white and red and brown in the clay. I stepped towards the truck and knelt to inspect a slender rillet of blood. Already tiny spiders skated across the black surface and moths lit there to rest their wings, uncoiling dark tongues to feed. With one finger I touched the sticky surface and raised my hand to the light.

There was too much blood. She had not been breathing. The right side of her face had paled to the color of lilacs, and I had glimpsed the rim of bone beneath her cheek, the broken lip spilling blood into the earth. Now behind me two sets of footprints marked the mountain road, and I could hear a woman's distant voice, a child's faint reply. I wiped the blood from my finger, and slowly returned to the truck to help Cass up the steps. Gently I eased him onto the freezer, pushing his shoulders until he sat there quietly. Then I settled myself beside the wheel. I started the engine, tentatively pressing pedals until the truck heaved forward, and drove crouched at the edge of the seat, squinting into the halo of light that preceded us. Behind me Cass toyed with his glasses, dropping them once and retrieving them from the floor. I saw him reflected in the truck's mirror like a trick of the light, his eyes fixed upon the passing hollows, the dark and tossing trees that hid from us a wonder.

After that I rode with Cass every morning on the town route. And as each afternoon struggled to its melancholy peak we'd start for the bearded lady's house. Sometimes we'd take one or two of the children with us, Kimberly and June Bug flanking me atop the freezer or playing with the radio dials. But usually we'd just find them all waiting for us when we arrived, racing through the tall grass behind Eva: Little Eva always running, running to hug Cass's knees and slip slyly past me when I stooped to greet her. Cass would bring a six-pack of True Blue Beer, and we'd squat beside Sam on the flimsy back porch, drinking and watching the children play.

The months marched past slowly. Our afternoons lingered into evenings when we took our cue from the hoarse voices of mothers hailing their children home. One night we stayed until moonrise, waving goodbye to the children as they took their hidden paths through the pinegroves. Their chatter was of school starting in the valley: new clothes and classrooms, a new teacher. The three Kims were the last to leave, and Cass handed each a popsicle as they passed the truck.

"Too cold," Kimberly squealed, and tossed hers into the weeds. Cass nodded sadly as we walked back to the porch, tugging at his collar against the evening chill. Eva sat yawning in Sam's lap, and the old man stroked her hair, humming to himself. I could scarcely see Maidie where she stood at the edge of the field, her face upturned to the lowering sky. Cass and I settled beside Sam, Cass reaching to take Eva into his arms.

"Will you miss me when it's too cold for ice cream, Eva?" he asked mournfully. "When the three Kims are all drinking hot chocolate?"

She stared at him solemn-eyed for a moment as he gazed wistfully across the field. Then she slid from his lap, pursing her lips to kiss his chin, and pulled at Sam's shoulder. "Show him what you can do, Sam," she said imperiously. "That thing. Show Cass."

Sam smiled and looked away.

"Show him!" She bounced against his side, pulling his union suit until he nodded and rose sighing, like a bear torn from his long sleep. Cass looked at me with mock alarm as Sam lumbered down the steps to the willow tree.

"Watch!" Eva shrilled, and Maidie turned to face us, her white face cold and impassive.

About the willow tree honeysuckle twined, wreathing it in gold and ivory trumpets. Sam reached and gently stripped the tiny blooms from a vine, disturbing the cicadas that sang there. In his hands the flowers glowed slightly in the dusk. I glanced up and marked where bats stitched the sky above him, and pointed for Eva to look.

"I see," she said impatiently, pulling away from me. "*Watch*, Cass."

Sam wheeled to face us, inclined his head to Eva and smiled. Then he flung his arms upwards, sending a stream of flowers into the air.

"See them?" cried Eva, clinging to Cass's hand.

I saw nothing. Beside me Cass squinted, adjusting his glasses. Sam tore more honeysuckle from the willow and flung another handful into the air.

A black shape broke from the sky, whipped towards Sam's face and fell away so quickly it looked like it was moving backwards. Another flicker of darkness inches from Sam's face, and another; and they were everywhere, chasing the blossoms he hurled into the night, flitting about his face like great black moths. A faint rush of air upon my cheek: I saw the bluish sheen of wings, the starpoint reflection of one tiny eye as a bat skimmed past. I shuddered and drew closer to Cass. Eva laughed and darted away from the porch, joining Sam and gathering the broken flowers from the grass. She stood with face tilted to where the tiny shadows whirled, striking at flowers and craneflies.

"Can you hear them, Cass?" she called. He stood, eyes and mouth wide as he looked from the two of them to me, and nodded.

"I do," he murmured.

Beside him I gripped the porch rail and shrank from them, the soft rush of wings and their plaintive song: a high thin sound like wires snapping. "Cass," I whispered. "Cass—let's go."

But he didn't hear me; only stood and watched until Maidie called to Eva and her sharp voice sent the bats flurrying into the night. Her voice stirred Cass as well; he turned to me blinking, shaking his head.

"Let's go," I urged him, and he took my hand, nodding dazedly: Sam walked to the porch steps and looked up at us.

"You be by tomorrow," he said, and for a moment he held my other hand. His fingers were cold and damp, and when he withdrew them I found a green tendril in my palm, its single frail blossom crushed against my skin. "To say goodbye."

"We'll be here," Cass called back as I led him towards the truck.

When we drove up the following afternoon it was late, the sun already burning off the tops of the mountains. Cass had bought a case of True Blue back in Zion. We'd been drinking most of the day, mourning the end of summer, the first golden leaves on the tulip poplars. From the top of the rise Maidie's house looked still, and as we coasted down the hill I saw no one on the porch. The chairs and empty beer bottles were gone. So was the broom that Cass had made into a hobby-horse for Eva, and the broken pots and dishes that had been her toys. Cass parked the truck on the grass and looked at me.

"What the hell is this?" he wondered, and opened another beer. For several minutes we sat, waiting for Sam or Eva to greet us. Finally he finished his beer and said lamely, "Guess we better go find out."

On the porch Eva's half-grown kitten mewled, scampering off when Cass bent to pick it up. "Jeez," he muttered, pushing tentatively at the screen door. It gave gently, and we hesitated before entering. Inside there was nothing: not a chair, not a rag, not a glass. Cass stared in disbelief, but put on a nonchalant expression when Sam trudged in.

"Looks like you been doing your spring cleaning," Cass said uneasily.

Sam nodded. "I got to go. This time of year . . . take the girl with me." He smiled vacantly and crossed to the back door. Cass and I looked at each other, perplexed. Sam said nothing more and stepped outside. I followed him, peering into the single other room that had held a cot and mattress. Empty.

I found Cass outside, weaving slightly as he followed Sam to the porch's crumbling edge. "Where're you going?" he asked plaintively, but Sam only shook his head in silence, leaning on the splintered rail and gazing out at the field.

There was no sign of Maidie, but I could hear Eva chanting tunelessly to herself in the thicket of jewelweed at wood's edge. Cass heard, too, and called her name thickly. The golden fronds, heavy with blossoms and bees, twitched and crackled; and then Eva raced out, breathless, her face damp with excitement.

"Cass!" she cried, and scrambled up the porch steps to hug him. "We got to go."

"Where?" he asked again, resting his beer against her neck as he smoothed her tangled hair. "You going off to school?"

She shook her head. "No. Sam's place." Eva hugged his legs and looked up at him imploringly. "You come, too. Okay, Cass? Okay?"

Cass finished his beer and threw the bottle recklessly towards the field, to crash and shatter on stone. "I wish someone'd tell me where you all are going," he insisted, turning to Sam.

The old man shrugged and eyed Little Eva. "You about ready?"

Eva shook her head fiercely. For the first time since I'd known her I saw her eyes blister with tears. "Sam—" she pleaded, yanking Cass's hand at each word. "I want Cass, too."

"You know that ain't up to me," Sam replied bluntly, and he turned and went back inside.

Cass grinned then, and winked at me. "Just like a girl," he remarked, tousling her hair.

Faint high voices called from the woods. From the brush scrambled the three Kims, tearing twigs from their hair and yelling to us as they clambered over the fence. Beside me Little Eva stiffened, slipping her hand from Cass's as she watched her friends waving. Suddenly she let out a yell and sprang to meet them with arms flung wide, her hair a blazing flag in the sunset. Cass called after her, amused.

"That kid," he laughed, then stopped and cocked his head.

"What?" I glanced back at the sagging porch door, wondering where Maidie and Sam had gone.

"Hear that?" Cass murmured. He looked at me sharply. "You hear that?"

I shook my head, smoothing the hair from my ears. "No. The kids?" I pointed to the girls greeting Eva in the tall grass.

"Singing," Cass said softly. "Someone's singing." He stared intently after Eva.

Above the field the sun candled the clouds to an ardent sea. A chill breeze rose from the west, lifting a shimmering net of bees from the jewelweed and rattling the willow leaves. In the grass the girls shrieked and giggled, and as we watched the other children joined them for their evening games of Gray Wolf and Shadow-Tag, small white shapes slipping from the darkening trees with their mongrels romping underfoot. Eva pelted her friends with golden-rod while the boys tussled in furrows, their long blue shadows dancing across the grass until they were swallowed by the willow's roots. Cass watched them, entranced, his head tilted to catch some faint sound on the wind.

"What is it?" I asked, but he only shook his head.

"Can't you hear?" He looked at me in wonder, then turned away and walked across the field towards the children.

"Cass!" I called after him; but he ignored me. For several min-utes I waited, and finally stepped back to the door. And stopped.

Someone *was* singing. Perhaps I had already heard without real-izing, or mistaken the refrain for the cry of the crickets or nightjars. I cocked my head as Cass had done and tried to trace the music; but it was gone again, drowned by the children's voices. I caught the bellow of Cass's laughter among their play, then faint music once more: a woman's voice, but wordless or else too far off for me to understand her song. At the doorway I paused and looked out at the field. The sun scarcely brushed the horizon now above the cir-rus archipelago. Lightning bugs sparked the air and the children spilled through their trails, Cass lumbering among them with first Kim and then Little Eva hugging his narrow shoulders. For a long while I watched them, until only Eva's amber hair and Cass's white shirt flashed in the dusk. Finally Cass looked up and, seeing me for the first time, beckoned me to join them. I smiled and waved, then bounded down the steps and across the field.

From the grass hundreds of leafhoppers flew up as I passed, the click of their wings a soft and constant burr. Last light silvered the willow bark and faded. The wind was stronger now, and with the children's voices it carried that faint music once more, ringing clearly over the whir of insects. I halted, suddenly dizzy, and stared at my feet as I tried to steady myself.

When I glanced up the children had fallen still. They stood ranged across the field, their dogs beside them motionless, ears pricked. I turned to see what held them.

As though storm-riven the willow thrashed, branches raking the sky as if to hurl the first stars earthward. I swore and stepped back in disbelief. Beneath me the ground shuddered, buckling like rotten bark. Then with a steady grinding roar the earth heaved. A rich spume of dirt and clover sprayed me as the ground beneath the tree split like a windfall apple.

The roaring stopped. A second of utter silence; and then song poured from the rift like a flock of swans. I clapped my hands to my ears and fell to my knees.

The dogs heard first. I felt the heat of their flanks as they streamed past me, heard their panting and faint whimpers. I forced myself to look up, brushing dirt from my face.

Above a gaping mouth in the red earth the willow reared. In its shadow stood Maidie, arms outstretched. She was singing, and the dogs streamed past her, vaulting into the darkness at her feet. I stared amazed. Then from behind me I heard voices, the soft stir of footsteps. I glanced back.

The field lay in gray half-light. Abruptly the darkness itself shivered, broken where the children ran laughing across the field, in twos and threes, girls clutching hands to form a chain across the waving grass, the littlest clinging to the bigger boys shouting in excitement. I yelled to them, but my voice was drowned by their laughter. They did not see me as they raced past.

She drew them, head thrown back as she sang on and on and on, her voice embracing stone and tree and hound and stars, until her song was the children and she sang them all into the earth. Her glasses fell from her face, the gaze she turned upon the children no longer blind but blinding: eyes like golden flowers, like sunrise, like autumn wheat. My hands were raw from kneading the clay as I stared, boys and girls rushing to her and laughing as they disappeared one by one into the rift at her feet. Her hands moved over and over again in a ceaseless welcoming wave, as though she gathered armfuls of bright blossoms to her breast. But I could not move: it was as if I had become that tree, and rooted to the earth.

Final footsteps pattered on the grass. Cass and Eva passed me, running hand in hand to join the rest, now gone beneath the willow. I screamed his name and they halted. Cass stared back dimly, shaking his head as though trying to recognize me. The woman I had known as Maidie raised her arms and fell silent. Then she called out a word, a name. Little Eva smiled at Cass, standing on tiptoe to kiss him. He smiled and kissed her forehead, then gathered her into his arms to carry her the last few steps to the willow. I watched as the woman waiting there took his hands; and lost him forever.

Another figure stepped from the tree's shadow. He stooped to take the child from Cass's arms. I saw Cass turn from Sam to the woman beside him, the woman whose wheat-gold eyes held a terrible sorrow. And suddenly I understood: knew the mother's eternal anguish at losing the child again to him, that bleak consort, He Who Receives Many; knew why she gathered this bright harvest of playmates for a sunless garden, attendants for the girl no more a girl, the gentle maiden doomed to darkness the rest of the turning year.

One last moment they remained. The child raised her hand to me and opened it, once, in a tiny farewell. The ground trembled. A sound like rushing water rent the air. The willow tree crashed into darkness. A crack like granite shattering; a smell like ash and grinding stone. They were gone; all gone.

The night was silent. Before me stretched the empty field, an abandoned cottage. Then from the woods echoed a poorwill's wail and its mate's echoing lament. I stumbled to the fallen tree and, kneeling between its roots, wept among the anemones hiding children in the earth.

I wrote this on the typewriter in the office of a defense contractor where I was working in 1986, after I quit the Smithsonian. On weekends I was in the mountains around Charlottesville, Virginia, riding on the ice cream truck with the boy who was briefly my husband and his best friend, Eddie Dean. Eddie is now a D.C.-area journalist and a terrific writer; in the story he became Cass Tyrone.

That was a pretty spectacularly happy time for me: even though I spent my days as an office manager in the dreaded Military Industrial Complex, I was writing and had the exhilarating sense that I might actually make it work. Everything in "On the Town Route" is true; as I wrote when it was published, "anyone who's spent much time in those mountains can tell you, some truly weird stuff happens there." This was my first story to delve into the Greek mysteries, the boy in the tree notwithstanding.

The Boy in the Tree

What if in your dream you dreamed, and what if in your dream you went to heaven and there plucked a strange and beautiful flower, and what if when you woke you had the flower in your hand?

—Samuel Taylor Coleridge

Our heart stops.

A moment I float beneath her, a starry shadow. Distant canyons where spectral lightning flashes: neurons firing as I tap into the heart of the poet, the dark core where desire and horror fuse and Morgan turns ever and again to stare out a bus window. The darkness clears. I taste for an instant the metal bile that signals the beginning of therapy, and then I'm gone.

I'm sitting on the autobus, the last seat where you can catch the bumps on the crumbling highway if you're going fast enough. Through the open windows a rush of Easter air tangles my hair. Later I will smell apple blossom in my auburn braids. Now I smell sour milk where Ronnie Abrams spilled his ration yesterday.

"Move over, Yates!" Ronnie caroms off the seat opposite, rams his leg into mine and flies back to pound his brother. From the front the driver yells "Shut up!", vainly trying to silence forty-odd singing children.

> *On top of Old Smoky*
> *All covered with blood*
> *I shot my poor teacher*
> *With a forty-four slug . . .*

Ronnie grins at me, eyes glinting, then pops me right on the chin with a spitball. I stick my fingers in my ears and huddle closer to the window.

> *Met her at the door*
> *With my trusty forty-four*
> *Now she don't teach no more . . .*

The autobus pulls into town and slows, stops behind a military truck. I press my face against the cracked window, shoving my glasses until lens kisses glass and I can see clearly to the street below. A young woman is standing on the curb holding a baby wrapped in a dirty pink blanket. At her ankles wriggles a dog, an emaciated puppy with whiptail and ears flopping as he nips at her bare feet. I tap at the window, trying to get the dog to look at me. In front of the bus two men in uniform clamber from the truck and start arguing. The woman screws up her face and says something to the men, moving her lips so that I know she's mad. The dog lunges at her ankles again and she kicks it gently, so that it dances along the curb. The soldiers glance at her, see the autobus waiting, and climb back into the truck. I hear the whoosh of releasing brakes. The autobus lurches forward and my glasses bang into the window. The rear wheels grind up onto the curb.

The dog barks and leaps onto the woman. Apple blossoms drift from a tree behind her as she draws her arms up alarmed, and, as I settle my glasses onto my nose and stare, drops the baby beneath the wheels of the bus.

Retching, I strive to pull Morgan away, turn her head from the window. A fine spray etches bright petals on the glass and her plastic lenses. My neck aches as I try to turn toward the inside of the autobus and efface forever that silent rain. But I cannot move. She is too strong. She will not look away.

I am clawing at the restraining ropes. A technician pulls the wires from my head while inches away Morgan Yates screams. I hear the hiss and soft pump of velvet thoughts into her periaqueductual gray area. The link is severed.

I sat up as they wheeled her into the next room. Morgan's screams abruptly stilled as the endorphins kicked in and her head flopped to one side of the gurney. For an instant the technician turned and stared at me as he slid Morgan through the door. He would not catch my eyes.

None of them will.

Through the glass panel I watched Emma Harrow hurry from another lab. She bent over Morgan and gently pulled the wires from between white braids still rusted with coppery streaks. Beside her the technicians looked worried. Other doctors slipped from adjoining rooms and blocked my view, all with strained faces.

When I was sure they'd forgotten me I dug out a cigarette and lit up. I tapped the ashes into my shoe and blew smoke into a ventilation shaft. I knew Morgan wouldn't make it. I could often tell, but even Dr. Harrow didn't listen to me this time. Morgan Yates was too important: one of the few living writers whose readers included both rebels and Ascendants.

"She will crack," I told Dr. Harrow after reading Morgan's profile. Seven poetry collections published by the Ascendants. Recurrent nightmares revolving around a childhood trauma in the military crèche; sadistic sexual behavior and a pathological fear of dogs. Nothing extraordinary there. But I knew she wouldn't make it.

"How do you know?"

I shrugged. "She's too strong."

Dr. Harrow stared at me, pinching her lower lip. She wasn't afraid of my eyes. "What if it works?" she mused. "She says she hasn't written in three years, because of this."

I yawned. "Maybe it will work. But she won't let me take it away. She won't let anyone take it."

I was right. If Dr. Harrow hadn't been so anxious about the chance to reclaim one of the damned and her own reputation, she'd have known, too. Psychotics, autists, artists of the lesser rank: these could be altered by empatherapy. I'd siphoned off their sicknesses and night terrors, inhaled phobias like giddy ethers that set me giggling for days afterward. But the big ones, those whose madnesses were as carefully cultivated as the brain chemicals that allowed myself and others like me to tap into them: they were immune. They clung to their madnesses with the fever of true addiction. Even the dangers inherent to empatherapy weren't enough: they *couldn't* let go.

Dr. Harrow glanced up from the next room and frowned when she saw my cigarette. I stubbed it out in my shoe and slid my foot back in, wincing at the prick of heat beneath my sole.

She slipped out of the emergency room. Sighing, she leaned against the glass and looked at me.

"Was it bad, Wendy?"

I picked a fleck of tobacco from my lip. "Pretty bad." I had a rush recalling Morgan wailing as she stood at the window. For a moment I had to shut my eyes, riding that wave until my heart slowed and I looked up grinning into Dr. Harrow's compressed smile.

"Pretty good, you mean." Her tight mouth never showed the disdain or revulsion of the others. Only a little dismay, some sick pride perhaps in the beautiful thing she'd soldered together from an autistic girl and several ounces of precious glittering chemicals. "Well," she sighed, and walked to her desk. "You can start on this." She tossed me a blank report and returned to the emergency lab. I settled back on my cot and stared at the sheet.

PATIENT NAME: Wendy Wanders

In front of me the pages blurred. Shuddering I gripped the edge of my chair. Nausea exploded inside me, a fiery pressure building inside my head until I bowed to crack my forehead against the table edge, again and again, stammering my name until with a shout a technician ran to me and slapped an ampule to my neck. I couldn't bear the sight of my own name: Dr. Harrow usually filled in the charts for me and provided the sedatives, as she had a special lab all in gray for the empath who couldn't bear colors and wore black goggles outside; as she had the neural bath ready for another whose amnesia after a session left her unable to talk or stand or control her bowels. The technician stood above me until the drug took effect. I breathed deeply and stared at the wall, then reported on my unsuccessful session with the poet.

That evening I walked to the riverside. A trio of security sculls silently plied the river. At my feet water striders gracelessly mimicked them. I caught a handful of the insects and dropped them on the crumbling macadam at water's edge, watched them jerk and twitch with crippled stepladder legs as they fought the hard skin of gravel and sand. Then I turned and wandered along the river walk, past rotting oak benches and the ruins of glass buildings, watching the sun sink through argent thunderheads.

A single remaining restaurant ziggurat towered above the walk. Wooden benches gave way to airy filigrees of iron, and at one of these tables I saw someone from the Human Engineering Laboratory.

"Anna or Andrew?" I called. By the time I was close enough for her to hear I knew it was Anna this time, peacock feathers and long blue macaw quills studding the soft raised nodes on her shaven temples.

"Wendy." She gestured dreamily at a confectionery chair. "Sit."

I settled beside her, tweaking a cobalt plume, and wished I'd worn the fiery cock-of-the-rock quills I'd bought last spring. Anna was stunning, always: eyes brilliant with octine, small breasts tight against her tuxedo shirt. She was the only one of the other empties I spoke much with, although she beat me at faro and Andrew had once broken my tooth in an amphetamine rage. A saucer scattered with broken candicaine straws sat before her. Beside it a fluted parfait glass held several unbroken pipettes. I did one and settled back grinning.

"You had that woman today," Anna hissed into my ear. Her rasping voice made me shiver with delight. "The poet. I think I'm furious."

Smiling, I shrugged. "Luck of the draw."

"How was she?" She blinked and I watched golden dust powder the air between us. "Was she good, Wendy?" She stroked my thigh and I giggled.

"Great. She was great." I lowered my eyes and squinted until the table disappeared into the steel rim of an autobus seat.

"Let me see." Her whisper the sigh of air brakes. "Wendy—"

The rush was too good to stop. I let her pull me forward until my forehead grazed hers and I felt the cold sting of electrolytic fluid where she strung the wire. I tasted brass: then bile and summer air and exhaust—

Too fast. I jerked my head up, choking as I inadvertently yanked the connector from Anna. She stared at me with huge blank eyes.

"Ch-c-c—" she gasped, spittle flying into the parfait glass. I swore and pushed the straws away, popped the wire and held her face close to mine.

"Ahhh—" Anna nodded suddenly. Her eyes focused and she drew back. "Wendy. Good stuff." She licked her lips, tongue a little loose from the hit so that she drooled. I grimaced.

"More, Wendy. . . "

"Not now." I grabbed two more straws and cracked one. "I have a follow-up with her tomorrow morning. I have to go."

She nodded. I flicked the wire into her lap along with the vial of fluid and a napkin. "Wipe your mouth, Anna. I'll tell Harrow I saw you so she won't worry."

"Goodbye, Wendy." She snapped a pocket open and the stuff disappeared. A server arrived as I left, its crooked wheels grating against the broken concrete as it listed toward the table. I glimpsed myself reflected in its blank black face, and hurried from the patio as behind me Anna ordered more straws.

I recall nothing before Dr. Harrow. The drugs they gave me—massive overdoses for a three-year-old—burned those memories as well as scorching every neural branch that might have helped me climb to feel the sun as other people do. But the drugs stopped the thrashing, the headbanging, the screaming. And slowly, other drugs rived through my tangled axons and forged new pathways. A few months and I could see again. A few more and my fingers moved. The wires that had stilled my screams eventually made me scream once more, and, finally, exploded a neural dam so that a year later I began to speak. By then the research money was pouring through other conduits, scarcely less complex than my own, and leading as well to the knot of electrodes in my brain.

In the early stages of her work, shortly after she took me from the military crèche, Dr. Harrow attempted a series of neuro-electrical implants between the two of us. It was an unsuccessful effort to reverse the damage done by the biochemicals. Seven children died before the minimum dosage was determined—enough to change the neural pattern behind autistic behavior, not enough to allow the patient to develop her own emotional responses to subsequent internal or external stimuli. I still have scars from the implants: fleshy nodes like tiny ears trying to sprout from my temples.

At first we lived well. As more empaths were developed and more military funding channeled for research, we lived extravagantly well. Dr. Harrow believed that exposure to sensation might eventually pattern true emotions in her affectively neutered charges. So we moved from the Human Engineering Laboratory's chilly fortress to the vast abandoned Linden Glory estate outside the old City.

Neurologists moved into the paneled bedrooms. Psycho-botanists tilled the ragged formal gardens and developed new strains of oleander within bell-shaped greenhouses. Empties moved into bungalows where valets and chefs once slept.

Lawrence Linden had been a patron of the arts: autographed copies of Joyce and Stein and the lost Crowley manuscripts graced the Linden Glory libraries. We had a minor Botticelli and many Raphaels; the famed pre-Columbian collection; antiquarian coins and shelves of fine and rare Egyptian glass. From the Victorian music room with its Whistler panels echoed the peacock screams of empties and patients engaged in therapy.

Always I remained Dr. Harrow's pet: an exquisite monster capable of miming every human emotion and even feeling many of them via the therapy I make possible. Every evening doctors administer syringes and capsules and tiny tabs that adhere to my temples like

burdock pods, releasing chemicals directly into my corpus stria-
tum. And every morning I wake from someone else's dreams.

Morgan sat in the gazebo when I arrived for our meeting, her hair
pulled beneath a biretta of frayed indigo velvet. She had already
eaten but servers had yet to clear her plate. I picked up the remains
of a brioche and nibbled its sugary crust.

"None of you have any manners, do you?" She smiled, but her
eyes were red and cloudy with hatred. "They told me that during
orientation."

I ran my tongue over a sweet nugget in a molar and nodded.
"That's right."

"You can't feel anything or learn anything unless it's slipped into
your breakfast coffee."

"I can't drink coffee." I glanced around the Orphic Garden for a
server. "You're early."

"I had trouble sleeping."

I nodded and finished the brioche.

"I had trouble sleeping because I had no dreams." She leaned
across the table and repeated herself in a hiss. "I had no dreams. I
carried that memory around with me for sixty years and last night I
had no dreams."

Yawning I rubbed the back of my head, adjusting a quill. "You
still have all your memories. Dr. Harrow said you wanted to end the
nightmares. I am surprised we were successful."

"You were not successful." She towered above me when she
stood, the table tilting toward her as she clutched its edge.
"Monster."

"Sacred monster. I thought you liked sacred monsters." I
grinned, pleased that I'd bothered to read her chart.

"Bitch. How dare you laugh at me. Whore—you're all whores
and thieves." She stepped toward me, her heel catching between the
mosaic stones. "No more of me—You'll steal no more of me—"

I drew back a little, blinking in the emerald light as I felt the
first adrenaline pulse. "You shouldn't be alone," I murmured. "Does
Dr. Harrow know?"

She blocked the sun so that it exploded around the biretta's peaks in resplendent ribbons. "Doctor Harrow will know," she whispered, and drawing a swivel from her pocket she shot herself through the eye.

I knocked my chair over as I stumbled to her, knelt and caught the running blood and her last memory as I bowed to touch my tongue to her severed thoughts.

A window smeared with garnet light that ruddles across my hands. Burning wax in a small blue glass. A laughing dog; then darkness.

They hid me under guise of protecting me from the shock. I gave a sworn statement to the military and acknowledged in the HEL mortuary that the long body with the blackened face had indeed shared her breakfast brioche with me that morning. I glimpsed Dr. Harrow, white and taut as a thread as Dr. Leslie and the other HEL brass cornered her outside the Emergency Room. Then the aide Justice hurried me into the west wing, past the pre-Columbian collection and the ivory stair to an ancient Victorian elevator, clanking and lugubrious as a stage dragon.

"Dr. Harrow suggested that you might like the Horne Room," Justice remarked with a cough, sidling two steps away to the corner of the elevator. The brass door folded into a lattice of leaves and pigeons that expanded into peacocks. "She's having your things sent up now. Anything else you need, please let her know." He cleared his throat, staring straight ahead as we climbed through orchid-haunted clerestories and chambers where the oneironauts snored and tossed through their days. At the fourth floor the elevator ground to a stop. He tugged at the door until it opened and waited for me to pass into the hallway.

"I have never been in the Horne Room," I remarked, following him.

"I think that's why she thought you'd like it." He glanced into an ornate mirror as we walked. I saw in his eyes a quiver of pity before he looked away. "Down here."

A wide hallway flanked by leaded windows overlooking the empties' cottages ended in an arch crowded with gilt satyrs.

"This is the Horne Room," murmured Justice. To the right a

heavy oaken door hung open. Inside saffron-robed technicians strung cable. I made a face and tapped the door. It swung inward and struck a bundle of cable leading to the bank of monitors being installed next to a huge bed. I paced to the window and gazed down at the roof of my cottage. Around me the technicians scurried to finish, glancing at me sideways with anxious eyes. I ignored them and sat on the windowsill. There was no screen. A hawkmoth buzzed past my chin and I thought that I could hang hummingbird feeders from here and so, perhaps, lure them within reach of capture. Anna had a bandeau she had woven of hummingbird feathers which I much admired. The hawkmoth settled on a BEAM monitor beside the bed. The technicians packed to leave.

"Could you lie here for a moment, miss, while I test this?" The technician dropped a handful of cables behind the headboard. I nodded and stretched upon the bed, pummeling a pillow as he placed the wires upon my brow and temples. I turned sideways to watch the old BEAM monitor, the hawkmoth's wings forming a feline mask across the flickering map of my thoughts.

"Aggression, bliss, charity," droned the technician, flicking the moth from the dusty screen. "Desire, envy, fear," I sighed and turned from the monitor while he adjusted dials. Finally he slipped the wires from me and left. Justice lingered a moment longer.

"You can go now," I said flatly, and tossed the pillow against the headboard.

He stood by the door, uncomfortable, and finally said, "Dr. Harrow wants me to be certain you check your prescriptions. Note she has increased your dosage of acetlethylene."

I slid across the bed to where a tiny refrigerator had been hung for my medications. I pulled it open and saw the familiar battery of vials and bottles. As a child first under Dr. Harrow's care I had imagined them a city, saw the long cylinders and amber vials as battlements and turrets to be explored and climbed. Now I lived among those chilly buttresses, my only worship within bright cathedrals.

"Two hundred milligrams," I said obediently, and replaced the bottle. "Thank you very very much." As I giggled he left the room.

I took the slender filaments that had tapped into my store of memories and braided them together, then slid the plait beneath a pillow and leaned back. A bed like a pirate ship, carved posts like riven masts spiring to the high ceiling. I had never seen a pirate ship, but once I tapped a boy who jerked off to images of red flags and heaving seas and wailing women. I recalled that now and untangled a single wire, placed it on my temple and masturbated until I saw the warning flare on the screen, the sanguine flash and flame across my pixilated brain. Then I went to sleep.

Faint tapping at the door woke me a short while later.

"Andrew," I yawned, pointing to the crumpled sea of bed-clothes. "Come in."

He shut the door softly and slid beneath the sheets beside me. "You're not supposed to have visitors, you now."

"I'm not?" I stretched and curled my toes around his finger.

"No. Dr. Leslie was here all day, Anna said he's taking us back."

"Me, too?"

He nodded, hugging a bolster. "All of us. Forever." He smiled, and the twilight made his face as beautiful as Anna's. "I saw Dr. Harrow cry after he left."

"How did you get here?" I sat up and played with his hair: long and silky except where the nodes bulged and the hair had never grown back. He wore Anna's bandeau, and I tugged it gently from his head.

"Back stairs. No one ever uses them. That way." He pointed lazily with his foot toward a darkening corner. His voice rose plain-tively. "You shared that poet with Anna. You should've saved her."

I shrugged. "You weren't there." The bandeau fit loosely over my forehead. When I tightened it tiny emerald feathers frosted my hand like the scales of moths. "Would Anna give me this, do you think?"

Andrew pulled himself onto his elbows and stroked my breast with one hand. "I'll give it to you, if you share."

"There's not enough left to share," I whined, and pulled away. In the mirror I caught myself in the bandeau. The stippled green feath-ers made my hair look a deeper auburn, like the poet's. I pulled a few dark curls through the feathers and pursed my lips. "If you give this to me . . ."

Already he was reaching for the wires. "Locked?" I breathed, glancing at the door.

"Shh . . ."

Afterward I gave him one of my new pills. There hadn't been
much of Morgan left and I feared his disappointment would evoke
Anna, who'd demand her bandeau back.

"Why can't I have visitors?"

I had switched off the lights. Andrew sat on the windowsill, luring lacewings with a silver cigarette lighter. Bats chased the insects
to within inches of his face, veering away as he laughed and pretended to snatch at them. "Dr. Harrow said there may be a psychic
inquest. To see if you're accountable."

"So?" I'd done one before, when a schizoid six-year-old hanged
herself on a grosgrain ribbon after therapy with me. "'I can't be
responsible. I'm not responsible.'" We laughed: it was the classic
empath defense.

"Dr. Harrow wants to see you herself."

I kicked the sheets to the floor and turned down the empty
BEAM, to see the lacewings better. "How do you know all this?"

A quick *fizz* as a moth singed itself. Andrew frowned and
turned down the lighter flame. "Anna told me," he replied, and suddenly was gone.

I swore and tried to rearrange my curls so the bandeau wouldn't
show. From the windowsill Anna stared blankly at the lighter for a
moment, then groped in her pockets until she found a cigarette.
She glanced coolly past me to the mirror, pulling a strand of hair
forward until it fell framing her cheekbone. "Who gave you that?"
she asked as she blew smoke out the window.

I turned away. "You know who," I replied petulantly. "I'm not
supposed to have visitors."

"Oh, you can keep it," she said airily.

"Really?" I clapped in delight.

"I'll just make another." She finished her cigarette, tossed it in
an amber arc out the window. "I better go down now. Which way's
out?"

I pointed where Andrew had indicated, drawing her close to me
to kiss her tongue as she left.

"Thank you, Anna," I whispered to her at the door. "I think I
love this bandeau."

"I think I loved it, too," Anna nodded, and slipped away.

*   *   *

Dr. Harrow invited me to lunch with her in the Peach Tree Court the next afternoon. Justice appeared at my door and waited while I put on jeweled dark spectacles and a velvet biretta like Morgan Yates's.

"Very nice, Wendy," he commented, amused. I smiled. When I wore the black glasses he was not afraid to look me in the face.

"I don't want the others to see my bandeau. Anna will steal it back," I explained, lifting the hat so he could see the feathered riband beneath.

He laughed at that. I don't hear the aides laugh very often: when I was small, their voices frightened me. I thanked him as he held the door and followed him outside.

We passed the Orphic Garden. Servers had snaked hoses through the circle of lindens and were cleaning the mosaic stones. I peered curiously through the hedge as we walked down the pathway but the blood seemed to be all gone.

Once we were in the shade of the Peach Tree Walk I removed my glasses. Justice quickly averted his eyes.

"Do you think these peaches are ripe?" I wondered, twitching one from a branch as I passed beneath it.

"I doubt it." Justice sighed, wincing as I bit into a small pink orb like a swollen eye. "They'll make you sick, Wendy."

Grinning, I swallowed my bite, then dropped the fruit. The little path dipped and rounded a corner hedged with forsythia. Three steps further and the path branched: right to the *trompe l'oeil* Glass Fountain, left to the Peach Tree Court, where Dr. Harrow waited in the Little Pagoda.

"Thank you, Justice." Dr. Harrow rose and shook his hand. On several low tables lunch had already been laid for two. Justice stepped to a lacquered tray and sorted out my medication bottles, then stood and bowed before leaving.

Sunlight streamed through the bamboo frets above us as Dr. Harrow took my hand and drew me toward her.

"The new dosage. You remembered to take it?"

"Yes." I removed my hat and dropped it. "Anna gave me this bandeau."

"It's lovely." She knelt before one of the tables and motioned for me to do the same. Her face was puffy, her eyes slitted. I wondered if she would cry for me as she had for Andrew yesterday. "Have you had breakfast?"

We ate goujonettes of hake with fennel and an aspic of lamb's blood. Dr. Harrow drank champagne and permitted me a sip—horrible, like thrashing water. Afterward a rusted, remodeled garden server removed our plates and brought me a chocolate wafer, which I slipped into my pocket to trade with Anna later, for news.

"You slept well," Dr. Harrow stated. "What did you dream?"

"I dreamed about Melisande's dog."

Dr. Harrow stroked her chin, then adjusted her pince-nez to see me better. "Not Morgan's dog?"

"No." Melisande had been a girl my own age with a history of tormenting and sexually molesting animals. "A small white dog. Like this." I pushed my nose until it squashed against my face.

Dr. Harrow smiled ruefully. "Well, good, because *I* dreamed about Morgan's dog." She shook her head when I started to question her. "Not really; a manner of speaking. I mean I didn't get much sleep." She sighed and tilted her flute so it refracted golden diamonds. "I made a very terrible error of judgment with Morgan Yates. I shouldn't have let you do it."

"I knew what would happen," I said matter-of-factly.

Dr. Harrow looked at her glass, then at me. "Yes. Well, a number of people are wondering about that, Wendy."

"She would not look away from the window."

"No. They're wondering how you know when the therapy will succeed and when it won't. They're wondering whether the therapist is effecting her failures as well as her cures."

"I'm not responsible. I can't be responsible."

She placed the champagne flute very carefully on the lacquer table and took my hand. She squeezed it so tightly that I knew she wanted it to hurt. "That is what's the matter, Wendy. If you are responsible—if empaths *can* be responsible—you can be executed for murder. We can all be held accountable for your failures. And if not . . ." She leaned back without releasing my hand, so that I had to edge nearer to her across the table. "If not, HEL wants you back."

I flounced back against the floor. "Andrew told me."

She rolled her eyes. "Not you personally. Not necessarily. Anna, yes: they created Anna, they'll claim her first. But the others—" She traced a wave in the air, ended it with a finger pointing at me. "And you . . . If they can trace what you do, find the bioprint and synthesize it . . ." Her finger touched the end of my nose, pressed it until I giggled. "Just like Melisande's dog, Wendy.

"Odolf Leslie was here yesterday. He wants you for observation. He wants this—" She pressed both hands to her forehead and then waved them toward the sky, the fruit-laden trees and sloping lawns of Linden Glory. "All this, Wendy. They will have me declared incompetent and our research a disaster, and then they'll move in."

A server poured me more mineral water. "Is he a nice doctor?"

For a moment I thought she'd upset the table, as Morgan had done in the Orphic Garden, Then, "I don't know, Wendy. Perhaps he is." She sighed, and motioned the server to bring another cold split.

"They'll take Anna first," she said a few minutes later, almost to herself. Then, as if recalling me sitting across from her, she added, "For espionage. They'll induce multiple personalities and train them when they're very young. Ideal terrorists."

I drank my water and stared at the latticed roof of the pagoda, imagining Andrew and Anna without me. I took the chocolate wafer from my pocket and began to nibble it.

The server rolled back with a sweating silver bucket and opened another split for Dr. Harrow. She sipped it, watching me through narrowed gray eyes. "Wendy," she said at last. "There's going to be an inquest. A military inquest. But before that, one more patient." She reached beneath the table to her portfolio and removed a slender packet. "This is the profile. I'd like you to read it."

I took the file. Dr. Harrow poured the rest of her champagne and finished it, tilting her head to the server as she stood.

"I have a two o'clock meeting with Dr. Leslie. Why don't you meet me again for dinner tonight and we'll discuss this?"

"Where?"

She tapped her lower lip. "The Peacock Room. At seven." She bowed slightly and passed out of sight among the trees.

I waited until she disappeared, then gestured for the server.

"More chocolate, please," I ordered, and waited until it returned with a chilled marble plate holding three wafers. I nibbled one, staring idly at the faux vellum cover of the profile with its engraved motto:

HUMAN ENGINEERING LABORATORY
PAULO MAIORA CANAMUS

"'Let us raise a somewhat loftier strain,'" Andrew had translated it for me once. "Virgil. But it should be *deus ex machina*," he added slyly.

God from the machine.

I licked melting chocolate from my fingers and began to read, skimming through the charts and anamnesis that followed. On the last sheet I read:

Client requests therapy in order to determine nature and cause of these obsessive nightmares.

Beneath this was Dr. Harrow's scrawled signature and the HEL stamp. I ate the last wafer, then mimed to the server that I was finished.

We dined alone in the Peacock Room. After setting our tiny table the servers disappeared, dismissed by Dr. Harrow's brusque gesture. A plateful of durians stood as our centerpiece, the spiky green globes piled atop a translucent porcelain tray. Dr. Harrow split one neatly for me, the round fruit oozing pale custard and a putrescent odor. She grimaced, then took a demure spoonful of the pulp and tasted it for me.

"Lovely," she murmured, and handed me the spoon.

We ate in silence for several minutes beneath the flickering gaslit chandeliers.

"Did you read the profile I gave you?" Dr. Harrow asked at last, with studied casualness.

"Mmmm-mmm," I grunted.

"And . . . ?"

"She will not make it." I lofted another durian from the tray.

Dr. Harrow dipped her chin ever so slightly before asking, "Why, Wendy?"

"I don't know." This durian was not quite ripe. I winced and pushed it from my plate.

"Can't you give me any idea of what makes you feel that?"

"Nothing. I can't feel anything." I took another fruit.

"Well, then, what makes you think she wouldn't be a good analysand?"

"I don't know. I just—" I sucked on my spoon, thinking. "It's like when I see my name—the way everything starts to shiver and I get sick. But I don't throw up."

Dr. Harrow tilted her head thoughtfully. "Like a seizure. Well." She smiled and spooned another mouthful.

I finished the last durian and glanced around impatiently. "When will I meet her?"

"You already have."

I kicked my chair. "When?"

"Fourteen years ago, when you first came to HEL."

"Why don't I remember her?"

"You do, Wendy." She lifted her durian and took the last drop of custard upon her tongue. "It's me."

"Surprised?" Dr. Harrow grinned and raised the flamboyant sleeves of her embroidered haik.

"It's beautiful," I said, fingering the flowing cuffs enviously.

She smiled and turned to the NET beside my bed. "I'm the patient this morning. Are you ready?"

I nodded. Earlier she had wheeled in her own cot, and now sat on it readying her monitors. I settled on my bed and waited for her to finish. She finally turned to me and applied electrolytic fluid to the nodes on my temples, placed other wires upon my head and cheekbones before doing the same to herself.

"You have no technicians assisting you?" I asked.

She shook her head but made no reply as she adjusted her screens and, finally, settled onto her cot. I lay back against the pillow and shut my eyes.

The last thing I heard was the click of the adaptor freeing the current, and a gentle exhalation that might have been a sigh.

"Here we stand . . ."
   "Here we stand . . ."
"Here we lie . . ."
   "Here we lie . . ."
      "Eye to hand and heart to head,
      Deep in the dark with the dead."

It is spring, and not dark at all, but I repeat the incantation as Aidan gravely sprinkles apple blossoms upon my head. In the branches beneath us a bluejay shrieks at our bulldog, Molly, as she whines and scratches hopefully at her basket.

"Can't we bring her up?" I peer over the edge of the rickety platform and Molly sneezes in excitement.

"Shhh!" Aidan commands, squeezing his eyes shut as he concentrates. After a moment he squints and reaches for his crumpled sweater. Several bay leaves filched from the kitchen crumble over me and I blink so the debris doesn't get in my eyes.

"I hate this junk in my hair," I grumble. "Next time I make the spells."

"You can't." Loftily Aidan stands on tiptoe and strips another branch of blossoms, sniffing them dramatically before tossing them in a flurry of pink and white. "We need a virgin."

"So?" I jerk on the rope leading to Molly's basket. "You're a virgin. Next time we use you."

Aidan stares at me, brows furrowed. "That won't count," he says at last. "Say it again, Emma."

"Here we stand . . ."

Every day of Easter break we come here: an overgrown apple orchard within the woods, uncultivated for a hundred years. Stone walls tumbled by time mark the gray boundaries of a colonial farm. Blackberry vines choke the rocks with breeze-blown petals. Our father showed us this place. Long ago he built the treehouse, its wood lichen-green now and wormed with holes. Rusted nails snag my knees when we climb: all that remains of other platforms and the crow's-nest at treetop.

I finish the incantation and kneel, calling to Molly to climb in her basket. When my twin yells I announce imperiously, "The virgin needs her faithful consort. Get *in*, Molly."

He demurs and helps to pull her up. Molly is trembling when we heave her onto the platform. As always, she remains huddled in her basket.

"She's sitting on the sandwiches," I remark matter-of-factly. Aidan shoves Molly aside hastily and retrieves two squashed bags. "I call we break for lunch."

We eat in thoughtful silence. We never discuss the failure of the spells, although each afternoon Aidan hides in his secret place behind the wing chair in the den and pores through more brittle volumes. Sometimes I can feel them working—the air is so calm, the wind dies unexpectedly, and for a moment the woods glow so bright, so deep, their shadows still and green; and it is there: the secret to be revealed, the magic to unfold, the story to begin. Aidan flushes above me and his eyes shine, he raises his arms and—

And nothing. It is gone. A moment too long or too soon, I never know—but we have lost it again. For an instant Aidan's eyes gray with tears. Then the breeze rises, Molly yawns and snuffles, and once more we put aside the spells for lunch and other games.

That night I toss in my bed, finally throwing my pillow against the bookcase. From the open window stream the chimes of peepers in the swamp, their plangent song broidered with the trills of toads and leopard frogs. As I churn feverishly through the sheets it comes again, and I lie still: like a star's sigh, the shiver and promise of a door opening somewhere just out of reach. I hold my breath, waiting: will it close again?

But no. The curtains billow and I slip from my bed, bare feet curling upon the cold planked floor as I race silently to the window.

He is in the meadow at wood's edge, alone, hair misty with starlight, his pajamas spectral blue in the dark. As I watch he raises his arms to the sky, and though I am too far to hear, I whisper the words with him, my heart thumping counterpoint to our invocation. Then he is quiet, and stands alert, waiting.

I can no longer hear the peepers. The wind has risen, and the thrash of the beech trees at the edge of the forest drowns all other sounds. I can feel his heart now, beating within my own, and see the shadows with his eyes.

In the lower branches of the willow tree, the lone willow that feeds upon a hidden spring beside the sloping lawn, there is a boy. His eyes are green and lucent as tourmaline, and silvery moths are drawn to them. His hands clutch the slender willow-wands: strong hands, so pale that I trace the blood beneath, and see the muscles strung like young strong vines. As I watch he bends so that his head dips beneath a branch, new leaves tangling fair hair, and then slowly he uncurls one hand and, smiling, beckons my brother toward him.

The wind rises. Beneath his bare feet the dewy grass darkens as Aidan runs faster and faster, until he seems almost to be skimming across the lawn. And there, where the willow starts to shadow the starlit slope and the boy in the tree leans to take his hand, I tackle my brother and bring him crashing and swearing to earth.

For a moment he stares at me uncomprehending. Then he yells and slaps me, hits me harder until, remembering, he shoves me away and stumbles to his feet.

There is nothing there. The willow trembles, but only the wind shakes the new leaves. From the marsh the ringing chorus rises, swells, bursts as the peepers stir in the saw grass. In the old house yellow light stains an upstairs window and our father's voice calls out sleepily, then with concern, and finally bellows as he leans from the casement to spot us below. Aidan glances at the house and back again at the willow, and then he turns to me despairingly. Before I can say anything he punches me and runs, weeping, back to the house.

A gentler withdrawal than I'm accustomed to. For several minutes I lay with closed eyes, breathing gently as I tried to hold onto the scents of apple blossom and dew-washed grass. But they faded, along with the dreamy net of tree and stars. I sat up groggily, wires still taped to my head, and faced Dr. Harrow already recording her limbic system response from the NET.

"Thank you, Wendy," she said brusquely without looking up. I glanced at the BEAM monitor, where the shaded image of my brain lingered, the last flash of activity staining the temporal lobe bright turquoise.

"I never saw that color there before," I remarked as I leaned to examine it, when suddenly an unfocused wave of nausea choked me. I gagged and staggered against the bed, tearing at the wires.

Eyes: brilliant green lanced with cyanogen, unblinking as twin chrysolites. A wash of light: leaves stirring the surface of a still pool. They continued to stare through the shadows, heedless of the play of sun and moon, days and years and decades. The electrodes dangled from my fist as I stared at the blank screen, the single dancing line bisecting the NET monitor. The eyes in my head did not move, did not blink, did not disappear. They stared relentlessly from the shadows until the darkness itself swelled and was absorbed by their feral gaze. They saw me.

Not Dr. Harrow; not Aidan; not Morgan or Melisande or the others I'd absorbed in therapy.

Me.

I stumbled from the monitor to the window, dragging the wires behind me, heedless of Dr. Harrow's stunned expression. Grunting I shook my head like a dog, finally gripped the windowsill and slammed my head against the oaken frame, over and over and over, until Dr. Harrow tore me away. Still I saw them: unblinking glaucous eyes, tumbling into darkness as Dr. Harrow pumped the sedatives into my arm.

Much later I woke to see Dr. Harrow staring at me from the far end of the room. She watched me for a moment, and then walked slowly to the bed.

"What was it, Wendy?" she asked, smoothing her robe as she sat beside me. "Your name?"

I shook my head. "I don't know," I stammered, biting the tip of my thumb. Then I twisted to stare at her and asked, "Who was the boy?"

Her voice caught for an instant before she answered. "My brother Aidan. My twin."

"No—The other—The boy in the tree."

This time she held her breath a long moment, then let it out in a sigh. "I don't know," she murmured. "But you remember him?"

I nodded. "Now. I can see him now. If I—" And I shut my eyes and drifted before snapping back. "Like that. He comes to me on his own. Without me recalling him. Like—" I flexed my fingers helplessly. "Like a dream, only I'm awake now."

Slowly Dr. Harrow shook her head and reached to take my hand. "That's how he found Aidan, too, the last time," she said. "And me. And now you." For an instant something like hope flared in her eyes, but faded as she bowed her head. "I think, Wendy . . ." She spoke with measured calm. "I think we should keep this to ourselves right now. And tomorrow, perhaps, we'll try again."

He sees me.

I woke with a garbled scream, arms flailing, to my dark room bathed in the ambient glow of monitors. I stumbled to the window, knelt with my forehead against the cool oak sill and blinked against tears that welled unbidden from my burning eyes. There I fell asleep with my head pillowed upon my arms, and woke next morning to Dr. Harrow's knock upon my door.

"Emma," he whispers at the transom window; "Let me in."

The quilts piled on me muffle his voice. He calls again, louder, until I groan and sit up in bed, rubbing my eyes and glaring at the top of his head peeking through the narrow glass.

From the bottom of the door echoes faint scratching, Molly's whine. A thump. More scratching: Aidan crouched outside the room, growling through choked laughter. I drape a quilt around me like a toga and lean forward to unlatch the door.

Molly flops onto the floor, snorting when she bumps her nose and then drooling apologetically. Behind her stumbles Aidan, shivering in his worn kimono with its tattered sleeves and belt stolen from one of my old dresses. I giggle uncontrollably, and gesture for him to shut the door before Father hears us in his room below.

"It's fucking freezing in this place," Aidan exclaims, pinning me to the bed and pulling the quilts over our heads. "Oh, come on, dog." Grunting, he hauls her up beside us. "My room is like

Antarctica. Tierra del Fuego. The Bering Strait." He punctuates his words with kisses, elbowing Molly as she tries to slobber our faces. I squirm away and straighten my nightshirt.

"Hush. You'll wake Papa."

Aidan rolls his eyes and stretches against the wall. "Spare me." Through the rents in his kimono I can see his skin, dusky in the moonlight. No one has skin like Aidan's, except for me: not white but the palest gray, almost blue, and fine and smooth as an eggshell. People stare at us in the street, especially at Aidan; at school girls stop talking when he passes, and fix me with narrowed eyes and lips pursed to mouth a question never asked.

Aidan yawns remorselessly as a cat. Aidan is the beauty: Aidan whose gray eyes flicker green whereas mine muddy to blue in sunlight; Aidan whose long legs wrap around me and shame my own, scraped and bruised from an unfortunate bout with Papa's razor.

"Molly. Here." He grabs her into his lap, groaning at her weight, and pulls me as well, until we huddle in the middle of the bed. Our heads knock and he points with his chin to the mirror.

"*Did you never see the picture of We Three?*" he warbles. Then, shoving Molly to the floor, he takes my shoulders and pulls the quilt from me.

My father had a daughter loved a man
As it might be perhaps, were I a woman,
I should your lordship.

He recites softly, in his own voice: not the deeper drone he affected when we had been paired in the play that Christmas. I start to slide from bed but he holds me tighter, twisting me to face him until our foreheads touch and I know that the mirror behind us reflects a moon-lapped Rorschach and, at our feet, our snuffling mournful fool.

"*But died thy sister of her love, my boy?*" I whisper later, my lips brushing his neck where the hair, unfashionably long, waves to form a perfect S.

I am all the daughters of my father's house,
And all the brothers, too; and yet I know not.

He kisses me. Later he whispers nonsense, my name, rhyming words from our made-up language; a long and heated silence.

Afterward he sleeps, but I lie long awake, stroking his hair and watching the rise and fall of his slender chest. In the coldest hour he awakens and stares at me, eyes wide and black, and turning on his side moans, then begins to cry as though his heart will break. I clench my teeth and stare at the ceiling, trying not to blink, trying not to hear or feel him next to me, his pale gray skin, his eyes: my beautiful brother in the dark.

After this session Dr. Harrow let me sleep until early afternoon. The rush of summer rain against the high casements finally woke me, and I lay in bed staring up at a long fine crack that traversed the ceiling. To me it looked like the arm of some ghastly tree overtaking the room. It finally drove me downstairs. I ambled down the long glass-roofed corridor that led to the pre-Columbian annex. I paused to pluck a hibiscus blossom from a terra-cotta vase and arranged it behind one ear. Then I went on, until I reached the ancient elevator with its folding arabesques.

The second floor was off limits to empaths, but Anna had memorized a dead patient's release code and she and I occasionally crept up here to tap sleeping researchers. No medical personnel patrolled the rooms. Servers checked the monitors and recorded all responses. At the end of each twelve-hour shift doctors would flit in and out of the bedrooms, unhooking oneironauts and helping them stumble to other rooms where they could fall into yet another, though dreamless, sleep. I tapped the pirated code into the first security unit I saw, waiting for it to read my retina imprint and finally grant the access code that slid open the false paneled wall.

Here stretched the sleep labs: chambers swathed in yellowed challis and moth-eaten linens, huge canopied beds where masked oneironauts turned and sighed as their monitors clicked in draped alcoves. The oneironauts' skin shone glassy white; beneath the masks their eyes were bruised a tender green from enforced somnolence. I held my breath as long as I could: the air seethed with dreams. I hurried down the hall to a room with door ajar and an arched window columned with white drapes. A woman I did not recognize sprawled across a cherry four-poster, her demure lace gown at odds with the rakish mask covering her eyes. I slipped inside, locking the door behind me. Then I turned to the bed.

The research subject's hair formed a dark filigree against the disheveled linen sheets. I bowed to kiss her on the mouth, waiting to be certain she would not awake. Then I dipped my tongue between her lips and drew back, closing my eyes to unravel strands of desire and clouded abandon, pixie fancies. All faded in a moment: dreams, after all, are dreams. I reached to remove the wires connecting her to the monitors, adjusted the settings and hooked her into the NET. I did the same for myself with extra wires, relaying through the BEAM to the transmitter. I smoothed the sheets, lay beside her and closed my eyes.

A gray plain shot with sunlight. Clouds mist the air with a scent of rain and seawater. In the distance I hear waves. Turning I can see a line of small trees, contorted like crippled children at ocean's edge. We walk there, the oneironaut's will bending so easily to mine that I scarcely sense her: she is another salt-scattered breeze.

The trees draw nearer. I stare at them until they shift, stark lichened branches blurring into limbs bowed with green and gentle leaves. Another moment and we are beneath their heavy welcoming boughs.

I place my hand against the rough bark and stare into the heart of the greenery. Within the emerald shadows something stirs. Sunlit shards of leaf and twig align themselves into hands. Shadows shift to form a pair of slanted beryl eyes. There: crouched among the boughs like a dappled cat, his curls crowned with a ring of leaves, his lips parted to show small white teeth. He smiles at me.

Before he draws me any closer I withdraw, snapping the wires from my face. The tree shivers into white sheets and the shrouded body of the woman beside me.

My pounding heart slowed as I drew myself up on my elbows to watch her, carefully peeling the mask from her face. Beneath lids mapped with fine blue veins her eyes roll, tracking something unseen. Suddenly they steady. Her mouth relaxes into a smile, then into an expression of such blissful rapture that without thinking I kiss her and taste a burst of ecstatic, halycon joy.

And reel back as she suddenly claws at my chest, her mouth twisted to shout; but no sound comes. Bliss explodes into terror. Her eyes open and she stares, not at me but at something that looms before her. Her eyes grow wide and horrified, the pupils dilating as she grabs at my face, tears the hibiscus blossom from my hair and chokes a garbled scream, a shout I muffle with a pillow.

I whirled and reset the monitors, switched the NET's settings and fled out the door. In the hallway I hesitated and looked back. The woman pummeled the air before her blindly; she had not seen me. I turned and ran until I reached the doctors' stairway leading to the floors below, and slipped away unseen.

Downstairs all was silent. Servers creaked past bringing tea trays to doctors in their quarters. I hurried to the conservatory, where I inquired after the aide named Justice. The server directed me to a chamber where Justice stood recording the results of an evoked potential scan.

"Wendy!" Surprise melted into disquiet. "What are you doing here?"

I shut the door and stepped to the window, tugging the heavy velvet drapes until they fell and the chamber darkened. "I want you to scan me," I whispered.

He shook his head. "What? Why—" I grabbed his hand as he tried to turn up the lights and he nodded slowly, then dimmed the screen he had been working on. "Where is Dr. Harrow?"

"I want you to do it." I tightened my grip. "I think I have entered a fugue state."

He smiled, shaking his head. "That's impossible, Wendy. You'd have no way of knowing it. You'd be catatonic, or—" He shrugged, then glanced uneasily at the door. "What's going on? You know I'm not certified to do that alone."

"But you know how," I wheedled, stroking his hand. "You are a student of their arts, you can do it as easily as Dr. Harrow." Smiling, I leaned forward until my forehead rested against his, and kissed him tentatively on the mouth. His expression changed to fear as he trembled and tried to move away. Sexual contact between staff and experimental personnel was forbidden and punishable by execution of the medics in question; empaths were believed incapable of initiating such contact. I grinned more broadly and pinned both of his hands to the table, until he nodded and motioned with his head toward the PET unit.

"Sit down," he croaked. I latched the door, then sat in the wing-back chair beside the bank of monitors.

In a few minutes I heard the dull hum of the scanners as he improvised the link for my reading. I waited until my brain's familiar patterns emerged on the screen.

"See?" Relief brightened his voice, and he tilted the monitor so that I could see it more clearly. "All normal. Maybe she got your dosage wrong. Perhaps Dr. Silverthorn can suggest a—"

His words trickled into silence. I shut my eyes and drew up the image of the tree, beryl eyes and outstretched hand, then opened my eyes to see the PET scan showing intrusive activity in my temporal lobe: brain waves evident of an emergent secondary personality.

"That's impossible," Justice breathed. "You have no MPs, no independent emotions—What the hell is that?" He traced the patterns with an unsteady hand, then turned to stare at me. "What did you do, Wendy?" he whispered.

I shook my head, crouching into the chair's corner, and carefully removed the wires. The last image shimmered on the screen like a cerebral ghost. "Take them," I said flatly, holding out the wires. "Don't tell anyone."

He let me pass without a word. Only when my hand grasped the doorknob did he touch me briefly on the shoulder.

"Where did it come from?" he faltered. "What is it, Wendy?"

I stared past him at the monitor with its pulsing shadows. "Not me," I whispered at last. "The boy in the tree."

They found the sleep researcher at shift-change that evening, hanging by the swag that had decorated her canopied bed. Anna told me about it at dinner.

"Her monitors registered an emergent MP." She licked her lips unconsciously, like a kitten. "Do you think we could get into the morgue?"

I yawned and shook my head. "Are you crazy?"

Anna giggled and rubbed my neck. "Isn't everybody?"

Several aides entered the dining room, scanning warily before they started tapping empties on the shoulder and gesturing to the door. I looked up to see Justice, his face white and pinched as he stood behind me.

"You're to go to your chambers," he announced. "Dr. Harrow says you are not to talk to anyone." He swallowed and avoided my eyes, then abruptly stared directly at me for the first time. "I told her that I hadn't seen you yet but would make certain you knew."

I nodded quickly and looked away. In a moment he was gone, and I started upstairs.

"I saw Dr. Leslie before," Anna commented before she walked outside toward her cottage. "He smiled at me and waved." She hesitated, biting her lip thoughtfully. "Maybe he will play with me this time," she announced before turning down the rain-spattered path.

Dr. Harrow stood at the high window in the Horne Room when I arrived. In her hand she held a drooping hibiscus flower.

"Shut the door," she ordered. I did so. "Now lock it and sit down."

She had broken the hibiscus. Her fingers looked bruised from its stain: jaundiced yellow, ulcerous purple. As I stared she flung the flower into my lap.

"They know it was you," she announced. "They matched your retina print with the masterfile. How could you have thought you'd get away with it?" She sank onto the bed, her eyes dull with fatigue.

The rain had hung back for several hours, a heavy iron veil. Now it hammered the windows again, its steady tattoo punctuated by the rattle of hailstones.

"I did not mean to kill her," I murmured. I smoothed my robe, flicking the broken blossom onto the floor.

She ground the hibiscus beneath her heel, took it and threw it out the window. "Her face," she said: as if replying to a question. "Like my brother Aidan's."

I stared at her blankly.

"When I found him," she went on, turning to me with glittering eyes. "On the tree."

I shook my head. "I don't know what you're talking about, Dr. Harrow."

Her lips tightened against her teeth when she faced me. A drop of blood welled against her lower lip. I longed to lean forward to taste it, but did not dare. "She was right, you know. You steal our dreams . . ."

"That's impossible." I crossed my arms, shivering a little from the damp breeze. I hesitated. "You told me that is impossible. Unscientific. Unprofessional thinking."

She smiled, and ran her tongue over her lip to lick away the blood. "Unprofessional? This has all been very unprofessional, Wendy. Didn't you know that?"

"The tenets of the Nuremberg Act state that a scientist should not perform any research upon a subject which she would not undergo herself."

Dr. Harrow shook her head, ran a hand through damp hair. "Is that what you thought it was? Research?"

I shrugged. "I—I don't know. The boy—Your twin?"

"Aidan . . ." She spread her fingers against the bed's coverlet, flexed a finger that bore a simple silver ring. "They found out. Teachers. Our father. About us. Do you understand?"

A flicker of the feeling she had evoked in bed with her brother returned, and I slitted my eyes, tracing it. "Yes," I whispered. "I think so."

"It is—" She fumbled for a phrase. "Like what is forbidden here, between empaths and staff. They separated us. Aidan . . . They sent him away, to another kind of—school. Tested him."

She stood and paced to the window, leaned with a hand upon each side so that the rain lashed about her, then turned back to me with her face streaming: whether with rain or tears I could not tell. "Something happened that night . . ." Shaking her head furiously she pounded the wall with flattened palms. "He was never the same. He had terrible dreams, he couldn't bear to sleep alone— That was how it started—

"And then he came home, for the holidays . . . Good Friday. He would not come to Mass with us. Papa was furious; but Aidan wouldn't leave his room. And when we returned, I looked for him, he wasn't there, not in his room, not anywhere . . .

"I found him. He had—" Her voice broke and she stared past me to the wall beyond. "Apple blossom in his hair. And his face—"

I thought she would weep; but her expression twisted so that almost I could imagine she laughed to recall it.

"Like hers . . ."

She drew nearer, until her eyes were very close to mine. I sniffed and moved to the edge of the bed warily: she had dosed herself with hyoscine derived from the herbarium. Now her words slurred as she spoke, spittle a fine hail about her face.

"Do you know what happens now, Wendy?" In the rain-streaked light she glowed faintly. "Dr. Leslie was here tonight. They have canceled our term of research. We're all terminated. A purge. Tomorrow they take over."

She made a clicking noise with her tongue. "And you, Wendy. And Anna, and all the others. Toys. *Weapons.*" She swayed slightly as she leaned toward me. "You especially. They'll find him, you know. Dig him up and use him."

"Who?" I asked. Now sweat pearled where the rain had dried on her forehead. I clutched a bolster as she stretched a hand to graze my temples, and shivered.

"My brother," she murmured.

"No, Dr. Harrow. The other—who is the other?"

Smiling she drew me toward her, the bolster pressing against her thigh as she reached for the NET's rig, flicking rain from the colored wires.

"Let's find out."

I cried out at her clumsy hookup. A spot of blood welled from her temple and I protectively touched my own face, drew away a finger gelled with the fluid she had smeared carelessly from ear to jaw. Then, before I could lie down, she made the switch and I cried out at the dizzy vistas erupting behind my eyes.

Aniline lightning. Faculae stream from synapse to synapse as ptyalin floods my mouth and my head rears instinctively to smash against the headboard. She has not tied me down. The hyoscine lashes into me like a fiery bile and I open my mouth to scream. In the instant before it begins I taste something faint and caustic in the back of her throat and struggle to free myself from her arms. Then I'm gone.

Before me looms a willow tree shivering in a breeze frigid with the shadow of the northern mountains. Sap oozes from a raw flat yellow scar on the trunk above my head where, two days before, my father had sawed the damaged limb free. It had broken from the weight; when I found him he lay pillowed by a crush of twigs and young leaves and scattered bark, the blossoms in his hair alone unmarked by the fall. Now I stand on tiptoe and stroke the splintery wound, bring my finger to my lips and kiss it. I shut my eyes, because they burn so. No tears left to shed; only this terrible dry throbbing, as though my eyes have been etched with sand. The sobs begin again, suddenly. The wrenching weight in my chest drags me to my knees until I crouch before the tree, bow until my forehead brushes grass trampled by grieving family. I groan and try to think of words, imprecations, a curse to rend the light and living from my world so abruptly strangled and still. But I can only moan. My mouth opens upon dirt and shattered granite. My nails claw at the ground as though to wrest from it something besides stony roots and scurrying earwigs. The earth swallows my voice as I force myself to my knees and, sobbing, raise my head to the tree.

It is enough; he has heard me. Through the shroud of new leaves he peers with lambent eyes. April's first apple blossoms weave a snowy cloud about his brow. His eyes are huge, the palest, purest green in the cold morning sun. They stare at me unblinking; harsh and bright and implacable as moonlight, as languidly he extends his hand toward mine.

I stagger to my feet, clots of dirt falling from my palms. From the north the wind rises and rattles the willow branches. Behind me a door rattles as well, as my father leans out to call me back to the house. At the sound I start to turn, to break the reverie that binds me to this place, this tree stirred by a tainted wind riven from a bleak and noiseless shore.

And then I stop, where in memory I have stopped a thousand times; and turn back to the tree, and for the first time I meet his eyes.

He is waiting, as he has always waited; as he will always wait. At my neck the wind gnaws cold as bitter iron, stirring the collar of my blouse so that already the chill creeps down my chest, to nuzzle there at my breasts and burrow between them. I nod my head, very slightly, and glance back at the house.

All the colors have fled the world. For the first time I see it clearly: the gray skin taut against granite hills and grassless haughs; the horizon livid with clouds like a rising barrow; the hollow bones and nerveless hands drowned beneath black waters lapping at the edge of a charred orchard. The rest is fled and I see the true world now, the sleeping world as it wakes, as it rears from the ruins and whispers in the wind at my cheeks, this is what awaits you; this and nothing more, the lie is revealed and now you are waking and the time has come, come to me, come to me . . .

In the ghastly light only his eyes glow, and it is to them that I turn, it is into those hands white and cold and welcome that I slip my own, it is to him that I have come, not weeping, no not ever again, not laughing, but still and steady and cold as the earth beneath my feet, the gray earth that feeds the roots and limbs and shuddering leaves of the tree . . .

And then pain rips through me, a flood of fire searing my mouth and ears, raging so that I stagger from the bed as tree and sky and earth tilt and shiver like images in black water. Gagging I reach into my own throat, trying to dislodge the capsule Emma Harrow has bitten; try to breath through the fumes that strip the skin from my gums. I open my mouth to scream but the fire churns through throat and chest, boils until my eyes run and stain the sky crimson.

And then I fall; the wires rip from my skull. Beside me on the floor Dr. Harrow thrashed, eyes staring wildly at the ceiling, her mouth rigid as she retched and blood spurted from her bitten tongue. I recoiled from the scent of bitter almond she exhaled; then watched as she suddenly grew still. Quickly I knelt, tilting her head away so that half of the broken capsule rolled onto the floor at my feet. I waited a moment, then bowed my head until my lips parted around her broken jaw and my tongue stretched gingerly to lap at the blood cupped in her cheek.

In the tree the boy laughs. A bowed branch shivers, and then, slowly, rises from the ground. Another boy dangles there, his long hair tangled in dark strands around a leather belt. I see him lift his head and, as the world rushes away in a blur of red and black, he smiles at me.

A cloud of frankincense. Seven stars limned against a dormer window. A boy with a bulldog puppy; and she is dead.

*   *   *

I cannot leave my room now. Beside me a screen dances with colored lights that refract and explode in brilliant parhelions when I dream. But I am not alone now, ever . . .

I see him waiting in the corner, laughing as his green eyes slip between the branches and the bars of my window, until the sunlight changes and he is lost to view once more, among the dappled and chattering leaves.

This began as a trope on Arthur Machen's classic story "The Great God Pan" and eventually grew into my first novel, *Winterlong*. An odd coincidence: M. John Harrison's story "The Great God Pan," another take on Machen, appeared about the same time, and grew into Harrison's extraordinary novel *The Course of the Heart*. (Peter Straub used the same tale as the inspiration for his *Ghost Story*.) "The Boy in the Tree" is more concise than the first part of *Winterlong*; certainly it works better as pure story than the novel does. I had sent it to the editor of the *Universe* anthology, who rejected it, saying the writing was elegant but the story's basic premise offensive. *But*—if I rewrote it, changing the first-person narrator and toning down some of the more unpleasant aspects of the Human Engineering Laboratory, *Universe* would consider buying it.

This was a tough call. I was broke, I'd made only one other sale ("Prince of Flowers"); but the thought of defanging the story made me sick to my stomach. Fortunately, I'd disobeyed Rule Number 3 for Fledgling Writers (*No Simultaneous Submissions*) and a week later Shawna McCarthy took it for Bantam's *Full Spectrum 2*.

Prince of Flowers

Helen's first assignment on the inventory project was to the Department of Worms. For two weeks she paced the narrow alleys between immense tiers of glass cabinets, opening endless drawers of freeze-dried invertebrates and tagging each with an acquisition number. Occasionally she glimpsed other figures, drab as herself in government-issue smocks, gray shadows stalking through the murky corridors. They waved at her but seldom spoke, except to ask directions; everyone got lost in the Museum.

Helen loved the hours lost in wandering the labyrinth of storage rooms, research labs, chilly vaults crammed with effigies of Yanomano Indians and stuffed jaguars. Soon she could identify each department by its smell: acrid dust from the feathered pelts in Ornithology; the cloying reek of fenugreek and syrup in Mammalogy's roach traps; fish and formaldehyde in Icthyology. Her favorite was Paleontology, an annex where the air smelled damp and clean, as though beneath the marble floors trickled hidden water, undiscovered caves, mammoth bones to match those stored above. When her two weeks in Worms ended she was sent to Paleo, where she delighted in the skeletons strewn atop cabinets like forgotten toys, disembodied skulls glaring from behind wastebaskets and book-shelves. She found a *fabrosaurus ischium* wrapped in brown paper and labeled in crayon; beside it a huge hand-hewn crate dated 1886 and marked WYOMING MEGOSAUR. It had never been opened. Some mornings she sat with a small mound of fossils before her, fitting the pieces together with the aid of a Victorian monograph. Hours passed in total silence, weeks when she saw only three or four people, cura-tors slouching in and out of their research cubicles. On Fridays, when she dropped off her inventory sheets, they smiled. Occasionally even remembered her name. But mostly she was left alone, sorting cartons of bone and shale, prying apart frail skeletons of extinct fish as though they were stacks of newsprint.

Once, almost without thinking, she slipped a fossil fish into the pocket of her smock. The fossil was the length of her hand, as per-fectly formed as a fresh beech leaf. All day she fingered it, tracing the imprint of bone and scale. In the bathroom later she wrapped it in paper towels and hid it in her purse to bring home. After that she started taking things.

At a downtown hobby shop she bought little brass and lucite stands to display them in her apartment. No one else ever saw them. She simply liked to look at them alone.

Her next transfer was to Mineralogy, where she counted mis-shapen meteorites and uncut gems. Gems bored her, although she took a chunk of petrified wood and a handful of unpolished amethysts and put them in her bathroom. A month later she was permanently assigned to Anthropology.

The Anthropology Department was in the most remote corner of the Museum; its proximity to the boiler room made it warmer than the Natural Sciences wing, the air redolent of spice woods and exotic unguents used to polish arrowheads and ax-shafts. The ceil-ing reared so high overhead that the rickety lamps swayed slightly in drafts that Helen longed to feel. The constant subtle motion of the lamps sent flickering waves of light across the floor. Raised arms of Balinese statues seemed to undulate, and points of light winked behind the empty eyeholes of feathered masks.

Everywhere loomed shelves stacked with smooth ivory and gaudily beaded bracelets and neck-rings. Helen crouched in cor-ners loading her arms with bangles until her wrists ached from their weight. She unearthed dusty lurid figures of temple demons and cleaned them, polished hollow cheeks and lapis eyes before stapling a number to each figure. A corner piled with tipi poles hid an abandoned desk that she claimed and decorated with mummy photographs and a ceramic coffee mug. In the top drawer she stored her cassette tapes and, beneath her handbag, a number of obsidian arrowheads. While it was never officially designated as her desk, she was annoyed one morning to find a young man tilted backward in the chair, shuffling through her tapes.

"Hello," he greeted her cheerfully. Helen winced and nodded coolly. "These your tapes? I'll borrow this one someday, haven't got the album yet. Leo Bryant—"

"Helen," she replied bluntly. "I think there's an empty desk down by the slit-gongs."

"Thanks, I just started. You a curator?"

Helen shook her head, rearranging the cassettes on the desk, "No. Inventory project." Pointedly she moved his knapsack to the floor.

"Me, too. Maybe we can work together sometime."

She glanced at his earnest face and smiled. "I like to work alone, thanks." He looked hurt, and she added, "Nothing personal—I just like it that way. I'm sure we'll run into each other. Nice to meet you, Leo." She grabbed a stack of inventory sheets and walked away down the corridor.

They met for coffee one morning. After a few weeks they met almost every morning, sometimes even for lunch outside on the Mall. During the day Leo wandered over from his cubicle in Ethnology to pass on departmental gossip. Sometimes they had a drink after work, but never often enough to invite gossip themselves. Helen was happy with this arrangement, the curators delighted to have such a worker—quiet, without ambition, punctual. Everyone except Leo left her to herself.

Late one afternoon Helen turned at the wrong corner and found herself in a small cul-de-sac between stacks of crates that cut off light and air. She yawned, breathing the faint must of cinnamon bark as she traced her path on a crumpled inventory map. This narrow alley was unmarked; the adjoining corridors contained

Malaysian artifacts, batik tools, long teak boxes of gongs. Fallen crates, clumsily hewn cartons overflowing with straw were scattered on the floor. Splintered panels snagged her sleeves as she edged her way down the aisle. A sweet musk hung about these cartons, the languorous essence of unknown blossoms.

At the end of the cul-de-sac an entire row of crates had toppled, as though the weight of time had finally pitched them to the floor. Helen squatted and chose a box at random, a broad flat package like a portfolio. She pried the lid off to find a stack of leather cutouts curling with age, like dessicated cloth. She drew one carefully from the pile, frowning as its edges disintegrated at her touch. A shadow puppet, so fantastically elaborate that she couldn't tell if it was male or female; it scarcely looked human. Light glimmered through the grotesque latticework as Helen jerked it back and forth, its pale shadow dancing across the wall. Then the puppet split and crumbled into brittle curlicues that formed strange heiroglyphics on the black marble floor. Swearing softly, Helen replaced the lid, then jammed the box back into the shadows. Her fingers brushed another crate, of smooth polished mahogany. It had a comfortable heft as she pulled it into her lap. Each corner of the narrow lid was fixed with a large, squareheaded nail. Helen yanked these out and set each upright in a row.

As she opened the box, dried flowers, seeds, and wood shavings cascaded into her lap. She inhaled, closing her eyes, and imagined blue water and firelight, sweet-smelling seeds exploding in the embers. She sneezed and opened her eyes to a cloud of dust wafting from the crate like smoke. Very carefully she worked her fingers into the fragrant excelsior, kneading the petals gently until she grasped something brittle and solid. She drew this out in a flurry of dead flowers.

It was a puppet: not a toy, but a gorgeously costumed figure, spindly arms clattering with glass and bone circlets, batik robes heavy with embroidery and beadwork. Long whittled pegs formed its torso and arms and the rods that swiveled it back and forth, so that its robes rippled tremulously, like a swallowtail's wings. Held at arm's length it gazed scornfully down at Helen, its face glinting with gilt paint. Sinuous vines twisted around each jointed arm. Flowers glowed within the rich threads of its robe, orchids blossoming in the folds of indigo cloth.

Loveliest of all was its face, the curve of cheeks and chin so gracefully arched it might have been cast in gold rather than coaxed from wood. Helen brushed it with a finger: the glossy white paint gleamed as though still wet. She touched the carmine bow that formed its mouth, traced the jet-black lashes stippled across its brow, like a regiment of ants. The smooth wood felt warm to her touch as she stroked it with her fingertips. A courtesan might have perfected its sphinx's smile; but in the tide of petals Helen discovered a slip of paper covered with spidery characters. Beneath the straggling script another hand had shaped clumsy block letters spelling out the name PRINCE OF FLOWERS.

Once, perhaps, an imperial concubine had entertained herself with its fey posturing, and so passed the wet silences of a long green season. For the rest of the afternoon it was Helen's toy. She posed it and sent its robes dancing in the twilit room, the frail arms and tiny wrists twitching in a marionette's waltz.

Behind her a voice called, "Helen?"

"Leo," she murmured. "Look what I found."

He hunched beside her to peer at the figure. "Beautiful. Is that what you're on now? Balinese artifacts?"

She shrugged. "Is that what it is? I didn't know." She glanced down the dark rows of cabinets and sighed. "I probably shouldn't be here. It's just so hot—" She stretched and yawned as Leo slid the puppet from her hands.

"Can I see it?" He twisted it until its head spun and the stiff arms flittered. "Wild. Like one of those dancers in *The King and I*." He played with it absently, hypnotized by the swirling robes. When he stopped, the puppet jerked abruptly upright, its blank eyes staring at Helen.

"Be careful," she warned, kneading her smock between her thumbs. "It's got to be a hundred years old." She held out her hands and Leo returned it, bemused.

"It's wild, whatever it is." He stood and stretched. "I'm going to get a soda. Want to come?"

"I better get back to what I was working on. I'm supposed to finish the Burmese section this week." Casually she set the puppet in its box, brushed the dried flowers from her lap and stood.

"Sure you don't want a soda or something?" Leo hedged plaintively, snapping his ID badge against his chest. "You said you were hot."

"No thanks," Helen smiled wanly. "I'll take a raincheck. Tomorrow."

Peeved, Leo muttered and stalked off. When his silhouette faded away she turned and quickly pulled the box into a dim corner. There she emptied her handbag and arranged the puppet at its bottom, wrapping Kleenex about its arms and face. Hairbrush, wallet, lipstick: all thrown back into her purse, hiding the puppet beneath their clutter. She repacked the crate with its sad array of blossoms, hammering the lid back with her shoe. Then she scrabbled in the corner on her knees until she located a space between stacks of cartons. With a resounding crack the empty box struck the wall, and Helen grinned as she kicked more boxes to fill the gap. Years from now another inventory technician would discover it and wonder, as she had countless times, what had once been inside the empty carton.

When she crowded into the elevator that afternoon the leather handle of her purse stuck to her palm like wet rope. She shifted the bag casually as more people stepped on at each floor, heart pounding as she called goodbye to the curator for Indo-Asian Studies passing in the lobby. Imaginary prison gates loomed and crumbled behind Helen as she strode through the columned doors and into the summer street.

All the way home she smiled triumphantly, clutching her handbag to her chest. As she fumbled at the front door for her keys a fresh burst of scent rose from the recesses of her purse. Inside, another scent overpowered this faint perfume—the thick reek of creosote, rotting fruit, unwashed clothes. Musty and hot and dark as the Museum's dreariest basement, the only two windows faced onto the street. Traffic ground past, piping bluish exhaust through the screens. A grimy mirror reflected shabby chairs, an end table with lopsided lamp: furniture filched from college dormitories or reclaimed from the corner dumpster. No paintings graced the pocked walls, blotched with the crushed remains of roaches and silverfish.

But beautiful things shone here, gleaming from windowsills and cracked formica counters: the limp frond of a fossil fern, etched in obsidian glossy as wet tar; a whorled nautilus like a tiny whirlpool impaled upon a brass stand. In the center of a splintered coffee table was the imprint of a foot-long dragonfly's wing embedded in limestone, its filigreed scales a shattered prism.

Corners heaped with lemur skulls and slabs of petrified wood. The exquisite cone shells of poisonous mollusks. Mounds of green and golden iridescent beetles, like the coinage of a distant country. Patches of linoleum scattered with shark's teeth and arrowheads; a tiny skull anchoring a handful of emerald plumes that waved in the breeze like a sea-fan. Helen surveyed it all critically, noting with mild surprise a luminous pink geode: she'd forgotten that one. Then she set to work.

In a few minutes she'd removed everything from her bag and rolled the geode under a chair. She unwrapped the puppet on the table, peeling tissue from its brittle arms and finally twisting the long strand of white paper from its head, until she stood ankle-deep in a drift of tissue. The puppet's supporting rod slid neatly into the mouth of an empty beer bottle, and she arranged it so that the glass was hidden by its robes and the imperious face tilted upward, staring at the bug-flecked ceiling.

Helen squinted appraisingly, rearranged the feathers about the puppet, shoring them up with the carapaces of scarab beetles: still it looked all wrong. Beside the small proud figure, the fossils were muddy remains, the nautilus a bit of sea-wrack. A breeze shifted the puppet's robes, knocking the scarabs to the floor, and before she knew it Helen had crushed them, the little emerald shells splintering to gray dust beneath her heel. She sighed in exasperation: all her pretty things suddenly looked so mean. She moved the puppet to the windowsill, to another table, and finally into her bedroom. No corner of the flat could hold it without seeming even grimier than before. Helen swiped at cobwebs above the doorway before setting the puppet on her bed-stand and collapsing with a sigh onto her mattress.

In the half-light of the windowless bedroom the figure was not so resplendent. Disappointed, Helen straightened its robes yet again. As she tugged the cloth into place, two violet petals, each the size of her pinky nail, slipped between her fingers. She rolled the tiny blossom between her palm, surprised at how damp and fresh they felt, how they breathed a scent like ozone, or seawater. Thoughtfully she rubbed the violets until only a gritty pellet remained between her fingers.

Flowers, she thought, and recalled the name on the paper she'd found. The haughty figure wanted flowers.

Grabbing her key and a rusty pair of scissors, she ran outside. Thirty minutes later she returned, laden with blossoms: torn branches of crepe myrtle frothing pink and white, drooping tongues of honeysuckle, overblown white roses snipped from a neighbor's yard; chicory fading like a handful of blue stars. She dropped them all at the foot of the bed and then searched the kitchen until she found a dusty wine carafe and some empty jars. Once these were rinsed and filled with water she made a number of unruly bouquets, then placed them all around the puppet, so that its pale head nodded amid a cloud of white and mauve and frail green.

Helen slumped back on the bed, grinning with approval. Bottles trapped the wavering pools of light and cast shimmering reflections across the walls. The crepe myrtle sent the palest mauve cloud onto the ceiling, blurring the jungle shadows of the honeysuckle.

Helen's head blurred, as well. She yawned, drowsy from the thick scents of roses, cloying honeysuckle, all the languor of summer nodding in an afternoon. She fell quickly asleep, lulled by the breeze in the stolen garden and the dozy burr of a lost bumblebee.

Once, her sleep broke. A breath of motion against her shoulder—mosquito? spider? centipede?—then a tiny lancing pain, the touch of invisible legs or wings, and it was gone. Helen grimaced, scratched, staggered up and into the bathroom. Her bleary reflection showed a swollen bite on her shoulder. It tingled, and a drop of blood pearled at her touch. She put on a nightshirt, checked her bed for spiders, then tumbled back to sleep.

Much later she woke to a sound: once, twice, like the resonant *plank* of a stone tossed into a well. Then a slow melancholy note: another well, a larger stone striking its dark surface. Helen moaned, turning onto her side. Fainter echoes joined these first sounds, plangent tones sweet as rain in the mouth. Her ears rang with this steady pulse, until suddenly she clenched her hands and stiffened, concentrating on the noise.

From wall to ceiling to floor the thrumming echo bounced; grew louder, diminished, droned to a whisper. It did not stop. Helen sat up, bracing herself against the wall, the last shards of sleep fallen from her. Her hand slipped and very slowly she drew it toward her

face. It was wet. Between her fingers glistened a web of water, loop-
ing like silver twine down her wrist until it was lost in the blue-
veined valley of her elbow. Helen shook her head in disbelief and
stared up at the ceiling. From one end of the room to the other
stretched a filament of water, like a hairline fracture. As she watched,
the filament snapped and a single warm drop splashed her temple.
Helen swore and slid to the edge of the mattress, then stopped.

At first she thought the vases had fallen to the floor, strewing
flowers everywhere. But the bottles remained on the bedstand, their
blossoms casting ragged silhouettes in the dark. More flowers were
scattered about the bottles: violets, crimson roses, a tendril rampant
with tiny fluted petals. Flowers cascaded to the floor, nestled amid
folds of dirty clothes. Helen plucked an orchid from the linoleum,
blinking in amazement. Like a wavering pink flame it glowed, the
feathery pistils staining her fingertips bright yellow. Absently Helen
brushed the pollen onto her thigh, scraping her leg with a hangnail.

That small pain jarred her awake. She dropped the orchid. For
the first time it didn't feel like a dream. The room was hot, humid
as though moist towels pressed against her face. As she stared at
her thigh the bright fingerprint, yellow as a crocus, melted and dissolved as sweat broke on her skin. She stepped forward, the orchid
bursting beneath her heel like a ripe grape. A sickly smell rose from
the broken flower. Each breath she took was heavy, as with rain,
and she choked. The rims of her nostrils were wet. She sneezed,
inhaling warm water. Water streamed down her cheeks and she
drew her hand slowly upward, to brush the water from her eyes.
She could move it no further than her lap. She looked down,
silently mouthing bewilderment as she shook her head.

Another hand grasped her wrist, a hand delicate and limp as a
cut iris wand, so small that she scarcely felt its touch open her
pulse. Inside her skull the blood thrummed counterpoint to the
gamelan, gongs echoing the throb and beat of her heart. The little
hand disappeared. Helen staggered backward onto the bed, frantically scrambling for the light switch. In the darkness, something
crept across the rippling bedsheets.

When she screamed her mouth was stuffed with roses, orchids,
the corner of her pillowcase. Tiny hands pinched her nostrils shut
and forced more flowers between her lips until she lay still, gagging

on aromatic petals. From the rumpled bedclothes reared a shadow, child-size, grinning. Livid shoots of green and yellow encircled its spindly arms and the sheets whispered like rain as it crawled towards her. Like a great mantis it dragged itself forward on its long arms, the rough cloth of its robe catching between her knees, its white teeth glittering. She clawed through the sheets, trying to dash it against the wall. But she could not move. Flowers spilled from her mouth when she tried to scream, soft fingers of orchids sliding down her throat as she flailed at the bedclothes.

And the clanging of the gongs did not cease: not when the tiny hands pattered over her breasts; not when the tiny mouth hissed in her ear. Needle teeth pierced her shoulder as a long tongue unfurled and lapped there, flicking blood onto the blossoms wreathed about her neck. Only when the slender shadow withdrew and the terrible, terrible dreams began did the *gamelans* grow silent.

Nine thirty came, long after Helen usually met Leo in the cafeteria. He waited, drinking an entire pot of coffee before he gave up and wandered downstairs, piqued that she hadn't shown up for breakfast.

In the same narrow hallway behind the Malaysian artifacts he discovered her, crouched over a pair of tapered wooden crates. For a long moment he watched her, and almost turned back without saying anything. Her hair was dirty, twisted into a sloppy bun, and the hunch of her shoulders hinted at exhaustion. But before he could leave, she turned to face him, clutching the boxes to her chest.

"Rough night?" croaked Leo. A scarf tied around her neck didn't hide the bruises there. Her mouth was swollen, her eyes soft and shadowed with sleeplessness. He knew she must see people, men, boyfriends. But she had never mentioned anyone, never spoke of weekend trips or vacations. Suddenly he felt betrayed, and spun away to leave.

"Leo," murmured Helen, absently stroking the crate. "I can't talk right now. I got in so late. I'm kind of busy."

"I guess so." He laughed uncertainly, but stopped before turning the corner to see her pry open the lid of the box, head bent so that he could not tell what it was she found inside.

A week passed. Leo refused to call her. He timed his forays to the cafeteria to avoid meeting her there. He left work late so he wouldn't see her in the elevator. Every day he expected to see her at his desk, find a telephone message scrawled on his memo pad. But she never appeared.

Another week went by. Leo ran into the curator for Indo-Asian Studies by the elevator.

"Have you seen Helen this week?" she asked, and Leo actually blushed at mention of her name.

"No," he mumbled. "Not for a while, really."

"Guess she's sick." The curator shrugged and stepped onto the elevator. Leo rode all the way down to the basement and roamed the corridors for an hour, dropping by the Anthropology office. No Helen, no messages from her at the desk.

He wandered back down the hall, pausing in the corridor where he had last seen her. A row of boxes had collapsed and he kicked at the cartons, idly knelt and read the names on the packing crates as if they held a clue to Helen's sudden change. Labels in Sanskrit, Vietnamese, Chinese, English, crumbling beside baggage labels and exotic postage stamps and scrawled descriptions of contents. WAJANG GOLEH, he read. Beneath was scribbled PUPPETS. He squatted on the floor, staring at the bank of crates, then half-heartedly started to read each label. Maybe she'd find him there. Perhaps she'd been sick, had a doctor's appointment. She might be late again.

A long box rattled when he shifted it. KRIS, read the label, and he peeked inside to find an ornate sword. A heavier box bore the legend SANGHYANG: SPIRIT PUPPET. And another that seemed to be empty, embellished with a flowing script: SEKAR MAS, and the clumsy translation PRINCE OF FLOWERS.

He slammed the last box against the wall and heard the dull creak of splintering wood. She would not be in today. She hadn't been in for two weeks.

That night he called her.

"Hello?"

Helen's voice; at least a man hadn't answered.

"Helen. How you doing? It's Leo."

"Leo." She coughed and he heard someone in the background. "It's you."

"Right," he said dryly, then waited for an apology, her embarrassed laugh, another cough that would be followed by an invented catalogue of hayfever, colds, flu. But she said nothing. He listened carefully and realized it wasn't a voice he had heard in the background but a constant stir of sound, like a fan, or running water. "Helen? You okay?"

A long pause. "Sure. Sure I'm okay." Her voice faded and he heard a high, piping note.

"You got a bird, Helen?"

"What?"

He shifted the phone to his other ear, shoving it closer to his head so he could hear better. "A bird. There's this funny voice, it sounds like you got a bird or something."

"No," replied Helen slowly. "I don't have a bird. There's nothing wrong with my phone." He could hear her moving around her apartment, the background noises rising and falling but never silent. "Leo, I can't talk now. I'll see you tomorrow, okay?"

"Tomorrow?" he exploded. "I haven't seen you in two weeks!"

She coughed and said, "Well, I'm sorry. I've been busy. I'll see you tomorrow. Bye."

He started to argue, but the phone was already dead.

She didn't come in the next day. At three o'clock he went to the Anthropology Department and asked the secretary if Helen had been in that morning.

"No," she answered, shaking her head. "And they've got her down as AWOL. She hasn't been in all week." She hesitated before whispering. "Leo, she hasn't looked very good lately. You think maybe . . ." Her voice died and she shrugged, "Who knows," and turned to answer the phone.

He left work early, walking his bicycle up the garage ramp and wheeling it to the right, toward Helen's neighborhood. He was fuming, but a sliver of fear had worked its way through his anger. He had almost gone to her supervisor; almost phoned Helen first. Instead, he pedaled quickly down Pennsylvania Avenue, skirting the first lanes of rush hour traffic. Union Station loomed a few blocks ahead. He recalled an article in yesterday's *Post:* vandals had destroyed the rose garden in front of the station. He detoured through the bus lane that circled the building and skimmed around the desecrated garden, shaking his head and staring back in dismay. All the roses: gone.

Someone had lopped each bloom from its stem. In spots the cobble-stones were littered with mounds of blossoms, brown with decay. Here and there dead flowers still dangled from hacked stems. Swearing in disgust Leo made a final loop, nearly skidding into a bus as he looked back at the plundered garden. Then he headed toward Helen's apartment building a few blocks north.

Her windows were dark. Even from the street the curtains looked filthy, as though dirt and exhaust had matted them to the glass. Leo stood on the curb and stared at the blank eyes of each apartment window gaping in the stark concrete façade.

Who would want to live here? he thought, ashamed. He should have come sooner. Shame froze into apprehension and the faintest icy sheath of fear. Hurriedly he locked his bike to a parking meter and approached her window, standing on tiptoe to peer inside. Nothing. The discolored curtains hid the rooms from him like clouds of ivory smoke. He tapped once, tentatively; then, emboldened by silence, rapped for several minutes, squinting to see any movement inside.

Still nothing. Leo swore out loud and slung his hands into his pockets, wondering lamely what to do. Call the police? Next of kin? He winced at the thought: as if she couldn't do that herself. Helen had always made it clear that she enjoyed being on her own. But the broken glass beneath his sneakers, windblown newspapers tugging at the bottom steps; the whole unkempt neighborhood denied that. Why here? he thought angrily; and then he was taking the steps two at a time, kicking bottles and burger wrappers out of his path.

He waited by the door for five minutes before a teenage boy ran out. Leo barely caught the door before it slammed behind him. Inside, a fluorescent light hung askew from the ceiling, buzzing like a wasp. Helen's was the first door to the right. Circulars from conve-nience stores drifted on the floor, and on the far wall was a bank of mailboxes. One was ajar, stuffed with unclaimed bills and maga-zines. More envelopes piled on the steps. Each bore Helen's name.

His knocking went unanswered; but he thought he heard some-one moving inside.

"Helen," he called softly. "It's Leo. You okay?"

He knocked harder, called her name, finally pounded with both fists. Still nothing. He should leave; he should call the police. Better still, forget ever coming here. But he was here, now; the police would question him no matter what; the curator for Indo-Asian Studies would look at him askance. Leo bit his lip and tested the doorknob. Locked; but the wood gave way slightly as he leaned against it. He rattled the knob and braced himself to kick the door in.

He didn't have to. In his hand the knob twisted and the door swung inward, so abruptly that he fell inside. The door banged shut behind him. He glanced across the room, looking for her; but all he saw was gray light, the gauzy shadows cast by gritty curtains. Then he breathed in, gagging, and pulled his sleeve to his mouth until he gasped through the cotton. He backed toward the door, slipping on something dank, like piles of wet clothing. He glanced at his feet and grunted in disgust.

Roses. They were everywhere: heaps of rotting flowers, broken branches, leaves stripped from bushes, an entire small ficus tree tossed into the corner. He forgot Helen, turned to grab the doorknob and tripped on an uprooted azalea. He fell, clawing at the wall to balance himself. His palms splayed against the plaster and slid as though the surface was still wet. Then, staring upward he saw that it *was* wet. Water streamed from the ceiling, flowing down the wall to soak his shirt cuffs. Leo moaned. His knees buckled as he sank, arms flailing, into the mass of decaying blossoms. Their stench suffocated him; his eyes watered as he retched and tried to stagger back to his feet.

Then he heard something, like a bell, or a telephone; then another faint sound, like an animal scratching overhead. Carefully he twisted to stare upward, trying not to betray himself by moving too fast. Something skittered across the ceiling, and Leo's stomach turned dizzily. What could be up there? A second blur dashed to join the first; golden eyes stared down at him, unblinking.

Geckos, he thought frantically. She had pet geckos. She *has* pet geckos. Jesus.

She couldn't be here. It was too hot, the stench horrible: putrid water, decaying plants, water everywhere. His trousers were soaked from where he had fallen, his knees ached from kneeling in a trough of water pooling against the wall. The floor had warped and more flowers protruded from cracks between the linoleum, brown fronds of iris and rotting honeysuckle. From another room trickled the sound of water dripping steadily, as though a tap was running.

He had to get out. He'd leave the door open—police, a landlord.

Someone would call for help. But he couldn't reach the door. He couldn't stand. His feet skated across the slick tiles as his hands tore uselessly through wads of petals. It grew darker. Golden bands rippled across the floor as sunlight filtered through the gray curtains. Leo dragged himself through rotting leaves, his clothes sopping, tugging aside mats of greenery and broken branches. His leg ached where he'd fallen on it and his hands stung, pricked by unseen thorns.

Something brushed against his fingers and he forced himself to look down, shuddering. A shattered nautilus left a thin red line across his hand, the sharp fragments gilded by the dying light. As he looked around he noticed other things, myriad small objects caught in the morass of rotting flowers like a nightmarish ebb tide on the linoleum floor. Agates and feathered masks; bird of paradise plumes encrusted with mud; cracked skulls and bones and cloth of gold. He recognized the carved puppet Helen had been playing with that afternoon in the Indonesian corridor, its headdress glittering in the twilight. About its neck was strung a plait of flowers, amber and cerulean blossoms glowing like phosphorescence among the ruins.

Through the room echoed a dull clang. Leo jerked to his knees, relieved. Surely someone had knocked? But the sound came from somewhere behind him, and was echoed in another harsher, note. As this second bell died he heard the geckos' feet pattering as they fled across the ceiling. A louder note rang out, the windowpanes vibrating to the sound as though wind-battered. In the corner the leaves of the ficus turned as if to welcome rain, and the rosebushes stirred.

Leo heard something else, then: a small sound like a cat stretching to wakefulness. Now both of his legs ached, and he had to pull himself forward on his hands and elbows, striving to reach the front door. The clanging grew louder, more resonant. A higher tone echoed it monotonously, like the echo of rain in a well. Leo glanced over his shoulder to the empty doorway that led to the kitchen, the dark mouth of the hallway to Helen's bedroom. Something moved there.

At his elbow moved something else and he struck at it feebly, knocking the puppet across the floor. Uncomprehending, he stared after it, then cowered as he watched the ceiling, wondering if one of the geckos had crept down beside him.

There was no gecko. When Leo glanced back at the puppet it was moving across the floor toward him, pulling itself forward on its long slender arms.

The gongs thundered now. A shape humped across the room, something large enough to blot out the empty doorway behind it. Before he was blinded by petals, Leo saw that it was a shrunken figure, a woman whose elongated arms clutched broken branches to propel herself, legs dragging uselessly through the tangled leaves. About her swayed a host of brilliant figures no bigger than dolls. They had roped her neck and hands with wreaths of flowers and scattered blossoms onto the floor about them. Like a flock of chattering butterflies they surged toward him, tiny hands outstretched, their long tongues unfurling like crimson pistils, and the gongs rang like golden bells as they gathered about him to feed.

———

This was my first published story, bought by Tappan King for *Twilight Zone* magazine in 1987; it appeared early in 1988. In a phone conversation, Tappan said that I would be a good writer for the 90s, because my work had "heart and also sharp little teeth."

At the time I was living in Washington, D.C., and working at the Smithsonian Insitution. The demonic puppet of the title was something I bought on my lunch hour one afternoon, walking from the Mall to a dim little shop called The Artifactory. I fell in love with the puppet and paid fifty dollars for it, a huge chunk of my meager paycheck; but when I brought it back to my cubicle at the National Air and Space Museum I announced that it would bring me luck. It did: shortly thereafter I wrote the story, and even though it took a year or so, I finally sold it.

World Fantasy Award-winner ELIZABETH HAND is also the author of *Glimmering, Winterlong,* and *Waking the Moon.* She lives in Maine with her two children.